A VIGIL IN THE MOURNING

SOULBOUND IV

HAILEY TURNER

Don't miss out on sneak peeks, exciting news, and more!
Sign up for Hailey Turner's newsletter
to stay up to date on her upcoming books.

WELCOME TO THE WORLDS OF HAILEY TURNER

Urban Fantasy
Soulbound

Science Fiction Romance
Metahuman Files

Steampunk-inspired Epic Fantasy
Infernal War Saga

To Aimee Nicole Walker
For the encouragement, the cat pictures, and the friendship.

1

The alarm went off at exactly 0600, dragging Special Agent Patrick Collins out of sleep. He didn't even bother opening his gritty eyes, just blindly reached for his cell phone on the nightstand to flip it over and shut off the alarm. The silence afterward was blissful, even though he knew it would only last ten minutes. But that was ten extra minutes, and every single one counted when you'd gone to bed at 0300.

The arm slung over his waist curled tighter, pulling him back against the warm body he shared the bed with. Jonothon de Vere nuzzled at Patrick's bare shoulder, making him drag up the duvet to keep out the cooler air of the bedroom. Jono was a god pack alpha werewolf and had a higher core body temperature, which meant their bed was too warm half the time, even in winter. February was still winter, and the body heat seeping into his was welcome right now.

"Don't wanna get up," Patrick muttered. "You can't make me."

Jono's soft chuckle echoed in the quiet of their bedroom. "You have a meeting."

Patrick turned his face into the pillow, words coming out muffled. "I don't *want* to have a meeting."

Jono stroked his hand up Patrick's chest, his touch warm until it wasn't. The scars from Patrick's childhood that were carved into his chest came with some degree of nerve damage. The near-mortal wound might have been healed by a goddess, but Persephone's care had only gone so far. Jono's touch came and went as he settled his hand over Patrick's heart.

Time was he would've hooked his fingers over the chain of Patrick's dog tags, but Patrick had finally set those aside on New Year's Eve. He'd been part of the Mage Corps until he was twenty-six, fighting on behalf of the government against the darker aspects of all the hells. At twenty-nine—going on thirty next month—Patrick had worn his dog tags for years after he'd stopped wearing a uniform.

After everything that had happened with the Hellraisers and Captain Gerard Breckenridge in December, Patrick was learning to let go of things that used to define himself even as he held on to other bits. One of those was Jono, the man he was soulbound to, the man who loved him—and the man who wouldn't let Patrick sulk even when the situation warranted it.

"You need to get up, love," Jono murmured.

Patrick made a disagreeable sound. "Five more minutes."

The alarm going off again indicated he wasn't getting those five minutes.

Patrick groaned and reached for his cell phone, actually lifting it up this time to turn off the alarm with a swipe of his thumb. He set it down and turned over in Jono's arms to press his face against that warm, hard chest. Patrick breathed in deep, smelling faint hints of stale alcohol and the last traces of Jono's cologne. He'd already been in bed when Patrick had stumbled home that morning, his managerial shift at Tempest ending before closing.

Patrick, on the other hand, had spent the last four days hunting down a possessed Catholic priest before locating the man in question in Hoboken, New Jersey. Patrick's tainted magic might make it easier for him to hunt down demons, but he was shit at sending them back to where they'd come from if they were still tied to a human soul. The possessed priest was currently contained in a warded cell at the Supernatural Operations Agency's New York field office. Last Patrick heard, the Catholic Church had sent an exorcism team to deal with the man.

Patrick hadn't stuck around to face the Church's hypocrisy regarding magic. As with most conservative religious organizations, the Catholic Church had banned magic centuries ago, but magic was part of the world, whether they liked it or not. No ban had ever been enough to stop demons from crossing the veil and wreaking havoc on humanity. The Catholic Church allowed magic use only for exorcisms, but that was lip service as far as Patrick was concerned. The Spanish Inquisition was testament to it.

The priest case had left Patrick catching cat naps at the office and at home, and the three hours of sleep he'd managed that morning was definitely not enough to make the upcoming meeting palatable.

Nothing would be enough to put him in a good mood when it came to dealing with SOA Director Setsuna Abuku.

"I'll make you coffee while you shower," Jono said, stroking his back.

Patrick hummed thoughtfully. "With whiskey."

"No. Now get up."

"Wow. I can feel the love in this room."

Jono snorted and rolled away, getting up. He turned on the bedside lamp as he did so. "You know I love you, but you're a right wanker when you don't have coffee in you."

"I could have you in me, and then I bet that would put me in a better mood."

Patrick watched as Jono stood and stretched, putting his naked body on display with a teasing smirk on his face. His black hair was bed messy rather than sex messy, and his wolf-bright blue eyes seemed to glow in the dim light.

He snagged a pair of underwear from the dresser and put them on. "That would make you late for your meeting."

Patrick flopped over on his back, glaring up at the ceiling. "I was trying to make you my excuse to get out of it."

"I know."

"Is it working?"

Jono laughed on his way out of the bedroom. "I'll get the coffee started."

"I'm hiding your tea," Patrick yelled after him.

If Jono responded, Patrick didn't hear him. Swearing under his breath, Patrick rubbed at his dry eyes, trying to find the willpower to get up. He'd much rather stay in bed with Jono, but his job couldn't wait. Working for the SOA was a headache most days, but at least he was no longer flying around the country and living out of hotel rooms and suitcases like he had been before being transferred to New York last year.

Patrick might no longer be attached to the SOA's Rapid Response Division, but some cases that came down the pipeline could only be handled by a mage with his expertise. The ongoing case about the Morrígan's staff was one example, even if very few people in the SOA knew about the problem.

It's probably why Setsuna is in town.

Some things weren't safe to talk about on a phone line—secret burner phone or otherwise. Patrick didn't believe Setsuna had uncovered all the Dominion Sect traitors in the SOA. The director coming to New York City just proved it.

Patrick finally shoved the blankets off himself and got up. He fumbled his way into a pair of jeans, a long-sleeved Henley, and battered combat boots. His gods-given dagger was sheathed and resting on the nightstand. Patrick strapped it to his right thigh and anchored a strap to his belt with practiced fingers. His semiautomatic HK USP 9mm tactical pistol was in the lockbox on top of the dresser, and he opened it up.

While he doubted he'd need a handgun for his upcoming meeting, Patrick didn't go anywhere unarmed while on duty. Unlike most magic users who never imagined they wouldn't have access to their magic, Patrick knew it was always a possibility, one he perpetually lived with. Mages were the only magic users who could access external magic outside the human soul. The soul wound he'd taken during the Thirty-Day War meant he could—technically—no longer tap a ley line or nexus.

The soulbond with Jono had changed that.

Patrick clipped his badge to his belt before grabbing his leather jacket from the closet. February had been rainy, wet, and cold so far, with a few snow days. The bitter winter cold from December when the Wild Hunt and the Sluagh had ridden the stormy skies above the city had thankfully settled into normal weather a few days after Christmas.

December had been a roller coaster that Patrick would've paid money at any point to get off of. Learning that his old captain was in truth an immortal had been one of those moments where everything about living just *hurt*. The gods had fucked with Patrick his entire life, and to learn that someone he considered a brother and brother-in-arms had betrayed him like that was still a raw wound deep down inside.

He'd forgiven Gerard though, because Patrick had learned—with Jono's help—that closing himself off from everyone wasn't helpful. Sometimes the gods themselves didn't get a choice. Gerard had proven that when, as the warrior Cú Chulainn, he had promised the goddess Cailleach Bheur he would return to Ireland once the Morrígan's staff was found.

It was finding the damned thing that was the problem.

Once locked away in the United States' Repository, it had been stolen by Medb after the Thirty-Day War ended three and a half years ago. They'd all thought Ethan Greene and the Dominion Sect had been behind the theft, but it turned out the gods weren't above stealing from each other. In the fight at the Gap of Dunloe on winter solstice, the Dagda had forced Medb to keep her promise and tell them where the Morrígan's staff was.

There was only one problem with that win. The fae of any court were experts at twisting words, and Medb had only said it was in the mortal world. After weeks of chasing down leads gleaned from chatter, the SOA—along with the Preternatural Intelligence Agency and the US Department of the Preternatural— had agreed it was most likely going to be sold on the black market.

They just didn't know *where*.

Something must have come up though. Setsuna had called Patrick yesterday while he was in the field to tell him she would be in town for a few days, and that they were meeting that morning. Patrick hadn't seen her in person since last June when he was in the hospital recovering from breaking up Ethan's sacrificial spell and getting his soul bound to Jono's. Patrick wasn't looking forward to today's meeting at all.

Whiskey in his coffee would've made everything better, but Jono was a stingy bastard.

When Patrick stepped into the living room of their top-floor Chelsea apartment, he was greeted with a kiss and a mug of coffee that had cream and nothing else in it.

"I'll pour my own whiskey," Patrick muttered against Jono's lips.

Jono laughed, nipping gently at his bottom lip. "You'll do no such thing. Are you hungry? I'll make you a fry-up."

"You can go back to bed, you know that? Only one of us is working today."

Jono pulled away and retreated to the kitchen. "I don't mind getting up with you."

Patrick watched him go, a warmth settling in his chest that had nothing to do with the central heat that Jono had turned up. The gods might have maneuvered Jono into his life, but Jono was everything Patrick never knew he needed.

He joined Jono in the kitchen, relishing their time together. Breakfast was a quick affair, and they ate it standing at the counter rather than at the dining room table. Patrick leaned against Jono as he ate, sipping at his second cup of coffee every now and then.

"Anyone come to the bar for help last night?" Patrick asked.

Jono shook his head. "No, but we were busy enough."

Busy was an understatement. Ever since Jono had accepted Emma's pack near the beginning of December and two more packs on Christmas Day as his responsibility, more and more packs had come to Tempest asking for protection. The other god pack of New York City, headed up by Estelle Walker and Youssef Khan, still maintained control of the five boroughs, but Jono's announcement of his own god pack meant the werecreature community was a ticking time bomb these days.

Most of the packs who had switched allegiance were smaller ones, located outside Manhattan proper. Nearly half the independent-ranked werecreatures who called the five boroughs home had asked Jono for protection before the end of January. Patrick anticipated the rest would shift allegiance before the end of February. Nearly every single pack who had asked to be governed by their god pack had been accepted—except for one.

The Falcon pack, out of Manhattan, was a moderately large pack of werewolves whose alpha had come to Tempest one night three weeks back. Eduardo had been earnest and willing to submit to Jono's rule, ready to show throat, but Jono had taken one look at the man and told him *no*.

Sage Beacot, their dire, had promptly kicked Eduardo out, along with the few pack members he'd brought. When pressed, Jono had simply said the Falcon pack couldn't be trusted. Later, Jono had confessed to Patrick that Fenrir had told him not to take the pack on. Patrick usually didn't trust gods, but the immortal

Norse wolf that had teeth and claws sunk deep in Jono's soul wasn't one they could argue with.

Rarely did animal-god patrons bestow werecreatures with their guidance and blessings. Given the choice, Patrick would wish Jono free of the immortal, but he could grudgingly admit that Fenrir gave their pack a legitimacy no one else had—they just weren't announcing the god's favor yet to anyone outside their pack. Whenever they did, Patrick knew shit would go down.

Right now, bringing in packs and independent werecreatures they could trust made it easier for them to expand their pack boundaries. Their small, four-person god pack literally only had one werecreature who carried the god strain of the werevirus. Jono was enough though, and the rest of them backed him. So far, the people who'd opted to accept their protection were fine with taking orders from a werewolf, a mage, a weretiger, and a fledgling fire dragon, even if most people thought Wade Espinoza was just an annoying teenager.

"See you tonight?" Jono asked as he walked Patrick to the front door.

Patrick slapped his hand against the doorframe, strengthening the threshold wrapped around their apartment with a quick burst of focused magic. "Monday nights at the bar are always my favorite."

"We won't stay late. I know you need to sleep."

"Just because I need to sleep doesn't mean I can let pack duty slide." Patrick rose on his tiptoes to kiss Jono goodbye. "I'll be there."

Jono pressed a hand to the small of Patrick's back, keeping Patrick close as he deepened the kiss just enough to be a tease. Patrick groaned, hating that he had to go to work.

"Be safe," Jono said when he finally pulled back. "I love you."

"I will."

Patrick didn't say the other words back—hadn't said them since Jono first confessed his love on Christmas Eve. They were buried down deep, spread through actions and touches, but never voiced. Some part of Patrick was too scared to say them and then lose what mattered most in his life these days.

The gods had given Jono to him as a weapon after all, and what the gods gave, they could take away.

"See you tonight," Patrick said as he left the apartment.

The door didn't close until he rounded the landing below. Patrick went to work with a smile on his face, Jono's care warming him better than the fae-given heat charms embedded in his leather jacket.

THE COFFEE in the SOA's New York field office tasted like burned sludge, but Patrick drank it anyway. Fueling his bad mood with shitty coffee was just par for the course some days. He checked the time on his cell phone again, but the numbers still showed that his meeting with Setsuna—which was supposed to start at 0900—was delayed. It was nearing 1000 and she was still ensconced with SAIC Henry Ng on a different floor.

Patrick was going to take his lunch break early at this rate, whether she liked it or not.

He frowned at the low battery on his phone, realizing he'd been too tired to remember to charge his phone last night. Jono and their bed had overridden all other thoughts at the time. Patrick leaned over to yank open the bottom desk drawer, certain he had a spare charger in the mess hidden there. Who knew how much crap he'd managed to hoard over the last nine months?

I'm picking up Wade's hoarding habits.

That was a terrifying thought.

Someone knocked on his office door and opened it without waiting for him to answer. "Collins. You have a visitor."

Patrick peered over his desk at the receptionist from the floor's front desk, still digging for a cell phone charger. "Is the director finally finished?"

The woman shook her head and stepped aside for someone else. "Not the director."

The person who entered Patrick's office was definitely not Setsuna.

One of the United States of America's only true god-touched seers looked like he'd gone on a full weekend bender and hadn't made it home. Marek's hazel eyes were bloodshot, brown hair messy in a way that wasn't stylish and had more to do with fingers running through it than anything else.

Patrick stared at Marek, noting the way his hands shook ever so slightly, the tightness around his mouth, and how hard he was clenching his jaw, as if he were trying not to throw up. Patrick abandoned his search for a charger in favor of helping Marek before the seer passed out.

"Sit down before you fall down," Patrick ordered as he got to his feet. "Where's your better half?"

Marek offered him a wan smile before sinking gingerly into one of the two chairs in front of Patrick's desk. "Work. Where I'd be if I hadn't gotten interrupted."

Patrick knew Marek's patrons were rarely kind when they forced a vision onto him. The Fates, in Patrick's experience, didn't care about anyone's feelings, and he had a soulbond to prove it.

Patrick waved away the woman who had escorted Marek to him and closed the door behind her. He wrote out a silence ward on the door, pushing magic out of his damaged soul. Static washed through the office before settling into the walls around them. He might work for the government, but that didn't mean he trusted everyone around him.

"Did you leave work?" Patrick asked as he went to the corner where one of the office administrators had installed a small minifridge for him one weekend last year. Magic users burned through a lot of energy, mages in particular, and Jono had gotten tired of Patrick coming home in a crappy mood because he hadn't eaten enough. Patrick's solution was useful.

"Never made it in," Marek confessed.

Patrick pulled out a bottle of Gatorade and a protein bar. "Did you let Sage know?"

"I'll call her after."

Sage was Marek's fiancée aside from being Patrick and Jono's dire. She was a weretiger who worked as an attorney for the fae law firm Gentry & Thyme. She was not one either of them wanted to get on the bad side of.

Patrick opened the Gatorade and handed it to Marek. "Drink. Slowly, because if you puke in my office, the janitors will hate me."

Marek stared at the bottle in his hand with a queasy look on his face. "I might puke anyway."

"Tell me you didn't drive here."

"Took a cab." Marek sipped carefully at the Gatorade. "No one was home to drive me, and the Norns wanted me to find you."

Patrick would never get used to the way all the gods seemed to love fucking with his life. "You should've let someone know. You're not safe when you're like this and no one is around you."

"I doubt Estelle and Youssef would try anything."

"That's you being a fucking idiot." Patrick leaned back against his desk and crossed his arms over his chest. "They're looking for weak spots, and you go down hard after a vision."

Marek pressed the cold plastic bottle against the side of his face, blinking slowly. His hazel eyes weren't washed out in the way they got when he was channeling the Norns. Patrick only hoped they'd leave Marek alone now that he was here.

"The government would arrest them."

"The government is already trying to arrest them, but the shine case is still being investigated. I'm not in favor of making the attorney general's job easier because you're dead."

Marek smiled tightly. "I knew you'd say that."

Patrick dragged a hand over his face. "Fucking immortals. What do they want?"

Marek very carefully reached out to set the Gatorade down on Patrick's desk. He wavered a little on the chair, and Patrick steadied him with a careful hand. Marek closed his eyes, and when he opened them again, the hazel coloring was gone, washed out into white. His aura cracked wide open and scraped against Patrick's shields in a way that felt like a punch to the gut from old magic.

Shining through the strands of a human soul's reach was the brighter, deeper presence of a god. Patrick sucked in a sharp breath and tasted ozone on his tongue. He knew it was no longer just him and Marek in the office now.

"*The Allfather is in danger,*" one of the Norns said, Marek's voice a mix of his own and the goddess using him as a mouthpiece. "*You must go to him.*"

Ice replaced the blood in Patrick's veins. "Are you fucking kidding me?"

Marek's body stood, the immortal controlling him trapping Patrick against the desk. Patrick held his ground, the edge of the desk digging into his upper thighs, but he refused to lean back as the immortal brought Marek uncomfortably close.

"*He does not believe it so, but Muninn and Huginn have heard the thoughts that whisper in the minds of men who would harm him.*"

"If Odin's ravens can find the fucking bastards, then why do you need me?"

"*Your family hides from us. They always have. Immortals aid their secrecy the way we aid you.*"

Patrick's lips curled. "I don't call what you do for me aid."

"*You owe us. Which means you will save the Allfather. It was chance his ravens heard anything at all.*" The immortal twisted Marek's mouth into a hard smile. "*Or fate.*"

Really. Fuck the gods.

"I'm a little busy tracking down that staff you lost. Can't you send someone else?"

Cold fingers grabbed his chin and dug into the skin over his jaw. The power shining out of Marek's eyes left Patrick worried the seer was going to lose another color, putting Marek one step, one shade closer to blindness and insanity. Seeing the future came with the cost every seer had to pay.

"Go to Chicago. The Æsir will be waiting for you."

The knowledge that Patrick would have to deal with the Norse gods left him wanting to punch something.

The immortal's presence disappeared at the same moment the door to his office opened. Marek's knees gave out, and Patrick caught him under the arms, holding him up. Swearing, Patrick shifted Marek back onto the chair.

"Patrick?" Setsuna asked after she had crossed through his silence ward.

Patrick ignored where Setsuna stood just inside his office, with SAIC Henry Ng blocking the doorway behind her. All of Patrick's attention was on Marek, not liking how he looked. Patrick cradled Marek's pale face in his hands, wincing at how cold Marek felt.

"What do you need?" Patrick asked.

When Marek didn't respond, merely swallowed thickly, Patrick went to grab the plastic recycling bin under his desk and brought it around to shove it between Marek's legs. Marek promptly leaned over and got sick. Patrick sighed as the smell of vomit filled his office.

"I'll handle this, Henry," Setsuna said.

Henry, unlike Patrick, knew better than to argue with the director. He murmured a quiet goodbye before leaving, closing the door behind him. Setsuna turned and tapped the tip of her intricately carved rosewood cane against the door, layering Patrick's silence ward with her own.

"I wasn't aware you had a visitor," Setsuna said.

Patrick glanced away from Marek to meet Setsuna's steady gaze, scowling at her. Patrick and Setsuna weren't close. The secrets they shared ensured he would never trust her. She was still his superior, and still in charge, no matter what the Norns demanded he do.

The woman who had been his guardian for ten years after he was delivered to her care at the age of eight didn't look her age, despite turning fifty-two at the end of last year. Her black hair was still cut in the shoulder-skimming bob she favored, and what wrinkles she had were faint.

The cane she carried was more a weapon than a need for balance. The carved Shinto shrine at the top and the winding steps leading up to it from the bottom tip were layered with kanji. Setsuna's witch magic had turned the cane into an artifact, and she never went anywhere without it.

"I didn't know Marek was stopping by until he did," Patrick said.

Setsuna's expression didn't change as she came forward. "What do the Fates want from you now?"

Marek slowly sat up. Patrick handed him the box of tissues on the desk to wipe his mouth with. "They want me to go to Chicago to save Odin."

"How fortuitous."

Patrick scowled at her. "Is that what you're here about?"

"I have your orders, yes, if that's what you're asking."

"You still owe me a trip to Maui. Next time, maybe order me to go there."

Before Setsuna could answer, Marek reached out with a shaky hand to grab Patrick's shirt. He tipped his head back, eyes closed to mere slits, looking like every movement hurt. "What staff?"

Patrick grimaced, knowing the months of keeping that mission out of their friends' awareness was over. "A problem you don't need to worry about."

"Urðr thinks otherwise."

Patrick passed Marek the Gatorade again, ignoring that statement. "Take small sips."

"Patrick."

"If the gods want me in Chicago, I guess I'm going to the Windy City. Seems you wasted a flight, Setsuna."

"Visiting you is never a waste of my time," she replied, moving to stand by the other chair.

Patrick turned so he could keep an eye on them both. "If you say so."

Setsuna pulled out a folded piece of paper from the inner pocket of her precisely tailored suit jacket and offered it to Patrick. "Eyes Only. The spell is curated to your magic. Lower your shields to read it."

Some days Patrick was terrible at following orders. Other days, he knew he didn't have a choice. He lowered his personal shields, letting his tainted magic slip free. Patrick took the piece of paper with careful fingers, skin burning briefly as whatever spell was embedded in it brushed against his magic.

When he unfolded it, all he saw was a swirl of black ink. Then the paper beneath his fingertips glowed briefly, the shine running along the edges of the paper. The ink started to move across the paper, orienting itself into lines of text. The Eyes Only warning sat below the header, which wasn't the SOA seal like Patrick was expecting. Instead, the US Department of the Preternatural seal was stamped there, indicating the information had come from outside his agency. The internal designation was for the joint task force put together to find the Morrígan's staff.

"A courier brought it to me on Friday from the Pentagon," Setsuna said.

"Knew you didn't come to New York because you missed me," Patrick muttered.

Patrick skimmed the memorandum, a cold feeling settling in his gut. No wonder it hadn't been sent by electronic means, and instead written out with magic for personal delivery to only those the spell was keyed to. If anyone used magic to try to read it, the paper would go up in flames.

As it was, he wished someone had burned the damned thing before it ever reached his hand.

Patrick stared at the name slashed across the bottom of the paper with a heavy heart. "General Reed signed off on it. Has anyone else in the joint task force received the same information?"

General Noah Reed was currently overseeing the US Department of the Preternatural, but he'd been the one to sign off on the missions Patrick's old team were given. Reed was a fire dragon hiding in human form, who hoarded information the way banks hoarded money. The intelligence officers working under him almost always had information they could trust.

If Reed said the Dominion Sect was actively working in Chicago, then it was probably true.

Setsuna curled both hands over the top of her cane. "I explained to everyone involved that you would be the one best able to handle this problem."

Marek tugged at Patrick's shirt, not having let go yet. The twist of his mouth was more scowl than frown. The pain he must have been feeling from channeling an immortal wouldn't deter him from the information he'd suddenly become privy to. Patrick was well aware of the degrees of Marek's stubbornness when he sought to get his way or get answers. Patrick wondered if that was a trait gained from being a CEO or a seer.

"What staff are the Norns worried about?" Marek demanded.

Patrick sighed and folded the paper into quarters before shoving it into his back pocket. "I hate Mondays."

2

a low voice.

Her brown eyes narrowed, but she didn't move from her position on the couch because Marek was using her lap as a pillow. Emma was a tiny Chinese American alpha werewolf who co-led the Tempest pack, one of Marek's oldest friends and business partners, and a woman Patrick never wanted to be on the wrong side of. Unfortunately, that wasn't an option right now.

"Uh, we weren't?" Patrick said.

Jono snorted as he held up the potion Victoria Alvarez had dropped off on her way home to help with Marek's migraine. She was a nurse and working nights this month, but luckily the timing had worked out.

"We couldn't," Jono corrected, eyeing the handwritten label. "The mission came from a general, and the gods made it clear they didn't want us to gossip about how they fucked up. Marek, you need to drink all of this."

"I'm not sitting up," Marek mumbled.

Leon Hernandez, who'd been standing behind the couch,

turned and headed for the kitchen in Marek and Sage's apartment. "I'll get you a straw."

Emma didn't watch her partner leave, more interested in burning a hole through Patrick's head with her glare. "You should've told us you got another mission from the gods. How are we supposed to help you if we don't know what's going on?"

"Technically, the mission came from the government," Patrick said.

"The Norns say otherwise."

Marek raised his hand and patted at Emma's face. "Shh. Too loud."

Marek didn't look much better since Patrick had half carried the seer out of his office. He'd called Emma and Leon to give them a heads-up because Marek belonged to their pack, and they were always overprotective of their friend when the Fates fucked with him.

Patrick had told Setsuna he was taking a long lunch in order to bring Marek home. The Art Deco building—more an enormous mansion from a bygone era—that Marek had bought some years back had been sectioned off into individual apartments. He and Sage owned the top two floors while Emma and Leon lived in the level below. The rest of the space was rented out to certain members of the Tempest pack. Patrick and Jono still came over for pack nights when they could, though work had been getting in the way of a lot of things lately.

The entire place felt like a home to Patrick's senses, the threshold surrounding the building strong but easy for him to work with. Casting magic within the building was never a fight, not how it could be in some of the places he'd ended up in over the years.

Leon came back and handed Jono the straw. Jono unscrewed the cap of the potion bottle, stuck the straw in, and passed it to Emma. She lowered the potion bottle and pushed the straw into Marek's mouth.

"Drink," Emma ordered, and Marek obeyed. "Is Ethan after this staff?"

Patrick rubbed at his mouth. "Yes."

"All right. So what's the plan?"

Before Patrick could answer, the front door opened, and Wade came inside, shoving the last bite of a candy bar into his mouth. Sage walked in behind him, her wool coat slung over one arm. She unceremoniously dropped her Birkin bag by the door, along with her coat. Patrick hadn't heard them arrive because of the silence ward wrapped around the apartment.

"Has he lost another color?" Sage asked.

"Possibly a shade of blue," Patrick told her apologetically.

Sage patted his shoulder on the way over to her fiancé. "It's not your fault."

"Kind of feels like it."

Sage knelt by Marek, smoothing his hair back and talking softly. She took the potion bottle from Emma and held it for Marek while he finished the medicine.

Leon sat down on the other end of the couch and pulled Marek's feet into his lap. Despite being engaged to Sage, Marek wasn't part of Jono's god pack. He remained a member of Emma's Tempest pack, and whenever the Norns knocked him down like this, Emma and Leon were always extra touchy-feely with him.

"What's this staff do?" Leon asked. "And how can we help?"

"We don't know." Patrick shrugged in the face of Emma's disbelieving stare. "The government didn't know what it was when they had it. Speculation is it's within the realm of necromantic magic, but we can't be certain because no one has seen it for years."

"Medb ended up stealing it and keeping it hidden in the mortal world. We couldn't get a straight answer out of her on where it was located though," Jono said.

"Is that what the whole mess in December was about? Not just Gerard's missing fiancée?" Emma asked.

"Something like that."

"Who's Aksel Sigfodr?" Wade wanted to know as he sat down on the arm of the couch next to Leon. "And why do you have to go to Chicago?"

Patrick looked over in surprise at where Wade was squinting at the memorandum that had been in his back pocket. "Stop pick-pocketing your pack leaders."

Wade snorted, a faint curl of smoke puffing out of his nostrils. "How else am I supposed to know what's going on?"

Leon reached up and swiped the piece of paper out of Wade's hand. "There are Pop-Tarts in the pantry. Go eat a box."

"Hell yes," Wade said, perking up.

He made a beeline for the kitchen while everyone else stayed put. Leon frowned at the piece of paper before looking over at Patrick. "This looks like a Pollock painting, not a memo."

"Eyes Only and the spell is geared to my magic's signature. You won't be able to read it," Patrick said, stepping forward to retrieve what Wade had momentarily stolen. "If you had magic and tried, it'd burn up."

"Wade can read it."

"Magic doesn't work on dragons."

"Then tell us what it says and who Aksel Sigfodr is."

Patrick sighed before sitting down in the closest armchair. "This was supposed to be an off-the-record mission."

"Yeah, packs don't work that way," Emma replied dryly.

"The federal government does."

"That's nice. You're still going to tell us."

Patrick made a face, knowing he couldn't keep quiet on this mess. Emma's pack was too entangled with theirs, and willing to help them fight on any number of fronts. It had taken Patrick months to come to terms with the fact that he had people he could call for help. Setsuna might be putting a lot of faith into the joint task force, but Patrick didn't trust its existence would remain outside the bulk of the SOA's awareness.

He'd come to learn that having allies in unexpected locations was never a bad thing. Jono had drilled into him that pack was family, and while they were both keenly aware of how family could hurt, Patrick was learning to trust the family they'd chosen. It wasn't always easy, but that's what made it worth it in the end.

"Aksel Sigfodr is a key player in Chicago politics. He also has ties to the criminal underworld, but no one's been able to pin any crime on him or his family."

Emma arched an eyebrow. "So he's part of the mob?"

Patrick shrugged. "Who the fuck knows? Organized crime has never been my specialty. Reed's people seem to think he might have some information on the staff's possible location."

"And that would be enough to bring the Dominion Sect to Chicago?"

"Yeah. More than enough."

"Well, fuck," Leon said. "Is this going to turn into another crazy sacrifice mess?"

"Now you've jinxed us," Wade muttered around a mouthful of strawberry Pop-Tart as he returned to the living room.

Jono looked over at Patrick. "When do you have to be in Chicago?"

Patrick grimaced. "I fly out tonight. Setsuna signed off on sending me to Chicago under the guise of a different case. Something about a corrupt candidate that needs looking into. I'm to meet with Sigfodr separately."

"Sounds like regular old Chicago politics to me," Sage said dryly. "Why would the SOA need to get involved?"

"I'll find out when I read the file and get there."

"Who's going with you?"

"You know I don't have a partner. I'm going by myself like I always do."

Sage shook her head. "That might've worked before you declared our god pack, but not anymore."

"I'm traveling under SOA jurisdiction."

"Pack law still matters. You're going to need to ask for pass-through rights from the Chicago god pack. Since you're one of our pack's alphas, whether or not you're a werecreature, you shouldn't go alone."

"I'm trying my hardest not to have the rest of the SOA know about my pack. As a government agent, it puts my cases in jeopardy to have so obvious a bias. Me waltzing into Chicago with a request to talk to the god pack alphas there isn't good PR for my agency."

Jono frowned, the worry in his eyes easy enough to read. "I'm with Sage on this one, Pat. I don't like you going alone."

"You can't come with me. I leave all the time for my job, but right now, we can't afford for you to be missing from our territory. One of us needs to stay."

The borders they claimed were still too fragile, and Estelle and Youssef weren't going to stop testing them. As much as Patrick hated not being able to have Jono with him, he disliked it even more that he'd have to leave Jono behind for the duration of this mission. He wouldn't put it past Estelle and Youssef to strike while he was gone.

Patrick trusted their own pack and a handful of their allies; he just didn't trust anyone else.

Sage pulled the straw away from Marek's mouth and set the potion bottle aside. "I can't go. I have a motion for summary judgment due on Friday, and I'm crunched for time as it is."

"Sorry," Marek mumbled.

Sage leaned down to kiss him lightly on the lips. "Not your fault."

"I can go," Wade said.

"You have class," Patrick reminded him.

Wade shrugged. "I'll get my therapist to write a note and excuse me. Worked during December."

"You're still making up classwork from December."

"I'm still pack. I can go."

Patrick would've preferred Wade stay in New York and keep

working toward getting the equivalent of his high school diploma. But choice was a big thing for Wade, and it was something Patrick refused to take away from him. Wade had spent four years fighting to the death as entertainment for the rich. He hadn't known what he truly was after being kidnapped and enslaved by the god Tezcatlipoca. Wade's ignorance was the only reason the immortal had been able to keep control of the teenager over the years.

Being free didn't mean life was immediately easy. Wade still saw a therapist weekly to help him work through years of trauma. Getting to have control over his life and make choices was an integral part of his recovery. Patrick and Jono might set limits for the safety of the pack, but they were careful about giving Wade orders because they both understood losing bodily autonomy in a way most people didn't.

"I think you should take Wade," Jono said after a brief pause.

Wade fist pumped the air before pulling out the second Pop-Tart from the silvery wrapper. "I've always wanted to try a Chicago-style hot dog."

"Of course you'd make it about food," Patrick muttered as he stood.

"You can call me if you have any pack law questions," Sage said.

Emma smoothed her hand over Marek's messy hair before clearing her throat. "I'm pissed you kept this from us, but I get it. The gods don't give you a choice about what you're allowed to share. If you need backup, I can send some of our pack along with you."

Patrick wasn't close to anyone in Emma's pack outside the core leadership. He liked them well enough—everyone was loyal to her and Leon—but he couldn't afford for knowledge of his ties to immortals to get out into the general public.

"Thanks for the offer, but Wade should be enough help. If shit goes down, he's a good ace in the hole. No one expects a dragon as backup."

"Just like no one expected the Spanish Inquisition," Wade said with a snicker.

"You are banned from watching any more Monty Python."

Jono snorted. "Now you're asking for the gods to throw a spanner in the works."

Patrick shrugged. "I expect that on a daily basis."

"What time does your flight leave?"

"Six o'clock," Patrick replied, remembering to use civilian time. "I need to go home and pack."

Wade frowned. "I need to pack. Do I even have a suitcase?"

"Yes," Jono said. "We found one when we cleaned out your apartment last month."

"Right."

"Pack a jacket. You need to act like Chicago is cold. It's February and it's still snowing over there," Patrick told him.

Wade made a face but didn't argue. Being a fire dragon, he ran a lot hotter in human form and forgot about appearing human in the dead of winter. Walking around in a T-shirt and jeans while it was snowing outside was not the best way to hide what he was. Reminding him to act human was second nature these days as Wade settled in to what he was.

"Send me your flight information and I'll get Wade's ticket. Hopefully there are seats available," Sage said.

Wade ripped open his last packet of Pop-Tarts. "I could just fly there on my own. I have wings."

"No," everyone said in unison.

Jono went to fetch Sage's Birkin and coat, carrying both over to her. He spoke quietly to her for a moment before straightening up and looking at Patrick. "Ready?"

"We'll pick you up at your apartment in two hours, Wade," Patrick said as he and Jono headed for the door.

Patrick snapped his fingers, disengaging the silence ward. A chorus of goodbyes followed them out of the apartment.

"I hate separating like this," Jono said when they were finally in the Mustang and driving back home.

"Can't be helped," Patrick replied, typing on his phone while Jono drove. He shot off an email to Sage with his flight details. "You know how my job is."

"I know how the gods are."

"Yeah, well. I'd tell them to fuck off if I could."

Jono hummed a wordless response. Patrick sighed and reached over to settle his hand on Jono's thigh. The heater was running in the car because it was a gray, dreary day outside. Jono was warm to the touch, body heat seeping through his jeans and into Patrick's chilled fingers.

"You'll need to be careful with the Chicago god pack. They aren't one Estelle and Youssef have an alliance with," Jono said.

"Isn't that a good thing? Means we can try to get them on our side."

"Alliances take time to form. A couple of days isn't going to be long enough."

"Somehow I doubt I'll be in Chicago for only a couple of days."

Jono sighed heavily. "Yeah."

They drove the rest of the way home in silence, with Jono managing to find a parking spot one block over from their apartment. Patrick shoved his hands into the pockets of his leather jacket, the heat charms embedded in it keeping most of him warm in the face of a cold winter wind.

Gray slush was all that remained of the last snowfall, shoved to the edge of the sidewalk and roads. Puddles that hadn't quite iced over littered the cement as they walked to their apartment building.

After climbing five flights of stairs, Patrick let them inside and immediately found himself pushed up against the front door. He tipped his head back, staring up into Jono's eyes. Jono lifted his hand and wrapped it loosely around Patrick's throat. Patrick swallowed, feeling Jono's fingers move with the motion. His cock twitched with interest, and despite needing to pack for his flight, Patrick had no intention of moving unless Jono wanted him to.

"Be careful in Chicago," Jono said, his voice coming out low.

"Would you believe me if I said I was always careful?"

Jono pressed his thumb against the edge of Patrick's jaw, tilting his head back farther. "You're a bloody liar."

"Good poker face though."

"I'd like your face"—Jono's other hand slipped between his legs—"and your cock, and all the rest of you, to come back in one piece."

Patrick licked his lips, canting his hips into Jono's touch. "Asking for a miracle."

"Pat."

"I'll do my best. Now shut up and kiss me."

Jono obliged in the best way, stealing the breath from Patrick's lungs, caging him in against the door. Jono kept Patrick there with a hand around his throat that had broken bones in dozens of fights but would never break his. Jono's preternatural strength was a turn-on for Patrick and always would be. There was something about finding safety in a man who could pick up a car and throw it when the need arose, then turn around and touch Patrick with a gentleness he'd rarely been given in his life.

Patrick tangled his fingers in Jono's shirt, pulling him closer. Jono moved his hand against Patrick's throat until he could press his wrist against the pulse point there. Patrick couldn't smell the scent that lived in Jono's skin and which he knew was seeping into his. The pack scent was something Jono pressed into his skin every day, and this moment was no different.

"Need to pack my suitcase," Patrick muttered against Jono's mouth.

Jono nipped at Patrick's bottom lip before sinking to his knees. The smile that curved his mouth was positively filthy. "So go pack."

Patrick banged his head against the door and swore. "Like I'm going anywhere when you're looking at me like that. What kind of willpower do you think I have?"

"You're the most stubborn bloke I know."

"Not when it comes to you."

Which was true in a way that would've made Patrick panic even six months ago. Now, it left him feeling like he didn't want to be anywhere else but here. He reached out and ran his fingers through Jono's black hair, pushing it out of his eyes. Jono's smile shifted into a teasing smirk before he undid Patrick's belt and pulled down the zipper on his jeans.

Patrick spread his legs, his dagger and service pistol weighing down the right side of his clothes, but the thigh straps ensured they wouldn't slide down. Jono made no move to get him completely undressed. Instead, he leaned forward and pressed his mouth over Patrick's quickly dampening underwear. Jono sucked at his cock through the thin material, the scrape of spit-soaked cotton a tease against sensitive skin that made Patrick's nerves buzz with want.

Jono mouthed his cock through his underwear for another minute or so until he finally got tired of the flimsy barrier. Jono pulled down his underwear to free his half-hard cock, tucking the elastic band under his balls. He licked roughly at the head of Patrick's cock. Patrick sucked in a breath that got stuck in his throat when Jono swallowed him down.

Patrick could feel Jono's breath against the skin of his stomach, and he moaned when Jono swallowed. The tight constriction around his cock that came and went had him tightening his hold on Jono's hair. He couldn't decide if he wanted to yank Jono off or drag him closer, and settled for just holding on as Jono took him apart with embarrassing ease.

"Is this because we didn't get a lie-in today and now I'm leaving?" Patrick gasped out, hips circling to push his cock deeper into the wet, willing heat of Jono's mouth.

Jono pulled off him, which wasn't what Patrick wanted *at all*, and he tugged pointedly at Jono's hair. Jono huffed out a laugh, his breath ghosting over the sensitive skin of Patrick's cock.

"I want the god pack in Chicago to know who you belong to when you go before them."

Patrick shivered at those words, moaning loudly when Jono dragged his tongue up the length of his cock before sucking at the tip. "Pretty sure that won't be a problem."

Jono didn't respond, choosing instead to swallow Patrick back down. Patrick pressed his shoulders against the door, fingers tightening on Jono's hair and shoulder. He swore when Jono tugged on his balls, playing with them. Warmth pooled in his belly as everything narrowed down to his cock and Jono's mouth and how badly he wanted to come.

The apartment felt almost too warm, but Patrick figured it was just him. He tried to thrust deeper into Jono's mouth, but Jono pressed his hips against the door, pinning him in place. Patrick whimpered, half curling over Jono as his cock throbbed between Jono's lips.

It was easy to let go like this, to let Jono draw out his pleasure with lips and tongue and the knowing touch of his hands. Jono knew what Patrick liked, what made him come apart at the seams, and it wasn't long before he was coming down Jono's throat, shivering through his orgasm.

"*Jono.*"

Moments like this—safe in Jono's hands—felt like a prayer when Patrick didn't believe in them.

Jono pulled off and rose to his feet, still holding Patrick's softening cock in one hand. At some point he'd undone his own jeans, and his hard cock pressed against Patrick's stomach, making a mess on his skin. Patrick let his forehead fall against Jono's shoulder as Jono started to jerk himself off, breathing in the smell of them.

Jono shifted against him, and Patrick lifted his head, breath catching in his throat when Jono's teeth scraped against the side of his neck. The pressure sharpened but didn't break skin when Jono came, hot cum falling over Patrick's spent cock. He hissed when Jono rubbed it into his sensitive skin, smearing it over his balls.

"I'm not flying with your dried cum on me," Patrick muttered.

Jono licked at his throat, the touch making Patrick wish they had more time to get undressed and mess up the bed.

"You can shower. My scent will still be on you."

Patrick tugged Jono down for a kiss that tasted like a mix of both of them. When they broke apart, Patrick gently scratched at the back of Jono's neck. "Pack my suitcase?"

"Of course." Jono pressed a kiss against his temple. "Love you."

Life was easier these days with someone else to lean on. Patrick didn't know what he'd find in Chicago, but he knew home would be waiting for him when he came back.

Patrick shoved the TSA badge, a set of janitor keys, someone's paper boarding pass, and a lanyard with LaGuardia printed on it into his jacket pocket, fingertips glowing from a look-away ward. Sparks of his magic twisted through the air in their immediate area as the ward directed everyone's attention away from them.

"I *told* you to keep your hands to yourself when we went through security," Patrick hissed.

"Maybe people shouldn't leave stuff lying around waiting for someone to take it," Wade muttered.

"They were wearing the damn things!"

Wade shrugged, gaze darting around as they walked through O'Hare, apparently unrepentant of his thieving ways. "I want a hot dog."

Patrick rolled his eyes and kept walking. "I spent fifty dollars on the plane feeding you. Can we get out of O'Hare first?"

"But Chicago Style Hot Dogs is *right there.*"

Wade's wheedling was the tone of a starving, dramatic teenager who wouldn't be deterred. Patrick didn't want to deal with a long ride into downtown Chicago listening to Wade whine about how hungry he was.

"Fine. Get your hot dog. I'll be waiting right here."

Wade ran off like the hounds of hell were after him, backpack bouncing on his shoulders. Patrick grabbed the handle of Wade's carry-on and dragged it with him out of the way of people rushing back and forth. It was late, and while Patrick was hungry, he wanted to get to the hotel first. He hated airport food. Room service wasn't much better, but he could at least order delivery at a hotel.

Patrick rubbed at his chest, frowning as the knit of his sweater scraped over his scars. The soulbond was muted in his soul the way it always was when he traveled, only it seemed stretched thinner and tighter this trip. He figured it was the distance—almost half a country was farther than half a state. He just hoped it wouldn't be a problem.

Ten minutes later, Wade returned, holding a paper bag that already had bright yellow mustard staining the sides. He had a half-eaten hot dog in one hand and looked pleased with himself as he took another bite, losing a bit of neon green relish off the side. Luckily, it fell into the paper wrapper the hot dog rested on and not the floor.

"Happy now?" Patrick asked as he grabbed the handles of both their carry-ons and started walking.

"I got six, so yeah."

"Consider that your dinner."

"What? No! I'm still getting room service."

"The government won't pay for it."

"You can pay for it."

Patrick snorted. "No, I won't."

"So does that mean I'm getting my own room?"

"No. You're staying with me."

"Then I'm getting room service."

Patrick quit arguing with Wade in favor of getting out of O'Hare and to the rental car location, because trying to win a fight with Wade over food was a losing battle. The sooner they got to the hotel, the quicker they could eat and sleep.

He followed the signs to baggage claim, peeling off toward the exit once they were past security. The second they stepped outside on the lower level, icy cold wind hit him in the face. Patrick winced, while Wade just hunched over his hot dog, eating faster, the jacket he was supposed to be wearing tied around his waist.

"It's cold," Wade muttered around a bite.

"Of course it's cold. It's still winter," Patrick said.

"No, I mean, my hot dog is cold now."

"Do *not* warm it up with your fire breath."

Wade rolled his eyes. "Whatever."

Patrick scanned the signs for the shuttle bus area, finding it a few seconds later and leading Wade over to it. They didn't have to wait long for the bus to come, though the bundled-up driver did give Wade a stern look when they boarded.

"Don't make a mess," the driver said.

"I won't," Wade said around a mouthful of hot dog. "These are good. Not gonna waste them."

Patrick made a face. "Chew with your mouth shut."

Wade made a point of chewing with his mouth open wide for a few more bites before finding his manners again. Patrick sighed heavily. He could see how this trip was going to go, judging by Wade's attitude.

The drive to the rental car facility didn't take long. Patrick didn't have to deal with the line at the desk due to the SOA's membership with the rental car company. They followed the signs to Pick Up for the SUV Patrick had reserved. He opened the car door, finding the key in the ignition with the engine off.

Wade chucked their luggage and backpacks into the trunk once Patrick unlocked the doors. Then he climbed into the front seat and pulled out another hot dog while Patrick adjusted all the mirrors before starting the engine and turning on the heater. He took a minute to plug the downtown Marriott hotel address into his GPS app before texting Jono.

ON THE WAY TO THE HOTEL.

Jono's response came less than thirty seconds later. GET SOME REST. RING ME IN THE MORNING.

They'd promised daily check-ins, and Patrick was going to try to keep to that. Considering the extra formalities governing his arrival in Chicago, Patrick knew he couldn't afford to keep anything from Jono, not if it would put their already tenuous pack position in more trouble.

They got on the road. The ride to downtown Chicago wasn't terrible, taking around forty minutes. Wade finished the last of his hot dogs fairly quick, then pulled out his phone and started playing a game on it. By the time they turned onto North Michigan Avenue, Patrick was ready to crawl into bed. It'd been a long Monday, and traveling with a teenager made him wistful of the days he used to travel alone.

When they finally pulled up in front of the Marriott, the doorman and a valet worker approached almost immediately.

"Valet parking?" the valet asked.

"Yeah," Patrick replied.

Wade handled getting their luggage out of the SUV while Patrick agreed to the daily rate for off-site parking and took the valet ticket before handing over the car keys. Then he and Wade headed for the entrance to the hotel.

Warm air greeted them in a blast once they stepped inside, and Patrick sighed in relief as he looked around. The lobby reminded Patrick of a poor man's Las Vegas casino, but the décor was less of a problem than the recognition that spiked through his magic.

Patrick sucked air through his teeth and didn't get his shields tightened down in time to hide. He hadn't expected to have to deal with werecreatures within an hour and a half of getting off the plane. Patrick watched as one of the front desk clerks' heads snapped around, his attention zeroing in on them despite the handful of other people scattered around the lobby, seated on chairs and couches.

"Ohhh," Wade said, drawing out the word. "Shit."

He was smart enough not to say anything else, sticking close to Patrick's side as they approached the front desk. The werecreature in a suit waved off his coworker so that he could be the one to help them.

"Checking in?" the man asked politely. He was taller than Patrick, of Indian descent, and Sikh, judging by his dastaar. The name tag pinned to his suit said Ekam. His eyes were a dark brown, which meant he wasn't god pack. Patrick didn't know what kind of werecreature Ekam was, and he knew better than to ask.

"Yeah. One room, two double beds if you have it available. Reservation is under Collins. I can give you the confirmation number if you need it," Patrick said, pulling out his phone.

The man nodded slowly, keeping his eyes on the computer screen. He stopped typing a couple of seconds later, gaze flicking back to Patrick and staying riveted to his face. "Patrick Collins?"

Ekam said his name with a weight to the syllables that Patrick didn't like. It made him wonder just how much of the shit going down in New York lately had traveled outside their territory borders. "Yeah. Special Agent Patrick Collins."

Since he knew the guy would be asking for ID, Patrick pulled out his SOA badge from his inner jacket pocket, flipping it open for Ekam to see. The other man's eyes moved from the badge to Patrick's face.

"Out of New York?"

"Says so on the badge, doesn't it?" Wade said.

"Quiet," Patrick said without looking at him. "It's been a long flight, and we just want our room."

Ekam drew in a breath that Patrick knew was meant to get their scent. Patrick didn't know what he'd get off them—Patrick's shields were locked down now and Wade's aura had been human to his senses since they'd gotten on the plane at LaGuardia. If it was Jono's scent somehow, well, he'd be fine with that at least.

Ekam turned his attention back to the computer. "I have a double deluxe on a midfloor ready for you. I'll need a credit card."

Patrick handed over his card, signed what he needed to, then shoved the card back into his wallet once it was returned. Ekam handed over two electronic room key cards, and Patrick promptly gave one to Wade. "Don't lose it."

Wade pocketed it and burped. "Okay. I'm hungry."

Patrick hoped the minibar in their room came with decent alcohol. "What's our room number?"

"You're in room 1209," Ekam said, polite enough. "Enjoy your stay."

If this little interaction was anything to go by, that wasn't going to happen. Patrick grabbed the handle of his suitcase and jerked his head in the direction of the elevator. "Let's go."

Wade followed after him, chewing on a fingernail. He kept looking around at everything, his curiosity obvious. It made Patrick wonder how often Wade had ever been in a hotel growing up before he was kidnapped. He didn't linger too much on that thought. If Wade wanted to talk about his past with them, he knew he could. Patrick wasn't going to ask prying questions because he knew how much someone's past could hurt.

"Twelfth floor, coming right up," Wade said as he pressed the button once they were in the elevator. "If that guy was a werecreature, are we moving hotels?"

Patrick chewed on his bottom lip, watching the floor numbers flash by. "Wouldn't really do much good now that they know we're in town. I'll lay down a threshold once we're in the room."

It wouldn't be as strong as the ones wrapped around their homes because hotels were technically public domains. People might stay in them, but they weren't a home. Magic wasn't going to seep into the foundation of the building and protect it against people or monsters who had no right to be there when a hotel was meant for everyone.

Patrick still did his damnedest to wrap their hotel room with a threshold while Wade decided which bed he wanted. He was picky about where he slept. Patrick still remembered the three hours they'd spent at Macy's in Manhattan last summer helping him decide on a mattress. It had been annoying at the time, but they'd stayed until Wade had lain on every bed at least twice before finally making his decision.

"This one is mine," Wade said, flopping down on the one closest to the window.

The curtains were open, allowing them to see the lit-up Chicago skyline. Patrick dropped his backpack on the other bed before approaching the window and staring out at the view for a few seconds. Then he pulled the curtains shut.

"Unpack and get ready for bed. I need to be at the local field office at 0800 tomorrow, and I want to sleep," Patrick said.

"But I'm still hungry," Wade whined.

Patrick sighed and headed for the nightstand that separated the two double beds. He picked up the phone, checked which extension was room service on the little welcome booklet, then looked at Wade. "What do you want?"

Wade smiled smugly, looking pleased with himself now that he was getting his third meal of the night. "A hamburger. Two of them. With extra fries. Oh, and dessert. Cheesecake if they have it."

Patrick had a feeling he was going to run through his allotted travel stipend for food within the first twenty-four hours of being in Chicago. He wondered if Setsuna would accept *kept fledgling dragon fed so he didn't eat the locals* as an excuse for reimbursements.

3

She couldn't quite keep the discomfort out of her expression when she shook Patrick's hand in the conference room upon first meeting, but she was polite enough not to mention it. Patrick was pretty sure it had to do with his tainted magic because he hadn't bothered shielding completely since leaving the hotel earlier. Possibly also because he was flying in and taking over a case someone else already had.

Either way, her annoyance was noted.

"Collins. Nice to meet you," Kelly said, sounding only slightly dubious. "This is my partner, Special Agent Benjamin Garcia."

She waved at the stocky older man standing beside her who looked like mornings were the enemy, or maybe just Patrick. The man was older than Patrick by at least ten years, with bits of gray scattered through his dark brown hair and a face that was a little pockmarked on the cheeks. He felt human to Patrick's magic, which was a normal status for many SOA agents.

Benjamin reluctantly offered his hand for Patrick to shake. The two might not like him being in Chicago, but they were all technically on the same side, which meant everyone had to pretend to be polite. Patrick took that with a grain of salt, knowing Setsuna still hadn't eradicated all the people with Dominion Sect sympathies out of the SOA. Cleaning house was never easy.

"Were you briefed?" Benjamin asked.

"With what was sent over, but you two have been working the case, so why don't you tell me what's going on," Patrick said.

Letting local agents take the lead in the beginning usually helped smooth things over, but not always. Considering the last time Patrick had been in Chicago he had *maybe* been responsible for a fire demon scorching the Bean, and, well, it was no wonder no one was happy to see him.

"What do you know about the candidates running for mayor in Chicago?" Kelly asked as she sat down at the conference table. Benjamin took the seat beside her, and Patrick opted to sit opposite them.

"Nothing? Chicago isn't my city, so I don't pay attention to your politics unless something hits the national news," Patrick admitted.

Rather than look annoyed, Kelly just shrugged. "This case might make it there."

She pushed a folder across the table, and Patrick dragged it closer to him, flipping it open. Inside was documentation he'd familiarized himself with on the plane, along with case notes that hadn't been included, either due to time or classification levels. Considering they were dealing with politics, it was probably the latter.

Dean Westberg was a man in his late thirties, handsome in a fashion model way, rich by way of a local real estate empire, and looking to break into politics. He seemed to fit the mold of a politician well enough with his background, and had been married for nearly ten years to a socialite, with no known affairs.

His platform was generally that of a conservative democrat, though Patrick could read between the lines easily enough. Westberg might say he didn't care that people had magic or were part of the preternatural world, but his personal bias was pretty clear. He offered up practiced lip service when it came to those of the preternatural world—meaning he didn't personally care for them, or the rights accorded them, but would follow the law. His views on magic ran about the same, and Westberg hinted it was his faith that shaped his worldview.

"Looks fine on paper. What's he hiding underneath?" Patrick asked.

"This is Chicago. You want to do politics here at any level, you have to kiss some rings to do it," Kelly said.

"Digging up dirt is an Olympic sport in this city. Westberg came to our attention when a criminal informant let us know he was taking rent payments from tenants at some of his slum properties with bits of people's souls instead of money," Benjamin said.

Patrick kept his eyes on the file and forced himself not to react to that news. He'd known there was a reason Setsuna had given him this case as cover for searching for the Morrígan's staff, but he'd had no idea it had to do with criminal actions against a person's soul. That classified information hadn't been included in the case file sent over through electronic means, encrypted or otherwise.

"Do you have proof?" Patrick wanted to know.

"Not enough to charge him with anything. Our criminal informant isn't missing parts of their soul, but the people we've tried to interview haven't been willing to talk. We can't read their auras without their permission, a warrant, or a subpoena. Westberg has to know we're investigating him because subpoenas have gone out to third parties and he's hired lawyers, but the attorney general's office doesn't want to tip their hand too much. We're being as careful as we can not to draw attention until we have an airtight case, and Westberg doesn't want this in the news with the election so close, so he's not talking," Kelly said.

Patrick drummed his fingers against the table for a few

seconds. "Housing is difficult to come by if you don't make a living wage. Desperate people do desperate things, but selling your soul is pretty far out there. I find it strange Westberg would make that a requirement for his tenants when he doesn't personally care for magic and is in the middle of a mayoral campaign that's just a stepping stone to a Senate run once his term is over if he wins."

"Winter here is brutal. It's not surprising people wouldn't want to lose their home, with nowhere to go, when the temperature is below freezing."

She had a point. Patrick knew from personal, painful experience that the way to get someone to agree to a shitty proposition was to wait until they were backed into a corner with no other options available. Coercion wasn't always done by force, but by the necessity of the person being asked to agree to the impossible.

"You said not enough proof, which means you have something." Patrick looked up from the file to stare at the other two agents. "What is it?"

Benjamin pointed at the left-hand side of the open file folder. "The pawnshop slip should be clipped in that stack. There's only the one, and it's a photo of it because the person in question wasn't willing to hand it over, but her daughter convinced her to at least show us."

Patrick flipped through the pages in question, sliding free the color copy of the pawnshop slip. The writing on it was faded, not because it was old, but because it was carbon copy. He didn't even know people still used that form of record-keeping anymore.

The name printed and signed in shaky handwriting read Margaret Jones. The item being sold was listed as a *favor*, the cost set at *to be determined*. It was innocuous enough if one didn't know the background details of the transaction.

People sold favors all the time. They were binding, like any promise—a valid contract the courts routinely upheld when challenged by people who regretted offering what they shouldn't. Patrick pulled out his phone and took a picture of the pawnshop record number, as well as the address. When people sold things, the items in question were kept in a shop's inventory as collateral until the person paid off their loan and retrieved it, or failed to do so and the item was put up for sale.

"Have you talked to the owner about this yet?" Patrick asked.

"Twice," Benjamin said. "With no warrant, he wouldn't give us a damn thing."

Patrick stood and shoved his phone into his back pocket. "I'm going to pay him a visit."

Kelly frowned at him. "Do you really think the third time will be the charm?"

"We'll find out."

"Good luck."

She sounded like she didn't believe Patrick would get far, but there was a reason Setsuna gave him the hard cases over the years. His record for closing out cases stood on its own.

Patrick left the SOA field office and crossed the street for the warded parking garage that belonged to the government. Patrick had parked the rental on the fifth level, and he half expected to be greeted by a god when he arrived, but the seats were all empty.

Patrick plugged the pawnshop address into the GPS on his phone before shoving the key into the ignition. The route was taking him to the New City neighborhood on the southwest side of the South Side district.

"Great," Patrick muttered.

He was going to stand out, he wasn't going to be welcomed, and he doubted anyone he met would be willing to talk.

CHICAGO WAS A SPRAWLED mess of a city where the divide of haves and have-nots wasn't as starkly noticeable as in other metropolitan areas. Patrick could still pinpoint when the shift in neighborhoods happened. Buildings gradually turned from the gleaming skyscrapers of downtown to the tree-lined streets of the well-off, before thinning out to narrow brick buildings that had seen better days and dilapidated storefronts that still served a marginalized community.

Patrick eventually made it to The People's Pawn Shop, a small business bracketed on either side by a Dunkin' Donuts and a corner store. The small parking lot was half-full, with the Dunkin' Donuts doing more business than the other two. A handful of men hanging out by two low-riders watched him get out of the SUV. Patrick didn't bother with a look-away ward on his gun or dagger, and the badge hanging from his neck was easy enough to make out.

His face stung from the cold winter wind until he entered the pawnshop, passing through two sets of doors that helped keep heat in and the cold out during winter.

A bell chimed overhead, and the hint of magic that washed over Patrick's shields wasn't human in the least. He shoved his sunglasses up onto his head, taking in the pawnshop. Glass display cases took up most of the floor, with shelves lining the three walls filled with items accessible only to employees. The windows up front were bare of items, the security bars on the outside made of iron and filled with magic.

Patrick doubted the owner had a problem with break-ins, despite the neighborhood.

A pair of Hispanic men in winter parkas, jeans, and boots looked up from whatever they were perusing in a glass case. The rapid conversation they had in Spanish ended with them heading for the exit, abandoning whatever they'd come to look at. The employee who had been helping them didn't watch them go, his dark brown eyes focused on Patrick.

The recognition burning through Patrick's soul and magic was one he hadn't felt in years, not since he was on the Hell-raisers and they'd run a mission in the Kandahar mountains. Ifrits tended to prefer the countryside over the density of mortal cities, but beggars couldn't be choosers in a rapidly developing world.

"Long way from your ancestral home," Patrick said in greeting as he walked forward.

The ifrit smiled slightly and picked a tray filled with small idols and loose items off the glass countertop, returning it to the display case below. "Certainly more profitable."

"Yeah, I can see that. Is the owner in?"

"You're talking to him."

Patrick came to a stop in front of the ifrit, sizing the demon up. His fingers twitched with the urge to reach for his dagger. The ifrit looked human, with dark brown skin, black hair and beard, and a smile that wouldn't look out of place on a car salesman selling secondhand vehicles. He wondered why Kelly hadn't mentioned the owner was an ifrit, unless she didn't know. Witches weren't mages on the power scale, and most mages didn't have Patrick's unenviable ability to recognize and hunt the darker aspects of the preternatural world.

Patrick looked away from the demon to take in some of the items for sale in the display cases before him and the shelves on the wall. Magic of varying power was embedded in some of the pieces, making them artifacts in their own right. Even more were nothing more than common, everyday items.

The place looked legitimate, but the owner—by virtue of what he was—said it wasn't.

Patrick hooked a thumb around the chain his badge hung from and lifted it for the ifrit to see. The badge didn't have his name, just his agent identification number on it. The less information he gave up here, the better. "I'm with the SOA. I'm here to ask you a few questions."

"Of course you are." The ifrit smiled. "Words are fine. I deal in words all the time. But if you don't have a warrant or subpoena for anything else, I'm afraid I can't help you."

Patrick hummed thoughtfully before unsheathing his dagger

and laying it down on the glass countertop. The ifrit froze, his smile becoming tacked on as he stared at the matte-black blade resting between them, all the power of the heavens and their many prayers capable of incinerating him with one little cut bound to the weapon.

"I'm not from around here," Patrick said mildly. "I know what you are, just like you know what this dagger can do to you. I'll come back with a search warrant if need be, but you're going to tell me the truth when you speak today."

Patrick kept his fingertips resting on the hilt of the dagger, his attention locked on the ifrit's pale face. The demon leaned away from the counter a little, putting some distance between himself and the threat of death in the shape of sharp edges.

"Ask your questions," the ifrit spat out, the veins on his face pulsing fiery red, like lava, beneath his skin for a second before calming down.

"People are selling you favors, but we both know that's not what they're actually giving you."

The ifrit licked his lips. "I don't know what you're talking about."

Patrick dug out his phone and unlocked it, finding the photo from earlier of the pawnshop slip. He turned the phone around so the ifrit could see the screen. "Don't you?"

Brown eyes flicked from the phone to Patrick's face. "Favors are legal."

"Souls aren't."

"I don't see souls mentioned in the itemized line."

Patrick smiled thinly and put his phone away. "Of course you don't. This favor someone sold to you. I want to see it."

"I can't show you."

"I don't need a warrant to see something I want to buy."

The ifrit shook his head. "It's been bought already."

Patrick knew if he asked to see the records on who had purchased it, he'd be denied. That was information he'd need a warrant for, but getting one required probable cause, and the SOA didn't have any they could use yet. It was up to Patrick to find it. Hearsay wouldn't hold up in the courts after all.

Patrick picked up his dagger and flipped it around with deft fingers, sliding it back into the sheath on his right thigh. The ifrit didn't relax even after the weapon was put away, glaring at Patrick and keeping his distance.

Patrick rapped his knuckles on the glass countertop. "See you around."

He left the pawnshop, feeling the ifrit's gaze boring into his back on the way out. Once outside in the cold, Patrick didn't lower his shields. The group with the low-riders was gone, but the car now parked in one of those spots carried its own set of problems.

The black woman sitting behind the wheel wasn't looking at him, but her phone. She might have been just another person running errands if his magic didn't recognize her as a werecreature. There'd been one in the hotel lobby that morning, and one walking past the SOA field office when he'd arrived. He hadn't seen one when he'd left, but it was looking more and more like Patrick was being followed, judging by the latest arrival.

Patrick got into the SUV and started the engine. He backed out of the spot and headed for the street. He kept half his attention on the road and the rest on the rearview mirror. He wasn't surprised in the least to see the black Chevrolet follow him onto the street ten seconds later.

Patrick cast a silence ward in the SUV, static washing through the frame of the vehicle. He lifted his hips to get to his phone, glancing at the screen a couple of times in order to unlock it and call Wade.

"Where are you?" Patrick said when Wade picked up.

"Uh, why? Are you in trouble?" Wade asked.

"Not yet, but I'm being followed."

"Werecreatures? I saw a couple this morning before I lost them."

Patrick scowled and drummed his fingers against the steering wheel. "And you didn't think you should go back to the hotel once you identified them?"

Wade snorted. "The hotel doesn't have good snacks. I'm at Target getting better ones."

"Of course you are."

"It's not like I can't tell what they are, and I'm good at ditching people in a crowd. I'm not being followed right now. Trust me, I'd know if I was."

"Get back to the hotel, Wade."

"After I get snacks. And maybe another hot dog."

"*Wade.*"

"Food first, fight later, bye."

Wade ended the call, and Patrick swore. "Fucking teenagers."

Patrick shoved his worry aside, knowing Wade could fend for himself these days. Patrick and Jono had made sure he could. That didn't stop Patrick from wishing Wade would *listen*.

He didn't know what was more annoying that morning: an uncooperative teenager or the werecreatures who kept following him around Chicago. When Patrick finally made it back to the hotel room for a late lunch and found Wade on the bed, surrounded by an overabundance of chips, candy, crackers, and other snacks, he decided it was teenagers.

Wade shoved a handful of goldfish crackers into his mouth. "I'm not sharing."

Patrick rolled his eyes.

Definitely teenagers.

4

JONO PARKED THE MUSTANG IN FRONT OF A CLUSTER OF RED-bricked residential buildings in the Brooklyn neighborhood of Midwood. It was a couple blocks from the Q stop, but it was late enough and cold enough that Jono had opted to drive rather than take the subway.

Leon opened the passenger-side door and took a deep breath. "I don't smell anything out of the ordinary."

Jono finished texting Patrick an update before he got out of the car. He breathed in and got a lungful of icy winter air, the wind smelling like snow and the metal-and-smoke scent that permeated the New Rebels pack territory. Beneath it was the usual mix of urban street smells, but Leon was right. Jono couldn't smell any trace of Estelle and Youssef's New York City god pack.

"It doesn't mean they won't show up," Jono said.

The door leading to the closest apartment building was pushed open and a man almost as tall as Jono stepped out. He was lankier though, with a friendly smile on his face.

"Thanks for coming out," Austin Capaldi said, sounding relieved as he approached the pair.

"That's what I'm here for, mate," Jono replied as he and Leon stepped onto the sidewalk.

Austin came to a stop in front of Jono and tilted his head to the side, showing throat in an act of submission that always looked easy for him when it was Jono standing in front of him. Jono had seen Austin show throat to Estelle and Youssef in the past, and it always looked like the DMZ between North and South Korea in physical form.

Austin's pack had come to them in early January, looking to switch alliances and ready to argue their case if Jono had any doubts. Not that there'd been any. Austin and his beta had come to Tempest one night, introduced his pack, managed to get two sentences into his request for protection before Jono had agreed to take them on.

With fifteen werewolves in their pack, all of whom called Brooklyn home within three blocks of where they stood, the New Rebels might have been small in numbers, but they made up for it in connections. Austin originally hailed from Los Angeles and had followed his wife to New York City for her medical residency. He'd left behind his old pack whose alpha had been married to a member of the Los Angeles god pack.

That two-hundred-member god pack was the largest in the United States, young in terms of years active, but not without power. Bringing Austin's pack into Jono's circle of protection meant they had an avenue of communication with the Los Angeles god pack, something Estelle and Youssef lacked.

Most god packs tended to honor pass-through rights of visiting members from outside their territory. Estelle and Youssef's rigid pack laws over the years had made entering New York City difficult for many. Whatever goodwill had existed before they came to power had definitely been squandered.

The only god pack Jono had opened up communications with was the San Francisco god pack. That one was small, half their numbers made up of werecougars rather than werewolves, but he'd had to broker pass-through rights for Emma's pack due to their work in the tech industry. Jono hadn't reached out to the Los Angeles god pack yet, but he knew when the time came, Austin's willingness to support Jono's god pack would go a long way toward a good first impression.

Still, Jono knew he'd have to make more of a stand, take on more of the packs within New York, for any of the other major god packs in the country to acknowledge his status. Until then, he would continue to care for the packs that came to him for help.

Jono dropped his hand away from Austin's throat. "Any sign of Nicholas tonight?"

Austin shrugged. "Haven't caught his scent or anyone else's from their god pack."

"Your newest all right?"

"Lira is a little rattled, but she gave as good as she got until we arrived to back her up. I told her she didn't have to come tonight, but she insisted."

Behind him, a couple more werecreatures came out of the building, wearing light jackets like he and Jono were. Werecreatures ran hotter than mundane humans, and it was easy to forget they weren't cold when they needed to act like it to keep their identities hidden.

Lira Tran was a slender Vietnamese American woman in her early twenties. She didn't look like she could bench-press a car, but looks were always deceiving. She smiled tentatively at Jono before showing throat.

"Hey, love," Jono said gently before scent-marking her. "Heard you had a bit of a rough go of it the other night."

"I'm okay," Lira said.

The handful of others who'd come to support their alpha showed Jono their throat, and he went through the ritual greeting quickly. Then he stepped back and nodded at Leon. "Keep watch here while we get their borders marked."

"Be careful around the playground," Leon warned.

"I know." Jono gestured at Austin and the others as he started down the pavement. "Let's go."

Patrick had joked once that werecreatures could just piss to mark their territories. Jono had smacked him in the face with a sofa pillow. Werecreatures marked territories by a pack member walking it daily and touching designated spots. It built up over time, creating a marker that surrounded a pack's territory. The scent people carried—both their own and their pack scent—could only be tracked by someone with preternatural senses, and werecreatures were better at it than most.

It was why pass-through rights existed, allowing someone to cross a territory that wasn't theirs without retribution. Lately, Estelle and Youssef had taken to breaking through all marked territories of the packs Jono had laid claim to and assaulting the people under his protection. It was a challenge he refused to let slide, and he had a few ideas on how to handle it.

"Where's Patrick?" Austin asked.

"Working," Jono replied.

He didn't go into detail, and the others didn't ask. Patrick co-led their pack, and any decisions Jono made, he knew Patrick would back him up.

Austin pointed out the locations of his pack's markers on the walk around their small territory: light posts, post boxes, certain bricks on building corners, a sewer grate, and more. Solid items that would rarely be moved or replaced were the best for carrying scent. Jono pressed his hand to every spot, overlaying his god pack scent into the territory claimed by the New Rebels.

They were three-quarters finished when the wind picked up, carrying the faint hint on the breeze of something that smelled bitter and rotten. The bitterness reminded him a little bit of Patrick's scent—a recognition that had Fenrir howling a warning that made Jono's soul twist.

Jono reacted on instinct, hauling Austin away from the

manhole cover the other man was about to crouch next to and mark. "*Scatter!*"

Preternatural speed meant none of them got hit by the four crossbow bolts that cut through the air, hitting asphalt and someone's car instead of live bodies. The smell of silver and aconite hit Jono's nose hard, making his eyes water. He shoved Austin behind a parked car on the other side of the street, in the opposite direction the bolts had come from.

"What the fuck was that?" Austin hissed. "Who the fuck uses *crossbows?*"

"You'd rather whoever the fuck they are use a gun instead?" Jono retorted.

Austin made a face. "No."

Jono grimaced, not liking what the unusual choice of weapon meant. Crossbows weren't normally most people's first choice of a weapon in a fight against werecreatures, but they did the job of keeping the shooter out of the range of teeth and claws. In an urban environment, when people didn't want to catch the attention of authorities, weapons other than guns were sometimes preferable. They made less noise and could be just as deadly.

All Jono knew was that the people who used those sorts of weapons never saw his kind as anything other than monsters to be hunted. If the people shooting at them were hunters, then he needed to get Austin's pack out of the line of fire and bring a proverbial gun to the fight.

He knew just where to find one.

"Go to your apartment building and get inside," Jono ordered.

"We're not leaving you," Austin told him.

"Austin—"

"*No.* This is my pack's territory, and we're going to fight for it."

Jono didn't have time to argue. None of them did. "Then get to the playground and make some noise when you arrive."

Austin flexed his hands, claws replacing his fingernails. "What about you? I can't smell whoever is out there."

Magic could go a long way toward hiding a person's scent. Sage's pendant necklace doubled as an artifact, and Patrick's personal shields had been anchored by a goddess. Picking them out as anything but human in a crowd was impossible sometimes. What Austin didn't know was that Jono had a connection to Fenrir, and he hoped the god was up to helping him out tonight.

"I'll draw them out. I have a feeling I'm the reason they're here."

It would be just like Estelle and Youssef to pay a third party to kill him. Patrick couldn't kill the perpetrators who came at the packs under their protection due to the bad press it would cause. The packs who were accosted never wanted to press charges, and Jono would never force them to. Estelle and Youssef's inability to challenge Jono directly just proved they were scared of him and what he represented. Either way, someday soon, they'd all have to meet in the challenge ring, and that was a fight Jono was determined to win.

Just like this one.

"Ready when you are," Austin said.

Jono nodded. "Go."

The pack members of the New Rebels tapped into their preternatural speed and ran down the street in zigzag motions, being careful to stay behind cover when they could. The sound of more crossbow bolts releasing reached Jono's ears, but he didn't hear any screams. He used the sound of the release to narrow down the position of their attackers. That, paired with the calm heartbeats of four people buried beneath the rush of city noises and people packed together, was enough for Jono to figure out their general locations.

Jono crossed the street in a blur, crossbow bolts cutting harmlessly through the air in his wake. He was too fast to get hit, and the reflexes behind the shots were human, of that he was certain.

He just wasn't sure what else the hunters carried in their souls.

Jono found the first attacker crouched in the bushes lining one of the residential apartment buildings, a moving shadow that Jono headed right for. He dodged the bolt aimed at his heart, nostrils flaring at the poisonous scent of silver and aconite left in its wake. Jono shoved down the memories of silver weapons cutting into his body in favor of getting his hand around the man's throat.

He slammed the man against the building, hard enough to daze the fucker. Jono yanked the crossbow out of the man's loose grip, breaking the finger curled over the trigger. The man didn't scream, lips curling away from his crooked teeth in an ugly grin as he kicked out at Jono with a quickness that reminded him of Patrick's training.

Jono dodged the kick, digging claws into the man's throat rather than fingernails as a warning. Blood trickled over his fingers, and the smell of it was rotten.

The eerie sound of a wolf's howl broke through the night, sounding out of place amidst the nighttime noises that permeated Brooklyn. Jono took that as his cue to move. He slammed the crossbow against the side of the building to break it before tossing the weapon aside. The sound of another crossbow releasing had him spinning on his feet, pulling the man in front of him.

The bolt meant to hit Jono in the back instead targeted the man's chest. It wasn't a life-threatening hit, because Jono could feel the shape of a tactical vest beneath the man's winter jacket that prevented the bolt from piercing skin. It would've been nice if the bastard had taken the hit in the heart.

The smell of silver and aconite stung Jono's eyes, but he didn't let that stop him from retreating, putting distance between himself and the enemies closing in. He didn't let go of his human shield, hauling the bleeding, struggling man with him down the block toward the playground.

"Who sent you?" Jono growled.

His grip on the man's throat eased just enough for the arsehole to get some air, but all that came out was a vicious "Fuck you."

"Nah, not my type. I like gingers."

Jono didn't bother asking more questions. He picked out the

shadows following at a quick pace, yellow light from streetlamps glinting off their weapons. They weren't using guns, but that didn't mean they didn't have any. Jono bared his teeth and picked up the pace, keeping his prisoner close.

"Jono!"

Leon's shout came from his right as he reached the corner, but Jono didn't look. He ran into the street, dodging in front of a car so fast the driver didn't start to brake until Jono reached the other side. He could see Austin's pack scattered through the playground, the scent of their uncertainty and traces of fear about being in territory that wasn't theirs carrying on the wind.

The playground had minimal coverage—just a few trees lining the sidewalk outside the fencing. A building took up space on one half of the block to the left of the playground. They had nowhere to hide out in the open, but hiding wasn't his intention. Jono put on a burst of speed, vaulting over the fence that enclosed the play-ground, hauling the bleeding man in his arms with him. They landed on the other side, and Jono slammed the man face-first into the ground. Jono drew in a breath, the scent of the city and the New Rebels pack mingling with the distinct smell of the undead.

"This isn't your territory, wolf. Get the fuck out."

Jono narrowed his eyes at the vampire who dropped down to the ground in front of him from the nearby building, eliciting warning growls from Austin's pack. Jono would've been thrilled he'd pissed off the Brooklyn Night Court by crossing uninvited into their territory, but the man on the ground suddenly heaved upward with a strength that wasn't human.

Jono grunted as the man twisted in his hold, ramming an elbow into Jono's side. He rolled out of the way, the faint sound of metal leaving metal reaching Jono's ears. He swore, letting the man go and throwing himself backward, but he wasn't fast enough to escape the knife that caught him in the ribs.

The silver blade, laced with aconite, burned like acid. Jono felt it in every centimeter of skin and bone the knife grated over before he could knock it aside. Jono stumbled a little in his attempt to get out of range. Before the man could close in for another strike, Leon grabbed Jono by the shoulders and hauled him out of reach.

The man got to his feet with a serpentine movement that made the hairs on the back of Jono's neck stand on end. Jono tried to ignore the deep ache growing in his chest, but he knew what silver and aconite poisoning felt like. His rapid healing wasn't going to fix this wound.

"The fuck is that?" Leon asked, his grip on Jono growing tighter.

Jono blinked, trying to steady his vision. The man standing in front of them didn't seem to feel the severely broken nose on his face. It was flattened and bent to the side, the blood still trickling out of it black in the shadows cast by the nearby streetlamp. Jono had a feeling the man's blood would be black even in broad daylight.

Possession is nine-tenths of the law when it comes to demons.

Patrick's voice echoed in his mind from a past conversation as Jono sought to straighten up and shake off Leon's hand. Jono's breath came out in a puff of white as blood slid down his side and soaked into the jumper he wore. He pressed his hand against the wound, fighting against the sickly heat spreading away from it through his chest.

"Jono," Austin said in a tight voice as he came up to flank them. "What the fuck?"

"Stay back," Jono growled.

They were downwind, and the breeze that blew over the playground carried with it a mix of human and the rotten egg stench of sulfur. Whatever artifact the hunter had carried to hide his scent must have been damaged or lost in their scuffle. Jono wanted to scrub the smell out of his nose and mouth, but he'd settle for figuring out how to kill a demon taking up space in a human body without magic.

Most laws on the books still considered it murder if you killed a possessed man. Jono knew the courts didn't favor the self-defense excuse when used by werecreatures unless it was within claimed territory. Even then, it was a gray area, but Jono wasn't about to go down without a fight.

"The only good werecreature is a dead one," the demon said around swollen lips and broken front teeth.

Jono flexed his fingers, claws lengthening at the tips. His attention skipped from the demon-possessed man in front of them to the ones crossing the street, no longer hiding in the shadows.

A rushing sound echoed in Jono's ears as more vampires jumped off the surrounding buildings to land in the playground. The vampires surrounded the werecreatures but didn't immediately attack them.

Fenrir's presence seeped through Jono's soul, and he didn't have the capacity to hold his ground against the god, not with poison running through his veins.

Don't, Jono said, trying not to beg. *Don't show them who you are.*

The number of people who knew about his patron was growing, but Jono knew now wasn't the time for word to get out about Fenrir. Enough of the wrong people already knew—Lucien and Ethan—that Jono couldn't afford for rumors to start to grow. His pack wasn't ready yet for the civil war heading their way.

Fenrir howled through his soul but let Jono keep control of his body and mind.

"We should get out of here. I don't like what I'm smelling," Leon said in a tight voice.

"Because they're demons," Jono said, breathing a little harder. The ache in his ribs was getting worse, the burn of silver and aconite making him sweat in a way he wasn't used to.

The man with a bruised and broken face smiled at that, flexing the hand with a broken finger. Another silver knife dropped out of his jacket sleeve into his hand. Leon's grip tightened on Jono.

"The bounty on your head was worth the drive north," the

demon said. The skin on his face seemed to move, black veins briefly showing through what skin wasn't covered in blood. The smell of sulfur grew stronger, making Jono gag.

Before anyone could respond, one of the hunters on the other side of the fence was slammed to the ground by the force of the person that landed on him. Jono heard bones crack, the gurgle of a scream broken off by virtue of a throat being torn out. He heard blood spatter on cold pavement like rain before the vampire moved, flinging himself over the fence and into the playground with a speed that few others in the preternatural world could match.

"You wasted all that gas for nothing and came driving through my territory without asking," the newcomer said.

Jono heard Austin swear from behind him as the master vampire for the Brooklyn Night Court landed amidst his followers. Jamere's physical appearance was that of a teenager, but the vampire was over four hundred years old, and how he looked had no bearing on the viciousness he employed when it came to holding his territory.

"Bounty isn't on your head, but we'll kill you for the fun of it," the demon said.

Jamere's laugh was low and deep. The smile on his dark face showed off a mouthful of jagged fangs. "You wouldn't be the first hunter to try."

Whatever signal Jamere gave, Jono never saw it, never heard it. One second the vampires of the Brooklyn Night Court stood like silent shadows in the dark playground. The next, they were blurs of motion that Jono's eyesight couldn't keep up with.

Vampires couldn't fly, but they moved with a speed that lay the foundation for the myths that had propagated over the centuries. The remaining two hunters beyond the playground scattered rather than fight, which told Jono they probably weren't sharing their soul with a demon. Not standing their ground was their first mistake. Jono tuned out their screams in favor of making sure he got answers.

"Don't kill the demon," Jono said.

"This isn't your territory," Jamere reminded him as he darted in close underneath the demon's quick knife thrust to bury his clawed hand in the body's gut. "You don't give the orders here."

"The New Rebels pack is under my protection, which means you and I are overdue for a chat about borders."

Jamere ripped out a coil of intestines, tossing the ropy organ away from him. The tactical vest the hunter wore had torn like so much wet paper in the face of the vampire's strength. The body in his hands jerked, a few more loops of intestines falling out of the hole. Blood and the acidic smell of a punctured stomach gave the cold breeze a sour undertone.

The sound of thunder when no lightning had struck echoed loudly in Jono's ears. Gray light haloed the hunter for a split second before fading. The sulfur scent diminished as the demon fled.

There went any hope of getting answers.

Wherever the demon had escaped to, it wasn't to anyone around them. Vampires had no souls, and the black magic powering the werevirus made possession too difficult most of the time for demons to attempt it on a werecreature. Jono only hoped they hadn't damned anyone in the neighborhood to demonic possession.

Jamere dropped the body and turned to look at Jono. "You must be fucking special to have the Krossed Knights coming after your ass. Maybe I should leave you to the fuckers next time or put you out of your misery myself."

Jono froze at that bit of information. Hunters of all things that went bump in the night had grown out of the Crusades in the western hemisphere, their numbers fluctuating over the centuries. They'd had more influence in the times where magic wasn't looked upon as something useful. The last couple of centuries hadn't been kind to their numbers, and they, in turn, had never been kind to the people and monsters they hunted.

Different branches had broken off and drawn up their own laws over the centuries as they migrated across the world. The Krossed Knights were predominantly found in the United States, and a problem Jono had managed to steer clear of until now, it seemed.

"Lucien wouldn't like that," Jono said in a low voice, gambling on the thinnest of associations with one of the most notorious vampires in the world to keep him and everyone else alive tonight.

Jamere smiled nastily as he stalked forward. "Way I hear it, Lucien might consider it a favor."

Jono pushed through the creeping sense of wrong in his body to keep his focus, digging in his heels when Leon would've pulled him backward and away from the threat. "You want to chance that? Then be my guest."

"Between the two of you, I thought Patrick was the only one with a death wish. You need to stop trying to one-up each other," Leon muttered.

Jono hadn't realized he was leaning so much of his weight on Leon until he tried to straighten up. Pain lanced through his ribs, and more blood seeped out of the wound. It still hadn't healed, and Jono was starting to feel like the time he'd had the flu when he was a kid.

Jamere came to a stop in front of Jono, neither of them giving ground. In the distance, Jono could hear sirens, the sound getting closer with every second that passed. But the bodies lying on the ground were technically in vampire territory, and the Krossed Knights were hunters no one would mourn over.

"Those weren't the only hunters after your ass. You're real popular these days," Jamere said.

Jono idly wondered what the bounty on his head was, and if it was something he should immediately warn Patrick about. "First I've heard of it."

"You're difficult to reach with that mage around you all the time. Where is he?"

Jono thought about Patrick's absence, about how half their pack was gone and he had hunters harassing their borders. "Tell Lucien I want a meeting."

"Jono," Leon said warningly.

Jamere's fangs cut into his lips when he smirked, half his face in shadow. "I ain't no messenger."

Jono leaned in close, Leon's hand keeping him steady. "I'm the alpha of the New York City god pack. I don't care about bloody demon-possessed hunters. I care about my territory. Tell Lucien I want to talk borders."

Leon's fingers tightened hard enough to bruise, and Jono knew he'd carry those marks for hours after they left the playground.

Jamere didn't move, didn't breathe, the undead smell he carried reminding Jono of a grave. The sirens were getting louder, and none of them could afford to get caught by the police. Not tonight.

"Been years since your kind has wanted to talk." Jamere blinked, face moving with an animation to it that came as an afterthought. "I think I prefer the fighting."

Jamere blurred away, his vampires following him. Jono blinked, stumbling a little when Leon hauled him around, taking on more of his weight.

"We need to get out of here," Leon said tightly. "You're still bleeding."

"Silver and aconite," Jono muttered.

"Yeah, I fucking *know*. Victoria is working tonight. We can swing by Mount Sinai on the way home."

"No hospitals. They have to report attacks like this."

"You're a stubborn asshole. Stop trying to be like Patrick."

Austin darted forward and settled in on Jono's left, helping him to stay upright. "Is it safe for you to leave with the police coming? You can stay at my place until they're gone."

Jono shook his head, letting them guide him toward the locked gate, which Leon easily kicked open. "Get your pack inside, Austin."

He was worried about their ability to keep their privacy intact if they were seen with him. Jono's eyes could never let him hide, and he'd spent years taking public hits for himself alone. Taking them for the packs under his protection was new, but that's what he was supposed to do. He'd bear that cost, and gladly.

Somehow, Leon and Austin managed to haul him back to the Mustang before the police made it to the playground. Leon dug the keys out of Jono's pocket to unlock the car, shoved him into the front passenger seat, and shut the door. Jono closed his eyes against the vertigo for a couple of seconds, listening to Leon fake a cheerful goodbye to Austin, casually acting like nothing was wrong as the police sped past. Then he got behind the wheel and started the engine.

"I left blood at the scene," Jono muttered.

"Blame it on the vampires if Casale comes around," Leon said as he pulled onto the street at a normal speed.

Somehow, Jono didn't think Jamere or Lucien would appreciate that.

Leon pulled out his mobile and unlocked it without taking his eyes off the road. "I'm calling Sage."

"If Patrick calls her for advice, tell her not to say anything about what happened tonight. Goes for everyone."

Jono needed Patrick to focus on his case in Chicago and not to worry about what was happening in New York. Jono could handle things on his own.

"You're going to be in for a world of hurt with that order."

Jono didn't care, one hand pressed to the knife wound that wouldn't heal. "Just drive."

5

text message from Jono he'd missed earlier while driving back to the hotel that evening.

IN BROOKLYN TO CHAT WITH THE NEW REBELS PACK ABOUT BORDER BREACHES.

Patrick frowned, hating the fact he wasn't there to help Jono out with the problem. He was about to text Jono back when recognition ran through his magic with the subtlety of a semitruck crashing on a highway and going up in flames.

Werecreatures.

"Motherfucker," Patrick said, scowling at the entrance to the hotel.

He'd returned to the Chicago field office after checking on Wade during his lunch break earlier in the day. Getting brought up to speed on a case like this took time. While his side trip to the pawnshop had been a necessary stop, it meant staying late to ensure he knew the parameters of the case down to the last detail.

The current case was dovetailing with his need to carve out time to speak with Aksel Sigfodr. The man featured prominently in Chicago politics, and keeping the two cases separate was going to require some delicate juggling. Patrick had a small list of people he needed to interview, research to do, and case notes he had to finish cross-referencing for both cases he was working. All of that would have to wait until he dealt with whoever was waiting for him inside.

Patrick shoved the valet ticket into his pocket for easy reach and headed for the entrance. He traced a look-away ward over the leather sheath that held his dagger strapped to his right thigh. Patrick didn't care if people spotted his gun, but he'd rather their eyes slide over the blade carrying magic gifted by the gods.

Patrick locked down his personal shields to keep his magic hidden before he even stepped foot inside the hotel. Having active shields didn't stop him from picking out the werecreatures scattered around the lobby once he arrived, from the front desk clerk to the bartender in the lobby's circular bar, to every single person lounging in the chairs and couches in the center pretending to be guests.

Patrick counted an even two dozen, not all of them god pack. The only ones who carried the god strain of the werevirus in their veins were sitting on the large yellow leather couch near the staircase leading up to the second floor. He could see the brightness of their amber eyes from meters away.

Seated directly across from them was Wade, surrounded by plastic Target bags filled with mostly empty snack wrappers. A family-sized bag of Doritos rested beside him on the cushion while his jacket was thrown over the back of the couch. As Patrick watched, Wade dug into the bag of chips, grabbed a few more, and popped them into his mouth. He chewed slowly, never taking his eyes off the four god pack werecreatures watching him eat with wary looks on their faces.

"I thought I left you in the hotel room?" Patrick asked as he approached the tense, silent standoff, ignoring all the eyes on him.

"Yeah. I got bored." Wade grabbed another handful of chips,

picked out the biggest one, and shoved it into his mouth. "Also hungry. You said you'd be back for dinner an hour ago."

"Got caught up in a meeting." Patrick eyed the multiple Target bags scattered on the couch and shook his head. "You went out again after I left, didn't you?"

"Yup." Wade popped the *p* on the word before licking his fingers clean of bright orange nacho cheese powder. "Had to get more snacks. Guess who followed me back?"

Wade didn't take his eyes off the werecreatures on the yellow couch, but he did pause long enough to crunch up the now empty bag of Doritos and shove it into the nearest overflowing Target bag. He knocked a few of them to the floor, making room for Patrick on the two-person couch. He seemed more annoyed than anything else about the werecreatures surrounding them, which was better than fear.

Wade had gotten better about standing up for himself and for the pack with the help of therapy and a vital support network. Facing off against strange werecreatures alone wasn't something Patrick had thought he'd leave Wade to do today, and he felt a little guilty it had happened.

Patrick came to a stop beside the small couch but didn't immediately sit beside Wade. Instead, he studied the four god pack werecreatures, taking their measure and trying to figure out which one was in charge. Patrick didn't have enhanced senses to sniff everyone out like Jono would if he were here. Despite being a mage, Patrick was human when it came to everything else, and he wasn't going to be ashamed of that fact.

The three men and one woman were a mix of ethnicities, though they shared the same intense, wolf-bright amber eyes. Patrick's gaze darted over each of them before he made a wild guess and focused on the woman. In his experience, women were usually the ones in charge, hiding behind society's perception that they weren't.

"I'm here on SOA business, not pack business. You didn't need to show up with the welcome committee like this," Patrick said.

The woman didn't blink, merely gave a careless, one-shoulder shrug at his statement. She was dressed in a business suit, a long camel-colored wool coat draped over the low table in front of her. Her Afro was teased out a couple of inches from her skull, bleached and dyed to a honey brown. The shade matched the nude color of her lipstick and the high-heeled boots she wore.

"You're still in our territory without permission," she said.

Patrick tapped the badge hanging from around his neck. "This gives me all the permission I need."

The woman rolled her eyes. "Pack law still matters, whether you're a federal agent or not. Our god pack alphas want to see you."

"What happens if I say no and go upstairs to my hotel room to order room service?"

"Are you?" Wade asked, perking up. "Because I'm starving and I want a hot dog."

"Room service doesn't offer that dish. Should've ordered delivery."

"Aw, man."

The woman's gaze darted from Patrick to Wade, lingering on the teenager in a way Patrick didn't like. To Patrick, Wade seemed human, his aura dimmed down to how he'd been taught to project it in order to pass as something he wasn't. Maybe the werecreatures smelled something different that was tipping them off.

Wade was their pack's ace in the hole, because no one ever expected a dragon to show up for a fight. They wanted him to keep what he was a secret not only as a last resort, but also so he could live as normal a life as possible. It was why, whenever General Reed asked about Wade, Patrick always changed the subject. If the military wanted Wade, they'd have to go through Patrick first.

"I'm here at the request of my alphas to bring you before them for trespassing," the woman said.

Patrick weighed her words and the intent behind them, picking through all the ranks of werecreatures he could be talking to and coming up with just one. "Dire?"

She smiled in a way that showed off just a hint of fangs, but the look in her bright amber eyes reminded him of Sage at her most implacable. "Good guess. Monica Woodard, though I'm not at your service."

"And the rest of your pack?"

"You don't need to know their names."

Patrick shrugged. "Fair enough."

Too many out there who called the preternatural world home took currency in names. The whole mess in December just proved it was a shitty payment system. Patrick couldn't be mad about someone not wanting to give out a name that didn't belong to them.

"How are we doing this? Are your alphas coming here? Is that why you have such a huge entourage?" Patrick asked.

"They don't come to you. You go to them."

"Nah, I don't play that game. We'll meet on neutral ground. I'm here for work, but if you want me here as a god pack alpha, then you need to respect that rank."

Monica's mouth curled in disdain. "You are no werecreature."

"I'm still pack, and everyone in New York who we protect considers me an alpha the same way Jono is. You either treat me as an alpha or the meeting you want isn't happening. I'm here in Chicago for my job, not to make trouble."

"The way I hear it, trouble follows you wherever you go," the man sitting to Monica's left said.

Wade slowly ripped open a box of Pop-Tarts, the sound of tearing cardboard drawing everyone's attention to him. Patrick watched him wiggle his fingers over the packets inside before choosing one from the middle. He tore it open, pulled a Pop-Tart out, and took a large bite of the corner, flashing sharp teeth in a not so subtle way.

"Put your teeth away," Patrick told him.

"They are away," Wade retorted around a mouthful of food.

His eyes were still brown, with human pupils, and no hint of red scales was showing through his skin. It was a miniscule shift of mass to change his teeth, but it was enough for a flicker of unease to cross Monica's face. She leaned back on the couch, her gaze lingering on Wade for a few more seconds before she focused on Patrick.

"What is he?" she asked.

"He's pack," Patrick replied, deliberately misinterpreting the question.

Monica narrowed her eyes. "My alphas will deal with you alone."

"I don't think so," Wade said, brushing crumbs off his shirt. He poured out the packets of Pop-Tarts and twisted around to shove them in his jacket pockets before getting to his feet. "I go where Patrick goes. You don't like it, then oh fucking well."

Wade glared at the god pack werecreatures with an intensity that made some of the surrounding werecreatures drift closer, sensing a threat. Patrick leaned over to grab Wade's jacket off the couch and hand it to him.

"Put your jacket on," he said.

Wade made a face. "Does that mean no room service?"

"Jacket now. Room service later."

Wade grumbled under his breath before making a show about putting it on. He left his garbage where it was, and Patrick would've told him to pick up after himself, but he figured the werecreatures on staff could deal with the mess.

Patrick turned to look at Monica. "Neutral ground, or I'm going upstairs and staying there, and anyone who tries to get inside my room is going to regret it."

Her mouth flattened into a tight line before her gaze strayed back to Wade. Whatever she thought he was, it was enough of a threat to get her to agree. Patrick wasn't mad she didn't consider him a threat, but the teenager with a bottomless pit for a stomach scaring her almost made him laugh.

"Your manners are terrible," Monica said as she stood.

"So I've been told. What's it going to be?"

"I'll call them."

Patrick watched her walk off, putting distance between them so he couldn't hear. Wade could, and his eyes never left her as she spoke on the phone.

"They don't wanna come out," Wade reported dutifully. "They're saying we're in the wrong. Oh, now she's saying she doesn't trust me in front of them."

Wade seemed pleased about that admission, giving Monica a smug smile when she looked over her shoulder at them. He waved at her before getting distracted by the candy bar Patrick found amidst the wrappers and stuck in front of his eyes.

"Oh, nice. I thought I ate that one," Wade said, quickly swiping it out of Patrick's hand.

Wade happily tore it open and took a bite, content to save his Pop-Tarts for later. He kept watching Monica, brows furrowed as he listened in on her conversation. Then his expression cleared, and he turned to face Patrick.

"We're going to some monk's bar on the Loop. Will I be allowed inside?" he asked.

"We'll find out," Patrick replied.

Wade was underage, and magic didn't work on him. Patrick couldn't hide his presence with a ward, and no one would believe Wade looked twenty-one. Sneaking him into a bar was going to take some doing.

Monica eventually returned to where they stood, eyeing them both. "I assume you heard?"

Patrick was already looking up the bar's address on his phone. "We'll take a taxi there."

He knew from past experience trying to find parking at night in any city's downtown was a fool's errand. Neutral ground at a bar wasn't unheard of, but he wondered about the ownership's ties to the preternatural world. If a god pack was showing up en masse in such a public space, then the bar had to have a policy geared toward accepting them.

"One of my pack will go with you to ensure you actually arrive."

"They aren't getting in a taxi with us. If you're worried about us going back on our word, then you and your paranoia can tail us later. Right now, I'm going upstairs to make a phone call."

"Hiding already?"

"I'm betting it'll take time for your alphas to get to the bar. You can hurry up and wait for us. Let's go, Wade."

Patrick gestured for Wade to follow him, and they made their way to the bank of elevators. None of the werecreatures attempted to follow them, but Patrick figured that wouldn't last for long. That meant, as soon as they got back to their hotel room, Patrick wrote out a silence ward on the back of the door, wrapping the space in static.

"Why aren't we leaving?" Wade asked.

"I'm not sitting out in the open while we wait for people to show up." Patrick dug out his phone and speed-dialed Sage. "Keep an ear out, will you?"

Wade mock saluted before throwing himself on the bed to play a game on his phone. After two rings, Sage picked up.

"Patrick," she said in greeting.

"So, hypothetically, if I never asked for permission from the local god pack to come to Chicago to do my actual job and they got pissed about that, what are my options?"

Sage sighed over the phone in such a way that Patrick could envision the annoyed look on her face. "Maybe I should have gone with you after all."

"You've taken enough time off from work to deal with pack business as it is. I can handle this. I just need to know how to get out of the corner I've found myself in."

"You should've asked for pass-through rights when you landed."

"Kind of busy with a case. I can't really say no to my job, remember?"

"Being our alpha is just as important. You need to apologize without apologizing. You can't afford to be seen as lesser because that puts our pack on uneven footing."

"I know that."

"Then find a way out of your *hypothetical* situation."

Patrick winced. "Are you mad at me?"

"I'm mad at the stupidity of males in general right now. Try not to make any promises or enter into a bargain. Your track record with those is terrible."

Patrick wondered who had pissed Sage off today other than himself. "I'll do my best."

"Call me after the meeting. Don't call me during. That'll just make you look like you don't know what you're doing."

Wade laughed at that, and Patrick thought about chucking a pillow at him. "I know what I'm doing."

"We can only hope. Good luck."

She ended the call, and Patrick shoved his phone into his pocket. "She thinks I suck at this."

"You kind of do," Wade said.

Patrick grabbed the nearest pillow and threw it at his head.

***

MONICA and some of her pack were waiting for them outside the hotel when Patrick decided enough time had passed for the Chicago god pack to have made it to the neutral territory.

"Took you long enough," Monica said.

"You're just mad you couldn't eavesdrop," Patrick retorted.

Monica shrugged, not denying she'd sent someone up to their floor to try to listen in on their conversation. Wade had heard them, even if the person in question hadn't been able to hear anything through Patrick's silence ward.

The doorman hailed them a cab that Patrick planned to pay for with cash because he didn't want the trip logged on a ride-share app for the SOA to track. Pack business wasn't the government's business.

"Where to?" the driver asked.

"The Monk's Pub," Patrick replied.

Wade buckled up, making sure the seat belt didn't crush his Pop-Tarts. Patrick wrote out a look-away ward on his handgun because people sometimes got uncomfortable about someone bringing a gun into a packed bar. He left his badge where it was, wanting to make it clear about his reason for being in Chicago.

It didn't take long to get to the bar, and Monica must have called ahead about their arrival because two god pack werecreatures were standing outside waiting for them. Patrick paid the taxi driver and got out, eyeing the Monk's Pub façade. It had been designed to look like a medieval building; the wooden doors had wards carved into the top, and the amount of witch magic emanating from the foundation told him it probably belonged to a coven.

"Our alphas are waiting for you," the petite blonde woman said as she shoved open the bar door.

A couple more cars and taxis pulled up on the street behind them. Patrick looked over his shoulder in time to see Monica getting out of a sleek sports car. Patrick's skin crawled with the feeling of being boxed in, and his fingers twitched toward his dagger. Wade stepped closer, arms crossed over his chest as he scowled at everyone around them.

"What if I eat them?" Wade asked.

Patrick rolled his eyes. "No. They'd taste bad. Get inside and I'll order you food. The place has a kitchen, and you're allowed to stay even though you're underage so long as the kitchen is open."

"They better have hot dogs."

Patrick entered the bar first, a wall of warm air hitting him in the face. Glass chandeliers and other light fixtures hung from the ceiling and protruded from the walls, giving off bright light. Wooden tables were scattered around the bar counter itself, nearly every seat taken. The booths along the walls were just as full.

Recognition pulsed through Patrick's magic, letting him know werecreatures and magic users alike were gathered in the bar, along with a decent amount of mundane humans. Patrick scanned the room, picking out the exit signs and ignoring the people who glanced their way.

"This way," Monica said as she passed them by.

Patrick and Wade followed her deeper into the bar toward a couple of tables near the back that had been pushed together. Some seats were open, enough for the three of them to sit down. Monica took the empty seat to the right of a Native American woman whose bright amber-eyed gaze never left Patrick's face. Next to her sat a Mexican man who sported tattoos across his bare arms that were unexpectedly familiar.

Patrick eyed the designs. "Anahuac Cartel?"

The man smiled, showing off sharp teeth. "Good guess."

"Not a guess. I know the vampire who's in charge of that cartel. You have his ownership inked on your skin." Patrick reached out and tugged Wade toward an empty chair. "Sit. I'll get you a menu when the waitress comes by."

"I got a few," Wade said, holding up two food menus, a drink menu, and a set of someone's keys with a building security badge attached.

Monica tensed in her seat across the table. "Those are mine."

"Oops. Must have fallen out of your purse."

Patrick snorted at the faux-innocent tone of Wade's voice. "Give them back to her."

Wade tossed Monica's keys across the table to her before sitting down in one of the two empty seats situated across from the Chicago god pack alphas. He held a menu up in front of his face, more interested in the food on offer than everyone seated around the table. Patrick sat beside him, trying not to reveal how much having his back to the room at large made him tense and uncomfortable. He looked away from Wade to meet the gazes of Monica's alphas.

"Your dire said my manners suck. I didn't think I needed to ask your permission to run a case in this city on the SOA's orders," Patrick said, keeping his voice even.

"You've crossed eight different pack territories in a single day, breached my god pack's borders without permission, and never once reached out to us to apologize. Your manners *do* suck," the woman said.

Patrick shrugged. "You want an introduction? Special Agent Patrick Collins, at your service. I'm one of the alphas of the only New York City god pack that matters and Wade's babysitter."

"Hey!" Wade protested, not looking away from the menu. "I can take care of myself. Aw man, they don't have hot dogs."

"Get a hamburger."

"I'm getting *three*."

"Not a good babysitter if your boy is that hungry," the man directly across from Patrick said.

"Wade is always hungry. He'll eat anything at any hour. Pizza, hamburgers, demons—"

"Gross. Not getting seconds on those," Wade muttered. "Can I get fried pickles?"

Patrick sighed and raised a hand, catching a waitress' attention. He waved her over and pointed at Wade. "I need to feed him."

The woman—a witch, judging by her aura and the spark of recognition that ran through Patrick's magic—arched an eyebrow before eyeing Wade. "What would you like?"

Wade rattled off a list of food that could have fed three grown men. Patrick resigned himself to a triple-digit charge, but if it kept Wade happy, it would be worth it.

"If you want to talk, I want to know who I'm dealing with," Patrick said once the waitress left to go put in the order.

"You're in no position to demand things of us," the woman said.

Patrick bit back a scowl and tried not to say the first thing that came to his mind. Sage would be proud he wasn't starting off with insults if she were here. "Like I said. I'm here because I work for the SOA. I'm not here looking to take your territory. Maybe I should've called, but it's not like any of my pack had your number."

"Your agency and the Chicago police know where we live."

"Yeah, they don't need to know about this. I gave you my name. I'd like yours in return."

She smiled thinly at him, the thick braid draped over one shoulder swaying as she leaned back in her seat. "Naomi White Hawk."

"Alejandro Perez," her partner said.

Patrick didn't see any wedding bands, so he figured they weren't married how Estelle and Youssef were. He couldn't rely on smell like Jono could for a situation like this, but Patrick was good at reading body language. None of the werecreatures seated at the table or in the surrounding bar area seemed fearful of their alphas. It was a stark difference from whenever he'd seen Estelle and Youssef interacting with their werecreature community.

"It's just me and Wade here. Our pack isn't looking to leave New York City anytime soon," Patrick said.

"That's not what we've heard," Naomi said.

"Any rumors you've heard about us leaving are false. Those are lies being spread by Estelle and Youssef."

"We've also heard you're stealing territory," Alejandro said before taking a sip of his beer.

"It's not stealing if the packs in question offer it to us and ask for our protection."

Naomi and Alejandro shared a brief look that Patrick couldn't read. He felt a little out of his comfort zone, unable to follow cues Jono or Sage would have no problem picking up on.

"Is that how you see it?" Naomi asked.

Patrick shrugged. "Estelle and Youssef are shit at looking out for the people they're supposed to protect. They're terrible alphas."

"And you, a mage who will never carry the werevirus in your veins, think you're better than them?"

"I know I am, and I believe that of my pack as well."

"Easy for you to say."

"You want proof they're good alphas?" Wade asked irritably. "Because I'm living proof if you need it. Patrick and Jono weren't the ones who sold me to vampires. That was—"

"Wade," Patrick interrupted calmly. "Be quiet."

Wade closed his mouth with a snap and glared at the table. Patrick reached over and pulled a packet of Pop-Tarts out of Wade's jacket pocket, ripped it open, and offered him one. Wade scowled, but couldn't resist his favorite snack.

"We heard about the change in the Manhattan Night Court," Alejandro said into the tense silence that followed Wade's outburst.

"From contacts I assume you still have in the Anahuac Cartel?" Patrick asked. "Would those be the same ones who were summoned to New York last year for a street block party-style coup?"

Alejandro studied him through narrowed eyes. "You said you knew the vampire who's in charge of that cartel."

"Something like that. I work for the SOA. Dealing with the preternatural world is a requirement of the job."

It wasn't a lie, even if it wasn't the entire truth. With his shields up, Patrick knew no one would be able to tell one way or the other. He wasn't about to name-drop Lucien though, not with a pack he didn't know and couldn't trust.

He caught sight of their waitress coming toward them carrying a couple of plates. He stayed quiet as Wade was served, the teen's mood lightening instantly once he had food.

"The rest will be out momentarily. Are you sure you're going to eat all this?" the woman asked in a dubious voice.

Wade had already taken a too-large bite of his hamburger to respond, so he just nodded. She left, and Patrick turned his attention back to the table at large.

"We didn't mean to break any rules by coming here without giving you a heads-up first. But I'm here for work, we aren't interested in Chicago, and we'll reciprocate pass-through rights in New York if any of your people ever come into our territory."

"There are two god packs who lay claim to that city. What makes you think you can keep your word if the other pack denies us entry?" Naomi asked.

"Because they don't have the alliances we do, and they won't be around for long."

"I'd eat those assholes if you'd let me," Wade said around a mouthful of fries.

"I don't need that paperwork in my life."

"Shame."

Naomi frowned at Wade, her nose twitching ever so slightly. "What are you?"

Wade burped, then smiled meanly. "Pack."

"Will you grant us pass-through rights for the duration of my stay in Chicago for the case I'm handling?" Patrick asked, wanting to steer the conversation away from Wade's background.

"Asking after the fact isn't how it's done," Alejandro said.

"I'm still asking."

He wasn't going to back down—he *couldn't* back down. Walking away would be as bad as showing throat to the enemy. The Chicago god pack wasn't their enemy though, and could maybe be a possible ally in the future if they played their hand right. Patrick just had to not fuck up any more than he already had.

"If you weren't a federal agent, I'd drive you to O'Hare myself and watch you get on a plane," Naomi said after a long moment.

"Does that mean you'll grant us pass-through rights?"

"I know human laws. I can't stop you."

"That's not a yes."

Naomi shoved her chair back and stood. "Do your job, Special Agent Patrick Collins. Just make sure none of the packs in this city are caught in the crossfire or we will have words."

He felt she was asking for a miracle there, but Patrick wasn't going to tell her that. "I'll do my best."

Around them, werecreatures were heading for the door, but Naomi had yet to move. Alejandro downed what was left of his beer before getting to his feet, standing shoulder to shoulder with her in a solidarity no one could miss.

"I met Estelle and Youssef once before when I spoke in front of the United Nations on indigenous rights some years back. They would have never asked permission one way or another if they came to Chicago. You did." Naomi pursed her lips. "Eventually."

"We'll remember that," Alejandro said.

Patrick didn't know what to say to that, so he kept quiet rather than dig himself a hole he couldn't get out of. He watched the Chicago god pack leave the bar and didn't breathe easy until they were gone.

"That probably could've gone better," Patrick said.

"Yeah," Wade agreed, then shoved a plate closer to Patrick. "Fried pickle?"

Patrick went for the mozzarella sticks instead.

6

"You should call Patrick."

Jono decided the better part of valor right then was to pretend Sage wasn't glaring at him at half past nine on a Wednesday morning. He grimaced as Victoria finished washing out the knife wound on his side with saline and started to apply the poultice. Her thick black hair was tied back in a ponytail, and her scrubs that morning had kittens playing with yarn balls on them.

"Stop moving," Victoria told him, never taking her eyes off his ribs.

She was seated on the coffee table, her potions case open and supplies scattered around her. Victoria worked as an RN at Mount Sinai and had a standing contract with Marek to help heal the migraines he got from his visions. It had expanded into caring for multiple pack members when needed, and she didn't seem to mind the extra work.

Jono rarely needed her services, but silver and aconite poisoning was something every werecreature needed help with. His body couldn't heal the damage on its own in a timely manner. He'd spent the better part of the night after Leon drove him home getting sick in the toilet. Leon hadn't left his side, and everyone else had met them at the flat. Which meant there was no escaping Sage's wrath, but at least Emma and Leon were making breakfast for him.

"*Jono*," Sage said.

"He doesn't need to know about this right now," Jono gritted out as Victoria started taping a bandage over the poultice.

Sage frowned at him, mouth twisting angrily. "You should have let me tell him what was going on when he called last night."

Jono shook his head sharply. "I don't want to worry him."

"The Krossed Knights are hunting you and you think Patrick will be fine being the last to know?"

"He won't be," Emma called from the kitchen.

Jono lifted a hand to rub at his eyes, wincing at the pull in his ribs. His skin felt clammy, and his head hurt. Sage's anger was only making his shit mood worse, mostly because he knew she had a point.

"You know why Patrick was sent to Chicago. It's not like he can just up and leave from working this case. I want him to keep his head in the game. If Patrick is worrying about me, he won't be worrying about himself," Jono said.

"All I'm hearing is an excuse. Patrick hates being lied to. You *know* that," Sage argued.

"This isn't lying. It's…just not telling him the whole story."

"Obfuscation doesn't make this situation *better*."

"No, but it'll keep Patrick focused."

"A hundred dollars you're sleeping on the couch for the next few months when he finds out," Marek said as he came out of the kitchen.

"A hundred dollars he'll be sleeping on *our* couch," Sage retorted.

Victoria straightened up and began putting bottles and jars away. "All right. I've done what I can. The purge potions are in the fridge. Take one bottle every six hours for the next two days. That should clear your system of the poison, but you're going to find shifting difficult until it's all out of your system. I'd advise against changing forms until you feel completely better in your human body."

Marek approached Victoria and handed her several hundred dollars in cash from his wallet. "Thanks for coming by this morning. Do you need a ride home?"

Victoria held up her mobile. "I'll catch an Uber."

"Charge it to me."

"Later. I'm going to sleep when I get home."

Victoria pulled on her puffy coat and waved goodbye before leaving the flat. Jono glanced down at his chest and grimaced at the red and black lines branching away from the bandaged knife wound. At least he was no longer bleeding, but he still felt like shit.

"When Patrick finds out we kept from him the fact you were nearly killed, he's going to be pissed at all of us," Sage said in a low voice.

"Then don't let him find out until he's home," Jono said stubbornly.

Sage glared at him, hands on her hips, the scowl on her face clearly showing her displeasure. Jono pushed himself into a more upright position on the sofa, the ache on the right side of his body making him clench his teeth. The pain burrowing into his muscles had faded some with the help of Victoria's potions, but Jono wasn't used to feeling so weak. The werevirus meant pain was an afterthought most days. Having to deal with it was annoying.

Sage spun on her heels and stalked over to the dining room table where she'd left her leather Louis Vuitton tote bag. "I'm going to work. Let me know if you come to your senses."

Jono knew she wouldn't tell Patrick because he'd given her that order before she even answered Patrick's first call last night. He didn't want Sage angry at him, but neither did he want Patrick in the wrong frame of mind while working an out-of-state case.

Sage left the flat, the front door shutting firmly behind her.

Jono winced, almost wishing she'd slammed it. He'd always admired her furious control, just not when her icy temper was directed at him.

"Should you be moving?" Leon asked as he came out of the kitchen carrying two mugs of coffee and one with a tea bag string dangling over the side.

"Shouldn't you be at work?" Jono replied.

"It was decided, while you were puking your guts out all night, that Emma and I will be crashing in your guest room until the threat passes." Leon set the mugs down on the coffee table, a serious expression on his face. "Sage gave that order. I listen to my god pack's dire."

"But not your alpha?"

"Not when you're being stupid," Emma retorted, coming out of the kitchen with her own cup of coffee in hand. "Leon and I can telecommute for the rest of the week. We'll take our meetings through videoconferencing."

"Patrick warded the flat," Jono reminded them.

"Patrick isn't here. We—"

Emma broke off and immediately looked at the front door, as did Leon, and their expressions told Jono he wasn't going to like what had pissed them off.

"Who is it?" Marek asked.

Before either could answer, the front door was thrown open and Sage strode back inside. The faint flush to her cheeks was partly from anger and partly from the sexual desire that seemed to pour off Carmen like bad perfume.

Emma immediately put herself between the succubus and Jono. Leon joined her in guarding where Jono sat on the sofa while Sage stood between Carmen and Marek. Jono stayed where he was, wishing he'd thought to put his shirt back on after Victoria had left so his wound was hidden.

Carmen leaned against the doorjamb, her long, curly black hair falling loose to her waist. She smiled at Jono, and the stink of her power filtering into the flat grew stronger, making Jono growl.

"Down, boy," Carmen purred.

"Carmen," Jono ground out.

She sauntered inside on high-heeled boots, the leather pants she wore paired with an oversized red sweater. It almost matched the color of her irises when she dropped her glamour, the horns of her kind spiraling back over her skull. The scent of desire thickened in the air, and Jono thought about reaching for the ward carved underneath the coffee table. Patrick had hidden several such wards throughout the apartment, the embedded magic in them capable of being triggered by a non-magic user.

He stayed his hand.

Behind Carmen, a slim woman stepped onto the landing. Naheed blinked lazily, taking in the room at large, but she stayed put. Lucien's favorite human servant doubled as Carmen's bodyguard during the day, along with a few others. The weather outside was cold, but she'd foregone a scarf, putting on display the necklace of bite mark scars encircling her throat.

Carmen came to a stop on the other side of the coffee table, peering around Leon's tense form to smirk at Jono. "I hear there's a bounty on your head."

"You here to collect?"

"Over my dead body," Emma growled.

Carmen wriggled her fingers at Emma. "That can be arranged."

"Carmen," Jono said sharply, shooting Emma a warning look. "What do you want?"

"You crossed into Jamere's territory and demanded an audience with your betters."

"He shares that border with a pack under my protection. He's going to need to accept the new boundaries." Jono levered himself to his feet, refusing to show any hint of discomfort, despite the dull, throbbing pain that ran through his entire body. "And I have no betters."

Carmen's bloodred lips curved into a mocking smile, her gaze drifting down his body. The air thickened with the scent of sex and desire, and Jono wished Patrick were there to block her power. It wasn't affecting him, but the others were struggling to fight it.

"You certainly have few betters in the dick department, I'll give you that."

"Explain why you're here, or get the fuck out of my home."

Something pulsed in the walls of the flat, a brief flare of magic that smelled distantly bitter. The threshold wrapped around the flat was still active even without a mage present. Carmen's lashes fluttered a bit at that reminder, but her expression never changed.

"You asked for a meeting with my master. Lucien will see you tomorrow night at Ginnungagap."

"Is that it? You could've rang if all you needed to do was deliver a message."

"Of course not," Carmen said with a throaty laugh that made Jono wish Patrick was by his side, dagger in hand and mageglobe at the ready, soulbond humming between them. "I've brought you a gift. A, shall we say, special delivery to show what happens when people cross us."

"We've made no move against you."

Carmen arched an eyebrow. "You were in Brooklyn."

"I have packs there."

"You can discuss that tomorrow night with Lucien."

Footsteps down on the ground floor caught Jono's attention, and he dialed up his hearing to listen. Two people were coming up the stairs, the cadence of their steps indicating they were carrying something.

A minute later, two human servants maneuvered their way around the landing and through the doorway, carrying a heavy-looking plastic crate. The smell of blood was impossible to miss, cutting through the heaviness of sexual desire still in the air.

"Put it in the kitchen. I don't want bloodstains on the carpet," Sage snapped.

The two human servants looked at Carmen first for orders, and she lazily waved them toward the kitchen. "Do it."

Jono would've followed them into the kitchen to see what messy problem Carmen had delivered to them, but Emma reached out and snagged his wrist with strong fingers, though her grip was gentle.

"Don't even think about it," Emma replied in a low voice.

Leon went into the kitchen, coming back a few seconds later looking a little green in the face. "It's a body. The pieces look like they could've been someone who was a Krossed Knight. They're dressed like one of the fuckers from last night."

Jono ran a hand over his face. "This is not the sort of attention we need, Carmen."

Carmen extended her hand to the side, and Naheed stepped forward to place something small and smelling of metal in her palm. She held it up for Jono to see. It was a medallion with antiqued spaces surrounding a St. Andrews Cross, and the words *Deus Vult* curved around the bottom edge.

The symbol of a member in good standing with the Krossed Knights was one they all carried, either inked in skin or like what Carmen held between her thumb and forefinger. Proof of acceptance into an order of hunters who would never see Jono as anything other than a monster. He knew, like everyone else, that the Krossed Knights never stopped hunting until their prey was dead.

"We don't take kindly to breaches of our borders," Carmen said.

"Then you should've taken care of the problem when it first arrived and gotten rid of the bodies. Maybe dropped them in the river on your way back from Brooklyn. You're a shit neighbor for not warning us."

"You can't get answers from a dead man without a necromancer. *We* have no need to hire hunters to clean up our borders. That would be your favorite wolves."

Anger coursed through Jono so quick it left him feeling light-headed—or maybe that was the poison working itself out of his system. He swallowed, tasting bitterness in the back of his throat.

"Do you have proof?" Sage asked flatly. "Because if not, you can take the body with you when you leave."

Jono got a hold of his temper, letting Sage take the lead for the moment. Part of him hoped Carmen didn't have proof because that would mean he'd get to sleep and not deal with this mess right now.

Except he was turning out to have Patrick's form of luck this week, because Carmen pulled out her mobile, held it up so they could see the screen, and played a video for them. The scream that poured out of the speaker made Jono clench his teeth.

"He's the one in the crate," Leon said quietly.

The man in question was bloodied and terrified, with one eye gouged out and dangling from his left eye socket by thin threads of muscle and nerve endings. Both lips were split, as if someone had taken a knife and ran it vertically up his face.

He seemed young.

"Answer me," a calm voice asked from off-screen. Jono recognized the voice belonging to Einar, Lucien's right-hand vampire, as the speaker even if he didn't recognize the hand gripping the man's short hair to hold him up. "Who hired you?"

The hunter opened his mouth, blood trickling past damaged lips. "God pack alphas."

"I want names."

The syllables that slipped off his tongue were wrapped in a whimper. "Estelle."

The video cut out, and Carmen dropped her arm back down to her side. "There's your proof."

"Vampires can coerce anything out of humans. All I saw was a forced confession brought about by torture," Sage said.

"Which was fun." Carmen turned on her heels, the glamour her kind could wield wrapping around her body once more, making her seem human when she never would be. "Believe what was in the video or not, but the body is not our problem anymore. We'll see you tomorrow night."

Carmen and the human servants left. Jono watched her go, aware of his friends staring at him and waiting for him to argue or call her back.

He didn't.

"I'm borrowing your bathroom," Marek said into the strained silence, awkwardly walking away to deal with the problem in his pants. "Everyone keep your ears to yourself."

"What the hell are we going to do with the body in the kitchen?" Leon asked, sounding aggravated. "It's in *pieces*."

Jono stared at the door, fingers flexing, the bones in his hands feeling bruised as he tried to shift but couldn't. There was still too much silver and aconite in his body, and he was mindful of Victoria's warning.

"We're returning it to its sender," Jono said.

Sage rounded on him, a furious look on her face. "You can't shift and you want to go poke the damn hornet's nest? Here I thought Patrick took all the stupid ideas with him when he left for Chicago."

"The body can't stay here."

"Then you should've had Carmen take it with her. You know this could be a trap, right?"

"To what? Make me accuse Estelle and Youssef of something we all know they'd do? They sold werecreatures to Tremaine for money and territory. You think they wouldn't hire a hunter to try to murder me?"

"I know they would. But if you bring that body to their doorstep with your fingerprints all over the crate, the first call they'll make will be to the police."

Jono smiled grimly. "Then we better find the cleaning gloves."

"Jono—"

"You *all* wanted me to form my own god pack," Jono cut in harshly, his gaze snapping around the room. "You wanted me to take this city back from them. I'm doing that, Sage. That's what this is. I'm bloody well sick to the back of my teeth with their bullshit. If they want a fight, then we'll give them one, but I'm not letting them chase me down into a corner. Not anymore."

"Not all the packs under our protection can afford to fight."

"Then we'll rely on other people. That's what alliances are for."

Sage made a cutting gesture with her hand. "We don't have one with the Night Courts."

Jono thought about the promise Lucien owed Patrick and wondered what it would cost to make the master vampire acknowledge it outside the angry conversations it existed in.

"Then we'll make one."

Lucien made bargains with no one. That was an historical fact, but Jono rather thought he could make the master vampire agree to an alliance if he offered up a war.

Jono realized, with a bleakness that left him swallowing back bile, they had no choice but to go all in if they wanted to survive. War waited for no one. It arrived unexpectedly or crept into the background of a person's life without them realizing it—but it came with a relentlessness that killed.

Emma raised her hand. "I'm in favor of poking the hornet's nest."

"Wait. What are we doing?" Marek asked as he came back into the living room. He'd taken care of his forced erection and looked more comfortable in his own skin.

"Delivering the body to Estelle and Youssef."

Marek blinked at them. "Right now?"

Leon shrugged. "Why wait?"

Sage crossed her arms over her chest and met Jono's eyes. She didn't bother to hide her anger, but Jono knew from past experiences she'd accept his order. She might not like it, and there was a fair chance she'd greet him with an *I told you so* later on down the line, but she'd do what he asked.

"I don't suppose we can blame the silver and aconite poisoning and claim you're out of your mind, can we?" Sage asked.

Jono shook his head. "No."

"Then let's get you dressed. Emma? Leon? The crate won't fit in the Mustang's trunk or our Maserati. Load it into your Escalade. We'll be down in about ten minutes."

"What about me?" Marek asked.

Sage kissed him soundly on the mouth before following Jono into the bedroom. "Finish your coffee and go get the car."

The clothes he'd worn last night to Brooklyn were a mess and had been stashed in a plastic bag that now resided in Marek's Maserati. They'd get rid of it in some place that wasn't here. Jono shoved his track pants off while Sage dug out some clean clothes from the dresser for him.

"You better have a damn good apology ready for when Patrick finds out," Sage said quietly as she handed him a pair of jeans and a long-sleeved Henley.

"I'll think of something," Jono said.

Sage watched him carefully get dressed with an unreadable look on her face. "You still smell like you're hurt."

"If it's the blood, we can blame it on the body when we deliver it."

In response, Sage unclasped the turquoise pendant necklace she wore on a platinum chain, the fae magic embedded in the artifact a barrier that hid her scent and what she truly was. Her scent hit Jono's nose in a soothing way, and he ducked his head a little so she could hook the necklace around his own throat.

"You can't show weakness to them."

"Thought you didn't even want me to show them my face at all?"

Sage arched an eyebrow. "I agree we can't let their actions slide if they truly hired the hunters. I just think you're rushing in without thinking."

"So, like Pat."

"The two of you are the reason I drink some days."

Jono gingerly sat on the bed while Sage went to grab his boots and a clean pair of socks. Bending over made everything ache in a way he wished would go away.

Sage knelt in front of him and calmly put on his shoes for him, tying the laces so tight he thought she'd break them. When she stood and went to step back, Jono snagged her wrist, pressing his fingers into the pulse point there.

"If I don't stand my ground and take what's ours, they'll keep coming," Jono said quietly. "We're either ready to fight now, or we never will be."

Sage twisted her hand free to grab his wrist, raising his hand to her throat. She tipped her head to the side, giving him full access. Jono pressed his scent into her skin, the feeling of pack washing over them both. The steady beat of her heart was a comforting metronome beneath his fingertips.

"I'll talk to Tiarnán about putting extra security on your apartment. If you want to make a point, we can rub our alliance with the fae into Estelle and Youssef's faces."

Jono cracked a smile. "There's a thought. Now go to work. I'll have Emma and Leon with me all day."

"If you're sure."

"I think me showing up without any of the rest of our god pack will prove how little I think of them and care for their bollocks."

"Call me after you're done."

"Of course."

Sage helped him off the bed. They left the flat, every step down the stairs making the knife wound over his ribs throb a little. Despite the pain, it hurt less than when he'd first been cut, a testament to Victoria's skill with healing potions.

Marek was already behind the wheel of his Maserati, and Sage headed for her ride. Leon was parked behind them on the street in the Escalade, hazard lights on, with Emma waiting outside to help Jono into the front passenger seat.

"Let's go," Jono said once he was buckled up.

The drive to Estelle and Youssef's territory in the Upper Manhattan neighborhood of Hamilton Heights felt like it took forever, but that was mostly the pain talking. Jono watched the buildings flash by, swallowing against the nausea that came and went.

Leon stuck to the speed limit, slowed for yellow lights rather than run them, and in general, drove like an old person. Jono figured the body in the boot was the reason for Leon's caution. He couldn't say it bothered him. Getting pulled over by the police would make the morning even worse, and they wanted to avoid that mess.

"Are we just dumping the crate on their porch?" Emma asked from the back. "What about cameras?"

"I'd wager they don't want the police digging any deeper than they already are," Jono said.

He didn't have much of a plan other than return the body to the people who hired the Krossed Knights. If he was thinking clearer, maybe he wouldn't have opted to act so rashly, but he was done with Estelle and Youssef in every way.

They didn't deserve to claim New York City as their territory, and Jono was going to make it clear he wasn't taking their shit anymore.

Leon parked in front of a brownstone sometime later, the street the god pack lived on quiet despite the weekday morning hour. He put the hazard lights on and stayed where he was behind the wheel. Jono and Emma got out, and he left her to retrieving the crate from the boot. Despite her petite size, Emma carried the crate as if it weighed nothing. She followed Jono to the front door of the rival god pack's territory.

The brownstones clustered on the block belonged to the god

pack of New York City through leases passed down to every alpha, but Jono would never want to live here. He preferred his flat with Patrick, and all the memories they were making in it over the buildings that seemed to have fear embedded in their very foundations. The smell made Jono's nose twitch, along with the magic Estelle and Youssef had bought to secure their home.

Fenrir stirred deep in his soul, and Jono knew whatever wards their pack had bought, none of it would hold in the face of a god's anger.

Jono reached the porch, and rather than knock, he kicked open the door. The wound in his side and the poison still in his body made him a little shaky, but Fenrir steadied him. The door broke off its hinges and crashed to the floor. The sound of it landing on the floor seemed to notify everyone left in the home of their arrival.

Jono didn't wait for anyone to come. He stepped aside just enough for Emma to drop the crate inside, the dish gloves she wore almost too big for her hands. She never lost her grip though, and kicked the crate further into the building. It crashed into someone's legs as they arrived, but Jono didn't care about that. All he cared about was the person who appeared in the doorway.

"Hope you haven't eaten yet because we've brought you breakfast," Jono said to Estelle.

She glared at him, standing behind her home's threshold and looking one breath away from murder. Her auburn hair was loose around her face, wolf-bright amber eyes snapping with fury. "You're trespassing."

"Jamere took offense to the hunters you hired working in his territory. I took offense to you being a cowardly bitch. Carmen brought your mess to me, so I'm returning it. Next time you want to fight, come find me yourself. Quit hiding behind proxies and paying others to do your dirty work."

"Oh, fuck," someone breathed behind her. "This guy is in *pieces*."

The smell of blood grew thicker, mixing with the faint hint of decomposition that was starting to build up around the body. A mundane human wouldn't be able to pick it up yet, but werecreatures could. There was no mistaking the dead for what they were —just like there was no mistaking the sulfur curling through the air in the hallway.

"I don't know what you're talking about," Estelle said.

"Of course you don't. But the video we have of a confession courtesy of the Manhattan Night Court says otherwise." Jono smiled, half listening to Fenrir howl through his mind. "New York City doesn't belong to you and your pack. Get that through your sodding thick skull."

Estelle let out a harsh laugh, bracing both hands on the edge of the doorway. It was telling that she didn't take a single step past the threshold. "You think you can take it? From *me?*"

Jono stepped right up to the threshold's edge, magic flickering at the edges of his vision. He could see through it with Fenrir's help, some bit of the god's power pouring through his soul. The fae magic embedded in Sage's pendant hid it all, or Fenrir allowed it to be hidden. Jono knew now wasn't the time to reveal what he carried in his soul, and Fenrir seemed to agree.

He didn't have Patrick, and he didn't have an alliance with the vampires—yet. Estelle had more packs at her disposal, and Jono knew better than to rely solely on a god's fickle blessing.

"I know I can," Jono promised with the sureness of a man who knew nothing would get in his way from taking what was rightfully his.

Estelle's smile froze on her face, nostrils flaring. He didn't know what she got off him, what she saw in his eyes, but she made no move to go for his throat like back in December.

Jono stepped back, ignoring the pull of the wound over his ribs, refusing to show weakness to her. "Any retaliation against the packs who have left your sphere of protection for ours will be considered an act of war going forward. I am *done* letting you think you have the right to cross my territory."

He didn't demand a challenge because he knew one would never be fair with Estelle and Youssef. The only way to take control of New York City would be to fight for it block by block.

Jono was ready to do just that.

It was one thing to test borders, quite another to hire hunters driven by demons and invite them into everyone's pack territory. The Krossed Knights would come for him and then go after everyone else. Of that, Jono was certain. Hate like that was never content with just one kill.

But Estelle and Youssef didn't care about that, and if they wouldn't, then Jono would.

He turned his back on Estelle and walked away, trusting in Emma to keep him safe. They returned to the SUV and got back in. Leon didn't peel out, keeping to the speed limit so as to not arouse suspicion.

"Surprised she didn't try to gut you," Leon said.

Jono rubbed at his nose. "She had a guest."

"Oh?"

"A hunter." Jono leaned his head back against the seat rest and closed his eyes. "A demon."

"You think they're making another deal?" Emma asked.

"I think we're not the only ones looking for alliances."

If Estelle and Youssef were courting demons and hunters, then Jono was going to do whatever it took to get Lucien on their side.

7

"THANK YOU FOR COMING," A DEEP VOICE BOOMED OVER THE chatter of the brunch crowd. "I'm sorry I missed the original pancake breakfast last week, but I did say I'd make it up to all of you."

The crowd in the community center full of senior citizens cheered and clapped, most likely for the free food. An icy wind had blown up off Lake Michigan overnight with a strangely long reach, and it was freezing outside. The community center was on the same block as a senior-living housing complex in the West Town neighborhood. It could have been a hazardous walk to the campaign stop, but Westberg's campaign had sent out dozens of volunteers to escort the elderly to their free meal.

"Do we get to eat the food?" Wade asked.

"No. I'll feed you later," Patrick replied.

Wade grumbled and pulled out a candy bar from his jacket pocket. Patrick kept his attention on the tall man in a business suit who was putting on a white apron as a dozen people laughed. As with any politician during meet and greets, he never stopped smiling. Patrick found it creepy.

He and Wade were standing in the back of the room while volunteers dashed back and forth between the tables holding all the food and the ones where the senior citizens were seated. A couple of people with press lanyards hanging from their necks were milling about taking pictures, while others had come to just observe the candidate and take his measure.

Patrick had come with both his pistol and dagger warded so no one would notice. His badge was clipped to his belt and hidden beneath his leather jacket. He was there to get a feel for the man the SOA considered a criminal. Wade had tagged along because he was bored.

"I heard there's a Nutella café in this city. Can we go to it?" Wade asked.

"You can go to it later. Maybe tomorrow."

"I wanted to go today."

"I'm not stopping you." Patrick pointed at Wade without even looking. "Don't steal my car keys."

Wade grumbled something rude under his breath but pulled his hand away from where it'd been creeping toward Patrick's pocket. "*Fine.*"

Patrick went back to ignoring him, keeping an interested expression on his face as he watched Westberg work the room. While the candidate spent time serving up plates and ferrying them to a lucky few senior citizens, his campaign staff and volunteers discreetly passed out campaign information.

A slim woman with perfectly styled blonde hair and wearing a warm winter pantsuit seemed to be in charge of the event. She drifted through the room, answering questions from curious people in between directing the ones handing out food and flyers. It seemed inevitable she would make her way to where they were standing.

"Here to support Mr. Westberg?" she asked with a smile that was friendly enough.

Patrick shrugged, never taking his eyes off her face. In the high heels she wore, the woman was closer to Jono's height than his. "Just checking out my options."

"As a candidate, Mr. Westberg is the only choice you should make."

"I guess. Never really been one to vote, but this year's election seems like one I should pay attention to," Patrick said, lying through his teeth.

"As his campaign manager, I can assure you Mr. Westberg only has the well-being of all Chicagoans at heart." She extended her hand to him. "Kristen Lief."

Her hand was cold when Patrick shook it, declining to give his name. "Nice to meet you."

"Do you have a ticket for the brunch?"

"Nah. We had time this morning between errands and thought we'd check things out. We need to go soon."

"I want chocolate," Wade said.

Patrick rolled his eyes. "We should probably go now."

Kristen kept smiling, the practiced expression of a consummate public figure. "Hopefully we'll see you at a later campaign stop."

"It's possible."

She moved on, deftly transferring her attention to the next possible vote. Wade leaned in once she was out of earshot and whispered in a hesitant voice, "She smelled like how Tezcatlipoca always smelled."

The chill that shivered down Patrick's spine felt colder than the winter winds blowing outside. Patrick kept his expression calm, moving with a deliberateness he hoped no one would see through to the fear that made his heart pound in his chest.

"Let's find you some Nutella."

They left the community center, the wind blowing outside a cold, cutting thing that made Patrick duck his head and pull out his beanie from a jacket pocket. He yanked it on, tucking the wool over his ears. Wade knew better than to talk until they were back in the SUV and Patrick had set a silence ward throughout the vehicle.

"Are you sure?" Patrick said as he started the engine.

Wade hunched his shoulders, gaze distant for a few seconds before he shook himself free of whatever memory was making his breath come a little quicker than usual. "She smelled like electricity. It was subtle, like perfume, but there. Kind of got the feeling she was trying to hide."

Patrick tightened his hands on the steering wheel before he forced himself to loosen his grip so he could pull into the street. "Okay."

Patrick wasn't going to question what Wade had sensed. To him, Kristen Lief had seemed as mundane human as they came, but he knew from experience gods could hide themselves if they tried. Not to mention the ones who weren't worshipped as much or as often as the more well-known immortals were weaker, less likely to be noticed and more likely to pass as human.

Being forgotten was a lonely existence for a god, but it made it easier for them to cause trouble in the mortal world.

Patrick thought about the supposed souls being offered up in lieu of money for rent and wondered if Westberg was the problem or a victim.

"I need to interview Westberg," Patrick said, thinking out loud.

"Could've done it back there," Wade said.

"Too public, and I need to see if I can even get permission to do it first. The case is being worked under seal. I can't disrupt what's going on with this field branch of the SOA."

Wade slouched in the seat and put a foot up on the dash. "I don't wanna go to the office with you. I want my Nutella latte."

"Then I'll drop you off at the café."

It was on the way, so it wasn't a hardship. Wade fiddled with the SUV's satellite radio until he found a station he approved of. Patrick didn't mind the choice of music, nodding along to the beat occasionally as he drove east toward downtown. They were on I-

90 for a brief part of the drive before crossing over one of the tributaries of the Chicago River.

Eventually, Patrick turned right onto North Michigan Avenue, heading toward the skyscrapers in the heart of downtown Chicago. As they approached the DuSable Bridge, lightning flashed overhead, followed by the boom of thunder that Patrick swore rattled the SUV's windows. He peered up at the sky in time to see a sheet of rain fall toward the earth, sending pedestrians without umbrellas running for shelter.

"Uh, pretty sure the weather forecast said windy and cold, not rain for days," Wade said.

Patrick flicked on the windshield wipers, staring through the downpour at the bridge up ahead. Between one eye blink and the next, two ravens appeared, one perching on either side of the drawbridge pillars. Even from the short distance between them, Patrick could see the aura burning around the larger than normal ravens that no one else seemed to notice.

They spread their wings at the exact same time, launching themselves into the air, inky shadows against the cloudy sky. *Follow.*

The voices of Huginn and Muninn cracked through his mind, leaving behind a headache Patrick could've done without. "God damn it."

"Any chance we can get food first? Maybe a latte?" Wade asked plaintively, eyeing the ravens winging ahead of them.

"I don't think we should keep who they're leading us to waiting."

Wade crossed his arms over his chest and sulked, staring mournfully out the window as they passed the Nutella Café a few minutes later. "I hate gods."

"You and me both."

Driving south, Patrick navigated traffic, relying on Wade to keep an eye on the ravens and what direction they took.

"Oh hey, a restaurant. Maybe we can have lunch after all," Wade said, pointing at the slim stone overhangs covering the entrance and windows of a building to their right as they drove past.

"I wouldn't trust whatever they offer," Patrick said as he eyed the location signs giving directions to the nearest parking garages.

"Aw, come on. If I could eat fae food and be fine, I bet I can eat whatever they have on their menu."

"Your funeral."

Patrick circled back until he found the entrance for Grant Park North Garage. Wade stuck close as they left the garage, taking the stairs up to the street. Patrick expanded his personal shields to keep the rain off them both as they hurried down the block to the restaurant Muninn and Huginn were still perched over.

The immortals watched them approach with black, star-speckled eyes. Patrick couldn't meet their gazes for long without feeling as if he were going to fall into a void and never find his way out.

Inside, the ravens said, their voices echoing in Patrick's mind. *The Allfather is not one to keep waiting.*

Well. That answered his question on who they were there to meet.

The restaurant overlooked Millennium Park and beyond it, Lake Michigan. That told Patrick it was the kind of place where prices were never shown on the menu. A doorman pushed open the door to Au Hall, allowing them to enter and get out of the rain. Patrick drew back his shields before they entered but didn't drop them. Wade looked around curiously at the mahogany wood paneling carved with intricate designs that weren't as random as they looked after a second glance.

"Your table is ready," the hostess said with a smile and a vacant look in her eyes. "If you would follow me?"

"Creepy," Wade said under his breath.

The hours on the discreet sign out front had indicated the restaurant was open for lunch and dinner every day of the week in set blocks of time. Today it was almost entirely empty of a lunch crowd.

The restaurant was two stories tall, with a mezzanine that ran along the front of the restaurant for eye-catching views of Millennium Park and Lake Michigan. The stairs on either end leading up to it were made of wood with gold-leaf banisters. Multiple crystal and gold chandeliers hung from the ceiling, their light reflecting from the mirrors that lined the rear wall.

All the tables were empty, save one. The circular table in the center of the room could comfortably seat five. Three of the seats were taken, and its occupants watched them come with unblinking eyes.

The hair on the back of Patrick's neck stood on end as they approached. His skin felt electrified, and not in the good way when he was with Jono. The trio's auras were blinding, glowing like the sun, making it impossible for Patrick to look any of them in the eye. Within seconds the brightness faded, even if the heaviness of power in the large room didn't.

"So good to finally meet the mortal who wields my prayers," Odin said dryly before taking a sip of scotch.

Patrick's fingers twitched toward his dagger, but he didn't draw it.

The Allfather and titular ruler of the Æsir appeared middle-aged, blond hair silvered at the temples and blending into the closely trimmed beard he sported. He wore a dark gray suit that screamed wealth and status, the kind bought with a credit card that had no limits. Odin's left eye was a clear, deep blue, while his right was steely gray in color, though cloudy, the difference easily explained away by heterochromia.

He looked exactly like the picture of him the SOA had on file; the agency just had the wrong information. Despite Patrick's new knowledge, he would never be able to update the file.

"You may sit," the regal goddess positioned to Odin's right said.

She offered Patrick a gentle smile, but that would never be enough to ease his wariness when dealing with gods.

She was beautiful in the way most goddesses were, and revered by her people the way queens expected to be. The immortal passed these days as a middle-aged socialite whose designer winter clothing would've been coveted by Nadine Mulroney if his best friend were here. Her light brown hair was done up in a chignon, and the jeweled sort of headband she wore could've doubled as a crown of sorts.

"Oh, hey," Wade said happily. "Hot dogs!"

The table was covered in so many platters of food there was almost no room for the plates. The small tray piled high with plain hot dogs in buns was surrounded by tiny ceramic condiment jars. Wade plopped down in one of the empty seats and stared longingly at the tray of hot dogs until the god to his left picked it up and passed it to him.

"One should never go hungry," the dark-haired god said, his voice deep and amused.

Wade snatched the platter out of the god's hands and started to smother the hot dogs with all available toppings. Patrick didn't tell him to stop, choosing instead to sit quietly beside him, keeping all his attention on Odin.

"Should I call you Aksel Sigfodr?" Patrick asked slowly. "Or would you prefer Odin?"

"I am worshipped by many names. I answer to them all," Odin said easily enough, which wasn't an answer. There were so many ways to piss him off if he didn't like what name Patrick chose to use.

He figured *asshole* wouldn't be the best place to start.

Patrick's gaze flickered over to the goddess again, weighing who she could be and only coming up with one answer. "Frigg?"

Odin's wife, the titular queen of the Æsir, smiled at him in a way he was sure she thought was comforting, but which made Patrick want to run for the exit. Sitting there reminded him of the breakfast he'd interrupted on Hera's rooftop last summer. The only difference was he didn't have Jono with him to lean on for support.

"Well met," Frigg said.

Patrick nodded slowly at that statement, in no way wanting to repeat it, because the words would be false. The dark-haired god at the table passed over a tray piled high with bone-in prime rib. "Take some."

"I'm not hungry," Patrick said.

"I am," Wade mumbled around a mouthful of hot dog.

The god produced a knife from somewhere and transferred a thick slab of prime rib to Wade's plate. The teen hummed happily at the addition, and Patrick resigned himself to letting Wade eat whatever he wanted at this table.

"You've done well by the fledgling," the god said.

"We try," Patrick replied.

"I know."

The statement had Patrick eyeing the god warily, mind skimming through all the possibilities of who the immortal could be but unable to decide until he looked into eyes no mortal would ever have—pale blue with a thin rainbow of colors ringing black pupils that seemed full of stars. Eyes that saw everything, the way Muninn and Huginn could, only in a different way. Tasked with keeping an eternal watch for the onslaught of Ragnarök, Patrick wondered what the god saw these days.

Patrick swallowed dryly before reaching for the nearest glass of water. "Heimdallr."

The immortal that stories called the shining god smiled, flashing gold teeth. "Yes. I see your lessons stuck."

The knowledge that Heimdallr might have been watching him from a distance all these years made bile creep up Patrick's throat. He forced it down with more water.

"Your ravens said you wanted to talk," Patrick said, wanting this conversation over with as soon as possible. "The Norns wanted me to find you. They seem worried about your safety, but you're a god, so I think you'll be fine so long as you steer clear of the Dominion Sect. General Reed ordered me to find you. He thinks you might know where the Morrígan's staff is, but I don't think he knew you were immortal."

Odin didn't immediately answer and took his time choosing which piece of prime rib he wanted, slathering it with horseradish once it was on his plate. A waiter came over from the bar with an open bottle of what Patrick thought was wine, but turned out instead to be mead. It looked like liquid gold when poured into the wineglasses. Patrick waved off a pour for himself and Wade.

"It's rude to decline an offer from the gods," Frigg said mildly.

"My track record isn't great with your kind, and Wade is underage. We'll stick with water."

"My son brews it locally at Eiketre. It is offered at every bar in this city," Odin said.

"I don't drink while working a case."

Which wasn't exactly true, but no way was Patrick willing to deal with gods while impaired in some way. The last time he'd done that, he'd ended up with a soul debt.

"You might be better company if you did."

Odin raised his glass at Patrick in a mocking manner before taking a sip. Patrick dug his fingers into his thighs, trying to ground himself. "The Morrígan's staff. Where is it?"

"You expect me to know where something not of my own kind's making is?"

Odin's derision came through loud and clear, but Patrick pressed on anyway. "Medb left it in the mortal world. We've been trying to find it before the Dominion Sect does. Our intelligence says they're in town, so there's a good chance the staff is as well."

"Your mistakes aren't mine to care about."

"They will be if Ethan gets his hands on that staff and turns himself into a god."

Odin set the wineglass down, half the mead gone. "The Morrígan's staff cannot turn someone into a god. You need prayers and sacrifices for that."

Patrick bit down on the inside of his cheek before releasing it. "Ethan has the Dominion Sect to pray for him and control of Macaria's godhead."

"What is left of it," Heimdallr replied.

Patrick turned his head to look at the other god. "You've seen her?"

"Years ago, when you were but a child still before Hades hid her from my sight, and again last summer." Heimdallr looked thoughtfully at Patrick before shaking his head. "Macaria's godhead has driven your sister mad. What's left of your sister's soul is not worth saving."

Patrick's lungs locked up, his ears ringing at those words. He'd known ever since the Thirty-Day War that Hannah was lost to him, but some tiny shred of him always thought there could be a chance to save her. That the sister he'd loved for eight years before Ethan did the unthinkable could be pried free of Macaria's godhead.

But human souls were never meant to carry such power, no matter how weak a god was from lack of prayers and worshippers and being forgotten by the world at large. These days, Hannah was just a vessel for their father's machinations, a battleground for a future no Fates of any pantheon could see.

Patrick forced himself to take a breath, air whistling past his lips and teeth. "You're the head of your pantheon. Ethan has a known track record of coming after gods in your position."

"Let him," Odin said with a disdainful twist of his mouth. "I fear no mortal."

"He stole a godhead and carries its power in a mortal body for his use. Few have been so bold in the millennia we have walked Midgard," Frigg reminded her husband.

"And they will die because of it."

"The Norns wouldn't have sent me here to help you if they

didn't think there was a legitimate threat. If you know where the Morrígan's staff is, that would be reason enough for Ethan to come after you," Patrick said.

"If I knew where the Morrígan's staff was, I would retrieve it and carry it home to my cousin."

Patrick very much doubted Odin would be that generous. "If you don't know its exact location, then do you know how to find it? General Reed seemed to think your human identity had information we could use."

Odin smiled, his one gray eye reflecting the light shining down on them. "We are in Chicago. You must know a city such as this is built on favors and promises."

"And money, I assume."

Odin leaned back in his seat and gestured expansively with one hand at the empty restaurant around them. "A mayoral candidate is scheduled to hold a fundraiser dinner here this weekend. He will not be the only one to come into my abode and ask a favor. The name I am known by in this city is one that cannot be ignored if you wish to do politics here. The old way of tithing has been lost to history, but we've found other avenues to gain prayers."

Patrick grimaced. "That's blackmail."

"It is only blackmail if you can prove it." Odin pinned Patrick with a look that cut straight to his soul, making cold sweat slide down his back. "I do not fear the Dominion Sect. The Norns have not seen the future since Persephone offered you a choice, but the blindness runs both ways. The Moirai and those gods who ally themselves with Ethan will fight for a future that is not guaranteed, the same way we must. The only way to lay claim to it is to kill your past."

Frigg pushed her chair back from the table and stood. "Let me show you to the door. I believe the rain has stopped."

Patrick stood, tugging at Wade's arm to get him up as well. "Let's go."

Odin's searing gaze was one Patrick could not meet. "Remember what I said. You owe a duty to us."

"I was dying as a child and didn't know any better." Patrick turned away from the table, shoving his hands into his jacket pockets to hide how they shook. "We all make mistakes."

Frigg led the way to the doors of the restaurant, the front-of-house area now empty of workers. She came to a stop with one hand resting on the door handle, studying Patrick with kind blue eyes he didn't trust.

"My husband believes nothing can touch him in this city that belongs to us," Frigg said.

"I always wondered why Chicago politics and the general state at large were so corrupt. It makes sense now," Patrick said. "Also the homicide count."

Frigg's mouth twitched downward at the corners ever so slightly. "War exists in all places."

"Yeah, but a war god exacerbates it."

"Do you truly believe Odin is a target?"

Patrick shrugged. "Ethan went after Ra and Zeus. What makes you think he'd stop at two when there are hundreds of myths in the world to steal a godhead from? You and Odin aren't subtle with your whole pay-to-play scheme going on here."

"It is our right to survive."

"At the expense of everyone else?"

Frigg pushed open the door, letting in a cold breeze that didn't seem to bother her at all. "I worry for my husband. He thinks his ravens can keep him safe forever."

"Why?"

"Muninn and Huginn hear all thoughts and carry all memories to Odin's ears. They can remove what knowledge Ethan has gained about godheads and bring it to Odin for safekeeping."

Personally, Patrick wouldn't trust a god with anything like that. "Then why the fuck do you need me if you have them?"

"Because the Dominion Sect and the gods of all the hells keep

Macaria and Ethan hidden the same way we gods of the heavens endeavored to keep you safe as you grew to adulthood. With the way Ethan is bound to your twin and Macaria, erasing his memory risks erasing Macaria's existence. Persephone will never allow it."

"But she'll allow his death."

"Death severs all bindings. It is the way of things." Frigg nodded at the exit and the cars passing on the street beyond it. "The storm has passed, but I feel another is brewing. Odin may be cavalier about his safety, but I never have been. You should visit his son at Eiketre."

"You know, I actually do have a case I need to work on here. Making stops at bars while on the clock isn't a good look."

"Then go after your work is finished, but you will go."

The firmness of her words told Patrick arguing would be a lost cause. Patrick scowled as they left Au Hall behind, ducking his head against the fierce wind. Wade kept pace as they hurried down the block for the underground entrance that would lead back to the parking garage.

"What now? Are you going to the bar?" Wade asked.

Patrick sighed as they descended into the slightly warmer underground area, trying to ignore the headache growing behind his eyes. "Eventually. I need to set up a meeting with the SAIC out here about Westberg first."

"Are you going to tell them his campaign manager is a god in disguise?"

"No."

"Why not?"

"Because most people don't believe in gods, and I tend to not trust anyone in the SOA out of principle."

"Is that why you brought me along?"

Patrick glanced over his shoulder at the dark-haired teen. "You're pack, and I trust you."

Wade seemed pleased about that. "Does that mean I'm going to the SOA with you?"

"No. You're going back to the hotel where you'll stay put this time and do some homework."

Wade groaned. "That's not fun."

"Work never is. Welcome to adulthood."

"Adulthood sucks. I want to return it."

Patrick snorted out a tired laugh. "You and me both."

8

"How are things in Chicago?" Jono asked, pressing the mobile tight to his ear. He peered out the front door of the ground-floor landing in their building, eyeing everyone milling about on the pavement.

"A mess, like usual. I'm going to be here at least through Sunday," Patrick replied. He sounded annoyed and tired, but with no underlying hint of pain. Jono had gotten adept at parsing out the tone of Patrick's voice when he was trying to hide a wound.

"Do you think you'll come home next week?"

"Depends on what happens with the case."

Jono didn't ask, well aware of Patrick's reticence to speak about anything work related over an unsecured line. "I'm about to head out to work. Ring me later?"

"Always."

"Love you."

"Stay safe."

Patrick ended the call, and Jono shoved the mobile into his back pocket before opening the front door. He ducked his head against the cold wind and jogged to where everyone was gathered on the sidewalk. Slowing to a stop, he turned around and stared at the building.

"Is this really necessary?" Jono asked after a moment.

"Yes," Sage replied flatly.

"Did you talk to our landlord?"

"Gargoyles are allowed to choose what building they want to live on and the owners have to let them. Most people consider their presence an asset to the property value," Tiarnán said.

Jono eyed the trio of gargoyles sniffing about the front of the building, their stone bodies moving with a surprising smoothness as they searched for the best perches. "They eat pigeons and leave feathers everywhere."

"They also eat vermin."

"Does that include trespassing werecreatures?" Marek wanted to know.

Tiarnán's violet-eyed gaze was steady when he turned to look at Jono. "They don't care for the taste of your kind's blood. They'll tie themselves to the building's thresholds and settle in tonight. As guards, there are none better for living in a city."

"If you say so," Jono said, though he wasn't sure if their neighbors in the building would appreciate the new arrivals. He wasn't sure how Patrick would like their presence either.

But as Sage had said, Patrick wasn't here, so it was his decision to make, and he knew better than to stand in Sage's way when it came to legally protecting their pack.

"Right, that's sorted then." Jono extended his hand toward Tiarnán. "We appreciate you letting the gargoyles know the building had room for them."

They might have an alliance with the fae, but Jono still knew better than to outright thank them. Tiarnán grasped his hand in a strong grip. "I hope they serve you well."

The fae lord returned to his town car after the handshake. The dwarf driver chauffeuring him about barely waited for the door to shut before pulling onto the street and driving away, taillights bright in the darkness.

"Shall we?" Sage asked, hiking her tote bag higher on her shoulder.

Jono nodded. "Let's get this over with."

"I still think I should go with you," Marek said.

"If things go tits up, I'd rather not have to worry about your safety. We'll ring you when the meeting is over."

Marek made a face but didn't argue. Sage had already laid out the reasons he was staying behind before handing him her engagement ring for safekeeping. In the event she had to shift tonight, she hadn't wanted to lose it. She kissed Marek briefly on the mouth before following Jono to the Mustang.

"I'm driving," Sage told him. "Did you take your potion?"

Jono refrained from rolling his eyes, but just barely. He was halfway finished with the medicine Victoria had given him, which she knew. "Yes, mum."

"Hilarious. Get in the car."

Jono got into the front passenger seat, clenching his teeth against the dull throb in his ribs. The potions were doing their job; he just wished they'd work faster. Jono felt better, but the wound was only halfway healed, though the flulike symptoms had mostly abated. He felt weaker than usual, a fact he knew Lucien would exploit if the master vampire found out.

His only recourse would be Fenrir, and while Lucien knew about his animal-god patron, Jono didn't want to give over his body to the immortal in a fight with the vampire. Fenrir might opt to murder the arsehole, and that would make a mess of the Night Courts in New York City.

If Patrick came home to the vampires at war with them, Jono really would be sleeping on the sofa.

Emma and Leon followed them to Ginnungagap, refusing to let any car merge between them. They crossed through several known pack territories, none of them friendly, but didn't stop. The borders that touched up against Lucien's surrounding Ginnungagap were always fluctuating and continually growing in Lucien's favor as his Night Court kept making bloody excursions into pack territory.

The warehouse-turned-club in the Meatpacking District was popular these days with a younger crowd who enjoyed taking a walk on the dark side. Finding street parking, even on a Thursday night, was a crapshoot. The alleyway between the warehouse and the next building doubled as parking in a pinch, and that's where Sage steered them. The Mustang's headlights flashed over a familiar motorcycle before they went out.

"Do you want my pendant again?" Sage asked, one finger hooked over the platinum chain.

Jono shook his head. "I can't hide here."

Sage only nodded and didn't question his decision. They both got out of the car, the sound of the doors closing echoing in the cold air.

Emma tucked her hands into her puffer coat, her thick hair tied back in a loose fishtail braid. "This place always gives me the creeps."

"Let's get inside," Jono said.

They walked toward the mouth of the alleyway and turned onto the block, passing the queue of people waiting to get into Ginnungagap. Despite the chilly night, most everyone was in club clothes. Jono remembered how that was, queuing up for the clubs back in London that would actually let him inside. With his eyes, it was impossible to hide what he was, and he'd had too many doors over the years slam shut in his face.

The ones to Ginnungagap opened for them, the human servant manning the entrance well aware of who they were and that they were expected.

"VIP section," the man told them in a low voice. "Our master is waiting."

Jono ignored the quiet grumblings from those in the queue

who were pissed he and his friends were allowed entry without being dressed smart. Jono squared his shoulders and steeled himself to step into the club.

What lived inside the walls of Ginnungagap hadn't changed since the first time Jono had stepped foot in it. Whatever power resided here always made his skin crawl whenever he crossed the threshold. The noise of the club that had sounded muffled on the pavement was loud enough now to make his ears ring until he dialed down his hearing.

They came into the security foyer where human servants handled payment for the cover charge and the checking of any holy items behind a warded and bulletproof window. Jono shook his head, distracted by the unceasing, rumbling growl Fenrir was giving off in his mind. It didn't feel like a warning, but a welcoming, and Jono didn't like that at all.

"I should be at the office," Sage said as they bypassed security and entered the club proper.

"You could've stayed and kept working on your motion," Jono said easily enough.

"And let you argue your way through a bargain alone? Don't be stupid."

"I'm thrilled you trust me so deeply."

Sage rolled her eyes, the only visual cue of her annoyance as the flashing lights from the club skimmed over her face. "I trust you. I don't trust Lucien."

"Makes all of us," Leon agreed.

Jono nodded toward the stairs at the rear of the club that led to the VIP mezzanine level. "Let's get this over with."

Getting through the crowd of dancing, drinking clubgoers took a couple of minutes. Not everyone was human, and the multiple scents that assailed Jono's nose made him grimace. Sage remained on his right, guarding his weak point, refusing to let anyone get close enough to touch.

The undead scent of vampires permeated the air and walls,

leaving a disgusting taste in the back of his throat every time he breathed. Jono tracked half a dozen vampires in the crowd who only had eyes for his small group. He didn't trust any of them, didn't like being surrounded, but this wasn't his territory. He had no power here but what he'd pry out of Lucien.

And Jono wasn't leaving without a promise of an alliance.

Carmen met them at the bottom of the stairs leading to the VIP section, wearing a dress that was little more than a negligee. The red silk edged in black lace matched her pupils and hair, though she still kept most of her glamour intact. The bruise on the side of her throat was the perfect shape of Lucien's messy, jagged fangs. Vampire fangs as a whole weren't neat and orderly, and they used all of them to access the blood of their victims. Carmen and the human servants never seemed to mind the bruises and scars left behind.

"Where's Patrick?" Carmen asked.

Jono ignored the question. "Where's Lucien?"

Carmen's mouth curved in a too-knowing smile Jono didn't care for. She curled her fingers at him, the varnish on her long nails the same color as her dress. "This way."

She led them upstairs to a space that overlooked the main floor of the warehouse. The smaller bar up there was manned by a human servant, but the area was mostly empty. The only ones taking up seats were Lucien and several vampires from his personal Night Court that had become the Manhattan Night Court back in August.

The underlying quiet in the mezzanine area echoed strangely beneath the music—no heartbeats, no breaths, because vampires weren't alive in the traditional sense. The undead didn't need to breathe except for when they needed to speak.

Lucien's gaze settled on Jono, the expression on his pale face seemingly carved from stone. He wasn't dressed for the cold outside—ripped jeans, a gray T-shirt—and he wasn't unarmed. He carried several knives on him, all of them smelling a bit like magic.

"Where's Patrick?" Lucien demanded.

"Working a case," Jono replied.

Lucien's black eyes narrowed as Carmen went to sit on the low-backed leather sofa he'd claimed. "You smell like blood."

Jono refused to acknowledge the half-healed wound over his ribs. "Must be your club. Should hire some cleaners to sort out the mess your Night Court makes of its meals."

"The blood is coming from you." Lucien kicked up a boot against the edge of the table between them, jostling the tall bottle of vodka situated in the ice bucket. "I hear you're claiming territory that isn't yours to take."

Jono took a seat in a chair without asking for permission. None of the others with him sat down, merely circled his seat in a show of force and protection. "I have packs that live in every borough. I know you burned all existing contracts with Estelle and Youssef's pack when you took over the Manhattan Night Court, but I figure we can come to an understanding."

"I don't make bargains. I don't sign contracts. You're asking for rights you'll never get."

Jono leaned back in the chair he'd chosen, lifting his left leg to rest his ankle on his right knee. "I know you love war more than you love Carmen, and I'm here to offer you one in exchange for an acknowledgment of border rights."

Lucien's expression never changed. "I make my own wars."

"If you make one here, in New York City, the government will figure out you're where you shouldn't be. I'm offering to cover for you."

"I've been doing this a long, long time, wolf. I've seen governments rise and fall. Human laws mean nothing to my kind."

"They mean everything to everyone these days, whether you want to believe in them or not. They favor my kind more than yours, but I think we can come up with an agreement that will be worthwhile to us both."

Lucien leaned forward, jagged teeth bared in a hard smile. "You seem to think I give a fuck about your pack problems. They don't interest me."

"Estelle and Youssef are partnering with the Krossed Knights. You know those hunters are allied with demons. What makes you think I'll stay their only target?"

"Historically speaking, you won't," Sage said calmly from his right. "Your one and only meeting with Estelle and Youssef left a mark on them, Lucien."

"I cut her face open. Perhaps I should have cut her throat instead," Lucien said.

"They hold grudges. They know you own the Manhattan Night Court. I wouldn't put it past them informing the Krossed Knights of your presence in the city. Which means all your known businesses will come under scrutiny by the hunters, and quite possibly the government."

"You think I'm unaware of that? The hunters in Brooklyn weren't the first to enter my territory."

"What happened to the ones that came before?"

Lucien laughed, the sound harsh and low beneath the music of the club, but Jono still heard him. "We ate them."

"And the demons they shared their souls with?"

"I'm a vampire. We have no souls for the denizens of hell to lay claim to."

"I'd say it's a pity, but it's not like that would change you much."

"If you came here to ask for the same thing Estelle and Youssef offered Tremaine, you wasted your time."

"I don't think so. You made a promise to protect Patrick, remember? Acknowledging our god pack will help you keep your promise."

"Don't speak of things you know nothing about," Lucien hissed, eyes narrowing.

Jono put both feet on the floor, staring Lucien down as Fenrir seeped through his soul in a way he remembered from Underhill and didn't like but couldn't fight. "You think I don't know what happened during the Thirty-Day War?"

"You weren't there."

"Patrick was, same as you. Only he got to say goodbye to Ashanti and you never did."

Distracted by the god clawing through his soul and the howls filling his mind louder than the club music, Jono never saw Lucien move. He only saw Sage, Emma, and Leon react to the threat at the last second, but they didn't stand a chance in the face of Lucien's fury.

Regret was always a bitter weight to carry, heavier than guilt some days.

Jono's reflexes were a shade too slow to dodge Lucien when the master vampire launched himself across the table. Sage put herself between them, snarling with a voice that sounded more beast than human, but Lucien put her down with a vicious slice from one of his knives to her abdomen. Sage didn't scream, merely tried to keep her guts from falling out as her rapid healing kicked in.

Emma tried to haul Jono out of the chair, but he wrenched free of her grip, nearly causing her to lose her balance as other vampires closed in. Leon fought to keep some of them at bay, but he wasn't a match for them all.

Jono would apologize to his friends later for his decisions tonight.

The chair toppled backward from Lucien's attack, crashing to the floor. When Lucien's fingers wrapped around his throat, fingernails that felt like claws slicing through skin, Jono didn't try to fight him. Lucien's other hand dug into the half-healed knife wound, ripping it open all over again, fingers determined to break apart his ribs. Jono tilted his head back and let Fenrir speak, never looking away from Lucien's murderous gaze.

"You should have asked for a different place to have this talk," the god bit out around a laugh that sounded like breaking bones,

Jono's mouth shaping the words. *"Ginnungagap is what birthed me and mine."*

Power burst through Jono's soul, and the air became charged around them, the scent of burning ozone running across his tongue. Lucien's fingers never loosened from around his throat, nor did they withdraw from the spaces between Jono's ribs, as the veil tore open around them. The club, with its music and dance floor full of the living and undead, faded to nothing amidst gray fog.

The mundane world fell away in the face of a primordial void that was too vast for Jono to comprehend. It made him feel small and insignificant even as Fenrir basked in its presence.

"Jono!"

Sage's voice echoed through the fog, as if coming from a great distance when he knew she should've been less than a meter away.

Don't let them get lost, Jono told Fenrir.

Lucien hadn't removed his hands from Jono's body, but he paused in his attempt at murder. The fog drifting close to them wasn't thick enough to obscure his face. The master vampire seemed more contemplative than afraid, and Jono could see, in that moment, how Lucien had survived the centuries when others of his kind had perished beneath the growth and spread of humanity.

Lucien never ran from any threat—he defeated it, or turned it into an opportunity to aid him.

"Here I thought you'd never show your face, Fenrir," Lucien said in a silky voice.

The god moved Jono's hand, claws shifting out of his fingers despite the distant sickly pain it caused him. They pressed threateningly against Lucien's side. *"Let us go."*

Maybe it was the threat from the god or the risk of being lost in the veil between worlds that had Lucien shoving himself off Jono. Either way, Lucien stood but didn't offer Jono a helping hand. Jono disliked being a passenger in his own body, but considering it was Fenrir who had ripped open the veil, he had no choice. He watched through his own eyes as Fenrir stood as well, ignoring the blood staining Jono's clothes. The parts of the wound not tainted from silver or aconite poison were already healing.

Fenrir threw back his head and howled with Jono's voice, the sound an almost pulsating thing that pulled through the pack bonds tying him to the people Jono had come to Ginnungagap with.

The veil around them swirled and moved as dark shapes stumbled closer, materializing as Sage, Emma, and Leon. Jono couldn't turn his head to look at them, but he could smell them, could hear their hearts beating. They were alive, and that was all Jono cared about.

"Jono, your eyes," Emma said, staring at him in shock. "They're glowing."

Sage reached out with a bloody hand to grab Emma by the arm when the smaller woman would have stepped closer. "Don't interfere."

"If any of my Night Court are lost within the veil, you will find them and send them back to the mortal world, or this conversation you want will not happen," Lucien threatened.

"I have no use for your children here. They remain where they are on the other side," Fenrir said.

Lucien raised his hand to lick Jono's blood off his fingers. "What do you want?"

"A bargain."

"I bargain with no one."

"You make promises with gods. You will make one with me and my chosen vessel."

Lucien's eyes never blinked, though his mouth curved up to reveal his jagged teeth in an angry snarl. "The only promise to a god I've ever made was to my mother."

"You keep it in strange ways."

"I keep it how she would see fit." Lucien stepped forward, pure violence in every line of his body. "I'd break it if I could."

Jono's mouth twisted into a smile. *"But you don't."*

"Because I heeded my mother's warnings about the threat of new gods backed by the hells. My kind can't eat the dead." Lucien flipped the knife in his other hand around to a better grip, tapping the blade against his thigh. "But I could eat you."

"Isn't this a cozy little get-together," a new voice drawled. "Fenrir, you know better than to play with your food like this."

Jono's head turned fractionally to the right, just enough for him to see the figure that slipped free of the thick gray fog. Hermes smiled in a way that still made Jono want to punch the arrogance off his face. The messenger god's curls were dyed a bright blue this time around, his ripped jeans and band T-shirt beneath the studded leather jacket worn-in and comfortable-looking.

"Hermes," Fenrir said. *"This does not concern you, cousin."*

"Oh, but it always concerns me when mortals get lost in the veil."

"We are not lost."

"You're a few steps away from being eaten by that void of yours. I'd say you're lost." Hermes glanced around the group and arched an eyebrow. "Where's Pattycakes?"

Punch him, Jono thought. *Please.*

Fenrir ignored him, the bastard.

"I am here. I am enough," Fenrir said.

Hermes spread his hands and shrugged expansively. "If you say so."

Lucien looked over at Hermes before focusing on Fenrir again. Jono tried to see if he had control back, but the weight of the god in his soul and mind was a pressure he couldn't fight against.

"Your vessel's problem with the Krossed Knights isn't mine," Lucien said.

"The fight between god packs will only get worse," Fenrir said.

"Then show your favor."

The god lifted Jono's hand to wave aside those words. *"My favor will be known, but not yet. Yours, however, will give them pause."*

"You don't have it."

"Oh, but we will." Jono's body stepped forward, guided by the god, and Lucien never gave any ground. *"You who were turned by a goddess, who carries her direct blood in your veins, you will gain my prayers toward her memory."*

"No one remembers you enough for it to matter. Your prayers have no power here."

Jono's head tilted to the side, gaze drifting toward his pack and Emma's before returning to Lucien. *"If I was not prayed to, I would not be here as I am."*

"That's not enough to make a bargain with me. That's not enough to bring her *back*."

"How certain of that are you?"

Lucien's mouth twisted, black eyes like holes in his head against the gray fog surrounding them. "You, wolf, are not enough."

"Fenrir is right, you know," Hermes interrupted. "Faith comes in many forms. I had faith Ashanti would get the dagger to Patrick, and look what happened."

"She *died*," Lucien spat out, rounding on the messenger god. "Your fight stole our mother from us."

Hermes stared him down, power flashing across his gold-brown eyes. "Ashanti was a willing sacrifice. She knew what was at stake. She knew what your temper would cost our side if she didn't bind you with that promise to keep Patrick safe. Legitimizing their god pack only serves to keep your word."

Lucien turned his head to glare at Jono and the god in control. "I won't bargain with gods. Let me speak with your vessel."

Fenrir withdrew through Jono's consciousness far enough to give him back his voice. The god remained beneath his skin, in his soul, a burning presence that made Jono want to shift forms.

"Prayers in exchange for acknowledgment of territory rights. Is that what we're agreeing to?" Jono asked, sounding like himself rather than Fenrir.

"I haven't agreed to anything."

"But you're going to."

Lucien smiled, his expression a twisted, monstrous thing. "You think because you carry a god's favor you have the upper hand here? They gave you to Patrick as a weapon. You're nothing but that to them."

"Patrick doesn't see me like that."

"Patrick doesn't matter. It's what he needs to do that does."

"Kill Ethan?"

"And the rot his father grew in the Dominion Sect. Stealing godheads was a dream before Ethan turned it into a reality." Lucien stepped closer, eyes never blinking. "You get acknowledgment of your territory, and every last pack you rule over will pray to my mother, as will your god."

"It took millions of followers to worship Santa Muerte into existence. You can't possibly think we'll be enough?"

Lucien said nothing to that, and Jono wondered what the vampire knew that he didn't. Lucien trafficked in information the same way he trafficked in weapons, drugs, and people. Knowing something was worth its weight in gold some days.

"That's my price," Lucien said. "Take it or leave it."

"Prayers for the damned in exchange for recognition of the living in the eyes of the enemy," Fenrir said, clawing back control of Jono's voice. *"Done."*

"If we're finished, let's get away from your birthplace, Fenrir. I feel like it wants to eat me," Hermes said.

Hermes passed between Jono and Lucien, a lazy smirk on his face. Fenrir receded from his soul, giving back control of his body. Jono shook his head hard, the deep silence making his ears ring.

Sage stepped closer, settling her hand on his arm. She peered up at him before giving a faint nod. "Good. You're back. Let's get out of here."

Jono looked over her head at where Emma and Leon stood, both of them staring at him intensely with various degrees of shock and hurt in their eyes. Jono winced. Explaining what had happened wasn't going to be easy. He doubted they'd forgive him immediately for keeping this particular secret after telling them he had nothing else to hide.

"Let's go!" Hermes shouted through the fog, already just a dark shadow in the veil up ahead.

The five of them followed after the messenger god, the scent of ozone a trail they never deviated from. Traveling through the veil was difficult and rarely done by mortals, but gods slipped through more easily than most. Fenrir had taken them through the veil, but Hermes was the one to drag them back to the mortal world, pulling them out of the fog with determined hands.

When Hermes' hand grabbed his, Jono tried not to flinch, letting the messenger god haul him back into Ginnungagap. The silence disappeared, replaced by the muffled quiet of an empty club, the music long since turned off. Bits of fog evaporated, his eyes adjusting to the structures of a building rather than the never-ending grayness of the space between worlds.

A blur of black and red was all the warning Jono got before Carmen stood before him and pressed a pistol to the underside of his jaw hard enough to make his teeth clack together.

"Bit dramatic, don't you think?" Jono asked, knocking the barrel aside.

"If you *ever* take Lucien away like that again, they'll never find your body," Carmen promised, her face a mask of fury. She'd dropped her glamour, and the sexual desire she exuded was enough to make Jono's nose itch.

"I wasn't the one who took him."

"Back off," Sage said, appearing by his side in the mess of broken furniture Hermes had dropped them into.

Jono craned his head around, trying to see where the messenger god had gone, but Hermes seemed to have disappeared.

Whether back through the veil or to explore the empty club, it was anyone's guess.

"How much time did we lose?"

"It's Friday morning," Naheed said from her position by the stairs, the pistol in her hand pointed at the floor.

Which meant they'd lost hours since their arrival at Ginnungagap on Thursday night. Traveling to the other side of the veil was worse than traveling over the International Date Line in terms of losing time.

Jono glanced around the VIP area, noticing the vampires from the start of their meeting were no longer around. He pulled out his mobile to check the time, seeing that it was past sunrise by a good twenty minutes. Lucien was a daywalker though, one of the few vampires who could exist in sunlight without being killed. Jono doubted he'd have a difficult time getting back to wherever his Night Court called home.

"The bargain was made," Lucien said, glaring at him.

"You'll acknowledge our god pack?" Jono asked.

"As long as you pray to Ashanti."

"Keep your word and we'll keep ours."

"Covens pray to their chosen gods to keep them alive. You will be no different in your actions, but I'll know if you renege on your promise."

Jono narrowed his eyes. "You aren't Ashanti's priest."

Lucien's smile was a hint of the monster he was in human form. "I am her child. Now get the fuck out of my club."

Sage pushed gently at his arm, and Jono took the hint for what it was. He turned around, listening as Emma and Leon fell into step behind him. The only people left in the club were human servants, and none of them cared about their passage out of Ginnungagap.

Jono shivered as he stepped outside, less from the cold and more from the feel of power against his skin as they crossed the threshold of the building and what lived in its walls.

"Nothing left to hide, eh?" Emma said in a low, angry voice before stalking toward her car.

Jono winced, not knowing where to start when it came to the god in his soul. "Em."

"Save it. Let's just get you back home."

That she was still going to escort him back to the flat and stay there, despite how angry she sounded and smelled, left Jono feeling absolutely horrid.

"I really bollocksed that up, didn't I?" Jono asked once he and Sage were in the Mustang.

"If you're talking about the bargain with Lucien? You were more successful than Patrick would've been. If you're talking about keeping secrets from your friends? It could've gone better," Sage said in a neutral voice.

Lawyers never did sugarcoat anything these days. Jono rubbed tiredly at his eyes. "Bloody hell."

Sage glanced over at him before refocusing on the road. "When are we telling Patrick about this?"

"When he gets back."

The faint unease that rolled through him made Jono shift in his seat. Fenrir's worry was difficult to parse.

The Æsir are restless.

Jono grimaced. "Maybe sooner."

He hoped Patrick was okay in Chicago.

9

"I can't believe the SAIC signed off on this," Kelly said as she shut the car door behind her.

Patrick squinted at her over the rims of his aviator sunglasses. "Something interesting came up the other day."

Benjamin eyed him dubiously as he and his partner stepped onto the icy sidewalk. "Funny how that happened the second you arrived in Chicago."

Patrick shrugged, not in the mood to explain himself on a cold and windy late Friday morning. He'd spent ten hours yesterday on conference calls with Setsuna and the Illinois State Attorney General's office arguing about being allowed to interview Dean Westberg. His explanation to Setsuna about immortal interference in the campaign was enough to get her to listen, but coming up with a plausible excuse for the local government offices spearheading the Westberg investigation was a different problem.

Blaming the Dominion Sect seemed like the best way to circumvent the god issue. It wasn't as if Patrick would be lying. He'd just have to figure out a way to make that connection without perjuring himself later on.

"The media is going to have a field day once word gets out about our visit. That might put the people he's targeting at risk," Kelly said.

"*Might* isn't a sure bet. Now come on. The element of surprise is always the best weapon against politicians," Patrick replied.

The campaign headquarters for the mayoral candidate was on the third floor of an office building downtown. The location told Patrick that Dean had money to burn because no one sane rented downtown office space in any city on a short-term lease. The rent was always astronomical, but maybe it was a subtle threat to his fellow candidates—a pointed hint about his deep pockets.

They showed their badges to the security guard at the front desk to get access to the elevator. When they arrived in the campaign space, they were greeted by curious looks from the people who were hard at work manning phones for text messaging outreach.

Most of the people there were either college students probably working around their class schedules or older people volunteering on their days off. All of them were mundane humans, which wasn't surprising considering Westberg's own preferences.

Kristen Lief, Westberg's campaign manager, stepped out of an office with glass walls. She came their way with a polite smile on her face that Patrick didn't trust at all. He tried to see her aura, but it was locked down tight, nothing but human in the faint glow that surrounded her before he quit looking.

She appeared human this time, but Patrick doubted Wade had been wrong in his assessment. Whatever immortal Patrick was dealing with, she was good at blending in as human.

"Were you that impressed at brunch the other day? Here to volunteer for the campaign?" Kristen asked.

Patrick pulled his badge with ID out of his pocket and flipped open the thin leather wallet so she could see it. "Actually, we're from the SOA. We'd like to speak with Mr. Westberg."

Kristen's smile became tacked on. "I'm sorry, but he's currently unavailable."

Patrick peered over her shoulder at the other, bigger office, where the candidate in question was talking on the phone. "Looks available to me."

Patrick walked past her, and when Kristen would've tried to get in his way, Kelly stepped forward to distract her.

"Yeah, let's not do that," Kelly said. "How about you and I have a talk?"

Patrick could feel the immortal's eyes boring into his back, and the intense attention made his shoulders tighten. He couldn't help letting his hand stray toward the hilt of his dagger in a need for security.

Pushing open the office door without knocking, Patrick watched as Westberg looked away from his laptop, still talking on the phone. Patrick silently held up his badge again, and Westberg didn't miss a beat.

"You know what? Something just came up and I'll need to call you back. No, nothing terrible. Kristen just needs me for something. It's probably polling results again. We'll talk later. I'll see you at the fundraiser dinner if we don't," Westberg said before ending the call. The candidate stared at Patrick. "Can I help you?"

"Special Agent Patrick Collins of the SOA. I'd like to ask you a couple of questions," Patrick said. He didn't drop his shields, but no recognition sparked through his magic. Westberg felt human to his senses.

"Now's really not a good time. I was just about to leave for lunch with my wife."

"You can be late."

Westberg eyed him with an inscrutable look before his expression cleared, replaced with a politician's smile. His entire demeanor seemed to change, becoming more welcoming when Patrick knew no one ever welcomed government interference.

"Well, if it can't wait, please, take a seat. Can I get you anything to drink?"

"No," Patrick said, declining both the drink offer and a seat. "I understand you're the owner of about a dozen or so residential properties in Chicago."

"I disclosed my taxes when I filed my candidacy paperwork. All of my income for the past ten years is available. You didn't need to pay a visit to confirm that information. I haven't hidden anything."

"You have some payment irregularities in your records."

"If that were the case, I'd expect the IRS to come calling, not the SOA."

"Yeah, they'd come if it was about money."

"Then why are you here?"

Patrick knew from the case records that deposition subpoenas had been issued to the property management company that handled Westberg's real estate empire and collected rent from tenants. As with any case, following the money was the first step, and it had brought Patrick here.

"The SOA thinks someone in your personal orbit might be compromised," Patrick said easily enough. "Your ambitions make you a target for certain kinds of people in the world."

"The wrong people, I'm guessing?"

"In certain eyes, yes. We believe the Dominion Sect may be targeting you."

Westberg didn't even blink. "Then I must be leading in the polls if they believe I'm a threat. Unlike that group, I'm for everyone to have a right to freely access their magic."

Patrick didn't comment on that. "Can you think of anyone who might have a grudge against you?"

Westberg laughed as he got to his feet. "Special Agent Collins, I'm running for mayor of Chicago. There will always be people who will hold a grudge against me."

"Ones who work for you specifically?"

"I'm sorry, if you want any more information, you'll need to speak to my lawyer."

Patrick wasn't surprised by that comeback. "We're just having a friendly chat, Mr. Westberg."

"Nothing that comes out of your agency is friendly."

"If that's how you feel, I'll take your lawyer's number."

"DeLucca & Associates. Ask for Marcello."

Before Patrick could respond, the office door opened and a statuesque woman wearing a fur coat came inside. She blinked large blue eyes at them, her light brown hair swept back in a loose chignon. Her face lacked wrinkles and expression lines, probably from an overabundance of Botox. The square-cut emerald ring on her left hand was large enough it almost reached her second knuckle. Patrick's magic remained quiet at her arrival, no recognition searing through his soul.

"Darling, we'll be late for our reservations," the woman said.

"Of course, Phoebe." Westberg smiled politely at Patrick as he came around the desk, invading his personal space. "I hope that will be all, Special Agent Collins?"

Patrick tilted his head back to look the other man in the eye. "Aksel Sigfodr says hello."

The only sign of Westberg's discomfort was the faintest tightening of his jaw. Patrick only saw it because he was looking. "Did he? And how is Mr. Sigfodr?"

"Happy you've paid his tithes. I'm sure your fundraiser dinner this weekend will do well."

Patrick didn't wait for a response, merely turned on his feet and left the office. Phoebe looked down her nose at him as he left, ever the loyal politician's wife in the face of a threat to her husband. Patrick walked through the campaign work room, waving at Kelly and Benjamin, who were still engaged in a war of words with Kristen. The pair peeled away from her, the campaign manager seemingly glad to be rid of them.

"That was quick," Kelly said in a low voice as they waited for the elevator.

"He lawyered up," Patrick said.

"We could've told you that instead of wasting a trip down here and tipping our hand more than strictly necessary that he's being targeted. Politicians of any party never like the optics of a federal visit."

Patrick didn't say anything to that accusation. The three of them rode the elevator back down to the lobby in silence. Kelly and Benjamin headed for their unmarked car without a goodbye. Patrick headed for his SUV, ducking his head against the wind. The air was sharp and cold when he breathed, burning the inside of his nose with every breath. The weather had been strange ever since his lunch meeting with Odin, and Patrick didn't know what to make of that.

Unlike New York City, Chicago didn't have a nexus buried far beneath the city's foundation. The closest one was found beneath the waters of Lake Michigan, a possible contributing factor to all the legends about the monsters that dwelled within the fresh water.

Most people forgot that the lake *was* the monster. Sometimes nature was stranger and more terrifying than any story humans could tell.

Patrick drove away from the campaign headquarters. He drummed his fingers against the steering wheel before pulling out his phone and calling Jono. He hadn't set the rental for hands-free, and so kept the phone pressed to his ear while keeping both eyes on the road.

"Hey," Jono said through a yawn when he picked up.

"Hey," Patrick replied. "Did I wake you?"

"Doesn't matter."

"I can let you go back to sleep."

"I like listening to your voice more. What's going on?"

"Still working the case. Hitting some dead ends, but the place I'm going to tonight might give me more information."

"Yeah? That's good, innit?"

"Maybe." Patrick sighed tiredly. "How's everything in New York?"

"You know, the usual."

"I tried calling you last night, but you never picked up. Busy night at the bar?"

Jono yawned again, the sound crackling through the speaker. "It was late when I finally saw your missed calls. I didn't want to wake you, so I never rang back."

"I wouldn't have minded if you had. Have I mentioned lately how much I hate hotel rooms now?"

"Because you're sharing one with Wade?"

"Aside from that."

"I miss you, too, love," Jono said quietly.

Patrick's shoulders loosened a little at that confession. It always left a warm feeling in his chest knowing who he had waiting for him when he finished a case. "I know."

"Finish your case so you can come home."

"That's the plan."

"You're driving, so I'm going to let you go. Ring me later, yeah?"

"Will do."

Patrick ended the call and dropped his phone in the cupholder in the console between the front seats. As frustrating as each passing day in Chicago was becoming, talking to Jono always put him in a better mood.

***

EIKETRE WAS LOCATED IN ANDERSONVILLE, in the North Side of Chicago. Built on a narrow street facing the fenced-off Rosehill Cemetery, the bar wasn't near any residential buildings, which was probably a good thing. The raucous noise could be heard even through the closed windows. An empty patio beneath a snow-coated pergola indicated tables were probably in use during the summer, but they'd been stored for the winter. Strangely blooming vines twined through the low iron fence surrounding the front patio area.

The front of the building was covered with weathered wooden boards, giving it a rustic look. The bar's name was carved into one such panel over the door, the tiny designs surrounding the letters made up of intricate wards that were geared toward a healthy hearth and home. The bar was connected to an even larger building that looked as if it could have housed a small brewery.

Patrick tucked his keys into his jeans pocket and studied the exterior with a wary eye. Unlike with Westberg's campaign manager, he could feel the presence of gods in this place like it was the only lighthouse in a storm.

"They aren't subtle," Patrick mused.

Wade hummed low in the back of his throat. "Am I allowed inside?"

"You don't have to come with me."

Wade shoved his hands into his jacket pockets and hunched his shoulders. "Not gonna let you face them alone."

"Then come on."

They passed through the open gate and headed for the front door, pushing it open. A blast of warm air hit them in the face, and Patrick immediately started sweating from the heat. The sudden change in temperature didn't seem to bother Wade.

A very tall, very broad man sporting blond hair and a beard sat on a stool just past the door, blocking the entrance to the bar itself. He looked up from his phone, gaze skipping from Patrick to Wade. He shook his head. "No one under twenty-one allowed."

"He's with me," Patrick said.

"That's great and all, but you'll need to go somewhere else."

Patrick pulled out his badge and flipped it open. "He's with me."

The man squinted at the ID and SOA seal printed on it before grimacing. "Right. Is this an official visit?"

Patrick put his badge away, eyeing the leather corded necklace the man wore with the metal hammer pendant hanging from it. "We were told to speak to the owner."

The man's eyes narrowed, but he didn't argue. "He's working the bar tonight."

Patrick nodded, then gestured for Wade to follow him into the crowd. "Keep close."

Wade's hand latched onto his belt from behind. "Like I'm going anywhere."

"And keep your hands to yourself."

"Uh, sure."

Patrick didn't hold out any hope that Wade's sticky fingers wouldn't come away with other people's belongings, but now wasn't the time to argue. Getting through the Friday night crowd was an effort in elbow pushing. The bar was packed, the noise level deafening, and Patrick hated being surrounded by people he didn't know and couldn't trust.

Inside, the bar was warmly lit, the walls covered in the same wood paneling as outside. Runes were carved into the walls around bleached trophy skulls, many with horns, some without. Not all of the skulls were of native animals, judging by their size and shape. Some of them looked human-shaped, if a little misshapen, which was unsettling.

If you took away the general crowd and kept only the worshippers, the place could have doubled as an altar of sorts for the god pouring beer and talking loudly with the regulars drinking their weight in golden mead.

Thor was easily the tallest man in the room, with broad shoulders and muscled arms he showed off in a too-tight T-shirt, apparently unbothered by the winter weather outside. His pale red hair looked almost blond in the light. It fell loose past his shoulders in a messy tangle of waves, blending into the thick beard he sported that was a few shades darker. He laughed with his whole body in a way that was welcoming to his patrons, and the friendly smile on his face never disappeared.

If Patrick's magic wasn't so overwhelmed with the teeth-buzzing knowledge he was in the presence of a god, he might find Thor's attempt at passing as human friendly if he didn't know any better. But he did, and when Thor's keen, blue-eyed gaze swept the crowd to settle on him, Patrick nearly forgot how to breathe.

I hate feeling like prey.

Thor waved at his fellow bartender, a tall, blonde-haired woman who sported a ponytail half made up of braids. She listened to whatever Thor whispered into her ear, her gaze flickering their way. Then she nodded and took over Thor's spot with a smile, handling the orders from his customers.

Patrick reached behind and grabbed Wade's wrist, holding on tightly. "Come on."

Rather than stay where they were, Patrick headed over to the one open spot at the bar—the staff pass-through area everyone was steering clear of. Another electric jolt of recognition burned through his magic when they reached it. Patrick swallowed the taste of ozone, his right hand drifting toward his dagger. The person seated on the last barstool near the pass-through area twisted around to look over at them, dark brown eyes cut through with streaks of silver narrowing to slits.

"Maybe I should've taken your bet, Thor," the immortal said.

The black leather jacket he wore was decorated on the back with a large beaded motorcycle patch in the shape of a colorful bird's wings. Black fringe lined the front and back on the sides, arching over each shoulder. His black hair was shaved on the sides, with a central mohawk grown long and ending in a thick, tight braid that fell down his back, the end wrapped in red leather.

"Next time you should throw money in the pot, Otenai," Thor said mildly as he stepped out from behind the bar.

"When am I ever in Chicago long enough to join your favorite pastime?"

"Gambling is my second favorite pastime. I've made a living out of my first."

Otenai threw back his head and laughed, toasting Thor with the beer in his hand that wasn't the golden color of mead. "That you have, cousin."

Thor crossed his muscled arms over his broad chest and stared down at Patrick. The Norse god of thunder was taller than Jono, with a presence that made all of Patrick's hair stand on end. "What brings you to Chicago?"

Patrick swallowed dryly, finding his voice after a second. "I was told I should come speak with you."

Thor eyed him for a moment before his attention landed on Wade. "The fledgling is underage in this form. I could lose my alcohol license for allowing him in here."

"Then close up so we can talk."

"Is what you have to say so important?"

"It's about your father. He's in danger."

Thor's eyes narrowed before he nodded, more to himself than to Patrick. "Very well."

Thor went back behind the bar and grabbed a rope attached to an old iron bell that hung from the ceiling. He gave it several hard pulls, the deep clang of the bell echoing through the bar, cutting through all conversation.

"Last call," Thor boomed. "Drink up, my faithful."

Rather than the protesting groans Patrick expected to hear, almost everyone at the bar finished their drinks quickly, even if they'd just ordered. People started to cluster at the counter to close out their tabs, or left cash on the tables before leaving the bar. Within fifteen minutes, the only people who remained were the immortals, a couple of employees, Patrick, and Wade.

Patrick nudged Wade toward the bar counter, the two of them claiming stools several down from where Otenai sat. Thor eyed them before grabbing a clean glass from the workspace and pouring a pint of mead. He set the glass in front of Patrick, sliding it over the wood.

"On the house," Thor said.

"I don't drink while on the clock," Patrick said.

"It's rude to ignore hospitality."

"This isn't a home."

"Ah, but it is." Thor turned to pick a purple-skinned apple from a bowl near the register and set it next to the pint glass. "Don't worry. These do not come from Iðunn's orchard."

Realizing that he couldn't get out of performing hospitality under the god's sharp gaze, Patrick picked up the apple and took a bite. The fruit was crisp and flavorful, a far cry from the out of season ones in the grocery stores these days. He sipped at the mead, the honey flavor of it coating the inside of his mouth.

"Can I have one?" Wade asked, pointing at the fruit.

Patrick passed the apple over to Wade. If the fruit wasn't from Iðunn's orchard, then it wouldn't give Wade the promise of eternal youth. "Finish this."

"And the mead?"

"You're not drinking alcohol."

"I'd say a fellow warrior is always welcome to drink, but the laws in this country are not favorable toward those who fight," Thor said.

"Wade is eighteen," Patrick said coolly. "He's not drinking anything but water or soda."

"If the fledgling won't drink, I'll gladly take what you would offer him," Otenai said, sliding his empty glass across the counter.

Thor seemed amused by that request. "You have imbibed an entire barrel at this point."

"You exaggerate. Half a barrel, if that."

The other bartender poured another beer rather than mead for the immortal, setting it in front of him before leaving the bar area to go bus all the tables with the other workers. That left them in a small bubble of privacy Patrick wasn't taking for granted.

Otenai slipped off his stool and carried his beer closer, bringing with him the same electric feel to the air that crackled around Thor. The immortal claimed the stool next to Patrick, studying him with eyes that saw too much.

"Otenai isn't a name I'm familiar with," Patrick said, breaking the silence.

"The DMV out of New York is plenty familiar with Otenai Burning Sky," the immortal said. "Hinon is another matter entirely."

Patrick frowned. It took a minute or so for him to pinpoint that name, dredging up his knowledge of myths studied over the course of years. "You're of the Haudenosaunee."

Known more familiarly as the Iroquois rather than the name they called themselves, the Native American tribe called the northeast part of the country home. But gods, no matter their origin, had a tendency to wander.

Hinon smirked. "I am."

"Little far from your ancestral homeland, aren't you?"

"I follow where Oniare goes. There have been sightings of the beast in Lake Michigan this winter, so in Chicago I stay." Hinon raised his glass to toast Thor with a small smile on his face. "My cousin is good company. We thunder gods must stick together."

Thor leaned against the work counter behind the bar, his hair falling over his shoulder as he stared at Patrick. "Hinon is always welcome. You, however, bring trouble."

Patrick flexed the fingers of one hand against the edge of the bar counter. "I wouldn't be in Chicago if the Norns hadn't ordered me here."

Thor arched one thick eyebrow. "Did they now?"

"Frigg told me to come here. Odin is in danger, but he doesn't think he has anything to worry about."

"That sounds like the one-eyed bastard," Hinon mused.

"There's a good chance the Dominion Sect is in Chicago looking for the Morrígan's staff. If they know Odin is here, they won't pass up an opportunity to take him."

"The Morrígan's staff," Thor said with a slight nod. "If it was in Chicago, we'd know. We'd feel its presence."

"Our intelligence seems to think it could be."

"Then your intelligence is wrong."

Patrick curled his hand into a fist. "If the Morrígan's staff isn't here, then information about it is. I'm not passing that chance up. You need to convince Odin he's not safe. Maybe see about getting him to take a vacation in a warmer climate somewhere."

"Chicago is not Asgard. It is not our true home, but it gives us what we need while on Midgard." Thor straightened up and gestured at the nearly empty bar. "Worshippers to keep our memory alive."

"They won't matter if Odin winds up dead and his godhead stolen."

Thor's smile was slight and condescending. "You know little about our lives if you believe death would stop the Allfather. Ragnarök is a beginning and an end. It is a mourning and a celebration we all must dance to."

"The end of the world in your myths will look a hell of a lot different if the Dominion Sect rewrites it."

"They won't get the chance."

"If you say so." Patrick licked his dry lips and grimaced. "Can I get some water?"

Thor poured him a glass, nudging it closer. "Anything else?"

"Odin says no one can do political business in this city without going through him. He's got a fundraiser dinner happening this weekend for a candidate."

"Westberg," Thor said with a nod as he straightened up to his full height and started organizing the work area behind the bar. "I know of that candidate."

"Do you know his campaign manager is an immortal?"

Thor narrowed his eyes. "I never said I've met Westberg, just that I know of him. I follow news of the election online like everyone else."

"Not one to hang out with your old man?"

"Politics bore me. I prefer a more personal form of outreach."

Patrick pointed at the skulls and antlers hanging from the wall. "Listening to people drink their joys and drown their sorrows in your altar?"

"It isn't a crime to be worshipped."

"It is if souls are the currency." Patrick pulled out his phone and unlocked it, swiping through his pictures until he found the one of the pawnshop slip. He held it up for Thor to see. "The SOA is building a case against Westberg for collecting rent payments in souls through pawnshop deals. They sell their souls, bit by bit, and Westberg buys them up. Why?"

"You tell me."

"He's got to pay Odin's tithes with something. Money isn't going to cut it." Thor stared at him without blinking, and Patrick sighed tiredly. "But you knew that, didn't you?"

Thor shrugged expansively before starting to sort dirty glasses into a plastic bin. "Everything has a price."

Patrick glared at Thor, shoving his phone back into his pocket. "How many people have to die until he's satisfied with a candidate's tithes?"

"It depends on the soul's worth. You know that." Thor shook his head as he leaned over to check the kegs hooked to the draft spigots. "Odin asks for payment. If a candidate wants to win, they'll pay it."

"I find it real hard to believe that a man who spouts his hatred and disgust about magic would do a one-eighty and suddenly be willing to get down and dirty with the preternatural world."

"Mortals have always done crazy things for power. Why are you surprised?" Hinon said.

"Closeted about his beliefs is one thing. Having an immortal as his campaign manager means I can't discount the possibility he's a victim here." Patrick drummed his fingers against the bar counter. "If it's a god using him as a puppet, then which one, and why? If it's to get to Odin, then I'd put money on the Dominion Sect wanting his godhead."

"Your father needs to find a new hobby," Thor said. He picked up another apple and tossed it to Wade, who caught it easily. The teenager bit into it with a crunch that spoke of perfect ripeness.

"Thanks," Wade said around the fruit.

"If Odin is the target, then we need to keep him safe," Patrick said.

"The Allfather can take care of himself," Thor replied.

Patrick opened his mouth to argue, but he was cut off by the sound of glass shattering as something bright and heavy and smelling of the hells was thrown inside the bar, lighting everything up like a supernova.

THE SCORCHING HEAT OF A HELLFIRE BOMB WAS UNFORGETTABLE, A nightmare that should have only been found in a war zone, not a bar in the middle of Chicago on a Friday night.

Patrick threw himself off the barstool and took Wade down to the floor with him. He ripped his shields out of his bones, expanding the protection around the both of them while Wade shrieked in his ears. Hellfire splattered against the shields, the overwhelming smell of sulfur making Patrick gag as the stuff slid down the magical barrier.

Hellfire was like metaphysical napalm, and Patrick didn't want to be anywhere near it.

"What the *fuck?*" Wade yelled as the sprinklers went off, water sluicing over Patrick's shields.

"You really think Odin can take care of himself when whoever is after him is lobbing hellfire bombs at you?" Patrick shouted at Thor, even though he couldn't see the god through the rapidly encroaching smoke.

Warm hands grabbed him by the shoulders, shocking him with electricity, but they didn't let go. "You need to get clear."

Hinon's voice rang in Patrick's ears like thunder. When he looked at the god, it was like looking into the face of the sun. Huge wings the color of the sky in a Midwest storm arched away from the god's shoulders, lightning snaking around each feather. Hinon's aura was a halo of electricity that made Patrick's eyes water and his skin become staticky though his clothes.

Hinon yanked Patrick to his feet, and Wade scrambled to keep up. The Haudenosaunee thunder god raised a wing between them and the crackling, deathly burn of the hellfire bomb. Patrick jerked free of his grip, conjuring up a mageglobe, the pale blue light at odds with the sickly hellfire shine around them. He grabbed Wade by the shoulder with one hand and pulled his dagger free with the other. Heavenly fire crackled around the matte-black blade, the prayers in its making reacting to the presence of the hells.

"Get outside!" Patrick yelled.

He glanced over his shoulder at where Thor had jumped the bar and was coming to the rescue of the handful of employees who had stayed behind to close up. One of the women was unconscious and looked badly burned as he picked her up off the floor.

Patrick strengthened his shields and filled his mageglobe with raw magic, ready to form any offensive spell he might need. He took point on the way out of the bar, leaving warmth for freezing cold and a shock wave spell that caused his shield to ripple and bend from the force of it. Patrick layered his shields, channeling magic through his soul to shore up a defense a goddess had anchored in his bones.

Every window in the bar shattered from the hit, glass flying everywhere. The building shook on its foundations but remained standing. Patrick thrust out his arm and sent his mageglobe careening forward to test boundaries. Raw magic exploded against the shield surrounding two SUVs on the street, both vehicles ready to drive away from the scene of the crime. That they hadn't already meant trouble.

A handful of people stood on the street, magic sparking at their fingertips and in some of the focus circles drawn around their feet on the cold asphalt. Of the four magic users, the only one who mattered to Patrick was the man surrounded by a ring of red-black mageglobes, the concentric circles tattooed on his palms dripping blood.

"Isn't that the same guy we fought on the Skellig Islands?" Wade asked.

Patrick spun the hilt of his dagger between his fingers, getting a better grip on the blade. "Yeah."

"What if I eat him?"

"You know, I wouldn't stop you, but you might get food poisoning." Patrick raised his voice. "Hell of a way to knock, asshole."

"I wasn't sure you'd answer," Zachary Myers replied.

The last time Patrick had seen Ethan's right-hand acolyte, they'd been fighting over Órlaith's life in Ireland. Back then, Patrick had support in the way of his entire pack and the Hellraisers. Here, in Chicago, all he had was Wade, but he couldn't let a dragon loose in the Windy City. That was attention they couldn't afford.

Which left Patrick backed into a corner, and he never liked being in that position.

"You *dare* defile a place of worship?" Thor shouted, his voice echoing through the air.

High above in the cloudy sky, thunder rumbled menacingly. The wind picked up, blowing bitterly cold and making Patrick's lungs burn with every breath he took. Even as Thor called up a storm, the wind carried something else to them—the unforgettable scent of death.

"Really now, you used to have class," a throaty voice called out as one of the SUV doors opened. "Is this what you have been reduced to, Thor? Finding prayers in a modern-day drinking hall?

Drunken promises never amount to anything. I thought you would have learned that lesson after all these centuries."

The goddess who appeared was as tall as Thor, her generous curves filling out the all-white pantsuit she wore, which seemed to be missing a blouse beneath the suit jacket. The gold chain necklaces that lay over her cleavage matched the color of her high heels. Long white hair was braided back in an intricate style, with the braids tied off at the base of her neck. The loose hair beyond the ties whipped away from her body like a banner in the wind.

She looked like her perfume of choice would be Chanel No. 5, but the smell coming off her was that of a grave with a body rotting away inside it.

"Hel," Thor snarled, his voice at odds with the gentle way he handed over the unconscious woman he carried to another of his employees. "You dare show your face after being exiled from Chicago?"

"This city is no Asgard. I can come and go as I please," Hel hissed.

"You can go right back to the hole you crawled out of," Patrick said.

Hel walked forward, hellfire crawling away from every footstep she left behind. The sickly crimson glow wrapped itself around the low iron fence, melting the metal with a level of heat Patrick could feel through his shields. Her bony fingers curled into fists. The skin over her hands didn't match the youthful look of her face, and Patrick wasn't sure he wanted to know what was hiding beneath the surface.

"Hinon, take my worshippers to safety," Thor said, his blue eyes glowing white-hot in the glare of hellfire.

Hinon snapped his wings close to his back, bits of lightning trailing across the ground like electric pinion feathers. "Keep your wits about you, cousin."

Hinon gathered the three women into his arms, holding them with ease. He spread his wings with a snap that nearly deafened

Patrick. Thunder echoed in the air, a sound so deep Patrick felt it in his bones as Hinon flung himself into the sky on massive wings that trailed lightning in his wake.

Patrick only watched him go for a second before his gaze snapped back to Zachary and the Dominion Sect mercenary magic users the mage had brought with him. Zachary watched him with a smile on his face Patrick didn't like at fucking all.

"Don't leave my side, Wade," Patrick said.

"Wasn't planning on it," Wade replied, inching closer.

Hel came to a stop halfway up the path leading to Eiketre's entrance, hellfire curling around her body like serpents. "I offered you a better way than plying prayers out of the bottom of a glass, Thor. You declined."

"You want to bring Ragnarök to a world not ready for the end. The Allfather is the one who keeps us relevant in mortals' memories. You will kill us all with the worship of new gods," Thor said.

Hel laughed, the sound dry and hollow, stolen by the storm winds rising over the city. "I offered you *life*, not this faithless existence you have resigned yourself to. You declined to join me."

"Death does not give a life, it only ever takes one."

A lightning bolt careened down from the sky in front of Thor, half blinding Patrick when it hit. Blinking rapidly, trying to clear his vision, Patrick stared at the charred, split ground in front of the god and the ball lightning that crackled and burned in the air between the two immortals.

Thor reached for the ball lightning, fingers tearing into the electricity. They folded over a carved wooden handle that pushed through the electric sphere with ease. Drawn from the crackling, heated lightning, Mjölnir took shape in Thor's fist, the ancient weapon filled with enough magic it could level mountains if he so chose.

Since Chicago wasn't anywhere close to a mountain range, Patrick hoped Thor wouldn't level a skyscraper or two. That was property damage he really didn't want to have to explain to the SOA.

Mjölnir burned with the power of a god, but Hel wasn't fazed by it in the least. The goddess spread her arms wide, hellfire dripping from her fingers. "You chose the wrong side, Thor. The past can't keep us alive."

Thor strode forward. "The past is what makes us. I will take what is owed to me for the damage to my altar out of your skin."

"Oh, but yours isn't the only altar I've come to ruin."

She thrust both hands toward them, hellfire exploding away from her fingers. Patrick grabbed Wade's wrist and hauled them out of the way, hoping to all the gods his shields would hold. The hellfire crashed into the bar, doubling the conflagration already eating its way through Thor's altar.

"Enough of your desecration," Thor snarled, raising Mjölnir high over his head.

Hel ripped open the veil between them, gray fog spiraling out from the tear between worlds. "Odin will never see Valhalla again. My Hel is all he will ever know."

Thor hesitated in the face of that threat, the lightning cutting through the clouds above never striking earth. "What have you done?"

"Wouldn't you like to know?"

As taunts went, it was enough to make Thor race after her through the veil, the tear sealing up behind him. It left Patrick and Wade to face off against the Dominion Sect while hellfire burned the bar to the ground.

"I hear sirens," Wade said.

Patrick couldn't hear a thing over the crackling roar of the fire, but Wade's hearing was better than his. While they really needed the Chicago Fire Department on the scene, he didn't want to risk the lives of first responders. Zachary, Patrick knew from previous experience, was all about collateral damage. Patrick didn't need the Dominion Sect to take potshots at fire fighters.

Patrick conjured up another mageglobe and filled it with a shock wave spell. He was hampered from casting higher-level offensive spells by the scars in his soul and his inability to tap a ley line, which would've come in real handy right about then. The shock wave spell was pushing his abilities, but he had no choice but to try.

"Next time I decide to travel without Jono, tell me it's a dumb fucking idea," Patrick said.

"It was a dumb fucking idea," Wade agreed.

Patrick released the shock wave spell, grabbed Wade by the wrist, and started running. The spell tore down what was left of the low, half-melted iron fence, knocking over parked cars and the SUVs in the street—thankfully not theirs, which was parked farther away. The first layer of Zachary's shield was stripped away by the spell, the second one bending in places from the blow.

Zachary's affinity leaned toward blood magic, not offensive combat spells. He could cast them, but Patrick's were better. It bought them time—mere seconds—but that was enough for Patrick to put distance between them in order to play bait.

"That's the wrong way!" Wade shouted over the rising wind.

The first drops of cold rain splattered to the earth as Patrick conjured up another mageglobe and threw raw magic at the fence surrounding the Rosehill Cemetery. The blast ripped a hole in the fence, and Patrick dragged Wade through it with him right as what passed for a magical grenade crashed into his shields.

Patrick grunted, feeling a layer in his shield crack, but they stayed up. He channeled more magic through his soul, strengthening his shields. He opted for a look-away ward over a brighter mageglobe, magic spinning away from his fingers in their wake before winking out.

"Get us through the trees."

Wade's eyesight was better than his. In the dark cemetery, Patrick needed to rely on Wade over his magic. Any light would give them away, and they needed to gain whatever bit of upper hand they could in the next few seconds.

Wade twisted free of Patrick's grip and tugged on the sleeve of his jacket. "Follow me."

Patrick let Wade guide him through the sparse trees that gave shade to mourners in the warmer months. In winter, their branches were bare, providing no cover from the rain beginning to pour down. Patrick shrank his shields, swearing when that didn't help clear his vision as rain sluiced down the invisible barrier.

Wade dragged them behind a larger tree, and Patrick pinned him to the trunk, making sure they were both hidden. When Wade opened his mouth, Patrick covered it, shaking his head. Wade got the hint and snapped his mouth shut. Patrick let him go, easing his head around the trunk just enough to try to get eyes on the enemy if they were approaching.

Sheet lightning made the clouds above pulse with an inner light. The thunder that followed was loud and angry, coming directly overhead. Patrick squinted through the rain, trying to see through his shields at the shadows moving in the darkness. His night vision was shitty after being around hellfire.

It was still good enough to see the spell casting going on and to recognize what it meant.

"*Shit!*" Patrick ground out.

Patrick grabbed Wade by the shoulders and yanked him to the wet ground, pouring enough magic into his shields that they flickered pale blue in the dark.

The ensuing magical blast cut through the trees around them, incinerating them into ash. While he doubted the fire spell would hurt Wade, Patrick didn't want to put him in the line of fire unnecessarily.

"Should I shift?" Wade asked, his wide eyes reflecting the lightning above. This close and Patrick could see the reptilian slit of his pupils.

"No. Just stay behind me."

Patrick rolled to his feet, coming up with a handful of mage-globes. He instinctively reached through the soulbond for Jono—and felt like someone tried to yank his spine out of his body. He grimaced, trying to breathe through the pain of a stretched-too-thin soulbond.

"You're outmatched," Zachary yelled, his own mageglobes circling his body in tight orbits.

"Go fuck yourself," Patrick yelled.

He flung three mageglobes at the ones Zachary aimed at him, their magic meeting over a line of graves and exploding like fireworks that could kill. Beyond them, back on the street, the sickly hellfire light at the bar was joined by the flashing lights of the first fire truck to make it to the scene.

"Uh, we might have a problem?" Wade said.

"What?"

Wade pointed in a different direction. "Werecreatures."

That was a problem Patrick hadn't seen coming and one he could most definitely do without.

He threw his next mageglobe at the ground, his magic burrowing deep enough to make it through the shields the sorcerer had erected around his fellow mercenaries. Patrick wasn't sure they hadn't shielded into the ground, but he found out soon enough when his mageglobe exploded within the magic dome that suddenly disappeared in a flash of light. The scream the man let out was ear-piercing and full of agony as his legs were blown off from the knees on down.

Zachary took a step backward, away from the werewolf that landed between them out of the darkness. He knelt so he could drag his hand through the blood pouring out of the other man's legs, writing out glowing sigils, and smiled.

"All of you *get clear*!" Patrick yelled, pitching his voice to battlefield loudness to be heard over the storm and hoping to all the gods the werecreatures fucking listened.

He raised his dagger instead of conjuring up another mageglobe, bracing his other hand behind the hilt. The blood spell that cut through the air was one he'd seen only during his time in the Mage Corps. It could pull a person's blood out of their veins and drain them dry faster than a vampire. It killed in less than a minute, and Patrick couldn't let it hit anyone but him.

So he didn't move.

Patrick pushed his dagger through his shields, white heavenly fire exploding out of the matte-black blade when the blood spell hit. The prayers and magic that powered the gods-given dagger tore Zachary's spell apart—and something else tugged at Patrick's soul.

It left him reeling, sent him staggering forward a step as his magic fluctuated in his soul. He nearly got sick when he realized what it meant.

Who it meant.

Because it wasn't the soulbond he had with Jono, but something else. Some connection he'd thought had died in that basement in Salem all those years ago.

Patrick pressed a shaking hand to his chest, fabric scraping over the scars there as what had once tied him to Hannah before Ethan severed it scratched at his soul.

Twins knew each other, whether identical or not, and always would.

No amount of magic or trauma would ever change that.

The strike spell came out of nowhere, slamming into him with a strength that made the scars on his soul feel like they should bleed. Patrick's shields wavered, then were ripped ragged through a blood connection that was always everyone's forgotten back door into any spell.

He should've remembered that.

Patrick re-layered his shields as best he could, fighting the faint pull in his soul that sought to undermine his magic. The aftershocks of the spell made his skin burn, the rain slipping through his damaged shields not enough to cool it.

"Patrick?" Wade yelled, sounding worried.

Wind blew fog over the cemetery headstones as Hannah Greene walked toward them, slipping through the veil in the way only gods could. She looked mostly how she had back in June—starved to a thinness that looked painful. Hannah wasn't dressed for the weather. She was barefoot and wearing a silk nightgown the rain had plastered to her pale skin. Her long red hair was tangled around her body in wet waves.

Even from the distance between them, Hannah's aura was cracked open like a dying star, shining with a burn to it that Patrick only ever saw in gods. Its power was muted though, twisted through with mortal ties that held in place. Patrick's lungs locked up, panic making his heart beat so fast he could barely hear anything over the rushing sound of blood in his ears.

Because if Hannah was here, Ethan couldn't be far behind.

"*Shall I dig your grave?*" Hannah asked, giving voice to Ethan's wants. "*There are plenty here to put you in.*"

The cadence to her voice matched Marek's when the Norns spoke through him, or Jono when Fenrir took control. It was the voice of a trapped goddess having shredded his sister's throat over the years.

Patrick opened his mouth but couldn't find any words, his thoughts tangled up in white noise in his head.

He froze, when he couldn't afford to.

Wade, however, didn't.

A large red clawed foot slammed to the ground in front of Patrick as a wing swept down, blocking out everything. A roar that shook the ground shook Patrick out of his stupor as dragon fire burned through the rain and blood magic Zachary was casting.

"No!" Zachary yelled over the noise.

Scared yips and howls from the werecreatures who had shown up were joined by the surprised shouts of first responders beyond the cemetery fence. It was enough to force Patrick's fractured focus into something whole.

"I said don't shift!" Patrick called out in a hoarse voice.

The red wing moved and a wedge head with black horns snaked downward on a long neck. The golden eye with its reptilian pupil blinked at him before snorting out a disdainful puff of smoke and fire that charred the brown grass in front of Patrick's feet.

The fog started to dissipate beyond where Wade was crouched over Patrick. He tightened his shields and stepped around the dragon leg in his way, shoving his hand against Wade's scaly head to get eyes on the enemy.

The cemetery was empty where they had been.

The absence of Hannah and Zachary left Patrick feeling sick to his stomach rather than relieved. His gaze swept the cemetery, seeing a multitude of wolf eyes reflecting back at him, none of which were the color of a god pack.

"All of you need to get out of here. I'll make sure the police know none of you were present," Patrick said, not bothering to raise his voice. The werecreatures could hear him just fine.

The werecreatures slinked off into the darkness as silently as they'd arrived. Patrick would figure out later what territory he and Wade had ended up in and apologize for ruining the pack's Friday night.

"Wade, shift back to human."

Patrick cast a look-away ward with cold fingers, aiming it toward the damaged cemetery fence. He couldn't outright hide Wade since magic didn't work on the teenager, but he could keep the first responders distracted while he dealt with the remaining Dominion Sect mercenaries.

He approached where the mercenaries were sprawled on the cold, wet ground. Two of them were burned beyond recognition, their magic not enough to withstand a fire dragon's rage. The third one whose legs Patrick had partially blown off had already bled out, the lingering stain of Zachary's blood magic seeping into the body.

Patrick knelt beside the dead and stared at the bodies for a long moment. Then he pulled out his cell phone with a shaking hand and called Jono. When the line picked up, he didn't even wait for a hello.

"I need you in Chicago."

"Usually it's your other half who makes my life difficult," Chief of the NYPD's Preternatural Crimes Bureau Giovanni Casale said.

Jono eyed the folder Casale tossed onto the table in Interrogation Room One. "He's a bit busy."

Neither Jono nor Patrick had confirmed their relationship with Casale. They weren't obligated to, but Jono knew their privacy was bound to be challenged sooner rather than later now that he was actively laying claim to New York City. He wasn't surprised Casale had picked up on their relationship though. The man was a cop, after all.

Casale took a seat with a grunt. "I hear we have hunters in the city."

"What makes you say that?"

Casale flipped open the folder, revealing a crime scene photo of a body that looked like it had been crunched into the sidewalk. Jono didn't flinch away from the bloody, destroyed mess the man had been reduced to.

"I don't like finding out about an active group of the Krossed

Knights hunting in my city after the fact. A heads-up would've been nice," Casale said, staring at him.

"I don't know what you're on about. Didn't think hunters rated your direct interference," Jono replied.

Casale raised a thick black eyebrow. "It's not a serial killer like last summer, but these assholes tend to start wars between preternatural communities. Happened during my rookie year as a cop. It was a fucked-up time, and the homicide count made it into triple digits. Those deaths were the only ones we knew of, but there were plenty more I'm sure we never learned about. I don't want a repeat of history."

Jono didn't blink. "What makes you think that will happen?"

"I have one dead hunter and more blood that was at the scene than came from a single body." Casale leaned back in his seat and eyed Jono. "Word on the street is you're looking to challenge Estelle and Youssef for the New York City god pack."

"I don't hold with gossip."

"I think it's less gossip and more truth these days. Those two have been trouble since they took over the pack some years back. I never could figure out why they let you stay."

Jono shrugged. "I had a good negotiator."

"One with good eyes," Casale drawled.

They both knew he was talking about Marek, but Jono didn't say his friend's name. "I'm not familiar with the Krossed Knights. They aren't in England."

"I'd be surprised if you were. They come out of our south. You still have hunters where you come from though. Messy business no matter the country."

"They aren't sanctioned."

Casale smiled grimly. "They never are."

Jono scratched at the shadow of a beard he hadn't yet had time to shave off. "What do you want?"

"This hunter died in vampire territory. They left the body." Casale pulled a couple of photographs from the bottom of the stack and spread them out. The CCTV screenshot had Jono stiffening in his seat. "I'd ask where you were Wednesday night, but it's a moot point."

The slightly blurry image of Jono standing with Leon and Austin in the playground, surrounded by Jamere's vampires, made Jono's breath catch in the back of his throat.

Bloody hell.

Maybe he should've brought Sage after all, filing deadline or not.

"Now," Casale said grimly. "The Brooklyn Night Court will say they were guarding their borders. That's been their excuse for decades. The law says they have every right to do so, whether undead or not, within reason, especially in the face of hunters. What's your excuse?"

"Thought this was supposed to be a friendly chat?" Jono said slowly, staring at the photographs.

"Murder isn't friendly."

Jono looked away from the photographs to meet Casale's gaze. "Did you ask me to come down so you could arrest me?"

Casale shook his head. "The hunter died in vampire territory. They'll claim self-defense all the way to the courts. I have detectives working the case who will talk to Jamere and take down whatever story he chooses to give us. You're the outlier in this mess. I want to know what you were doing there and who is with you in the picture."

Jono straightened up, glad he had an easy answer to that question. "No."

"*No* isn't going to cut it."

"No, I'm not telling you who was with me. They're a pack under my protection, and they're granted their right to privacy under federal law."

Casale frowned, tapping a finger against the table in a slow metronome. "So the rumors *are* true about you forming a second god pack."

Jono stood, and Casale didn't tell him to sit back down. "I think we're done."

"I think we're just getting started." Casale stared at him. "Or you are."

"And if I am?"

"A civil war is never bloodless or victimless."

Jono smiled bitterly, thinking of Wade and the few werecreatures they'd saved from Tremaine last August. Of the packs who kept coming to Tempest looking for a drink and someone to save them.

"Certain people think I'm a problem." Jono nodded at the pictures. "Jamere didn't."

"Vampires aren't friendly with your kind."

"They're friendly enough with me."

"Since when?"

"Am I under arrest?"

Casale shook his head slowly. "No."

"Then we're done here. Call Sage next time you want to have a little chat with me."

Casale stood, the lines around his mouth deepening as he frowned. "New York City doesn't need a civil war."

Jono headed for the door. "Sometimes war is inevitable, mate."

He half thought he'd be arrested once he left the room, but Jono only got the odd look or two from some of the detectives seated at their desks in the bull room. One of them got to her feet, waving at him to follow her toward the exit.

"I'll escort you out," Detective Specialist Allison Ramirez said.

"Cheers," Jono said.

Jono didn't feel comfortable until he was outside the heavily warded building that housed the PCB in Lower Manhattan, breathing in cold winter air. He pulled his mobile out of his pocket and was about to ring his ride when a familiar Escalade pulled to the curb. The window rolled down halfway, and Emma stared at him from behind the steering wheel. The accusation in her gaze hadn't faded since Ginnungagap.

"Get in," she said flatly.

Jono bit back a wince. "Where did Leon go?"

"We swapped babysitting duties." Someone honked in the street behind her and she scowled. "Get *in*, Jono."

Jono climbed into the SUV and buckled up. Emma took her foot off the brake and stepped on the gas. She didn't look at him.

"Leon and I were supposed to go to Queens," Jono said.

"We swapped that duty, too."

Jono stretched out his legs and stared straight ahead. He knew why Emma was angry, that the row he could feel building was inevitable, but he figured the place to start was "I'm sorry."

Emma gripped the steering wheel so tight her knuckles went white. She clenched her jaw, muscles standing out in her slim throat. "I hate how your secrets keep getting doled out when we least expect it."

"They aren't just my secrets, Em."

"This one is." Emma flicked the turn signal before the next light, waiting to turn left. "Sage said she found out in December when you were all past the veil in Tír na nÓg and you told her not to tell us."

"You can't be mad at her for keeping my secret."

"You've had an animal-god patron guiding you since you were infected. Do you know how fucking rare that is? More than half the packs in the United States have stopped believing in them. The power they bring is just myths these days."

"Did it look like I was carrying a myth?" Jono asked quietly.

Emma snorted. "I'm assuming Patrick knows?"

"He's known since last summer." Jono leaned his head back against the headrest and grimaced. "Ethan knows because he saw what was in my soul in preparation for his sacrifice. Lucien and Carmen found out when I left to get Patrick after he'd stayed at the Crimson Diamond to save Kennedy in August. Gerard and Keith know because they were there with us in the Spring Queen's Court when I reinforced our bargain with the fae. Now you and Leon know."

"Ethan knows?" Emma asked after half a minute of silence.

Jono closed his eyes and tried not to think about that time spent in Ethan's hands. "He knew, somehow, about Fenrir, or that the gods were going to give me to Patrick. Either way, it made me a target at the time."

Emma didn't speak again until they were driving north on the FDR, heading for Queensboro Bridge. "It kind of feels like you don't want us to know anything."

"I…" Jono's voice trailed off, and he opened his eyes, staring blankly at the red taillights stretched out before them. Evening rush-hour traffic was fucking terrible no matter the city. "Fenrir didn't speak to me until after I got infected with the werevirus. I was making a right mess of things in London at the time. Then I woke up one day with his voice in my head and his claws in my soul and he wouldn't leave."

"Did Marek know? When he went to London to bring you here?"

Jono turned his head, staring at Emma's profile limned in the faint shine of headlights and taillights. "No. He never mentioned Fenrir when he made his offer."

"Maybe he knew and just never said anything. Like you."

"Em." Jono rubbed tiredly at his face. "Is this going to be a problem?"

"You lying?"

"Me obeying the gods because I had no bloody choice."

Some of the anger seemed to dissipate in her scent, her slim shoulders slumping. "I just don't know why you couldn't trust us."

Jono reached over and slid his hand beneath the thick fall of her hair to curl his fingers around the back of her neck. "I've trusted you since the day you picked me up from the airport when I first arrived. That's never going to change. This wasn't about trusting you, but about keeping you and the rest of your pack safe."

He took a breath, catching when the rest of her anger drained away into frustrated sadness, the sting of it making Jono swallow. Emma took her eyes off the road for a split second to glance his way, huffing out a sigh.

"We told you for years we'd follow you."

Jono tapped his fingers against her spine before pulling back. "I know, but Patrick wasn't here yet."

"Have you told him about what's happened this week?"

"No."

Emma rolled her eyes and focused on the road. "You're in for a world of hurt with that one when you finally do. My couch is ready for your dumb ass."

"Ta," Jono said wryly.

The tension that had been between them since leaving Ginnun-gagap finally disappeared on the drive to Queens. Jono was grateful for the respite. He knew he'd been a shit friend over that decision, but he also knew he'd been in the right. He hadn't been in any position to challenge anyone before Patrick showed up in New York City last year.

Their lives had become a right mess since then, but Jono didn't regret the path they were walking. He had a home and a pack now, just like Marek had promised. Jono wasn't giving those up without a fight.

Emma switched on the satellite radio and picked a music station at random. They didn't talk much on the drive into Queens, but Jono didn't mind. Traffic meant their progress was slow, but Emma eventually pulled off onto NY-25A, following it to Jackson Heights. The Queens neighborhood was blocks of resi-dential buildings and a destination for middle-class families looking to escape the high costs of Manhattan.

Several packs called Jackson Heights home, two of whom had asked Jono for protection. After the mess the other night, Jono had pushed back this meeting until he'd fully healed from being poisoned. Victoria's potions had done their job, and while Jono felt better, he wasn't keen on a repeat of the other night.

Which was why he and Emma weren't immediately heading for the packs, but to negotiate borders with Rajesh, the master vampire of the Queens Night Court.

Lucien owned the Manhattan Night Court and held brutal influence over the rest of the Night Courts in the five boroughs. He wasn't one to be crossed without consequences. Jono knew the master vampires outside Manhattan worked cautiously with Lucien when they had to, and tried to steer clear of him when they didn't.

An alliance with Lucien wasn't a guarantee of compliance from the other Night Courts though, but Jono would be damned if he didn't leverage Lucien's reputation to get what he wanted. Namely, some bloody fucking reprieve for the packs under his protection when it came to borders brushing up against vampire-held territory and interference from Estelle and Youssef's god pack.

"Huh," Emma said, breaking through his thoughts.

Jono blinked, recognizing that furious tone in her voice. "What is it?"

"Pretty sure we have a tail. That black Honda Civic has been following us since we got on the FDR."

Jono looked at the rearview mirror and the side mirror, picking out the car in question—two vehicles back, in the next lane over. He squinted, vision sharpening as he tried to make out who the driver was.

"You think it's a hunter?" Emma asked.

"No," Jono said slowly, catching the faintest gleam of amber in the driver's eyes. "God pack."

"They could have hunters in the back seat or following us in another car."

Jono knew that was a possibility they couldn't ignore. "Let's get to our destination."

Jackson Heights was a sea of red-bricked apartment buildings and the occasional storefront. Most of it could have doubled for suburbia in a midsized town if one squinted. People lived out here to escape Manhattan rents and to still keep the cultural experience of a big city. There was a specific block of apartment buildings that Jono knew belonged to the Queens Night Court and which housed a good portion of their willing human servants.

It was also, while not neutral territory, a potential kill box Jono was willing to risk to make a point.

Emma sped up, taking the next corner sharply on a yellow light. The car following them ran the red, and Jono kept an eye on it in the mirrors. Then a faint blur on a passing rooftop caught Jono's attention, and he angled his head to peer upward.

"Got company," he said.

Emma scowled. "Hold on. Two more blocks."

She drove the Escalade like it was one of her many sports cars —fast, professionally, and with only half a thought to speed laws. Jono undid his seat belt and kept the fingers of his other hand resting against the door handle. Emma turned off the street into the entrance of the car park situated in the center of the block between apartment buildings, getting out of sight of the general public.

Three cars followed after them, either not knowing or not caring about where they were. The second Emma braked to a halt, Jono was out of the vehicle, facing the car coming at them head-on. The driver didn't brake to a stop so much as was forced to a stop by the vampire who landed on the bonnet. The front of the car crumpled from the landing, his weight heavy enough that it caused the rear wheels to momentarily lift up before crashing back down. Brakes screeched as the other two other cars came to a stop, their passengers getting out.

Jono glanced up, eyes barely able to track movement against the clouds. Shadows blurred down from the rooftops, landing on the cement hard enough to crack it. The circle of vampires that surrounded them in the car park had Emma throwing herself out of the SUV, coming to stand by Jono's side.

Rajesh straightened up on the car he'd landed on, the dastaar of the Sikh religion he wore a deep, dark red. Then he moved, and the god pack werecreature behind the wheel of the car was dragged screaming through the windshield, shattered glass sticking out of her skin where it had broken off.

"Hands off!" Nicholas Kavanaugh snarled as he got out of the back seat of the damaged car.

Rajesh held the woman up by her throat, sharp fingernails cutting into skin and veins with preternatural force behind them before she could strike back or even shift. Blood poured over his fingers and down his wrist, soaking into the fabric of the jacket he wore. He easily dodged her weak attempts to fight back.

"You're trespassing," Rajesh hissed right before he tore out the woman's throat and then slammed her face-first down into the jagged metal of the damaged boot.

Nicholas snarled loudly, the bones in his face shifting a little, but he didn't move.

Rajesh let the woman go and jumped off the car; she never moved again. The vampire eyed Nicholas with disdain before turning to face Jono. He licked the blood off his hands with slow swipes of his tongue as he paced forward.

"I prefer human blood, but I'm never one to turn down werecreatures when they breach my territory," Rajesh said.

"Would've given you a ring, but I didn't have your number," Jono said.

"This is not your territory."

"Two of the packs under my protection reside in Queens. I've come to ensure they're protected from you"—Jono nodded in Nicholas' direction—"and from them."

"Those packs have been exiled and need to leave New York. The god pack alphas ordered it," Nicholas said.

Rajesh bared his fangs in a hard smile as he stared at Jono. "Did you?"

"My packs aren't leaving. I'm here to talk borders," Jono said.

Nicholas stepped forward. "That fucker isn't in charge."

Rajesh held up his bloody hand to Nicholas, but he never took his eyes off Jono. "Wasn't talking to you. One more word and I'll take your tongue in payment."

It was telling that Nicholas shut up. He might be the dire of Estelle and Youssef's god pack, but whatever treaties they'd managed to secure with the vampires when Tremaine was in charge had been ripped to shreds when Lucien took over.

Jono stood his ground. "Heard from Lucien, have you?"

Rajesh lowered his hand, flicking blood off his fingers onto the cement. "That one acts as the mouth to our mother. Disobedience earns us no favors."

Clever teeth, Fenrir growled in his mind.

Jono could admit the lie Lucien was telling as truth formed a sound enough story. Jono was mindful of Patrick's stories, of his guilt over the dead and how the world hadn't yet learned of Ashanti's death. He was aware of how her children still prayed to a goddess who would never hear their words again.

"Then I suppose we're going to have ourselves a chat. I have something to attend to first."

Jono moved past Rajesh and stalked toward Nicholas, not fazed by the god pack werecreatures who formed a protective half circle around the other man. Jono stopped in front of them, staring at Nicholas over their shoulders.

"You've been sniffing around the packs who are my responsibility," Jono said.

"They've been ordered to leave," Nicholas said.

"They came to *me*, asking for protection yours never gave them. My law rules them, not any of yours." Jono's fingers twitched, the shift from nails to claws a subtle change that came easier now that he was healed. "Your pack put a contract out on my head with the

Krossed Knights. I'd be flattered, but I don't hold with consorting with demons."

Nicholas' gaze cut away to the vampires who had them surrounded. "Seems you're consorting with them just fine."

"The undead aren't demons. Right bloody bastards, but the hells want nothing to do with them, unlike your masters." Jono nodded at the car with the body buried in its boot. "Take your dead and get out. You come sniffing about my packs and I'll let the Night Courts have their way with you."

"The Night Courts—"

"Have an understanding with me and mine. They aren't the only ones. You tell Estelle and Youssef if they want a fight, then they'll have one. Now get the fuck out."

Jono turned his back on them and walked with a measured stride back to where Emma stood. She kept her attention on the werecreatures behind him, fingers flexing, the claws at the tips curved and sharp.

"What about the car Rajesh crunched?" she asked.

"Not our problem," Jono said.

"It's got evidence on it."

"It will be dealt with," Rajesh replied.

Emma glanced his way, shoulders tight. She smelled angry, which was better than fear or stress. "Surprised the cops aren't here."

Rajesh licked blood off his jagged teeth, watching as Nicholas and the god pack members that had come with him got back in their remaining vehicles and fled the scene. "No one who lives here will call them, and the cops know better than to get in my way when I protect my territory."

Jono wondered if any of the police were on the take. Considering how long Rajesh had laid claim to Queens, the NYPD probably had a whole set of rules when patrolling to not piss off the master vampire.

"Let's—" Jono began but was cut off by his mobile ringing with the set tone that only meant Patrick. He pulled it out of his pocket and answered.

Patrick spoke first. "I need you in Chicago."

Jono stiffened, all his instincts immediately primed at the tone in Patrick's voice—flat and distant, as if he were in shock.

"Pat?" Jono asked.

Jono heard him swallow over the line, the wind on both their sides echoing badly through the speaker. "Where are you?"

Jono glanced at Rajesh, who seemed far too interested in the conversation. "Nowhere secure. When do you need me to be in Chicago?"

Emma already had her mobile out, rapidly texting someone. Jono hoped it was Sage.

"Tomorrow."

"I'll be there," Jono promised. "Are you all right?"

Patrick laughed, the sound ruined and bitter in the worst way. "Sure."

Bollocks. Jono bit his tongue, unwilling to call Patrick out on that lie in the midst of people he didn't trust. "I'm coming to you."

The sound of Patrick taking a deep breath wasn't comforting in the least. "Good. Call me when you're in a secured location. If I don't pick up, it's because I'm working."

Patrick ended the call, and Jono had to remember to loosen his grip on his mobile so he didn't break it. He looked over at Rajesh, wanting nothing more than to have Emma drive him to LaGuardia so he could get on the first flight out to Chicago to be by Patrick's side, but knew he had to finish this first.

"Let's chat."

12

behind when he got into the taxi. He tossed his leather duffel bag beside him in the back seat and didn't look at the driver when he said, "Marriott Downtown."

He hadn't taken off his sunglasses since leaving the private jet Marek had provided him for his early flight west. He wasn't about to risk getting thrown out of the taxi because he was god pack.

Jono checked his mobile again, hoping to see another text from Patrick, but the last five filling his queue were from Wade. Patrick had been working all night on a crime scene, though what exactly happened Jono still didn't know. Jono hadn't gotten home until around midnight, and Patrick hadn't been able to find time for a secured call.

Jono didn't like not knowing what was going on, but at least they were in the same city now. He pressed a hand to his chest as he stared out the window. The distant ache he'd blamed on the knife wound, but which hadn't been cured by Victoria's potions, was finally gone now. Jono figured it was the soulbond, no longer stretched so thin over almost half a country, settling back into place.

After the shit week he'd had, Jono would take the little things.

The drive into downtown Chicago was slower than he would've liked, but it was absolutely sleeting out. Jono could understand the driver's caution, but he really just wanted to get to where the rest of his pack was. That took some time, and when the taxi driver finally pulled in front of the hotel, Jono threw a wad of bills at him, letting the driver keep the change.

The doorman was wielding an umbrella like a professional, and while the bloke was shorter than Jono, he still held the umbrella high enough that Jono didn't bump his head.

"Thanks, mate," Jono said as he was led to the hotel's entrance.

He entered the hotel mostly dry and smelled the usual mix of travelers and bleach. Underneath that were distinct, overlapping pack scents that made him grind his teeth. The hotel seemed to have an overabundance of werecreatures working or visiting, and he chalked that up to Patrick's presence.

Jono pegged at least five of the people in the too-colorful lobby as werecreatures, but the only one who mattered was the tall, slim African American woman who stood from one of the leather sofas. He could see her bright amber eyes clear as day, and Jono reached up to take off his sunglasses, never looking away from her face.

Her stride never wavered as she approached, and she had a calmness around her that reminded him of Sage. She put herself between him and the lifts, which he didn't much care for.

"Get out of my way," Jono said in a low voice.

"Jonothon de Vere, I presume?" she asked slowly, her gaze flicking up and down to take his measure. "I heard you were British, so it must be you."

"Who are you?"

"Monica Woodard. Dire to the Chicago god pack."

Jono stared her down for a couple of seconds before he let his gaze lazily track every other werecreature in the large lobby. "I'm not here for your territory."

"That's what Patrick said, too."

"Then you should've taken it as truth." Jono stepped around her, but Monica moved smoothly to intercept him again. Jono went still, trying to get a grip on his rising temper. The lack of sleep and his worry over Patrick meant he wasn't in the mood for anyone's bullshit. "Get the fuck out of my way."

He had to give Monica credit. She didn't back down, refusing to lower her gaze. "Your pack member is safe."

"I'll be the judge of that."

This time she didn't try to stop him when Jono walked around her, striding toward the lifts. Wade had texted him their room number while he'd been en route. He could feel people's eyes on him, and it made his skin crawl and his temper worse. Jono shoved his anger down, trying to shake it off. He didn't want Wade to think Jono was angry at him.

Jono took the lift up and wasn't at all surprised to find Wade waiting for him literally right outside the doors when they opened on the twelfth floor. Wade blinked at him before darting in for a quick, hard hug, nearly bowling Jono over.

"I'm so glad you're here," Wade mumbled into his chest.

Jono wrapped his free arm around the teenager, hugging him tight and breathing in his scent. "Where's Pat?"

Wade pulled back and stepped out of the way so Jono could exit the lift. "Working still. He's been out all night. The only time he wasn't working was when he came to drop me off back here and told me to wait for you."

Jono jerked his head in the direction of the hallway for Wade to follow him. "You eat yet?"

"I ordered room service earlier."

"Right, then. Let's get my things in your room so we can be off."

"Patrick said not to leave the hotel. He said he'd call us when he was free."

Jono smiled tightly as he waited for Wade to unlock the door with the key card. "Yeah, that's not happening."

"Do you know what happened? Did he tell you?"

"No, and keep your gob shut about it. Too many ears about."

Wade made a face, his nose scrunching up. "Yeah, okay. Who's down there?"

"Met the Chicago god pack's dire." Jono tossed his duffel bag on the half-made bed, assuming it was Patrick's considering the other bed was unmade and filled with empty snack wrappers. "Clean up your mess, Wade. Don't be rude to housekeeping."

Wade grumbled but did as he was told while Jono texted Patrick that he was with Wade. He stared at the screen, hoping for a quick response, but none came. It was barely eight in the morning, and he knew from experience that cases could swallow Patrick for days at a time. Despite whatever had happened last night, Jono didn't want that to happen.

He needed answers, and he had to find some way to break it to Patrick about what was going on in New York.

"Did you rent a car?" Wade asked.

"No. Patrick has one. Figured that should be enough."

Jono's mobile buzzed in his hand, and he quickly unlocked it to check the text. He breathed a quiet sigh of relief to see it was from Patrick.

Meet at Eiketre at 1000.

Beneath it was a link to a web page, and Jono clicked on it. "He wants us to meet him at a bar called Eiketre in two hours."

"That's the place that burned last night."

Jono glanced at him and frowned. "Should you be chatting about that?"

Wade shrugged. "It's on the news."

Jono weighed their options, stared at the two empty room service trays dumped on the dresser, and decided he could sort the news out on his mobile somewhere else that wasn't crawling with werecreatures.

"Let's get you breakfast," Jono said.

Wade perked up, scrambling for his hoodie. Jono didn't know where his jacket had gone. "There's a café nearby we can walk to."

"It's bloody pouring out, mate. We're taking a taxi."

Killing time by feeding Wade seemed like the best course of action. It wouldn't ease Jono's nerves any, not until he had eyes on Patrick, but it would at least keep Wade occupied.

IT HADN'T STOPPED RAINING by the time they reached the bar by the cemetery a couple of hours later, but at least it had let up some. It was more a heavy sprinkle rather than a deluge, but the wind still blew hard and cold, shaking the bare branches of nearby trees. Jono paid the taxi driver in cash before getting out, holding the borrowed hotel umbrella over both himself and Wade.

The melted iron fencing around the front patio of the bar was wrapped in yellow crime scene tape still. Perhaps as a warning to pedestrians until the whole lot could be removed and replaced. The building itself seemed badly scorched, but the damage didn't seem destructive to the point the whole building needed to undergo construction.

"I thought you said it was a hellfire bomb?" Jono asked as they walked toward the bar.

"It was, and then we ran into the cemetery over there," Wade replied.

Jono followed where he pointed, seeing the blown-open fence across the street crisscrossed with yellow Police Line – Do Not Cross tape that moved rapidly in the wind. Considering the weather, he had a feeling it would be torn off before the day was over.

Jono breathed in deep, catching some of Patrick's scent beneath the underlying smell of wet cement and embedded smoke. The soulbond tugged in his chest, and Jono lengthened his stride. They reached the sidewalk in front of the bar right as the damaged door opened up. All the tension seeped out of Jono's body once he got eyes on Patrick.

"Pat," Jono breathed out, handing the umbrella to Wade.

He closed the distance between them, not caring about the rain. Jono framed Patrick's face with both hands, kissing him with a fierceness that had Wade groaning behind them.

"Oh my god, get a room," Wade told them.

Jono pulled back, smoothing his thumbs over the dark circles beneath Patrick's green eyes. "You look knackered."

Patrick shrugged tiredly. "I've been overseeing the processing of the crime scene, and I have a meeting with the SAIC this afternoon. The press finally left here about thirty minutes ago."

"What happened?"

Patrick waved tiredly at the entrance to the bar. "I'll tell you inside. Let's—"

He broke off as the sound of heavy, rumbling engines filled the air. Jono looked down the street in time to see the first of many motorcycles turn the corner and drive toward them. The riders were all women. The motorcycles ranged from Harley Davidsons to Indians to Suzukis, the sound of the engines like thunder in the air. They brought with them an overwhelming ozone scent that had Jono putting himself between his pack and the new arrivals, who parked in a line on the street in front of the bar.

The engines cut off, but none of the women immediately got off their bikes. Then the lead rider took off her helmet, gloved hands wet from the rain. Blonde hair tumbled out, falling down her back. A too-beautiful face was revealed, dominated by eyes the color of the fog that lived in the veil between worlds.

"I see you've finally come crawling home, wolf," the woman said.

Fenrir howled a name through Jono's mind, and he stared at the immortal—the valkyrie—in shock as he repeated it. "Brynhildr."

The valkyrie commander offered Jono a cold smile he couldn't be sure was meant for him or his animal-god patron, or both.

"I want one," Wade said, staring avidly at the motorcycles with a covetous look on his face.

"No," Patrick told him. "You don't even know how to drive a car yet."

"Those are *winged horses*. They can drive themselves."

"You already have wings. You don't need a pegasus in order to fly."

Jono eyed the motorcycles with a hefty dose of wariness. Rather than carrying the scent of oil and metal, the various motorcycles carried the same ozone burn as the valkyries who rode them. Glamour, maybe, or some other kind of magic to hide or change their form.

Brynhildr dismounted from her Harley, leaving her helmet on the seat. The other valkyries followed her lead, none of them bothered by the rain. Jono's gaze skipped from one to the next, taking in their different faces that all had the same strange gray eyes. All of them wore some combination of leather trousers, jacket, and gloves, though the styles were different. Each valkyrie wore a pendant of a carved wooden spear on a leather cord around their throats.

Fenrir howled restlessly in his soul, and Jono couldn't tell whether the god wanted to greet the valkyries or maim them a little. He turned to look at Patrick, raising an eyebrow. "Norse gods this time?"

Patrick grimaced, mouth pressing into a hard white line. "Not just them."

"Hel attempted to burn my altar down as a distraction while the Dominion Sect kidnapped the Allfather. I summoned the valkyries to aid us in his place," a deep voice said from behind them. "Well met, Brynhildr."

"Thor," the valkyrie in charge replied. "I wish it was under better circumstances."

Jono looked at the tall, broad-shouldered god who filled the charred doorway and had to bite back the instinctive growl that didn't come from him. Jono focused on the god's words through Fenrir's annoyance. "Odin was taken?"

Patrick sighed. "Ethan is like a one-trick pony with this stupid shit of his. Let's get out of the rain and behind some wards before we start talking."

Jono ran a hand through his wet hair, shivering a little in the face of the cold wind howling over the street. Thor stepped aside and Jono followed Patrick into the scorched bar. He curled his lip at the smell of smoke and the bitterness of hell that stung his nose. Fenrir didn't seem bothered by it at all, but then, if Hel was the one who had spearheaded the attack, this probably felt like home to the wolf right about now.

When Fenrir first started to speak to him and Jono realized he wasn't going insane, he'd dived headfirst into Norse mythology. Dry and half-forgotten as it was, he knew those stories better than the others he'd started to learn once Patrick came into his life.

"Hel did this?" Jono asked. "The place is still standing. Is she just that weak or have bad aim?"

The bar, for all that it was badly scorched and had lost many tables, chairs, and barstools, was mostly intact. The strange animal antlers on the wall were dirtied by smoke but not charred. If Jono squinted, he could see rune lines carved into the walls, bits of magic crackling through them here and there like electric sparks. Considering which god owned this place, that wasn't surprising.

Magic made Jono's ears pop as someone set a ward around the place. It wasn't Patrick, because Jono knew what his magic smelled like.

"Eir, I would have you see to the ones Hel harmed," Thor said.

A young-looking valkyrie took a seat at the bar, her dark hair twisted around her head in a crown braid. She'd been the one with cat ears on her motorcycle helmet. Her gray eyes were ringed by black eyeliner that ended in a cat-eye flick.

"It's what I'm here for," Eir said. Her gaze flickered Jono's way, and she nodded at him. "I can heal you, too, if you want."

Patrick's head snapped around, pinning Jono with a sharp, worried look. "What the fuck happened?"

Jono grimaced, figuring he was fine after Victoria's potions. He hadn't felt any symptoms for a while now. "Nothing."

"It's not *nothing* if Eir is offering to heal you."

"Later, okay? Let's deal with your problem first."

Patrick gave him a *look* that promised a row later on. Jono inwardly winced but pressed on with the gathering at hand.

A thunderous boom high overhead outside rattled the plyboard nailed over the broken windows. A man who smelled like electricity sauntered into the bar a few seconds later, brushing rainwater off his beaded and fringed leather jacket and smelling of ozone.

"My favorite wing mates," the man said with a pleased smile. "Any of you seen a serpent in the lake during your travels?"

"We came from the west, Hinon. Oniare would not be there," a red-haired valkyrie with a pixie cut said.

"A pity. He makes for a good hunt, Skuld."

The god joined them at the bar, taking the beer Thor offered him with a pleased smile on his face. The valkyries all received glasses of mead, Jono and Patrick declined anything but water, and Wade got an entire bowl full of strangely colored apples. He grabbed an apple in each hand and methodically started to eat them.

"They aren't fae fruit as far as I know," Patrick said with a shrug when Jono shot him a questioning look. "Not that the fae food he ate before did anything to him."

Wade stared at them both and deliberately took a bite of one apple, chewing loudly.

Thor crossed his arms over his broad chest, his gaze sweeping over everyone assembled before him. "Dominion Sect mercenaries attacked the Allfather as he was leaving Au Hall and took him captive."

"Have Muninn and Huginn found him yet?" Brynhildr asked.

Thor shook his head. "He is hidden from their power, and Heimdallr has not seen him."

"What of Frigg?"

"She is ensconced with the authorities today, as she was last night." Thor stared at Patrick. "Your people best treat her well."

"This isn't my field office, but no one will find out what Frigg is so long as she keeps up the deception that she's nothing more than human. You guys have been doing that for centuries. She'll be fine. We have bigger things to worry about with Odin missing and Ethan in town," Patrick replied.

"I thought that was the problem in general?" Hinon asked.

Patrick grimaced, listing a little against the bar as he rubbed at his face. "The nexus under Lake Michigan has been illegally accessed, and weather updates show a reactionary storm brewing. I thought it was you and Thor messing around, but what's forming over the water is ugly. The storm is likely going to hit today, and weather witches in the field office say a white-out blizzard might occur."

"That will make searching for the Allfather difficult, but not impossible," a dark-skinned valkyrie said.

"For you. It's a risk for my pack to be out in weather like that."

"Eir will ride with you," Brynhildr said.

"I wasn't asking for an escort."

"You'll have one anyway."

The coolness of the valkyrie's tone had Jono pressing against Patrick's back as he eyed her over Patrick's head. "We have one of yours with us already."

Brynhildr raised her glass to her lips, swallowing a mouthful of mead. "Loki's get is not one I trust."

Jono opened his mouth to reply, but his voice was stolen by

Fenrir, the god gaining control. *"This is not the story any of us need or want."*

Brynhildr slowly set her glass back down on the bar, staring at them. "Fenrir."

"Odin's least favored valkyrie."

"I have a name. Use it." Fenrir said nothing, and Brynhildr let go of her drink. "I have never trusted you. What's to say this is not an attempt by you to kill the Allfather?"

"Because this is not our Ragnarök, and the future remains uncertain. I chose your side to keep our stories alive. The gods of hell would throw their support behind a lie that will deliver nothing but forgetfulness and death to immortals. That aids none of us."

"Trickery works in such a manner."

"He's no trickster," Patrick said.

"He was birthed by one."

Jono fought for control of his body and mind, shaking his head to clear it once Fenrir receded into his soul once more. "You lot gave me to Patrick as a weapon. We're tied together by the soul-bond. That should be enough of a surety, because I would never betray him."

Brynhildr studied him with those fathomless gray eyes of hers. "You might not. I wouldn't put it past the wolf."

"Such faith you have in my children," a new voice said, the words echoing in the bar.

Thor punched the air in front of him, a sphere of ball lightning exploding around his fist that gave off so much heat Jono's skin burned. The god pulled Mjölnir free, the great stone head of the hammer sucking up the lightning.

"Loki," Thor growled. "Show yourself."

The largest deer skull on the wall shifted on its nails before lifting away. The bone was the only solidly real bit of the ghostly skeleton that jumped to the floor, transparent hooves making no sound upon landing. Patrick moved to put himself between Jono and the construct, dagger held in one hand.

The valkyries moved like lightning to surround the construct. They'd come into the bar empty-handed, but now each of them carried a spear in their hands, the differences in their carvings minimal, the magic in the weapons impossible to miss. The skull head swung from side to side. If it could grin, Jono thought it would.

"You've thrown your lot in with the wrong side once again," Brynhildr ground out.

"*I see nothing wrong about our freedom to choose,*" Loki's disembodied voice said through the construct.

"Where is the Allfather?"

The ghostly deer danced on its feet, and the head was tossed back, the solid antlers nearly hitting a blown-out light fixture. "*What makes you think I know?*"

"Because you're here to gloat. I'd sew your mouth shut if I thought it would do us any good."

"I have needle and thread in my bag. Say the word," Eir said, the spear in her hands not moving a millimeter.

Loki laughed in a way that made Jono's bones hurt. Fenrir sank his claws into Jono's soul but remained quiet. Jono didn't know if it was out of fear or self-preservation.

Thor vaulted over the bar counter, landing with a heavy thud. He straightened up to his full height, tiny lightning bolts arcing over Mjölnir's corners, the short handle swallowed up in his grip. "Too scared to show your face in person, Loki?"

"*I wouldn't have shown up at all if not for my traitorous son.*" The skull swung to face Jono, its eye holes glowing with an eerie yellow light. "*Hel will never welcome you again if you commit to this path. Would you give up your home for a war you can't win?*"

Jono's bones thrummed with a growl only he could hear. Patrick glanced back at him, and Jono half thought Fenrir would take control again, but the god remained silent.

Loki's laughter made Jono's skin crawl. "*If that is your choice, then war it shall be.*"

The ghostly skeleton flickered and disappeared, like a glitch on a computer screen. The bone skull clattered to the floor, every spear point following its fall.

Brynhildr spun her spear to rest the metal-shod butt on the floor. She looked over at Thor, mouth pulled into a taut frown. "What are your orders?"

"Ride," Thor said.

Brynhildr nodded sharply. She angled her spear to press the tip to her throat. Even as the weapon spun in the air, it shrank until it was once again the size of a pendant she hooked to the leather cord around her neck.

"We'll search for the Allfather. What will you do?" she asked.

"There is a fundraiser dinner scheduled at Au Hall tomorrow night. There are meetings I must take today in Odin's place."

"I thought you'd be out searching for him?" Patrick asked.

"Odin would be displeased if we ignored the business of politics in this city."

Patrick snorted. "Keeping the throne warm?"

Thor ignored him and turned to set Mjölnir on the bar counter near Wade, who stared at it with narrowed eyes and took a slow, contemplative bite of his apple.

"Don't steal his hammer," Jono warned.

"I wasn't going to!" Wade protested.

"You were thinking about it."

Hinon slid off his barstool and tugged his jacket straight over his shoulders. "I'll help with your search from on high."

"Thank you, cousin," Thor said.

The immortal headed for the exit, knocking a fist against Thor's shoulder as he went. "This is everyone's war, not just yours. We'll find Odin."

"What are we doing?" Wade asked.

Patrick sheathed his dagger, scowling at Jono. "I drive you guys back to the hotel and Jono here tells me why Eir offered to heal him before I go back to work."

This time, Jono couldn't bite back the wince.

13

"Wʜᴀᴛ ʜᴀᴘᴘᴇɴᴇᴅ?"

Jono sighed. "Can we not do this in the car? I'm fine."

Patrick didn't look away from the road. "But you weren't."

"I'm *fine*."

"Start talking."

"It can wait until you won't run someone off the road."

Patrick's hands tightened on the steering wheel. "Fuck you. I have better control than that. I'd just leave *you* by the side of the road."

"Not in this weather you wouldn't."

"Try me."

Jono scowled out the window at the snow that had started to fall sometime while they were in the bar. They'd arrived in rain and left in snow, and none of them had liked what that meant. If the reactionary storm was going to hit Chicago with a blizzard, there was very little time to get ready for it.

"Everything turned out fine," Jono said. "I'll tell you about what happened when we're behind your wards."

Patrick didn't respond, but his icy silence filled the car for the entire drive back. The one time Jono turned on the radio, Patrick reached over and turned it off. When he settled his hand on Patrick's thigh, it stayed there for two seconds before Patrick moved it to the gearshift. Then Patrick's scent cut out completely as he locked down his shields as tight as they could get. Jono couldn't read him at all, and he huffed out a frustrated breath.

"Ooh, you're in trouble," Wade said sotto voce from the back seat.

Jono resisted the urge to snap at him, knowing that yelling at Wade wasn't the right way to vent his frustration. Explaining himself had to wait until they were at the hotel and behind a silence ward.

It took time to get there, simply because the unexpected snow was snarling traffic. Chicago was used to snow, but usually the city had more of a warning than an hour's notice. If the reactionary storm was bringing a blizzard, no one was prepared for it.

When they finally made it back to the hotel, Patrick silently handed over the car keys to the valet. He wouldn't look at Jono as he strode toward the entrance with Wade on his heels. Jono followed them inside, taking a quick breath to get a read on who might be waiting for them. He smelled werecreatures, but not as many as before. When they made it to the lobby, he didn't see Monica, but the front desk clerk was there, wearing a dastaar.

It reminded him of the long meeting with Rajesh last night, and not in a good way. The master vampire had been reticent to acknowledge the borders Jono wanted to establish for the packs in Queens, but they had at least opened a dialogue. That was more than what Estelle and Youssef had with some of the vampires.

When they reached the lifts, Wade didn't get in with them. "You know what? I'm going to go find something to eat."

"It's snowing and only going to get worse. Stay in the hotel," Patrick told him.

"The hotel doesn't have Target snacks. *Target* has Target

snacks." Wade pointed finger guns at them and rocked back on his heels. "I'm gonna get some."

The door slid shut on his smirking face.

"At least he won't freeze," Jono said.

Patrick didn't respond, angrily stabbing the button for the twelfth floor. They rode up in silence, and Patrick exited first once the doors dinged open on their floor. Jono followed him to the hotel room, watching as he wrote a silence ward on the wall opposite the bathroom with angry motions once they were inside. Static bloomed outward through the wall, blocking out the distant sound of traffic below on the street.

"Start talking," Patrick ordered as he yanked off his jacket and tossed it on the bed closest to the bathroom. "Maybe strip while you're at it so I can see whatever wound you're sporting that made Eir offer to heal you."

"Victoria's potions were enough to fix me," Jono said.

Patrick glared at him. "What the *fuck* did you need potions for?"

Jono crossed his arms over his chest. "Remember when I texted you I was going to Brooklyn earlier this week?"

"For pack border issues, yeah, I remember. Don't tell me they were plants and betrayed you?"

"Austin? No, his pack is on our side. We found ourselves in a bit of a mess by the end of our territory marking."

"Define a *bit of a mess*."

"Ran into some hunters. Krossed Knights, to be precise. We led the arseholes into vampire territory, but one nicked me with his silver knife laced with aconite."

Patrick stared at him, quiet for all of two seconds before he lost his head.

"You're being targeted by the *Krossed Knights* and you didn't *tell* me the second you realized what was going on?" Patrick yelled.

Jono was glad for the silence ward, because the volume of Patrick's voice would've reached the end of the hall. "I didn't want you to worry when you were off doing your job."

"Because telling me after the fact is so much fucking better!" Patrick went still, his eyes narrowing as he glared at Jono. "Wait a minute. When I called Sage the other night, she was pissed off. Was that because she knew what had happened to you?"

"I told her not to tell you."

"You fucking *asshole*," Patrick ground out, taking a step forward, hands balled into fists. "Why the *fuck* would you keep something like this from me?"

"Because you were here in Chicago dealing with a case and gods again, and I didn't want you to worry," Jono snapped.

"You're being targeted for death by the Krossed Knights! What makes you think I wasn't going to worry no matter when you told me?"

"At least this way you could focus."

Patrick let out a harsh laugh. "I focused just fine on the front lines while in the military. Did you think I wouldn't be able to do my job if you told me? I'm a goddamn professional, Jono. I know how to fucking compartmentalize shit."

"I know you are, but I thought it could wait until you got home and I could tell you in person. What could you have done while out here? You couldn't leave."

"It doesn't matter because you never fucking told me before you got here!" Patrick raked a hand through his hair and shook his head. "For fuck's sake, Jono. The Krossed Knights have a higher kill rate than any other hunter group the SOA has in its database. Those fuckers don't mess around, and you didn't think it would be a good idea to tell me?"

"We handled it."

"By throwing them at the vampires?" When Jono hesitated in responding, Patrick zeroed in on that tell like a heat-seeking missile. "What else aren't you telling me?"

"Estelle and Youssef are the ones who hired the hunters. We don't have contractual proof, not enough to bring it to the police, but Estelle was meeting with one of the hunters at their home when I dropped off the body that Carmen brought us."

"Carmen brought you a body," Patrick said slowly, dragging out the words. "Why were you talking to her?"

"Because I told Jamere I wanted to meet with Lucien."

Patrick dragged a hand down his face before turning his back on Jono. He paced to the window before looping back around to where Jono stood by the bed. "You met with Lucien?"

Jono refused to look away, so he was in prime position to watch all the blood drain out of Patrick's face when he said, "I made a bargain with him."

"Lucien doesn't *make* bargains."

"He did with me. With our pack."

Patrick shook his head and turned his back on Jono again, lifting both arms so he could link his hands behind his skull. Jono watched the skin over Patrick's knuckles go white and tried not to feel like he'd made the wrong decisions when he knew he hadn't.

"I can't fucking believe you did that," Patrick ground out. "What did you give up? Lucien doesn't give anything away for free, if he gives anything at all. So what the *fuck* did you offer him in return?"

"That our pack and all the ones under our protection would pray to Ashanti."

Patrick's entire body stiffened, and Jono stepped closer, reaching for him. His fingertips brushed Patrick's shoulder, but the other man jerked away, spinning around on stumbling feet. He knocked Jono's hand aside, high spots of color on his pale cheeks from the anger Jono still couldn't smell through his locked-down shields.

"You *what?*" Patrick asked in a low, furious voice.

"We need to look after our borders. Estelle and Youssef keep breaching ours. None of the packs we protect are close enough to help each other if they go for a full attack, but we're all within Night Court territory. The vampires can get to the packs in trouble in the other boroughs quicker than we can. We have a fae alliance. I thought, why not get one with the vampires?"

"Because it's *Lucien* you fucking got one with! You can't trust him, Jono!"

"He's kept his promise to Ashanti about you," Jono shot back stubbornly. "It shows he'll keep his word."

"It proves he's biding his time to murder my fucking ass, is what it shows."

"I'd never let that happen."

"You'd never see him coming if he had the chance."

Jono crossed his arms over his chest. "Do you think so little of me that I wouldn't do whatever it takes to keep you safe?"

"I don't know what you were thinking when you went to him. Maybe it was the silver and aconite poisoning messing with your head. The poisoning you *didn't tell me about.*"

"I thought I was doing what was best for our god pack," Jono growled. "We don't have the numbers to fight Estelle and Youssef for territory. Alliances are all we have right now, and we needed more than just the fae."

"You didn't have to make one with Lucien."

"Are you mad because I made the bargain or that I didn't ask for your permission? Because I don't need it."

"We're supposed to make these kinds of decisions *together.*"

"You were in Chicago—"

"You could have fucking called me!"

"You have a job, and this is mine!" Jono snarled. "You need to trust me to do it."

"I don't trust *Lucien.*" Patrick stepped back, his face closing off with a blankness Jono hadn't seen since they first met. "And apparently you don't trust me."

"That isn't what this is about—"

"You should've told me the *second* you knew it was the Krossed Knights hunting you," Patrick cut in. "That group doesn't stop hunting until their target is dead. Do you understand that? I'm going to need to notify the police about their presence in New York City and that they're after you."

"Casale already knows."

Patrick stared at him, grinding his teeth so hard Jono could hear it loud and clear. "Were you smart enough to call him and put the PCB on notice you're a target?"

"The PCB found one of the bodies Jamere left on the playground. I got called in because they had screenshots from CCTV of us together."

"Fucking hell, Jono. You realize how that looks? You can't afford to get slapped with a murder charge. Hell, you can't afford *any* kind of charge, not when one could get your green card revoked and you kicked out of the country."

"I told Casale I was talking with the vampires about borders when the hunters attacked. I wasn't arrested."

"That doesn't mean you won't be when we get back."

It was a possibility Sage had made clear could happen, but Jono had faith in her ability to lean into the rights accorded a god pack alpha werewolf fighting for their territory. "That won't happen."

"You don't know that."

"I'm not going to apologize for making sure the packs under our protection are *safe*."

"You putting your life on the line isn't going to do that."

"How is that any different from what you do?" Jono shot back. "You having a sodding badge doesn't make your choices better than mine."

"Me having a badge complicates *everything* if you're arrested. If the government starts investigating you, then it'll start investigating *me*, and I won't be able to hide the soulbond from SOA agents with a goddamn warrant giving them the authority to go digging in our souls."

"We'd find a way around that if it happens, but since it hasn't, it's not an issue right now."

Patrick laughed in his face. "If you think it won't be, then you're wrong."

"What would you have had me do? You weren't *there* to make the decisions with me, so I did. I'm not going to bloody apologize for the choices I made."

"You should've called me," Patrick spat out, stalking past Jono.

"Where are you going?" Jono demanded, snagging Patrick's arm before he got very far.

"Work. You know, that thing I need my *sodding badge* for." The mockery in Patrick's voice didn't match the angry twist of his mouth. When he tried to jerk his arm free, Jono refused to let him go. Patrick smacked his other hand against Jono's chest, glaring up at him. "Let. Go."

Jono didn't listen, hating everything about this argument. "Drop your shields."

"Fuck you. I need to get to work."

Patrick twisted his arm to break the hold and Jono let him, unwilling to hurt him. Jono followed Patrick to the door and pressed his hand against it when Patrick tried to open it.

"You *asshole*," Patrick snarled, twisting around to press both hands against Jono's chest and push. Jono planted his feet and refused to move.

"The gods put you in too much fucking danger every time they waltz into our lives," Jono bit out, staring into Patrick's eyes. "You put enough on the line when they make you fight for them. I know you can compartmentalize shit, but I didn't want you to have to."

"You don't get to make that choice for me."

Those words cut through Jono like the hunter's knife, leaving him cold. He took a breath to steady himself, leaving more of his weight against the door so Patrick couldn't open it when the other man turned around to try again. He still couldn't smell Patrick, but that wasn't the only way Jono could read him.

He reached for the soulbond, the tie deeper than where Fenrir lingered in his soul. The soulbond was a warm connection that

Jono let wash over him, bringing with it a twisted sense of Patrick's emotional state. It wasn't easy to pick any one emotion out, but something still came through. Unlike in August and the fear Jono had sensed when Patrick had gone to the Crimson Diamond, all Jono got this time was a cracked sort of pain he knew he was responsible for.

Jono knew Patrick lied to survive but that he hated being lied to by the people who mattered. More than that, he hated having choices taken from him, because so much had already been stolen from him.

Jono *knew* that. He did.

But he'd still hurt Patrick in the worst way—and he couldn't take those decisions back.

"I'm sorry," Jono said thickly as he pulled his hand away from the door and tried to get Patrick to turn around and look at him. "You're right. I should've rang you about the hunters, but I still would've gone to Lucien."

Patrick shook him off, gripping the door handle with one hand even as he half turned to look Jono in the eye. "Even if I told you not to?"

Jono gave a slow nod, knowing he couldn't lie here. "We need more than what we have for this fight. You know that, and you have to know you're so bloody wrong about me not trusting you, Pat. Because I do. I always will."

"You have a real fucking funny way of showing it."

"I was just trying to keep you safe."

Patrick let out a hollow laugh. "Do you know who I saw in the cemetery last night? *Hannah.* News flash, Jono. I'm never safe."

Patrick yanked open the door, and Jono hooked an arm around his waist to haul him away from it. The door closed on its own, and Jono ignored Patrick's elbow digging into his side and the swearing in order to push him up against the wall and frame his face with both hands.

"Did she hurt you?" Jono asked in a low, furious voice. Anger and fear made Jono nauseous at the thought of Patrick facing his family alone. Because the thought of losing Patrick was a nightmare Jono never wanted to know.

Patrick's words, when he spoke, were like poison, flaying Jono worse than silver and aconite ever could. "I don't know."

The blankness of Patrick's expression was a mask Jono hated to see. It left Jono gutted, and he raised a hand to cup Patrick's face, but his hand was knocked aside.

"Don't," Patrick snapped.

"I'm sorry," Jono said, at a loss for words and not wanting to argue if it meant Patrick would stay. "Just don't go. *Please.*"

Jono leaned down and kissed Patrick with a fierceness that made their teeth clack together. Patrick let him, didn't pull away, hesitating only a second before kissing him back with the same intensity.

"I'm sorry," Jono breathed out like a litany of prayers between kisses. "I'm sorry I wasn't there."

"But you aren't sorry for not calling me."

Jono slid his hands down Patrick's body to grab his arse and pull him into his arms, nipping at his bottom lip. "Already said I was."

"Not about Lucien," Patrick said, kissing him back.

Jono carried him back to the bed that didn't have his duffel bag on it. Housekeeping must have been by, because it'd been made up and the rubbish everywhere taken away. "I'll make it up to you."

He dropped Patrick onto the bed, following him down, chasing after his mouth. Patrick's arms wrapped around his neck to hold him there, trying to breathe with the help of Jono's lungs. The soulbond hummed between them, stronger than it had been when they'd had so much distance between them.

He rolled his hips, dragging his clothed cock against Patrick's. They both groaned, and Patrick tore his mouth free, throwing his head back, giving Jono room to kiss his throat. Patrick's shields had been taken down, and Jono could finally breathe in the strangely bitter scent that meant home to him.

"Didn't pack lube," Patrick groaned when Jono worked a hand under his arse to lift him into the roll of Jono's hips again.

"I did," Jono muttered against his skin. Patrick grabbed his hair and gave it a good yank, the quick sting in Jono's scalp making him smile.

"Then fucking go get it."

Letting Patrick go took effort, and Jono didn't manage to get off the bed for another minute. Patrick's mouth and his scent were too enticing, but he finally made it to his duffel bag. Jono found the lube in thirty seconds, which was about the same amount of time it took Patrick to remove his combat boots, dagger, and pistol. The boots stayed on the floor while the weapons were put on the desk.

Jono stole a kiss on his way to the window to shut the curtains. Not that anyone would be able to see in through the heavily falling snow, but he wasn't willing to put Patrick on display for anyone. He turned back to the bed, stripping out of his shirt and tossing it on the floor. His jeans and underwear followed seconds later. Patrick was down to his underwear, which Jono helped pull off before kneeling down to suck the tip of Patrick's cock into his mouth.

Patrick's hips jerked upward, and Jono pressed him back down onto the bed with one firm hand. He swallowed Patrick down to the root, dragging his tongue over sensitive skin. Fingers tangled in his hair, pulling again as Patrick tried to strain upward, his heels digging into Jono's back.

"Fuck. *Fuck*," Patrick bit out, his entire body tense.

Jono pulled off, turning his head to bite gently at Patrick's inner left thigh before straightening up. He pulled Patrick's legs off his shoulders and crawled over him, hauling Patrick with him farther up the bed. Patrick distracted him by biting one nipple and scraping blunt fingernails over the other.

"Bloody tease," Jono grunted.

"Fuck you. I'm not the one who needs to apologize."

Jono uncapped the lube and poured it over his fingers. He leaned down and kissed Patrick to shut him up. He pushed Patrick's knee to the side, opening him up so Jono could push a finger inside him. He didn't go slow, knowing that's not what Patrick wanted right now. Jono still got undertones of anger in Patrick's scent, and taking his time as an apology wasn't going to be welcomed here.

Jono dragged his teeth over Patrick's jaw and down his throat. He traced scar tissue with his tongue as he pushed a second finger into Patrick. "Didn't mean to keep you out of the loop. I just wanted to keep you safe."

"You think I like finding out you could've died and I wouldn't have been there?" Patrick asked, his voice cracking slightly.

Jono curled his fingers and rubbed them against Patrick's prostate. Patrick arched against him, groaning loudly, so Jono increased the pressure. Fingers hooked over Jono's chin and tugged in a demanding way. He lifted his head, meeting Patrick's gaze without blinking. "Next time, I'll call."

"You better. I'm the one who makes stupid promises, not you, remember?"

"Rather you didn't."

"Shut up. You don't have any room to talk right now."

Jono pulled his fingers out and reached for the lube again, slicking up his cock. When Patrick reached for him, Jono grabbed his hands and pulled them over his head. Jono wrapped his hand around Patrick's wrists, pinning him to the bed. When he met Patrick's eyes, most of the green was gone, swallowed by black pupils. Jono kissed him because he could, because he never wanted to know what it would be like to watch Patrick walk out the door and leave him behind.

Jono dug his knees into the bed as he guided his cock to Patrick's hole, pushing into that tight heat with tiny rolls of his hips. Patrick's legs wrapped around his waist, and he swallowed loudly as Jono sank all the way in, his cock jerking between them. Jono flexed his fingers around Patrick's wrists, keeping him pinned as he pulled out and snapped his hips forward. The hard thrust drew a moan from Patrick that made Jono smile and do it again and again.

Jono didn't go slow, and he wasn't gentle, holding Patrick down with firm hands while he fucked him hard. Every moan, every hitched breath that escaped Patrick's mouth spurred Jono on. He didn't stop until Patrick came with a shout, Jono's name on his lips as he shuddered through his orgasm. Jono dug his knees into the bed as he chased his own release, grinding his cock into Patrick until he came with a harsh groan.

Patrick's eyes were closed, his fingers fisted tight over his head. Jono let his wrists go, the skin there red from pressure, but not bruises. Patrick blinked his eyes open when Jono touched his cheek with gentle fingers.

"We're in this together, and I'm always going to trust you. That's never going to change, love," Jono said quietly before pressing a gentle kiss to the corner of Patrick's mouth.

Patrick turned his head, catching Jono's mouth with his, kissing so sweetly that it felt like an apology when he had nothing to apologize for. Jono gently pulled out of him before getting them underneath the blankets. Jono wrapped his arms around Patrick, holding him close, refusing to let him go.

Patrick stroked calloused fingers over Jono's hips. "Where were you hurt?"

Jono shifted, grabbing Patrick's hand to place it over the spot on his ribs that was healed up now. "Didn't go deep."

"A silver knife laced with aconite doesn't need to go deep."

"Bloke is dead and the demon is gone."

Patrick rested his forehead against Jono's chest. "Demons are never gone."

Before Jono could reply, the hotel room door opened. He twisted a little on the bed to look over his shoulder as Wade walked in, one hand over his eyes and a bottle of air freshener probably stolen from housekeeping in the other.

"You better be decent," Wade warned.

"Decent enough," Patrick muttered.

Wade parted his fingers and cracked open one eye. Then he scowled and started to aggressively spray the air freshener. "That's *my* bed you're in. The other one was yours."

"We can switch."

"No. You can get me my own room."

Patrick lifted his head and squinted at Wade. "Did you steal that?"

Wade stood at the foot of the bed they were in and sprayed the blankets on every word he spoke. "My. Own. Room."

Jono's eyes watered and he sneezed. "I'll pay for it. Get out so we can get dressed."

Wade sprayed the bed one more time before leaving, grumbling under his breath. Patrick sighed and pressed his forehead against Jono's chest again. "I have a meeting I need to get to."

"Okay."

"I'm still mad."

"I know. I'm sorry. I'll make it up to you."

Patrick shifted in his arms and kissed him on the mouth before getting up and heading for the bathroom. "Make it up to me in bed like that and maybe I'll forgive you, or you can sleep on the couch when we get home."

Jono would make it up to him every night if that's what it took.

14

"I THOUGHT THE CHICAGO PCB HAD THE CASE?" PATRICK ASKED, staring through the doorway at the woman seated in the interview room on the fifth floor of the SOA field office.

"They did, but since the Sigfodrs are people of interest to our investigation into Westberg, the SOA took it over," Benjamin said.

Patrick took a sip of his coffee, the Starbucks deep roast a far cry better than the office brew Benjamin had. "I bet that's going to cause some friction."

"It always does."

"Who's interviewing her?"

Benjamin slapped Patrick on the shoulder, giving him a mean smile. "You are. We were waiting for you to get back from your nice little break."

Patrick gave him a sidelong look. "I was up for over twenty-four hours and got into a fight with Dominion Sect mercenaries."

"And that's why you got a break, but now it's time to work."

Patrick shook his head and took another sip of coffee. He mentally steeled himself before entering the interview room. He closed the door behind him but didn't lock it. The room had no windows and no cameras, giving them a false sense of privacy. Patrick didn't make the mistake of calling the goddess by the name people knew her by in myths.

"Good afternoon, Mrs. Sigfodr," Patrick said.

Frigg watched him take a seat with those unearthly eyes of hers. They were red-rimmed from crying, but her makeup looked perfect. Patrick wasn't sure if it was a show for the authorities or if she really had been crying over Odin. Immortal relationships were complicated, and Patrick didn't understand them at all.

"There is nothing good about today," Frigg said.

Patrick sat down at the small table across from her. He placed his coffee in front of him before discreetly writing out a silence ward under the table, letting static wash through the walls. "How are you holding up?"

"How do you think?" Frigg asked tightly. "The Dominion Sect has my husband."

"Yeah, I know. I tried to warn him."

"It is not your fault."

"It's not yours either."

"I was speaking to the kitchen staff when he was taken. If I was there—"

"If you were there, you'd have been taken as well." Patrick shook his head. "You think Ethan wouldn't love to have you both? The more gods he can tie to a sacrificial spell, the better. Ethan's people did a snatch and grab and got the fuck out of Dodge because that was the only way to get to Odin."

"They should not have been able to contain him."

"You guys might be taking tithes from politicians, and Thor might be accepting prayers as payment for his mead, but it's nothing how it was in the past for you. That doesn't give you power. It barely makes you something to remember. Ethan has Macaria and he's got the entire Dominion Sect praying for him."

Frigg folded her hands together on the table. "He is no god."

"He's trying to become one. He's gotten close twice. Now he

has Odin and is after the Morrígan's staff, which might very well be in Chicago. I can't see why they'd be here if it wasn't."

"It is not here."

Patrick wasn't sure if Frigg was speaking the truth, but he hoped she was. Dealing with a missing god needed to take priority right now. "What does it do?"

"Perhaps you should ask the goddess it belongs to."

"Or you could just tell me now. Odin's ravens were the ones who told me the staff was missing last year. You have to know something, even if it's not part of your pantheon. Ethan is only after two things these days. Godheads I understand, but this one particular artifact is different. Why?"

"Do you know what war is like?" Frigg asked.

"I've fought a war. I know exactly what it's like."

"I live with war, and I love him despite the suffering he brings." Frigg blinked, eyes flashing with power that made Patrick flinch. "You are asking the wrong question."

"Then what is the right one?" Patrick wanted to know, trying to keep the frustration out of his voice even as he kept a neutral expression on his face. They still had an audience on the other side of the glass window.

"What kind of god does Ethan want to be?" Frigg unfolded her hands and turned them over one at a time, palms to the ceiling. "He has Macaria's godhead, a child of one hell. He seeks the Morrígan's staff, a war goddess' weapon that raises the dead. An empty hell is a useless kingdom without followers. How many wars has Midgard seen? How many bones are buried in her dirt? How many restless souls do you think are out there? He who claims the dead can wage war on the living. You cannot become a god without first building your own myth, and to do that, you need the proper tools."

Patrick thought nothing could be colder than the blizzard beginning to rage through Chicago, but Frigg's words froze him down to his soul. They echoed Persephone's, the warning she'd given him by the River Styx filtering up through his memories.

"The Dominion Sect has tried for centuries to break the veil between worlds and allow hell to reign on earth," Patrick said slowly. "But that's not what they really want, is it? Another pantheon's hell is just a distraction. They never planned to give Earth up to any god of any hell out there. They never planned to share it. They want to make a brand-new one."

Ethan wanted to.

Frigg smiled with a bitterness that stung like salt in a wound. "Are you ready for your world to become what Asgard is now? What all the gods' homes are, whether in heaven or in hell? A story you hope someone will remember across the veil, in some other Earth that isn't yours?"

Patrick opened his mouth to speak, words a mess on his tongue, when the world upended itself.

Pain ripped through his soul, an echo of the pulse that rippled through the ley lines passing deep beneath Chicago. For a second, everything whited out. Magic that wasn't his burned the frayed edges of that long-forgotten tie to Hannah buried beneath the metaphysical scars he carried on his soul.

It was like the cemetery all over again, only worse.

Then the soulbond that tied him to Jono saturated his soul, blocking the old, worn-out connection like a wall that would never break. Patrick sucked in a shaky breath, blinking black spots from his vision as he stared up at the ceiling around Frigg's head.

Patrick unstuck his tongue from the roof of his mouth. "What…the *fuck* was that?"

"Someone drew too much power through a ley line," Frigg said, her eyes flickering with white fire. "The nexus will need to be guarded."

Patrick got an elbow underneath him and rolled to his side, feeling like his brain was about to leak out of his ears. "*Fuck.* That was backlash hitting the ley lines? Why did I feel it?"

He shouldn't have been able to, and if Frigg had an answer, she kept it to herself. She helped Patrick to his feet with firm hands, and he felt the room spin in his stomach. Then a cool finger touched the center of his forehead, and a rush of energy flowed through him. This time it didn't hurt, more like a balm that soothed the rubbed-raw edges of his soul.

Steadiness came back to him, just in time to be upright and not looking like death warmed over when Benjamin slammed open the door to the interview room. He took one look at Patrick before yelling over his shoulder, "Collins is conscious. What about the others?"

"Others?" Patrick asked.

Benjamin gestured at Patrick to follow him. "Every mage in the building just went down. We're checking on everyone and those who haven't made it in today. You should get checked out."

"I'm fine."

"You seem to be the only one."

Patrick grimaced, thinking about why. "Yeah. How's the SAIC?"

"Don't know."

"Let's go find out."

Benjamin left, already distracted by what was going on beyond the interview room. Patrick looked over at Frigg, who was pulling on the brown fur coat that had been draped over the back of her seat.

"I'll find your husband," Patrick promised.

Frigg nodded, looking for all the world like a queen, despite the drab surroundings. "See that you do."

The goddess left the interview room, perfectly capable of seeing herself out of the building. Patrick swore and pressed the heels of both hands against his eyes, rubbing them until colored spots were all he could see against the back of his eyelids. The sound of his phone going off had him fumbling it out of his pocket to answer it.

"Are you all right?" Jono asked without even a hello.

"Yeah. I'm fine," Patrick said.

"You're such a bloody liar. I *felt* that."

"Something hit the ley lines."

"So why would you feel it?"

Patrick hesitated. Without Jono, he couldn't tap a ley line. The only answer he could think of pointed at Hannah, and nothing good would ever come from that. "I can't talk about it here."

He didn't want to talk about it *ever*, but he knew he had to tell Jono as soon as they were alone.

"Right. Me and Wade are coming to you. We'll find a Starbucks near your building, or anything that is open in this bloody weather, and wait for you to pick us up. If you need *me*"—Jono stressed the word, making it obvious what he meant without outright talking about the soulbond—"I'll be close by."

Patrick bit the inside of his lip, holding back all the words he wanted to say but couldn't while in a building surrounded by SOA agents and workers. "Might have better luck with a Dunkin' Donuts."

"I vote Dunkins," Wade said loud enough that Patrick could hear him through the line.

"You *just* ate," Jono said.

Patrick snorted. "Stay warm. Talk to you soon."

He ended the call and went to find SAIC Andrew Dabrowski.

The Chicago SOA field office only employed about a dozen mages, half of which were assigned to the Rapid Response Division. The fluctuation had ricocheted through every mage, whether they were tapped into a ley line or not. It had caught people unawares, even through their shields.

Which means Ethan doesn't care if we know he's taking that power. Patrick grimaced as he got in the nearest elevator and pushed the button for the twenty-ninth floor. *Frigg is right. We'll need to shield the nexus.*

His thought seemed to be shared by Dabrowski, because the second Patrick stepped into the SAIC's crowded office and the older mage got eyes on him, Patrick became the center of attention.

"Collins," Dabrowski said, cracking open a potions bottle one of the witches on staff must have given him. He looked about as green as the potion he poured into a cut-crystal glass. "We're shielding the nexus."

"Hope you don't expect me to help with that, sir. My shields aren't the greatest, and I can't tap a ley line or nexus," Patrick replied from the doorway.

Dabrowski waved off his words. "I'm sending you and other agents to Lincoln Park. Special Agent Alara Bowen will locate the epicenter of the spell. Near as we can tell, the hit came from a ley line beneath that neighborhood. My guess is it's the same bastards who came after you last night. I want to know what the hell they're doing and why."

Hopefully not sacrificing a god, but Patrick didn't put the odds in their favor. "Understood, sir."

Patrick didn't know what they'd find in Lincoln Park, but he knew it wouldn't be good.

***

Wade stuck his arm between the two front seats, a frosted pink donut with sprinkles resting on a napkin. "Donut?"

Patrick didn't look away from the street he was driving down that had been recently cleared of snow, despite more falling. The snow plows and salt trucks were out in full force right now, and they apparently did not mess around. "Not now, Wade."

The donut disappeared. "Fine, then. More for me."

The sound of rustling paper bags came from the back seat of the SUV. "Don't make a mess."

"Yeah, yeah."

"Are you going to tell me what happened?" Jono asked from the front passenger seat.

Patrick tightened his fingers on the steering wheel, wishing the SUV had sirens. He'd picked up Jono and Wade from the Dunkin' Donuts where they'd found shelter, which put him behind the other agents in getting to the scene. The snowstorm was still terrible, but it wasn't whiteout level yet. Weather witches were fighting to break it up. The reactionary storm had stalled over Lake Michigan, still aiming at Chicago, and Patrick didn't know if that was due to magic or interference from any of the immortals running around Chicago looking for Odin.

"Aksel Sigfodr turned out to be Odin. General Reed's people were wrong about him knowing anything about the staff, but the government was right about him being a criminal."

"How so?"

"You know how I told you he's big in Chicago politics? Odin runs a pay-to-play scheme for politicians, but money isn't enough. Seems he wants souls instead of prayers for his pantheon. The Dean Westberg case I got assigned focuses on rent payment done through pawnshops, but they aren't giving up antiques as collateral, just pieces of their souls. I'm pretty sure Westberg buys them up, then gives them to Odin as tithes," Patrick said.

"Sounds bloody awful."

"Odin didn't think he was in danger. The Dominion Sect did a snatch and grab at the same time they hit Thor's bar." Patrick pushed at the windshield wiper controls, scowling when he realized they were already on their highest setting. "I don't know what they used to contain him, or who."

"What happened at the bar?"

"Zachary was there. He brought Hel along. Thor went after her, and I drew Zachary and his people into the cemetery. Hannah showed up in the cemetery. I felt her," Patrick said slowly as he flexed his fingers against the steering wheel, chewing on his bottom lip. "In my soul."

Jono's hand settled on his thigh, giving a gentle squeeze. Patrick was still pissed at him, but not enough to pull away. "How is that possible?"

"She's my twin. We had a connection when we were younger, but Ethan broke it with soultakers. At least, I thought he had."

"You've never felt her before, have you?"

Patrick shook his head. "Not since we were kids. When that connection cut, I thought she was dead. I kept thinking that until I saw her in Cairo."

"What about today?"

"Backlash hit the ley lines from a surge."

Jono frowned, turning his head to look at him. "You weren't tapped into a ley line through me though. How did you feel it? Because *I* felt it through the soulbond."

"I know. I think it was Hannah." Patrick laughed hollowly. "I don't know what Ethan *did* when he tried to kill us. I didn't think I had a connection, but maybe something stuck."

Some small, selfish part of Patrick hoped it hadn't. The idea that he might have had a connection to his sister all this time while she was at Ethan's mercy made him want to throw up. Because the thought that maybe he could have found her before now was something he didn't want to contemplate. He swallowed against the urge and instead focused on where his magic was leading him.

He hadn't been given an address when leaving the SOA field office, just a general direction to Lincoln Park. Fine-tuning the location was up to Bowen. He'd given her his cell phone number, but she hadn't called to give him an update yet. She was a mage who could follow the ley lines, and despite getting knocked on her ass from the backlash, she was back in the field doing her job.

What Patrick could pick up the closer they got to the urban park that carried the Lincoln namesake were traces of black magic. Whatever spell had been cast, the remnants of it were drifting on storm-driven winds, settling on snow-covered rooftops of people unaware their souls were in danger.

"Trying to track down everyone who might need their soul

stripped of black magic in this weather is going to be a mess," Patrick muttered.

Patrick's phone beeped with a text message. Jono picked it up for him and unlocked it. "It's an address."

"Plug it into the GPS, will you?"

Jono did, and the GPS recalibrated. When the computerized voice spoke the destination, Patrick blinked in surprise. "Wait, what's the address again?"

Jono repeated it and gave him a questioning look. "Do you know it?"

Patrick wanted to press on the gas, but speeding in this weather was a good way to slide into an unmoving object, like a parked car or the nearest powerline post. "That's one of Dean Westberg's personal properties."

"The candidate guy?" Wade asked. "Oh, man. That can't be good."

"Maybe someone got revenge on the bloke for messing around with souls," Jono said.

"We'll find out soon enough."

It took fifteen minutes to get three blocks over. When Patrick turned down the street in question, it was blocked by government cars taking up most of the street. Patrick put the SUV into park and activated the emergency brake. He left the keys in the ignition so the heater would keep running, but still wrote a heat charm onto the roof.

"Stay put," Patrick told them as he pulled on his gloves before opening the car door.

"I have one bag of donuts left," Wade warned.

Patrick rolled his eyes and left Jono to deal with Wade's never-ending hunger. He zipped up his leather jacket and shoved his gloved hands into the pockets to keep them warm as he trekked toward the house that was surrounded by agents. The beanie kept his head warm, and his boots held up in the snow well enough, but he'd rather be indoors and out of the elements.

Recognition was a bitter burn in his soul from the black magic lingering in the air. The house in question was a four-story, red-bricked mansion with a set of stone steps leading up to a porch and the front door. The lights were off, no one was home, but the entire building was leaking residual black magic like a broken dam.

"Anyone send out a shelter in place order yet?" Patrick asked once he made it past the perimeter and met up with Bowden on the sidewalk in front of the house.

"The SAIC is getting it issued," Bowden said, her breath coming out in white puffs. She glanced at him, her dark brown eyes reflecting the light of the vibrant green mageglobe that hovered near her shoulder. "No one answered when we knocked, but we can't get the door open."

"Warded?" Patrick asked.

Bowden shook her head. "Spelled. We can't get through it. I stopped anyone from trying once I got a read on the spell. The casting looks military grade to me. Figured that's more your expertise than mine."

Patrick sighed and took his hands out of his pockets, flexing his fingers. "I'll take a look. Anyone get in contact with Westberg yet?"

"Someone is handling it. This isn't going to look good for him once the media picks up on it."

"Maybe he shouldn't be dealing in magic, then."

There was a lot more that Patrick wanted to say, but he kept his mouth shut. Taking the steps two at a time to the porch, Patrick slowed to a stop in front of the closed door. The sickly magic emanating from it scratched against his shields with a familiar sort of deadliness he remembered from his time in the field with the Hellraisers.

"Trying to ruin everyone's day," he muttered under his breath as he raised both hands and conjured up a mageglobe. "Assholes."

The tripwire spell was a messy one, meant to turn whoever walked through it and anyone in the immediate area into so much meat. Patrick conjured up a tiny mageglobe, cradling it against his palm as he traced the spellwork with a single finger. Pale blue light sank into ugly red-orange, highlighting the lines of the spell and leading him to the origination point near the peephole.

It wasn't unlike the spells he'd cleared in hot zones while in the Mage Corps. Undoing it took some focus, a precise cut of magic, and the willpower to unravel the spell piece by piece. It took a couple of minutes, but Patrick eventually lifted what was left of the tripwire spell off the door and burned it with mage fire. The smell of the magic made him gag. To get away from the smell, he unlocked the door with a key charm that was strong enough to override the home's threshold.

The door swung open and Patrick unholstered his gun, switching off the safety. He heard Bowden and some of the other agents follow him inside as he cleared the front living area.

"Clear," he said loud enough for everyone to hear.

SOA workers worked to clear every room and level of the home. Patrick followed the heaviest traces of black magic to the third floor on unerring feet, coming into what might have been an entertainment room. It had been ruined by whatever high-level casting had happened in the home, one strong enough to send a wave of backlash through the ley lines and any mages within Chicago.

The pentagram burned onto the hardwood floor, the black and red candle wax melted into clumps around carved idols at the five points, and the concentric circles filled with the blood of a baby boar ruined the vibe of the place. The dead animal's throat had been cut, all its blood drained out, before being tossed into a corner.

Scattered in the spaces between the concentric circles were flower petals of a color not found on Earth. They reminded him of the plants blooming in the forests surrounding the Spring Queen's court in Tír na nÓg. Lying in the exact center of the pentagram was a single lock of dark red hair, burned at one end. It made him wonder what else Ethan's acolytes had stolen from the fae when they'd gone after Órlaith.

The residual in the room was black magic mixed with sex, reminding Patrick of how it felt to be around Carmen when she was really leaning into her power of desire. Beneath all that was a shadow charge of electricity that spoke of the presence of a god. Patrick wondered if Ethan had put Odin in the middle of that circle, or someone else, because it didn't feel as if a god had died here.

Patrick tightened his shields as he lowered his gun a little, staring at the sacrificial circle and wondering just what the hell sort of spell had been performed here. Despite the lingering traces of black magic, the space didn't feel like *death*.

It felt more like life.

Patrick didn't step any farther into the room, wanting to preserve the scene until the Evidence Response Team arrived. What he could see wasn't good, and he didn't like what it could mean.

"No one enter this room until the evidence is catalogued," Bowden said loudly. She pointed at another agent. "Stay here and keep watch. I don't want anyone to enter or disturb the scene."

"Is it safe?" the man asked.

"Whatever happened here is over, but you're not getting out of having your soul scoured clean."

Someone pounding up the stairs made both Patrick and Bowden turn around. The panting agent who arrived on the landing waved at them. "Got a body in the wine cellar."

"Westberg sure knows how to throw a party," Patrick said. "Speaking of that guy, do we know where he's at?"

"Not here," Bowden said as they headed downstairs.

"His alibi is going to be interesting."

Patrick was curious what sort of defense the guy would come up with to deny any involvement in whatever sort of ritual had happened in his hearth and home. Considering his platform, it wasn't a good look politically.

They made it to the wine cellar by way of a door next to the pantry on the first floor. Wooden steps led down to a temperature-controlled cellar filled with racks of wine Patrick assumed were expensive. At the bottom of the stairs was a body burned beyond recognition, curled in the fetal position, and smelling like they'd been dead for at least a week.

Patrick made a face at the smell, motioning for everyone to get back upstairs. "We need to preserve the evidence and call in the Medical Examiner."

"I can honestly say Westberg isn't getting *my* vote," Bowden said.

Patrick didn't care about votes, just where the bastard was. "Call it in to the SAIC. I'm going to get an update on his whereabouts. We need to bring him in."

He left the house and the lingering wrongness of the ritual on the third floor. He ducked his head against the wind and snow, jogging back to where Jono and Wade waited in the SUV. The engine had been turned off, but the heat charm he'd cast was doing its job when he opened the door.

"That was quick. Thought it'd be longer," Jono said.

"Someone did a ritual of some sort, and there's a dead burned body," Patrick said as he yanked the door shut.

Jono handed him the car keys, and he shoved them into the ignition. "So they sacrificed someone?"

"Don't know. The body was in the wine cellar, and the ritual happened upstairs." Patrick took a deep breath before starting the engine. "I think they did something to Hannah."

It was the only answer, because he couldn't have felt the backlash in the ley lines unless he was tied to Hannah, who was the focal point of a spell.

Jono grimaced. "Can't put that into the report."

"Nope."

"Any sign of Odin?"

Patrick ran the windshield wipers to clear off some of the snowfall before backing up. "Traces of a god, but I don't know if it was Odin. Could've been Hel or Loki for all we know."

"So are you done here if we're leaving?" Wade asked.

"Weather is getting worse. I'm going to drop you guys off at the hotel while I figure out where the hell Westberg is. We need to bring him in for questioning."

"You sure you don't want us nearby?" Jono asked.

"You're in Chicago. I can tap your soul from a couple miles."

They'd worked on doing that in New York after Christmas. It was easiest when they were fighting together, but if Patrick was on the other side of Manhattan from Jono, he could still tap a ley line through Jono's soul.

"If Westberg is a politician, will he ask for a lawyer?"

"Yeah." Patrick frowned before digging out his cell phone and calling Setsuna. There weren't that many people on the street in this area, not like downtown. "I might have a way around that."

"Truth potion?" Wade asked.

"Those are illegal. And no, he's already under investigation for a federal crime concerning souls. He can ask for a lawyer and keep his mouth shut all he wants, but I can get the dead to talk."

"Isn't *that* illegal?"

"Not if the government is doing it." The ringing in his ear cut off as the phone picked up. Patrick slowed a little as he turned right onto West Webster Avenue. "Line and location are secure."

"As is mine," Setsuna replied.

"Great. I need you to authorize a writ for habeus corpus et animum for me and push it through the courts."

There was a pause before Setsuna sighed heavily. "You do understand how difficult it is to get a judge to sign off on something on a weekday much less on the weekend?"

"You sent me out to help investigate the Westberg case. He's been dealing in souls; I've got a missing god we need to find and a dead body that might give us some answers. Will you authorize it?"

"Which god is missing?"

"Odin."

Setsuna went quiet for a few seconds. Patrick kept his eyes on the snowy road while he waited her out. "You're lucky Anika is back in DC. If Legal can convince a judge to sign off on the writ, she'll be there tomorrow. I'll need your affidavit for it."

"I'll get it to you within the next two hours. There's a reactionary storm heading our way, and traveling isn't easy."

"Judges hate being woken up, especially on weekends. Try to get it to me soon."

Setsuna ended the call as Patrick turned right onto North Clark Street. Wade leaned forward from the back seat, resting his forearms on both their headrests.

"Writ of what now?" he asked.

"We need to produce the body and soul of the dead guy we found in the house. Can't do that without a necromancer," Patrick said, eyes glancing at Wade in the rearview mirror. "Put your seat belt on."

Wade stared at him with wide eyes. "A necromancer?"

"The federal government employs two and a soulbreaker. Put your seat belt on."

Wade rolled his eyes and sprawled back on the seat, grabbing the shoulder strap of the seat belt. "It's not like we're going very fast. It's snowing and you drive like an old—"

Patrick jerked the wheel to the left as hard as he could, the feeling of hell exploding through his magic and in the back of his throat as a blast of hellfire ripped through where they'd been driving. Wade tumbled into the back of his seat with a yell, one arm tangled in the seat belt he hadn't been able to buckle as the SUV slid over snow and ice.

Patrick pumped the brakes, trying to regain control, when something heavy slammed into the SUV on the right side with a heavy crunch. The airbags deployed, keeping Patrick from breaking his nose on the steering wheel as powder floated through the air. The SUV was propelled across the center line and into oncoming traffic by the force of the hit—and kept going. The side wheels hit the curb, and the SUV tilted ominously before crashing onto its side. Patrick's head knocked against the window hard enough to hurt, a twinge running through his neck as the SUV rolled onto its roof.

"Patrick!" Jono yelled.

"Ow!" Wade cried out. "Oh, shit!"

He blinked his eyes open, thighs slamming against the steering wheel and the seat belt holding him in place upside down. Patrick turned his head and watched as the four massive black, blood-stained paws of a hellhound landed on the snowy ground outside his cracked side window. A huge head swung down, fiery red eyes coming into view over a jaw that wouldn't close properly over the fangs in its mouth.

"Fucking *shit*," Patrick ground out right before he threw a bolt of raw magic at the hellhound through the window in an attempt to buy them all time to *run*.

15

JONO SHIFTED CLAWS OUT OF HIS FINGERS AND POPPED THE AIRBAGS. The chalky taste of the deployment powder almost made him sneeze. He broke open the side passenger door with one strong shove of his hand, sending the door spinning into the street. He ripped his seat belt out of the vehicle's framework, slamming one hand against the roof of the car as gravity pulled him downward. He used his other hand to rip apart Patrick's seat belt, freeing the other man.

Fenrir howled through his mind as Jono hauled them both out of the SUV and into the cold snowstorm. The bitter scent of hell filled his nose, making him gag as they staggered to their feet. Patrick's magic pushed past him in a flash of pale blue light, surrounding them in a shield. The reprieve bought them time, but not much.

Jono punched a hand through the rear passenger door and ripped it off, tossing it away, then held his hand out to Wade. "Come on, mate. Let's go."

The teenager grabbed his hand in a bruising grip and scrambled out of the SUV, gold eyes wide in his face, red scales pushing through his skin. "What the fuck was that?"

Garmr, Fenrir snarled, the syllables buried so deep in growls that it took a couple of seconds for Jono to parse the name out and repeat it. "Garmr."

"That's not a name, that's a sound," Wade complained.

"He's Hel's hound," Patrick said, two mageglobes spinning close to his elbow. He clutched his dagger in his right hand, skin reddened over his temple from the hit he'd taken during the crash.

"You all right?" Jono asked.

Patrick didn't even look at him, eyes on the hellhound coming back their way. "Fucking peachy."

The hellhound gape-grinned at them, black saliva dripping off its fangs to hiss and bubble on the snow beneath its mouth. Jono shrugged out of his jacket and grabbed the collar of his shirt, yanking it off.

"Tap a bloody ley line," Jono growled right before he shifted forms.

Agony ripped through his nervous system before the pain receptors were turned off. The pressure of his body ripping itself apart over breaking bones to reset in a new form was a distant sensation. Thick fur sprouted through his skin as muscles reformed over new bones. His sight shifted from purely human to that of a wolf, the sharpness throwing the world into high relief.

When his nerves realigned, snapping on in his brain, Jono shook his wolf head to get rid of some of the blood from the shift and snarled a warning at the hellhounds closing in outside Patrick's shield. The pull of the soulbond steadied before breaking open in a familiar way. The rush of magic was easier to ignore these days, the feel of it like fire in his chest.

"We need to lead them deeper into the park," Patrick said. "We're too close to civilians here."

The snow coming down was enough of a deterrent to keep people inside, but it hindered a fast escape from the area. Cars had already skidded badly in the street to dodge theirs when it had crashed. Jono growled and stepped forward, putting himself in front of the other two.

"What do we do?" Wade asked.

"We run. You don't shift."

"But—"

"*No*, Wade. It's too public here, and it's the middle of the day. You can't risk it."

Wade didn't argue, but Jono could smell his frustration. Jono never took his eyes off the hellhound that came to a stop outside the barrier of Patrick's shield. Black lips pulled away from gray gums, revealing tarnished fangs.

"Be ready to run," Patrick said.

Jono felt magic surge through his soul, spiraling down the soulbond into Patrick. A mageglobe streaked through the shield and slammed into Garmr again, sending the hellhound skidding backward, far enough to give them room to run.

Patrick took point and Jono took up the rear, keeping Wade between them. They left the wreck behind them for the snow-covered depths of Lincoln Park. Patrick's magic cleared them a way through the circle of hellhounds, but that wouldn't be enough to stop them.

My sister's favored companion will not be evaded so easily, Fenrir said.

Then I'll tear out his throat.

Garmr is not so easily killed.

Jono could feel the god seeping into his consciousness, clawing for control. He growled a warning, snapping in the direction of a hellhound that threw itself at Patrick's shield as they ran. *No. Let me have this fight.*

Fenrir retreated in his mind, but not far, and Jono knew it was only a reprieve for however long the god granted him.

Lincoln Park was a sea of leafless trees and snowy ground. Patrick set off another mageglobe with a blast of magic that sent the hellhounds flying away from them. It gave them enough time to get over the first stretch of land before hitting asphalt again.

The street running through the park was empty. Up ahead were structures and a sign indicating the location of a Nature Boardwalk. No one was around, but continuing onward felt like a bottleneck.

"Is that a zoo?" Wade asked. "What if they eat the animals for snacks?"

"They won't do that until after they eat us," Patrick replied.

"I'm not gonna be dinner. What do we do?"

"You die," a new voice said.

Patrick spun on his feet, raising his dagger in the direction of the newest threat. "Hades."

Jono half turned, keeping himself between the other two and the god walking toward them. Hellhounds moved around his body in sinuous motion, the black animals with their fiery red eyes never looking away from their prey.

The Greek god of the Underworld wore a suit beneath a knee-length wool coat dusted with snow. His dark hair was stylishly trimmed, and his dark eyes stood out like holes in his corpse-pale face. Jono only vaguely recalled the god from his time as Ethan's hostage on the sacrificial circle, but the threat was enough for Fenrir to take over.

Getting shoved to the side in his mind was never easy to accept. Losing control of his body always left Jono with a bit of hindbrain panic that Fenrir would never give it back. But the situation didn't allow for dwelling on the unknown, just a threat.

"*Cousin,*" Fenrir said, the syllables coming out strangely in Jono's wolf mouth, like the cracking of bones.

"You seem to be on the wrong side of the hunt, Fenrir," Hades said.

"What did you do to Hannah?" Patrick demanded harshly.

Hades' attention turned away from Jono and Fenrir to Patrick, the ugly hate in the god's eyes making Jono want to raise his hackles. "I have done nothing to my daughter's vessel, nor to her."

"Bullshit. You only sold Macaria's life to Ethan."

Patrick held his dagger steady between them, his hair a mess. He'd lost the beanie in the crash, but not his nerve if his scent was anything to go by. The magic pouring through Jono's soul and into the ring of mageglobes that flared to life around Patrick was a steady rush not commanded by fear.

Hades' expression didn't change, but the ozone scent spiked with a rage that tasted like how static felt when it hit Jono's tongue. Fenrir moved his body to the edge of Patrick's shield, eyeing the hellhounds that stalked around them in a circle for a moment. Jono wanted to track their movements, but Fenrir chose to focus on Garmr. Hel's favored hound smelled electric, like the air after a storm.

Immortal, but no god, Fenrir told him.

Jono was never certain of the difference, but in a fight they were both dangerous. Fenrir pressed Jono's snout against Patrick's magic; the buzz of it echoed in his soul. With a snarl, they walked through the shield, the soulbond giving them a way through that wouldn't tear down the shield and hurt Patrick. Being tied together made it easier, or maybe Fenrir did.

"You chose the wrong side," Hades said, raising a hand to point in Jono and Fenrir's direction. "And your vessel will pay for it."

To that, Fenrir howled an unearthly challenge that drew the hellhounds to them in a pack of death Jono wasn't afraid to face. Fenrir charged to meet them, though several were blown aside by the mageglobe Patrick threw at the pack. Fenrir kicked one in the throat with a hind leg before spinning to face Garmr's advance.

Fenrir used Jono's body like the weapon it was, sinking into a killing focus that left acidic blood strewn across the snow. It reminded Jono of the fight at the Gap of Dunloe in Ireland, when they faced off against Medb's side. Less of the enemy, but the threat was the same.

Jono's claws sank into burning flesh, the acid scoring his fur and skin before healing in seconds. Fenrir's presence in him was enough to survive the sulfuric acid that gave the hellhounds life.

The attack aimed at them by Hades was a different story entirely.

Jono and Fenrir saw the hellfire bomb flying toward them through the snow and had only a single second to twist out of the way. It scorched his fur as they retreated, the smell of burning fur reaching his nose. It exploded close by, sending dirt and snow and burning bits of flame into the air. The only reason they didn't get a face full of hellfire was the shield Patrick erected between them and the bomb.

Fenrir launched them away from the epicenter and that wall of protection, dodging the fallout even as the hellhounds cut in close, surrounding them. Fenrir growled a furious warning—and the sound was echoed by the rumbling thunder of motorcycle engines.

The valkyries' battle cries cut through the air with a shriek that would've made Jono's ears twitch if he had control of his body. Fenrir snapped his teeth at the nearest hellhound, catching the edge of the beast's jaw and tearing through muscle before he slipped out of reach.

Garmr howled a warning, head snapping from side to side as the hellhound tracked the valkyries driving toward them from both ends of the street. The other hellhounds joined the cry, and it was answered by the more familiar howls of wolves. The wind blowing strong over Lincoln Park carried with it the scent of pack and wolves. Dark streaks raced over the snowy ground from the north as werecreatures came to join the fight.

Best give me back control, Jono warned Fenrir.

There was a moment when he didn't think the god would relinquish his body, but then control came back in a buzz of nerve connections that made Jono shake his great wolf head. He snapped his teeth together, shifting his position to be closer to Patrick and Wade where they still stood behind the shield.

Hades' hands dripped hellfire, the snow around his feet having melted into a puddle that stained his Oxfords. The god stared at Patrick with so much hatred in his eyes that Jono wanted to shield Patrick with his body.

"You should have died," Hades said.

"Talk to your wife," Patrick shot back.

A blur of motion cut through the air. One of the hellhounds arched its back from the hit, a valkyrie's spear protruding from its side. The valkyries were closing in, with Brynhildr leading one group and Eir the other. The motorcycles ate up the snowy ground easily, and before Fenrir relinquished his sight completely, Jono got a flash of winged horses overlaid on the vehicles the valkyries rode.

More spears cut through the air, one aiming for Hades' heart. It never found its home, as the god stepped backward through the veil, gray fog swallowing him before the weapon ever reached him. Garmr snarled viciously before racing away from the fight, heading east around Patrick's shield, and several hellhounds followed. Patrick stayed his hand due to the werecreatures that finally made it to their location, snarling and snapping at the few hellhounds who remained.

Several valkyries launched themselves off their motorcycles, the vehicles driving out of range on their own. They landed in the midst of the hellhounds, the small group a whirlwind of violence, their spears cutting open the beasts with well-placed thrusts. Brynhildr drove around Patrick's shield to pull the spear she'd thrown at Hades out of the ground, spinning it around with a practiced hand. Some of the werecreatures who had arrived gave her a wide berth.

Brynhildr shoved her visor up. "We heard Garmr's howl and came as quick as we could."

Jono shook snow and blood off his fur and changed back to human in a writhing twist of skin, bone, and muscles. Joints ground together and muscles snapped to attach to new locations.

The colors of the world became slightly muted, the sharpness fading. Standing naked in the snow, Jono ground his teeth together against the chill that wanted to make them chatter.

"They attacked us in the street," Patrick said as he lowered his shields. He conjured a mageglobe and sent it toward Jono. The heat pouring off it was welcome. "I'm betting the cops will arrive soon, so all of you need to go. I'll handle the authorities."

"What about the dead hellhounds?" Wade asked.

Patrick grimaced. "Leave them. They're evidence. I'll burn them after we get crime scene pictures."

"I don't think you'll have much time for evidence gathering in this storm," Jono said.

Two of the werewolves started to shift as well, their bright amber eyes the only things staying the same from wolf to human. Like Jono, neither of them cared about being nude with an audience. Jono assumed they were Naomi White Hawk and Alejandro Perez, the god pack alphas Patrick had dealt with earlier in the week.

"Our home is nearby. We can house you there," Naomi offered. She nodded at Jono, meeting his gaze with a steady one of her own. "Jonothon. My dire told us you were in town."

"Naomi. Alejandro. Haven't had a chance for a proper introduction. As you can see, we've been a bit busy," he said by way of apology.

"Killing hellspawn, dealing with dead bodies, trying to stay out of reach of the cops," Patrick said pointedly.

"We can escort all of you to your territory home," Brynhildr said to Naomi. The god pack alpha's expression never changed, but her scent took on a sharp, worried layer to it. Jono figured she and the rest of her pack had finally gotten a whiff of the immortals and didn't know what to make of them.

"Does that mean I get to ride a motorcycle?" Wade asked excitedly, practically dancing on his feet.

"You're still not allowed one when we get home," Patrick retorted. "Now all of you, get moving."

"I don't like leaving you alone," Jono argued.

Patrick glared at him. "I don't want to have to explain your naked ass to the Chicago PD. I'll be fine."

Knowing he didn't have time to argue, and that they'd argued enough lately, Jono gave in. He curled his fingers over Patrick's chin to tilt his head up for a quick, hard kiss. "Be safe."

Patrick smiled tightly, but it didn't reach his eyes. "Don't do anything stupid like last time I wasn't around."

Jono fought back a wince at the reminder he still wasn't entirely forgiven. Sighing, Jono stepped back. He, Naomi, and Alejandro wasted no time in shifting back to their werewolf forms. Jono was warmer once on all fours, shaking blood from the shift off his fur. He paused long enough to headbutt Patrick before nipping gently at his hand. Patrick scratched between his ears with gloved fingers.

"I'll find you after I deal with this mess," Patrick promised.

Wade brandished Jono's phone and waved it at them. "You can call him. I saved his phone after he shifted."

Jono snorted, breath coming out in white puffs, grateful for Wade's sticky fingers. He reluctantly walked away from Patrick to follow Naomi and Alejandro. Wade happily clambered onto a motorcycle, riding tandem with Eir and petting the motorcycle with a reverent hand. The motorcycle revved its engines without Eir's hands on the handlebars, proving that what he'd seen in that split second during their charge hadn't been a hallucination.

The valkyries put away their spears in the same manner as they had at the bar, the weapons dangling once more from their throats before getting tucked beneath their clothes. Brynhildr let Naomi and Alejandro take the lead. Jono stayed on their heels, the trek through snowy Chicago a quick one. The Chicago god pack's home was three blocks away from Lincoln Park, in a mansion that rivaled Westberg's.

Werecreatures stood guard outside the house in human form, and one took the stairs two at a time to open the front door. Jono followed Naomi and Alejandro up the stairs but paused on the porch to look back at where Wade was climbing off a motorcycle.

"We must keep searching," Brynhildr said from the street, her helmeted head turned toward him, the visor flipped up. She didn't raise her voice, and Jono could hear her even through the wind.

Jono nodded, then growled a warning at Wade when the teenager kept petting the motorcycle. Wade heaved out a sigh and jogged over to Jono, brushing snow off his shoulders as he climbed the stairs.

"I still want one," Wade announced.

Jono nipped at his heels, gape-grinning at the squawk Wade let out before the teen hurried inside. Jono followed him, walking into a pleasantly warm home where other god pack members patiently waited in the living room with changes of clothes. Naomi and Alejandro were already human and getting dressed. Monica was there, and she arched an eyebrow as she held up a stack of clothes.

"I have something for you to wear," Monica said.

Jono shifted back to human, going through the grinding change of bodies once more. When he was human again, he straightened up and took the clothes with a quiet "Cheers."

The tracksuit bottoms were a little short, hitting just above the ankles, and the T-shirt was tight across his shoulders, but Jono didn't complain. He'd ruined his shoes during the first shift, but he'd packed an extra pair. Jono ran a hand through his hair before nodding at Wade.

"Let me have my mobile," Jono said.

Wade handed it over only slightly reluctantly. His desire to steal and keep things that weren't his for a hoard they had to clean out monthly was a habit Jono and Patrick still hadn't gotten him to break.

The front door slammed shut and a few more Chicago god

pack members came into the living room. They spread out to keep watch, but none were blocking exits.

"Weather is getting worse," one of them said. "Doesn't feel normal."

"It's not. It's a reactionary storm," Jono said.

Naomi frowned at him. "The news isn't saying that."

Jono smiled thinly. "The news doesn't want to incite panic."

"I'm hungry," Wade announced.

Jono sighed. "We need to get back to the hotel. I know the weather is shit, but could one of your pack members give us a ride downtown? I lost my sunglasses in the crash, and getting a taxi with my eyes is difficult enough without a blizzard in the mix, as I'm sure you know."

"Every god pack member knows. Will our people be safe if they take you back?" Alejandro asked.

"I can't make that promise. I don't know what's out there in the storm."

Alejandro and Naomi glanced at each other, having a silent conversation. Finally, Naomi nodded. "I'll go. You stay."

"Take Monica with you," Alejandro said.

"Of course."

"I'll go start the car," Monica said.

She was the only one who left. The rest of the Chicago god pack who were present in the home remained where they were. Naomi approached, absently braiding her long hair with quick fingers and tying it off at the end.

"Patrick offered pass-through rights for any pack coming from Chicago who wanted to go to New York," she said.

"If that's what he offered, then I'm in agreement," Jono replied.

"And what of Estelle and Youssef?"

Jono gave Naomi a hard smile. "They want a fight, so we're giving them one. Our pack might be small in numbers, but our alliances include the fae and every Night Court in New York City."

"Every Night Court?" Alejandro asked sharply.

Jono nodded. "Yes."

Naomi eyed him. "You smell like truth."

"We've taken in the packs who've left Estelle and Youssef's protection, and we're doing our best to keep them safe. We'll do the same for whoever comes through *our* city from yours."

"There is a pack who settled here five years ago from New York. Fifteen people who uprooted their lives came to us and asked for permission to stay and for protection. They didn't trust the god pack alphas they left behind," Alejandro said.

"I wouldn't have either. I came to the States about four years ago, and I didn't care for how Estelle and Youssef handled things then or now."

"But they let you stay as an independent?"

"They didn't have a choice." At Alejandro's dubious look, Jono continued with "A seer brought me over from London. I got to stay because Estelle and Youssef couldn't say no to the government."

"You're going to have a war," Naomi said.

"We already have one, but my pack isn't backing down. Too many people will be hurt if we do."

Naomi and Alejandro were silent for a few seconds before she waved at him to follow her. "Come on. Let's get you back to the hotel."

Jono looked over at where Wade had oh so casually been perusing the mantle over the fireplace, noticing that half the knickknacks that had been there were now gone. He sighed. "Put them back, Wade."

"But they're *shiny*," Wade protested.

"And they're not yours, mate."

Wade scowled and sulkily pulled out at least ten knickknacks from his pockets and set them back on the shelf. "They could be."

Jono shook his head before offering Naomi and Alejandro his apologies. "Sorry about that. Wade was a pickpocket in a past life, and it's been tough breaking him of that habit."

"I think you mean *current* life," Wade muttered.

The pair eyed Wade a little warily before Alejandro snorted. "A pack under our protection said they'd seen a dragon at the cemetery the other night. We thought they had to be mistaken, or it was an illusion."

Jono didn't say anything into the silence that followed, and Wade thankfully kept his gob shut. Naomi smiled slightly at their reticence but didn't seem annoyed.

"Let's get you to your hotel," she said.

Naomi waved at them to follow her out of the home. Jono settled a hand on Wade's shoulder and steered him toward the front door and back out into the cold. The snow beneath Jono's bare feet was icy.

"Thanks for your help today," Jono said once they were in the back seat of Naomi's car.

She looked at him in the rearview mirror, amber eyes bright in her face. "The attack happened in our territory. We would have come no matter who was in trouble, but I'm glad it wasn't Estelle and Youssef. I don't like what I've heard about them."

Jono didn't blame her. If Estelle and Youssef ever needed his help, he'd never give it, not for all the money in the world.

16

"Arresting me in front of my colleagues was uncalled for," Dean Westberg snapped furiously when Patrick entered the interview room.

"You weren't arrested. You were just advised to come quietly to sort things out. It's not our fault you had the press there documenting the dinner," Patrick said.

Patrick sat down across the table from Westberg and his lawyer, Peter Stefan Mathys, a man whose tailored suit couldn't completely hide the gut he was sporting. Mathys had used all three names whenever he introduced himself to anyone after arriving. The condescending way he looked down his nose at Patrick wasn't unexpected, though it was irritating. Over the years, Patrick had dealt with lawyers who weren't that great at their jobs and others who based their worth on their over a thousand dollars an hour rate. Mathys was definitely in the latter group, and possibly in the former.

Either way, Patrick hated dealing with lawyers.

"The SOA would like to know where you've been for the past two weeks?" Patrick asked.

"Don't answer that. You're under no obligation to answer any of their questions if they haven't charged you with anything," the lawyer said.

Patrick opened up the file folder he'd brought with him and thumbed through a couple of crime scene photographs that had been rush developed for this interview. He slid one of the burned body in the wine cellar across the table for them to look at.

"We found a body in your home today, Mr. Westberg. The press staked out your Lincoln Park address for the entire time it took the SOA to process your house. Now, I'm not saying you killed the guy, but I'm pretty sure this isn't the kind of story you wanted in the news in the final stretch of your campaign."

Westberg's gaze stayed locked on the picture, even when his lawyer picked it up to review more closely.

"I had nothing to do with that. My Lincoln Park property isn't big enough for the events I needed to put on for my donors. My wife and I have been staying at our Gold Coast mansion," Westberg said.

"Hope your other property isn't hiding any more dead bodies."

"If you want to search my client's homes, you'll need to get a warrant," Mathys snapped.

"Fine. We'll look into that. I still need your whereabouts for the past two weeks."

Mathys opened his mouth, but Westberg lifted his hand in a wordless *shut up* gesture the lawyer surprisingly obeyed.

"If you're asking me to account for every single minute between now and whenever this person died, then I should simply forward you the itinerary Kristen gave me. I've been scheduled to be somewhere practically every hour of the day for the past two weeks."

Patrick tried not to react to the assumed identity of a goddess he was pretty sure was Hel. Tracking her down was turning into a wild goose chase according to the SOA agents assigned that task. Kristen Lief was nowhere to be found at the moment.

"Except you missed a day, didn't you? You made up for it at the senior brunch this past week that should've happened last week. What day was that again?" Patrick asked.

Westberg's eyes narrowed. "Rescheduling events happens during a campaign."

"Sure, but I have a dead body and you have a period of time you're unaccounted for."

"You have no proof my client has done anything wrong. If you did, you would have arrested him, or the Chicago PD would have. We'll be leaving now," Mathys said.

Patrick watched both men stand up, not moving from his own seat. "Someone performed a ritual in your home, Mr. Westberg. There was no sign of forced entry, but they left behind a spell that would've resulted in the very messy death of anyone who crossed it. I was under the impression you didn't care for magic."

"How *dare* you imply I've hired someone to use magic on my behalf in my home," Westberg spat out. "I don't care what other people do in their lives, but magic goes against my faith. Perhaps your time would be better spent investigating the pro-magic groups who've harassed my family since I entered the race. I wouldn't put it past any of them to break into my home and desecrate it as they've done."

"If that's the case, send me your itinerary."

Tracking down all the people they would have to interview to corroborate his locations for the past two weeks was a headache Patrick thankfully wouldn't have to share alone. The SOA was throwing more agents at the Westberg case than they had been now that a murder had hit the news. Patrick was curious about the spin Westberg's campaign would use to try to distance him from the mess.

Mathys shot Patrick a dirty look. "Get a subpoena. If you aren't charging my client with anything, then we're done here."

Mathys gestured for Westberg to precede him out of the room. Patrick didn't bother calling them back. He gathered up the photograph and sorted it back into the file. He carried the documents out of the room with him. A junior agent was seeing Westberg and Mathys out, but since Patrick was heading up to see SAIC Andrew Dabrowski, they all had to wait for the elevators for an uncomfortable minute.

Patrick's came first, and he took it up, stopping at a couple of floors along the way to let other people off. Despite it being late in the afternoon on a Saturday, Dabrowski hadn't gone home. He'd stayed after the backlash on the ley lines to coordinate the SOA's response to the threat. Patrick didn't have to resort to a phone call, merely knocked on the already open door before heading into the SAIC's office.

"Westberg and his lawyer left. They claim his whereabouts can be accounted for in the last two weeks. He missed an event last week that was rescheduled for this week. It'll be interesting what excuse he comes up with," Patrick said.

Dabrowski frowned. He looked better than he had earlier but still tired. "We've notified the attorney general's office about what's happened. Considering the other case in the pipeline, we couldn't keep this information from them."

"Too bad we couldn't keep it from the news."

"Or your fight with hellhounds in Lincoln Park. I heard you declined a ride to the hospital."

Patrick rubbed at the back of his neck, the twinge he'd felt there after the car accident gone thanks to a healing potion. "I didn't need to be held up in a hospital when a potion from one of your witches here worked just fine. The wreck wasn't that bad."

"If you're sure, though I'm concerned about the Dominion Sect targeting you twice now."

Patrick tried not to laugh. "Maybe they just don't like me."

Dabrowski rolled his eyes. "It's a problem if they're targeting SOA agents."

"I fought them in the Thirty-Day War. They're terrible with grudges."

"I'd offer you a temporary partner to watch your back, but the director said it wasn't necessary."

Patrick would've fought him on that offer if Dabrowski had gone through with it. "I'm used to handling my cases alone. I'll be fine, sir."

"Chicago might not be," Dabrowski drawled.

"I'll do my best not to allow demons to scratch the Bean again."

"It's ugly. I might look the other way if you do." Dabrowski sighed and leaned back in his chair, causing the leather to squeak. "We have witches in Lincoln Park working through the addresses affected from being within the radius of the spell's epicenter. Everyone's souls should be cleansed by tomorrow morning. If we miss anyone, we're telling them to call a support number rather than going to a hospital to keep contamination to a minimum."

"Want me to get Legal to work on subpoenas for Westberg's itinerary?"

"Send in the request, and have them work with the AG's office. I have a feeling we'll need to move faster on the rent payment by way of souls case. See if you can't track down Westberg's campaign manager."

Considering Patrick was pretty damn certain Kristen was Hel, he wasn't looking forward to that. "Right. Anything else?"

"Get it to stop snowing."

Patrick snorted. "I have zero affinity for weather magic. Sorry, you're stuck."

Dabrowski waved him off. "Report in when you find something. I'm going to be living at the office this weekend it feels like."

Patrick left the SAIC's office, intent on stopping by his borrowed one to update his report before heading back to the hotel. He didn't pay any attention to the other agent that got into the elevator with him until they spoke.

"Fancy meeting you here, Pattycakes."

Patrick's head snapped up, and he stared in disbelief at where Hermes lounged against the other side of the elevator, dressed in a generic suit, but still sporting his dyed curls. They were a neon orange tipped in fire truck red this time, ensuring he'd stand out in a crowd. Patrick assumed a lot of magical misdirection went into no one in the SOA building seeing the non-regulation hair color.

"What the fuck are you doing?" Patrick said.

Hermes wiggled his fingers at Patrick. "My job, Pattycakes. I hope you're hungry because I'm here to take you to dinner."

"I'm not eating with you."

"You're mistaken. I'm not the one you're having dinner with. That would be Persephone."

Patrick went cold. The thought of facing the goddess who owned his soul debt was not something he ever liked doing. He swallowed thickly, fingers tightening on the file he carried. "I had dinner plans already, and I'm in the middle of a case."

"Cancel. I'm to take you to her, and we both know she doesn't like to be kept waiting."

"Not through the veil," Patrick said sharply. "I can't lose any time."

"A few hours won't hurt you. It didn't hurt your wolf the other night."

Patrick stared at him. "What?"

Hermes shoved himself away from the wall as the elevator slowed to a stop. "Didn't he tell you? Fenrir dragged him and Lucien across the veil to have a friendly little chat in Ginnungagap."

Patrick swallowed, refusing to show the hurt and anger that Hermes' words dredged up. Jono had told him about Lucien, but not that they'd gone past the veil.

He's sleeping on the couch when we get back home.

"I need to put my case file away, and we're *driving*, Hermes," Patrick said flatly.

The god smirked, icy amusement in his gold-brown eyes. "Sure thing, Pattycakes."

Patrick had to remind himself that punching Hermes in the face would result in nothing but possible broken bones and some definite bruises—for himself.

Hermes followed Patrick out of the elevator and to the visiting agent office he'd been assigned since arriving in Chicago. He locked the case file in a filing cabinet, grabbed his leather jacket off the hook behind the door, and pulled on his beanie and gloves.

Patrick wasn't waylaid by anyone on his way out of the building. He figured Hermes had something to do with that, but didn't say anything. They walked in silence to the parking garage across the street, snow pelting them with every step they took. By the time Patrick made it to his second SUV he'd been given from the local motor pool, his nose felt frozen and so did his fingers.

"I hate reactionary storms," Patrick muttered as he started the car and turned the heater on full blast. "Where am I going?"

"Dunkin' Donuts on West Adams Street," Hermes said.

"I thought you said dinner?" Patrick stared at him. "Are you serious?"

Hermes tugged on his tie, and Patrick watched his clothes melt away as if they weren't real, revealing the outfit Patrick normally expected to see him in: ripped jeans, an old band T-shirt, and a spiked leather jacket.

"Persephone likes their donuts."

Patrick wasn't going to question a goddess' taste in food and so kept his mouth shut.

The drive to the particular Dunkin' Donuts spot would've taken fifteen minutes tops on a good night. In the middle of a snowstorm, it took closer to thirty. The roads were icy even with the snow plows and salt trucks having gone over the downtown streets. The Dunkin' Donuts on the corner was brightly lit, like a neon oasis in the storm. Patrick would've driven past it while looking for a parking garage, when Hermes pointed at the street in front of the business.

"Park over there," he said.

"Government plates aren't going to get me out of being towed in this weather," Patrick warned.

"No one will see your ride."

Whatever magic Hermes wanted to use on the SUV was fine by Patrick so long as he didn't lose the vehicle to Chicago tow trucks. Knowing the god, it was a distinct possibility, but he had to risk it, so he parked where Hermes told him to.

Not many people were inside the Dunkin' Donuts when they entered, but Hermes made a beeline for two women seated at a table by the window. The glass was fogged over a little from the inside heat, but not enough that one couldn't see the snow blowing past outside.

"I brought him, now where are my hash browns?" Hermes asked.

Persephone gestured at the white bag sitting in front of an empty chair. "All yours."

Patrick stayed where he was, heart pounding in his chest so hard it hurt to breathe as he stared at the Greek goddess and queen of the Underworld. He didn't realize his phone was ringing until Persephone smiled slightly at him and popped a donut hole into her mouth.

"You should answer that," she said.

Patrick blinked, the world reorienting around himself. He dug out his cell phone, pulling off his glove with his teeth so he could accept the call. Jono's voice came through the speaker before Patrick even had the phone pressed to his ear.

"Are you all right? You bloody well gave me a heart attack just now," Jono said.

Patrick realized the soulbond was a humming tie between them and most of the discomfort stemmed from his end. He took a moment to try to tamp it down, to shove it aside and ignore it.

"I'm fine," Patrick replied.

"You don't *feel* fine, Pat."

"Hermes is annoying. Don't worry, he didn't take us through the veil like Fenrir did for you." At Jono's startled silence, Patrick grimaced. "Yeah, forgot about that, didn't you?"

"Pat—"

"Later. I don't want to hear it right now."

Patrick ended the call. He gripped his phone to stop himself from digging his nails into his palms. Persephone never looked away from his face, the faint curve of her mouth knowing in a way he didn't like.

She was dressed in winter clothing, her gold-brown skin glowing healthily beneath the bright overhead lights. Her curly, dark brown hair was barely tamed beneath a beanie with a pompom. The freckles scattered over her nose and cheeks never seemed to change, no matter the months or years between their meetings.

"You've never met my mother," Persephone said, nodding at the woman who sat opposite of her.

Patrick's gaze snapped to the Greek goddess of harvest and so much more, mouth dry and at a loss for words. Demeter studied him with crystalline blue eyes, giving nothing away. Her straight white hair fell to her shoulders in a fashionable long bob, the faint wrinkles on her face barely aging her. Her winter clothes were more fashionable than Persephone's, and the black fur coat draped over the back of her chair dragged on the floor.

His fingers itched with an electric burn that caused them to exude a pop of static electricity when he pulled back a chair to sit down. He shoved his phone into his jacket pocket, letting it go with some effort. Half a dozen donuts were left in a box that held twelve, but Patrick didn't reach for one.

"So." Patrick cleared his throat. "Why are you in Chicago?"

"Because this is where Macaria is," Persephone said.

"Right." Patrick glanced at Demeter. "Are you here for emotional support?"

Demeter reached for a blueberry donut, tearing it into bite-sized pieces. "I am here because of the spell which was cast that pulled power from the nexus."

"It wasn't a sacrificial one."

"And yet, I hear Odin is missing."

"He's not dead yet."

Demeter popped a piece of donut into her mouth and chewed slowly. She didn't blink, and Patrick tried not to squirm beneath her gaze. Her aura was a flickering, golden glow around her that thankfully didn't burn his eyes. He wondered if she had dimmed it out of politeness for his presence or if the people who remembered her were thin on the ground these days.

"The spell wasn't for Odin," Persephone said.

What little warmth Patrick had felt walking into the shop evaporated at her words. A chill settled in his bones that no amount of heat charms embedded in his leather jacket could cure.

"Then who was it for?" he asked, thinking of the pentagram on that hardwood floor in Westberg's home. All the candles and figurines and blood spilled for a reason no one knew—except Demeter seemed to.

"They were *for* Macaria. They were *to* Freyr," Demeter said.

Patrick rubbed at his eyes hard enough he had to blink away black spots when he opened them again. "Freyr. He's—what? The Norse god of fair weather, which we could use, and—"

Patrick snapped his mouth shut so fast his teeth caught the edge of his tongue, cutting into it. The taste of blood filtered over his tongue, but he hardly noticed it. He stared at Demeter, stomach churning badly.

Persephone folded her hands together, nails digging into the sun-kissed skin over her bones. "Fertility."

Patrick shoved himself to his feet, hurried to the garbage bin near the door, and puked up everything left in his stomach from lunch and enough bile it came out of his nose. He heaved for a few seconds more, clammy and cold. It felt as if his world had been ripped apart all over again, the same way his soul had twisted from the backlash running through his twin's.

A warm hand settled on the back of his neck. He jerked away from the touch, breathing harshly through his mouth, wishing he had a bottle of whiskey at hand to wash away the sour taste.

"No," Patrick rasped out, staring at Persephone, only dimly aware that no one was paying any attention to them.

"Freyr may not be of our pantheon, but like knows like. Fertility spells resonate because of the life they gift to those asking."

"*No.*"

Persephone stepped closer, bringing with her the scent of spring that wasn't strong enough to overpower the taste and smell of bile in his mouth, in his throat. "You didn't take the shot in Cairo and this is where it led us."

Patrick flinched with his entire body, struggling to breathe. His phone started ringing, but he couldn't answer it when the effort to get air into his lungs hurt so much.

"You owe me my daughter's life, Patrick. That was my price when I saved you."

He swallowed so hard his throat clicked, the scars on his chest pulling tight. "I know."

Persephone touched his cheeks, wiping away the tears he hadn't known he'd shed. "You will pay your soul debt, no matter the cost."

She walked out of the shop and into the snow, disappearing into the white flurries and the veil tangled between each snowflake. Patrick scrubbed a shaking hand over his face, trying to get his bearings back. When he looked over at the table they'd been sitting at, he saw it was empty.

"Fuck," Patrick whispered quietly as he headed outside.

His phone stopped ringing before starting up again. Patrick fumbled it out of his pocket on the walk back to the SUV, Jono's name bright on the screen, a lifeline that could never save him. Patrick's thumb hovered over the green Accept icon before swiping over the red, sending the call to voicemail.

He needed a goddamn drink, not a conversation.

17

eyes.

"You smell like an alleyway behind a pub," Jono said from beside him on the bed.

"Put me out of my misery."

"Those bloody ravens came by while you were passed out. They said Frigg wants to have a chat over breakfast."

The thought of food had Patrick swallowing very, very carefully. "I said put me out of my misery, not make it worse."

Gentle fingers rubbed at his temples and the throbbing there that wouldn't go away. "Want to talk about it?"

The thought of talking about the atrocity done to his twin had Patrick struggling to a sitting position, eyes still closed, breathing heavily. Jono helped him to the bathroom, and Patrick fell to his knees in front of the toilet just in time to get sick. Nothing came out but bile and whiskey, but he didn't feel better afterward.

"Guess that answers my question."

Patrick listed to the side and ended up leaning against the tub. He kept his eyes shut, but that didn't stop the world from moving.

The hangover he was suffering through was caused by trying to drink his body weight in whiskey last night. Jono had eventually caught up with him at some dive bar downtown. He'd paid Patrick's tab, driven him back to the hotel, and poured him into bed, where he'd passed out rather than slept.

"Shower, and I'll ring the front desk for some paracetamol," Jono said in a quiet voice.

"They call it Tylenol here," Patrick muttered.

"Hush, you."

The thought of moving wasn't appealing, but Patrick knew he needed to. It wouldn't be the first time he worked while feeling like he wanted to keel over and die, though this time it was self-inflicted as opposed to an injury.

Moving hurt, but he did it anyway, slowly peeling out of the sleep pants he didn't remember putting on last night. Hauling himself to his feet, head pounding, Patrick turned on the shower and carefully stepped into the tub. The warm spray hit him in the face, and he flinched, the water like needles against his skin.

He tipped his head back to get a mouthful of water, swishing it around before spitting it out. It didn't get rid of the taste of vomit on his tongue, but it would do for now until he brushed his teeth.

Patrick moved with slow motions to get clean, trying to get his bearings. He was in the process of deciding if he wanted to actually shampoo his hair and make his headache worse by touching his skull when the shower curtain was moved so Jono could enter the shower with him. Jono didn't say anything, but he did take the soap and start to wash Patrick up.

Patrick let him, staring blankly at the bleached white tile surrounding them, thoughts catching on Persephone's words from last night.

"Ethan performed a fertility rite at Westberg's house," Patrick said slowly, the words coming out rough. He felt every single syllable in his head, but he couldn't keep quiet about this.

Jono's hands stilled on his body for a couple of seconds before resuming their soaping. "Fertility? Not sacrificial?"

Patrick closed his eyes, nausea in his belly and guilt a heavy weight on his shoulders. "Hannah."

He didn't want to think about the implications of a spell like that, but knew he couldn't ignore it. Pretending a problem didn't exist was a luxury Patrick would never get.

Jono gently tugged him backward. Patrick's shoulders settled against Jono's chest, strong arms wrapping around him to hold him close. "How do you know?"

Patrick swallowed, wanting desperately to brush his teeth but not wanting to leave Jono's warmth. "Hermes took me to see Persephone last night. She brought her mother."

"Demeter?"

"Yeah. Fertility goddess. She said Freyr was involved."

"Doubt the other Norse gods will be pleased about all this."

The thought of reporting back to Frigg about more betrayals in their pantheon made Patrick want to crawl back into bed and never leave it.

Jono pressed a gentle kiss to the top of Patrick's head. "Is that why you went drinking in a blizzard?"

"Not a blizzard yet. I think Thor might have broken up bits of it. The SOA has weather witches trying to keep the worst at bay right now."

"Pat."

"I keep not saving her. I keep fucking up."

"It's not your fault."

"I—"

Jono raised his hand and gently placed it over Patrick's mouth. His breath blew warm over the shell of Patrick's ear when he spoke. "Listen to me, love. You were eight when Ethan tried to murder you, and you thought Hannah had died during that spell. You spent years believing she was dead. What Ethan has done is not on you, it's on him. This is not your fault."

"It feels like it is," Patrick said after Jono removed his hand. "I'm her twin."

"That doesn't make you responsible for her."

"I'm older than her by seven minutes."

"Being older doesn't mean anything when you were that young." Jono gently turned him around, cupping his face with warm hands. "Whatever Ethan has done to her is *not your fault*. He should've been a father to you both, and never was. You aren't to blame for his selfishness."

Patrick listed forward and let his head slide free of Jono's hands to sink down onto his shoulder. "Still have to kill him."

"Yeah, love. I'll help."

Patrick sighed. "Okay."

Jono took charge that morning when Patrick would've preferred to stay in bed. He got Patrick in and out of the shower, made sure he brushed his teeth, and gave him tea instead of coffee, which Patrick thought was an utter betrayal. Patrick complained about the lack of coffee on the drive to Eiketre but still drank the damned tea.

Sunday morning had arrived with Chicago blanketed in snow and more still coming down. Ice was pushing against the shores of Lake Michigan, snow plows and salt trucks were running nonstop, and all flights in and out of O'Hare were delayed. Which meant Patrick's meeting with the SOA's only necromancer wasn't happening until late afternoon at the earliest.

"Fuck," Patrick muttered as he glared at the email from Setsuna while Jono parked in front of the bar. "Shit. I could've slept in."

"But breakfast," Wade whined as he got out of the SUV. "I'm hungry. Housekeeping wouldn't refill my minibar snacks."

Jono shook his head. "I told you not to touch the minibar in your room."

"Yeah, but I was *hungry*."

Patrick got out of the SUV, wincing at the cold that slapped him in the face. With all of the delays happening, Patrick should have spent his morning at the SOA field office working on the Westberg case now that it had blown up in everyone's faces. Instead, he, Jono, and Wade were at Eiketre. Patrick would've declined the breakfast offer, but when a goddess demanded you show up for a meal, he knew better than to ignore the order.

The front door was unlocked, and they let themselves inside. Magic slithered over Patrick's shields, making his headache spike and the tea he'd carefully sipped on the drive over threaten to crawl up his throat.

"Be welcome," Frigg said from where she and Thor sat at a pair of tables shoved together and overflowing with food.

The spread of fresh bread, cheese, meats, pâté, jam, and enough coffee to drown in was almost enough to make up for driving through heavy snowfall, if Patrick felt like eating. It wasn't quite a blizzard, but it was getting there. Patrick would give it another day, maybe less, before it reached whiteout conditions. The SOA's weather witches were working double shifts to try to break up some of the weather patterns, but they wouldn't be able to disrupt it all.

Patrick would choose freezing to death in a blizzard over breaking bread with gods, but Jono had vetoed that idea. Wade, however, was more than happy to eat what Frigg offered him.

"This is good," Wade said after sitting down and filling up a plate. He took a bite of fresh bread laden with three slices of meat, a smear of brie, and enough jam to make Patrick worried about the upholstery in their new rental.

"I could've sworn we taught you manners," Patrick said, keeping his head propped up with one hand.

Wade stared at him and took another overly large bite of his breakfast and chewed loudly.

"He's a growing dragon. Let him eat," Frigg said, giving Wade a motherly smile.

Wade smirked at Patrick and started picking out the next pieces of meat to go on another slice of bread. Patrick resigned himself to needing to pay a cleaning cost on the SUV when he returned it to the motor pool.

"It's good of you to care for him, though I hope you'll be able to tend to his needs," Thor said.

Patrick shrugged with one shoulder. "A friend of ours is a billionaire who owns a tech company. His pack tithes ours. We'll be able to keep Wade fed."

"You hope," Wade muttered around his food.

"Let's not make it a contest, yeah?" Jono said mildly. "Chew with your gob shut."

"Any news on Odin?" Patrick asked, leaving Wade to his food.

Frigg's expression never changed, though Thor looked as if he wouldn't mind murdering someone.

"The valkyries are still searching. Muninn and Huginn haven't heard the Allfather's thoughts since he was taken," Thor said.

"That does not mean he is gone. We would know if he was." Frigg arched an eyebrow at Patrick. "They said Chicago had visitors last night."

"Persephone and Demeter say hello, and that you should maybe jail Freyr since he apparently performed a fertility rite on my sister."

Thor grimaced, setting down his coffee mug. "Freyr would not abandon his convictions for the Dominion Sect."

"The Norns weren't worried about him. Maybe they should've been."

Patrick eyed the whiskey bottle on the table, then his coffee mug, and wondered if hair of the dog might cure him or kill him that morning. He reached for the bottle of Jameson, managed to get his fingers around the neck of it, before Jono grabbed his wrist.

"You have work today, and you're already hungover," Jono said.

"I'm late already. What's another shot?" Patrick protested.

"Going in with whiskey on your breath isn't the excuse you want."

Jono had a point; Patrick just hated it. Sighing, he let the bottle of whiskey go and accepted the top-up of his mug from the coffee pot on the table. "Westberg was brought in yesterday for questioning with his lawyer. The guy apparently owns three houses in Chicago just for him and his wife. They've been staying at their Gold Coast one for months due to his mayoral campaign. He swears he can account for every second of the last two weeks, but he missed an event one of the days. They're blaming whatever happened at the one in Lincoln Park on disgruntled activists who are against him. Without evidence, of course."

Jono snorted. "Convenient."

"That's politics for you. They're more pissed about not being able to go home to a place they stay at for a quarter of the year and hadn't been to since last September than they are about whatever happened there."

"Were they arrested?" Frigg asked.

"No."

She hummed thoughtfully, staring beyond where Patrick sat. "His fundraiser dinner is still set to happen tonight at Au Hall."

"Seriously? In this weather?"

"The election is soon. Perhaps he believes he doesn't have the votes."

"He's leading in the polls," Thor said.

Patrick gently rubbed at his temples, wishing he didn't feel like shit, knowing he only had himself to blame. "If the SOA waits any longer to charge him, he might get elected, and then removing him from office is going to be a pain in the fucking ass. Can't you, I don't know, cancel it because of the weather?"

"This is Chicago. A blizzard won't stop its citizens from going out."

"It *should*."

"There are tithes he owes us. Thor will accept them in Odin's place," Frigg said.

Patrick bit back the argument about accepting souls in lieu of prayers as tithes because it wouldn't get him anywhere except maybe thrown out on his ass. "Maybe I'll send some agents in to keep an eye on Westberg."

"Why not go yourself?" Thor asked.

"Because I have a dead body I need raised, and my necromancer is late flying in due to the weather."

Thor took a baguette and broke it in half with his big hands. "I have done what I can to mitigate the effects, though it has taken great effort to do so. If I undo it completely, the effects of the reactionary storm will grow elsewhere, and be worse."

Patrick was aware of that, but it still didn't make doing his job any easier. The general rule with a reactionary storm was to let it run its course where it was if at all possible. Choking it off just made the magic and weather worse when it came back.

"Why has it been hard? I thought you were the god of thunder? That counts as a weather god, doesn't it?"

Thor kept making his sandwich but didn't bother to hide his grimace as he spoke. "In a way, yes, but rain obeys Freyr more than it ever will me."

"No wonder the weather is shit," Jono said drolly.

Frigg's mouth thinned into a hard line. "I will speak to him."

Patrick snorted, then regretted the way it made his face hurt. "Good luck with that."

The door to Eiketre was pushed open, letting in a blast of cold air. Brynhildr and Eir walked inside, both brushing snow off their shoulders. Brynhildr carried her motorcycle helmet in one hand, which she placed on one of the brand-new bar tables. The scorch marks from hellfire had been cleansed, and while the foundation and walls of the place still stood, the furnishings had all needed replacing. Patrick was a little impressed at how quickly the place had been fixed up.

Wade perked up at their arrival. "Can I go say hi to Dynfari?"

"She's outside with the others," Brynhildr said.

Wade nearly tipped out of his seat in his hurry, snatching up another handful of meat and bread to carry with him outside.

"We're going to need to check his flat for a motorcycle after this trip," Jono said.

"He doesn't even know how to drive," Patrick muttered.

"That's not likely to stop him."

Brynhildr and Eir came over to the table. Patrick eyed Eir, who bypassed an empty seat to approach him. She reached for him, her hand hovering over his head. "May I?"

Patrick knew better than to accept help from gods, but the general grossness he felt at the moment from being hungover was enough to get him to cave. "Yeah. Have at it."

She brushed her fingers over his forehead, and a cool wave of magic washed through him. It dragged away his headache and lingering traces of nausea, took away the foul taste still coming up on his tongue from too much whiskey.

Patrick straightened up, feeling mostly human again. "Thanks."

"We need you in one piece," Eir said.

Patrick was never surprised by that answer. Jono shoved his plate over to Patrick and pointed at it. "Eat."

"Any news, Brynhildr?" Frigg asked.

The valkyrie dipped her head out of respect to the other goddess. "Nothing worthwhile, my lady. We believe Hades is helping to keep the enemy hidden from us, along with Odin, and the veil is thick in this city."

"Hades will die by my hand if need be," Thor said as he stood from the table.

"Persephone might beat you to it." Patrick paused before shaking his head. "Or she'll kill you."

Thor's smile was condescending. "I will welcome her attempts if she tries, for she will not win that fight."

Patrick wasn't so sure, but it wasn't worth arguing over. He pushed his chair away from the table and got to his feet. He grabbed the slice of bread with meat and cheese on it from Jono's plate and folded it in half. "I need to get going. I'll let you know if the dead have anything useful to say. Maybe see if you can't find Freyr and get any answers out of him."

Jono followed him out of the bar back into the snow. Wade was crouched between two motorcycles, petting the seats under the watchful eyes of a couple more valkyries.

"Let's go, Wade," Patrick called out.

Wade craned his head around to look at them. "Wow. You no longer smell like a distillery."

"Funny. Get in the car. I'm dropping you both off at the hotel."

Jono shook his head. "Drop us off at a coffee shop near your work."

"You'll be more comfortable at the hotel than in a coffee shop. I have a lot of work ahead of me."

"Yeah, and you might need us. We'll stick close by. It'll be cheaper to feed Wade at a restaurant rather than through room service or the minibar."

Patrick shrugged. "If you say so. I don't know how long I'll be."

"It doesn't matter. The hotel is too far away if something goes wrong."

"It might not be."

Jono smiled tightly. "Best not tempt fate."

Patrick would rather shoot the Fates, but he knew bullets couldn't kill a god.

***

Special Agent Anika Dandridge didn't make it to the Chicago SOA field office until close to 1700. Patrick felt her presence before he even saw her.

Is this how I feel to everyone?

Even through his shields Patrick could sense the shroud of death that surrounded Anika, saturating her aura with a darkness that wasn't bad, just cold. Patrick stood to greet her as she entered Dabrowski's office, eyes flicking from her dark face to the psychopomp trotting at her feet. It took the shape of a fat little pug, gray in coloring, with keen, otherworldly eyes.

Anika herself was an African American woman in her late forties, tall, her graying hair twisted into dreadlocks pulled back in a thick ponytail. Born and raised in New Orleans, Louisiana, Anika was a necromancer who owed her life to the government—literally. As with most black magic, it was illegal, but she had been granted a reprieve of life as a child after her case was appealed through all levels of the courts until it reached the United States Supreme Court. The nine justices had ruled unanimously to allow her to live.

Government interference at its finest.

"Special Agent Dandridge," Dabrowski said as he stood. "I wish your first trip to my field office was under better circumstances."

Anika left her carry-on by the door to come greet them. She didn't extend her hand in greeting, but Patrick did. She eyed him for a moment before accepting the handshake. Even through his shields, he could feel the pull of her magic, a hunger in her power that reached for his soul despite his shields.

"Thanks for coming on such short notice," Patrick said.

Anika shrugged, the ankle-length wool coat she wore shifting with the motion. "A judge signed off on my services. It's not like I could say no."

"I know how that is."

"Let's get you and your companion to the body," Dabrowski said.

Anika glanced down at the psychopomp sitting politely by her feet. "Selene. Is the body onsite?"

"In our morgue."

"And the supplies I requested?"

"Waiting for you. The videographer arrived about two hours ago and finished setting up the camera."

"Excellent." Anika graced them both with a polite smile, her eyes crinkling at the corners. "Then let's go wake the dead."

The SOA's morgue in the basement reminded Patrick of the one at the PCB back in New York. The dead always had to be handled with care, and the wards embedded in the walls and floors of the morgue were different than the ones sunk into the building's foundation.

Anika brought her luggage with her, and Selene never left her side. Patrick kept pace behind the psychopomp. As a pug, it was cute and would probably go unnoticed to mundane humans for what it truly was—a spirit guide for the dead.

Psychopomps were rare and only appeared to people whose magic dealt with the dead. Patrick had only met one before this. Spencer Bailey was an old friend from the Mage Corps and a soulbreaker with an affinity for the dead. His psychopomp had taken the shape of an ocelot with an attitude.

The head medical examiner had come in on his day off to oversee the resurrection of the body found at the Westberg home. Dr. Aaron Sheehan was a reedy man in his early fifties, a warlock, and greeted Anika with a smile that didn't look forced.

"Thank you for your help with this matter, Special Agent Dandridge," Dr. Sheehan said.

"Of course," Anika said, slipping out of her wool coat and handing it to Dabrowski. "Is that the body?"

Patrick looked over at the corpse laid out on an exam table, white paint having been brushed over the burned skin. The sigils on the corpse's chest were there to keep the body from turning into a zombie and walking out of the building.

The videographer had set up in the corner, his camera aimed at the body. He had a visitor badge clipped to his suit jacket, a coffee cup by his feet, and looked a little nervous.

"We have, uh, the chicken?" Dr. Sheehan said.

He pointed at the cage sitting on the adjacent exam table. The chicken standing inside it blinked at them and fluttered its wings before pecking at the metal cage. It let out a loud squawk before going to the bathroom.

Anika nodded. "Yes, that will do. Let me get out my tools before we officially begin the session."

Patrick took up a position that put him outside the frame of the video camera. He didn't care if his name was on the record for this, but he didn't want his face anywhere viewable. He watched as Anika knelt and opened her luggage. Inside were the personal supplies she used to do her magic, nestled inside padded pockets and boxes secured in the luggage with a multitude of straps.

Magic was personal, and always would be. Necromancy was a mystery to Patrick, mostly because it was rarely performed. Messing with a person's soul, whether they were alive or dead, was illegal. Necromancy was restricted for a reason, not the least for the blood magic it involved.

He watched as Anika pulled out a marble mortar and pestle set, two vials of different-colored liquid, a packet of dried ingredients, a box of matches, and a sharp, clean machete, its blade etched with spellwork. She laid everything out at the foot of the exam table, then clucked her tongue at Selene.

"Please come here," she said.

Selene trotted over to her, and Anika leaned over to pick up the psychopomp. The pug settled between the burned feet of the corpse, tongue lolling out as she looked up at Anika. Anika absently pet the pug as she glanced over at the videographer.

Anika nodded at him. "I'm ready."

The videographer cleared his throat. "I'll count down to three and start the recording. I was given a list of names of attendees. Can I confirm everyone is here?"

He listed off everyone on his attendance list, and Patrick spoke up when his name was said. The videographer typed something into his laptop and then nodded.

He counted down to three and then went through his oral statement that dictated his name, the time, place, and who was in attendance. The case chosen for the record was the federal one regarding real property and the souls for rent payment. Patrick wasn't surprised about that choice. When the videographer fell silent, Anika retrieved the chicken, grabbing it from the cage with sure hands.

She tucked the body beneath her arm, held its head to stretch out its neck with one hand, and used the machete to slit its throat. She drained its blood into the mortar, just enough to cover the bottom, before depositing the carcass back in the cage.

Patrick watched as Anika wiped the machete with a clean towel before calmly placing it against the charred left knee of the body, carving downward over the tibia. Burned flesh broke off, curling over the blade. When she had six inches of blackened, dead flesh to work with, she used the machete to carry it to the mortar and place it into the mixture.

She added several drops from two of the vials, and all of the dry ingredients. Then she picked up the pestle and mortar to grind the burned skin into the blood mixture. As she did so, the morgue grew colder, and Patrick could see his breath puff out in front of his face after half a minute. Anika kept grinding the mixture down until it thickened. Then she set the pestle aside and took a match from the box, striking it. The fire flashed a deep blood red, and she dropped the match into the mortar.

The fire that flared up from the mixture was an eerie yellow.

Anika dipped her fingers into the mortar, unbothered by the fire. When she drew her hand back, her fingers were stained with blood that she used to draw a sigil on the corpse's chest, over-writing the ones already there.

A breeze blew through the workroom, and Patrick shivered. They were in the basement, with no windows. Anika's magic filled the space they stood in, and Patrick was glad for his shields.

"I, Anika Dandridge, call for the dead, in the name of the living," Anika said.

Selene stood, standing strangely still between the corpse's feet. The psychopomp's eyes had turned completely white, and every time it breathed, fog escaped its nose and mouth.

"I call for the spirit, whose flesh from bone anchors you to this plane. I summon the soul from its endless wandering." She lifted her hand from the corpse, bloodied fingers spread wide, and the body followed after her like a puppet with its strings held by its master. "Rise, the nameless dead."

It felt almost as if Patrick were walking through the veil between worlds, but the fog was restricted only to Selene, Anika, and the corpse. The pressure against Patrick's personal shields was that of a force trying to reclaim the dead that Anika had summoned with the help of her psychopomp.

Bits of burned flesh broke off as the corpse's arm bent, stiff fingers touching its charred chest and stiff face. Its mouth opened, and flakes of dried flesh fluttered to the exam table. The corpse's teeth had all been broken down to the gum line post-mortem, making identification from dental records impossible. Fire had eaten through all but a few strands of muscles on the face, and Patrick could see through the mouth cavity to the other side.

"Where am I?" the corpse asked, voice rough and ruined, coming out an echo, as if from a great distance.

"In the body you left behind for the other side. You will be here only for a moment." Anika looked at Patrick, her brown eyes glimmering with magic. "Ask your questions, one at a time."

"What is your name?" Patrick asked, because they needed an identity for the record as much as they needed to know who had killed him.

"I…" The corpse bent its neck, what skin was left over its vertebrae splitting over bone. "My name?"

"Your name when you lived for the record," Anika coaxed, magic in her voice, at her fingertips, her psychopomp a bridge for souls of the dead to cross over.

The corpse had no eyes, only hollow, burned-out sockets. Patrick stared at the blackened and ruined skull as the spirit of a dead man said, "My name is Dean Westberg."

Patrick turned and *ran*.

18

"You'd think the one time I need a god, they'd be fucking *listening* for me," Patrick snarled as he ran a yellow light. "Hermes, you bastard. Where the fuck are you?"

The sirens in the SUV rang shrilly in Jono's ears, mingling with the noise coming from his mobile. He wished he could turn the bloody thing off.

"Do the Norse have messenger gods?" Wade asked from the back seat of the SUV.

"Not one I'd trust."

"You don't trust any gods."

"Shut up and put your seat belt on. Remember what happened the last time you weren't wearing one?"

The click of Wade's seat belt was loud in the SUV. The sound of the call switching over to voicemail yet again made Jono grimace. "No one is picking up at the restaurant."

Patrick glanced over at him. "It's a private event tonight. I'm not surprised the phone is being ignored."

Jono put his mobile away. "Yeah."

The windshield wipers were running at top speed, but it wasn't fast enough to clear all the snow falling down on them. The reactionary storm had gotten worse, and the blizzard the SOA's weather witches had tried to keep at bay was now blowing at the shores of Lake Michigan. Driving was a constant fight with the wheel, snow, and traffic, though Patrick seemed to be handling it well enough.

"Fuck," Patrick growled as he gunned it through another yellow light changing to red rather than brake for it. "I'd even take those annoying ravens right now, so long as a god actually listened."

"No you wouldn't," Hermes said from the back seat.

Wade yelled in surprise, twisting against his seat belt and lashing out at the god who suddenly appeared beside him. Jono turned around in his seat in time to watch Hermes get smacked in the face by Wade's hand hard enough the god's head snapped back.

"Fuck," Hermes said, voice coming out muffled. "Watch your strength, fledgling."

"No, please, hit him again, Wade," Patrick said.

Hermes glared at Patrick as he realigned his nose that Wade had unintentionally broken. "Do you want my help or not?"

"It's not a question of *wanting* your help."

Hermes arched an eyebrow. "I can leave?"

Jono rolled his eyes and faced forward. "Wish you would, but we need your help, so stay sat."

Patrick white-knuckled the steering wheel and kept driving. Jono reached over to settle his hand on Patrick's thigh. Patrick was shielded so tightly Jono couldn't get any scent off the other man, and he didn't like that.

"The SOA is investigating a local politician. We found a body in one of his homes, but it turns out the dead guy is actually the politician. Someone has been impersonating him, probably since last week. Whoever it is has a fundraiser going on right now they refused to cancel," Patrick said.

"Sounds like a party," Hermes said.

"Odin is *missing*, Hermes. Ethan did fuck knows what to

Hannah. Westberg's campaign manager is most likely Hel, and the person taking Odin's spot to receive tithes tonight is Thor. Someone needs to warn him and Frigg that they're probably the next targets."

"You mortals invented phones for a reason."

"Oh, fuck you. I would've called, but *I don't have their numbers*, and no one is picking up at the restaurant. Now be a good messenger god and go *warn* them."

Hermes shook his head, dyed curls flopping against his forehead. Jono never took his eyes off the god in the rearview mirror. "Wish I could, but the veil isn't where any of us want to be right now."

Jono felt the way Patrick's muscles tightened beneath his fingertips. Jono looked over his shoulder at Hermes and tried not to scowl. "What the bloody fuck do you mean by that?"

Hermes leaned forward, glancing at Jono before meeting Patrick's gaze in the rearview mirror. "It took me hours to get here to you when it shouldn't have."

"Why?" Patrick demanded.

"Because another realm is pushing at the veil, trying to break through, and it is not any ruled over by my pantheon."

"Ethan performed a fertility rite, not a sacrifice. There's been no sightings of soultakers in Chicago."

"Yes, but how many souls has Odin accepted as payment over the years for mortals to do business in his home away from home?"

Jono dug his fingers into Patrick's thigh. "Drive faster, Pat."

"Mother*fucker*," Patrick ground out and pressed on the gas.

Driving in the snow above the speed limit was always a risk, but maybe the Fates were looking out for them tonight. The SUV only skidded out of the lane twice, and Patrick managed to get the vehicle under control every time without injuring anyone else on the road. The lights and sirens on the SUV cleared them a path, but the way forward wasn't easy.

The reactionary storm had finally, fully made it to shore. Snow was dropping furiously all over the city. Jono wouldn't be surprised if whiteout conditions happened within the next half hour. All that mattered was that they got to Au Hall before visibility dropped to zero.

Patrick was focused on the road, the snow swirling in front of them dipping through the flashing colors of the SUV's emergency lights. Jono didn't try to draw him into conversation, but that changed when they drove across a bridge spanning the Chicago River. Jono didn't expect Wade to frantically smack them both on the shoulder.

"There's something in the water," Wade said.

Jono craned his head around, trying to peer through the snow beyond the window. He looked at Wade, who almost had his face pressed up against the fogged window.

"How the hell can you see anything in this weather?" Patrick wanted to know.

"I, uh, can feel it? It's big."

"Kid can sniff out gods," Jono reminded him, still squinting through the snow.

"The kid is right," Hermes said.

Wade scowled at Jono and Hermes, his brown eyes gold with reptilian slit pupils. "I'm not a kid."

"Hide your eyes, Wade," Patrick said. "Whatever is in the river can wait."

Jono wasn't so sure about that, but Patrick was in charge at the moment. Right now their priority was getting to Au Hall. If a monster was in the river, they'd deal with it after they saved Thor and found Odin.

They drove off the bridge, and Wade settled back down in his seat. No one spoke as Patrick maneuvered them through city streets, aiming for the stretch of road running parallel to Grant Park. When he finally turned onto South Michigan Avenue, the steering wheel slipped through his grip from the howling wind that slammed into the vehicle. Jono grabbed it and held it steady until Patrick got a better grip and straightened out the SUV.

"Thanks," Patrick muttered.

Jono let the steering wheel go. "'Course, love."

They'd left the wall of skyscrapers and its steel buffer behind them. The ferocity of the reactionary storm blew across the open shores of Lake Michigan with a roar that almost drowned out the SUV's sirens.

"If we have to fight in this, I'm going to freeze," Wade said.

"What do you mean *if*?" Patrick asked.

A single bright headlight flashed across the rearview mirror before disappearing. It was replaced by another, and being almost boxed in made Jono tense. A mageglobe flared into existence near Patrick's elbow, and Jono shifted claws out of his fingertips. The roar of a motorcycle cut through the storm, and Jono flexed his fingers. Jono tracked the shadow as the dark shape on Patrick's side of the road pulled up alongside the SUV.

"That's Brynhildr and Dynfari," Wade said, sounding excited. "And Eir!"

Jono forced his claws back, leaving his hands human-shaped for the moment. The valkyries followed them up the street as far as they could go until they hit a police blockade at the intersection near Au Hall. Patrick turned and pulled over to the curb. He killed the engine and tossed the keys in the glove compartment. The lights and sirens switched off, but the roar of the wind never faltered.

"Ready?" Jono asked, fingers curling over the door handle.

Patrick nodded. "Let's go."

Jono shoved open the SUV door and stepped out into freezing cold. Despite always running hot, the cold stung his skin. Brynhildr and Eir jumped the curb and pulled up onto the sidewalk. Jono rounded the SUV and helped Patrick get his door open so he could get out.

Both valkyries raised the visors on their helmets, Patrick's mageglobe washing pale blue light over their eyes and the grim expressions on their faces.

"We've been searching for you," Brynhildr practically yelled to be heard over the wind. "We can't reach Thor."

Jono closed Patrick's door once he was out of the way. Wade and Hermes had made it out of the SUV and onto the sidewalk. Jono had to grab Wade by the collar of his sweater and hold him back when the teenager would've gone to greet the valkyries.

"The SOA's necromancer raised the dead today. Body we found was Dean Westberg. Someone's been impersonating him since probably last week," Patrick said.

Eir turned her head, staring at Hermes. "Cousin. What are you doing here? You've never cared for Chicago."

Hermes wasn't dressed for the weather, but the cold didn't seem to bother him. "I've never cared for the bridges your pantheon builds to the other side. You've misplaced a hole in New York City. Feel free to take it back."

"Ginnungagap goes where it likes," Brynhildr said.

"I thought Lucien made a deal over that void?" Patrick asked.

Brynhildr shrugged. "His mother did."

"With Odin?"

"With Ginnungagap."

Patrick hunched his shoulders against the wind and started walking. "Hermes said the veil feels off."

Brynhildr swung herself off the motorcycle, not bothering with the kickstand, and took off her helmet. The motorcycle revved its engine, and she patted one of the handlebars before leaving it behind. "We cannot cross it."

"Is that normal?" Jono asked, practically shouting to be heard.

"Crossing the veil is always difficult these days, but something else fills it along the shores here."

"There was something in the river," Wade said.

"Chicago shares the edge of the world with Lake Michigan."

"It's a *lake*," Patrick said, lengthening his stride. "Not the damn Marianas Trench."

"This is no ordinary storm, and what is building in it is no ordinary pressure," Eir said.

"Fuck all you gods and your damn wars. If Chicago is ground zero for your Ragnarök, then I'm not getting a bonus this year because the government will pay for the property damage out of my paycheck."

"We have tithes," Jono reminded him.

"Shut up and let's go crash a party."

They were stopped at the entrance to Au Hall by someone who must have been hired to work the event. She was so bundled up that all Jono could really see was her eyes. "Private event. I need to see your invite."

Patrick unclipped his badge from his belt and held it up for her to see. "Special Agent Patrick Collins with the SOA. Step aside."

Her eyes widened and she hesitated, but gave ground when Brynhildr pushed past her with a confidence that could not be ignored. Brynhildr made it to the door—but that was as far as she got. The moment she touched the door handle, Brynhildr was thrown backward by a surge of magic.

Jono moved so fast the wind whistled in his ears, catching Brynhildr before she could hit the street. He grunted, feet sliding in the snow as he went down to one knee from her weight and the force of impact. He looked down at her fiercely angry face, tasting ozone in the back of his throat.

"All right, love?" Jono asked as he helped her back to her feet.

She looked down at her burned and blackened hands, strips of skin peeled off and hanging from the sides of her palms. The remains of her gloves hung from her wrists, half of the leather burned away. Then Eir was there, grabbing Brynhildr's wrists to get a good look at the wounds.

"Hold still," Eir said tersely.

She covered Brynhildr's hands with her own. Silvery magic

flickered at the edges of their joined hands for a couple of seconds. When Eir pulled her hands away, Brynhildr's were completely healed.

Brynhildr yanked the remnants of her gloves off. "That spell is god-made and not one that has ever lived in the walls of Au Hall."

"Hel?" Patrick asked.

Brynhildr grimaced. "I am not sure."

Patrick pulled his dagger free and flipped it to get a better grip on the hilt. "Right. Hermes is useless right now, but I'm betting you can call your sisters."

"Fuck you, too, Pattycakes," Hermes said, busy sending the woman who'd been guarding the door away with a push of godly suggestion.

Eir pulled out her cell phone and unlocked it, the screen bright even through the swirling snow. "On it."

Jono only half listened to Eir as she called one of her valkyrie sisters. He approached where Patrick and Wade stood near the door. The front windows of the restaurant were covered with cloth shades, more to keep the attendees from view than it was to hide the weather. The solid wooden door was the only way in, and Jono's skin itched from the hellish magic emanating from it.

"Hel might be inside. She was with Westberg, or whoever it is, all this week," Patrick said.

"Maybe she was the one controlling whoever took Westberg's place," Jono said.

"Or *whatev*er. They felt human every time I interacted with the guy."

"That means nothing," Brynhildr said from behind them.

"Yeah." Patrick raised the dagger, pressing the point of the blade against the center of the door. Magic burned and sparked from the touch, casting a malevolent, sickly color over the matte-black blade. "Get ready."

Jono watched as Patrick leaned his entire bodyweight against his grip to pierce the encasement spell wrapped around Au Hall.

White heavenly fire flared up around the dagger that burned bright. The spell wasn't strong enough to stand against hundreds of prayers from all the gods of heaven, and it disintegrated with a crackling hiss. Magic peeled away from the door with a rainbow flash of color.

"Clear?" Jono asked.

"Yeah," Patrick said.

Jono reached for the handle and yanked it up, breaking the lock and shoving it open with preternatural strength. They stepped inside the restaurant, a blast of warm air hitting them all at once. Jono's nose twitched with the stink of expensive perfume, cologne, and the sweat of way too many people in too warm of a place.

A woman standing in the hostess area to greet new arrivals froze when she caught sight of them before rallying. "Au Hall is closed tonight for a private event. I'll need to ask you to leave."

Patrick held up his badge again, not even looking at her. "This is my invitation."

He walked past her and into the restaurant proper, Au Hall packed with people despite the reactionary snowstorm raging outside. Jono stayed right by Patrick's side, scanning the crowded restaurant. He wondered how many of the people who had bought seats for the fundraiser dinner had done so because they had no choice.

Classical music poured from the surround sound speakers, white noise beneath the chatter of conversation. Dinner guests mingled between tables if they weren't already seated. Everyone was dressed for a black-tie affair, and Jono would've felt under-dressed if he gave a damn.

"Do you see Thor?" Patrick asked, keeping his right hand angled behind his hip to hide his dagger.

Jono scanned the first floor but couldn't see the god. "No."

"Then let's go upstairs."

"Do you have a plan for when we find him and whoever is playing at being Westberg?"

"Adrenaline and hope for the best."

Wade snorted. "That's not a plan."

"It's a Patrick plan," Jono muttered.

A set of stairs along the wall led up to a balcony area that would've offered up a fantastic view of Grant Park and Lake Michigan on a clear day. Jono took the steps two at a time, keeping pace with Patrick. He ignored the heads turning to watch them and the way conversation became muted below.

The commotion their group was causing by barging in on the fundraiser unannounced caught the attention of whatever was impersonating Westberg once they reached the landing. The balcony wasn't as crowded—probably reserved for high-dollar donors—most of whom looked annoyed at their arrival.

Half the guests up there were seated at their dinner tables. Others mingled in small groups. Jono caught sight of Thor immediately, the god towering over everyone else around him. The man standing next to Thor who wore Westberg's skin locked eyes with Jono. Whoever it was didn't hesitate to turn toward Thor—and run the god through with a wooden spear that flashed into existence in his hands.

"*No!*" Brynhildr yelled.

"That's Gungnir, Odin's spear," Eir snarled, shoving past Jono. "The Allfather would never willingly give it up."

Silence reigned for a handful of seconds, the length of time it took for Thor to fall to his knees, obscured by the tables and people between them. Then everyone started screaming. Guests lurched away from the tables, clogging the narrow path between chairs, rushing for the stairs.

Patrick swore and raced after the two valkyries. Jono went after him. Patrick didn't care about manners or niceties, and neither did Jono. They shoved aside anyone who got in their way, intent on making it to where Thor had fallen.

Then the crowd parted, tables flipping over as Patrick used magic to clear them a path across the balcony space. Plates and drinks went flying, sending food and alcohol into the panicking crowd around them. Brynhildr and Eir were golden blurs to Jono's eyes, but they still weren't quick enough to stop the man impersonating Westberg from planting his foot on Thor's back and yanking free Odin's spear.

A spray of blood arched away from Thor, splattering the imposter's face. Jono thought it was the smear of red that blurred his features—but then his face kept changing. The features shifted like so much clay, reforming into a sharply featured face that looked nothing like Westberg. Light brown hair framed eyes the color of rich earth, and the smile on his face was as cold as the snowstorm raging outside.

Brynhildr touched her throat, her hand coming away with a spear that grew in size. "*Loki.* You have given your last betrayal."

"I think not," the Norse trickster god said with a fierce grin.

He spun Gungnir in his hands before swinging it around to block Brynhildr's blow from her spear. The clash of the weapons made the air vibrate, bits of lightning sparking at the tip of Gungnir.

"That can't be good," Wade said from behind them, sounding a little scared.

Eir launched herself at Loki while Patrick dove for Thor. Jono swore, sticking with Patrick. The flash of Gungnir as Loki spun it had Jono launching himself at Patrick, taking his lover and Thor down to the floor as Odin's spear let out a crackling bolt of lightning. It cut through the air in a split second, making every light bulb in the chandeliers hanging from the ceiling explode. The restaurant was plunged into a twilight darkness, only the recessed lighting high in the ceiling surviving.

Loki swept the spear in an arc around him, forcing Brynhildr and Eir back onto the defensive. Jono rolled off Patrick, hands smearing in blood that had splattered onto the floor.

"Eir!" Patrick yelled, his voice high and frantic as he pressed his hands over the hole in Thor's chest. "*Eir!*"

The god of thunder wasn't moving.

Let me in.

Fenrir's voice roared through Jono's mind, and he didn't fight it. For once, he let the wave of power drag him under without searching for the surface and fighting control. Fenrir sank into his body and soul, and Jono shifted from man to wolf so fast that he *felt* the pain of the shift this time—raw and furious, like he'd been skinned alive down to his bones.

When Fenrir finally settled on all fours and blinked, it was with Jono's eyes, and Loki was looking right at them. The glittering point of Gungnir was aimed their way, Loki's hard smile a sliver of white behind the spark of lightning.

"You are no son of mine, Fenrir," Loki said.

"*Your faith is a lie, Father,*" Fenrir ground out around the wolf fangs in Jono's mouth.

"Faith is all we have when our stories are not enough."

The floor-to-ceiling windows behind Loki exploded inward, shredding the shades and turning glass shards into shrapnel. Pale blue light enveloped them in a shield—Patrick's magic keeping them safe amidst the storm. The glass shards bounced off the barrier, but everyone else wasn't so lucky.

Beyond Patrick's magic, Jono watched alongside Fenrir as Loki pitched himself into the snow beyond Au Hall, his laughter swallowed by the reactionary storm. Brynhildr threw herself after him with a wild cry that made Jono want to lay his ears flat against his skull. Lightning flashed in the distance, followed by thunder so close it shook the building.

Shook the ground.

The air pressure dropped so suddenly Jono's ears popped even in wolf form. The howling wind changed cadence in such a way that Jono wanted to run from it—because that wasn't the wind anymore.

Nature didn't sound like the dead were screaming.

"*Eir!*" Patrick yelled.

The other valkyrie rocked to a halt halfway to the windows, her hands white-knuckling her spear. Then she swore, spinning on her feet. She returned to them, and Patrick lowered his shields just enough to let her through.

Let me see, Jono demanded.

Fenrir obligingly turned his head, and Jono stared at where Patrick kneeled beside Thor, both hands slick with blood, while Wade hovered over them. Eir folded to her knees beside them, face a stone mask in the low light.

"The veil is tearing," Eir said as she pushed Patrick's hands aside. Jono watched as she dug her fingers into the ragged, gaping hole in Thor's chest, her words ringing like a death knell between them all. "Niflheim is coming home to rest at the roots of the world tree."

19

One of Patrick's hands was covered in Thor's blood. Patrick clutched his dagger in the other. He still almost shot Huginn and Muninn out of the air with a mageglobe when Odin's ravens came flying through the shattered windows. The pair didn't stop to aid them; instead they dived at the people on the stairs, their sharp beaks pecking at people's skulls.

"What the hell are they doing?" Wade asked, hands curled over his head as if to protect himself. "Are they hungry?"

"For memories. They'll take the thoughts and memories of what happened here tonight, and no one will be the wiser," Eir said, white magic covering her fingers so bright Patrick couldn't see them.

More blood gushed through Patrick's fingers from the hole in Thor's chest. "Forgetting isn't going to fix this mess. You said that's *Niflheim* coming to shore?"

The Norse realm of the dead was a threat no city or country could ever be prepared for. Patrick could fight the Dominion Sect with what power he had on hand until reinforcements arrived, but he sure as fuck couldn't fight an entire hell without an army.

Eir never took her eyes off Thor and the wound she was healing. "The Dominion Sect must have taken the tithes owed to Odin to break the veil. That is over a century's worth of souls."

Which meant it was maybe enough power to cause the end of the world.

"I'm not getting my yearly bonus," Patrick said, lifting his hand out of the way of Eir's so she had space to work. "You brought a hell to Chicago, and I know I joked about scratching the Bean, but I didn't mean like *this*."

Thor suddenly heaved beneath Eir's hands, spitting up blood. Patrick grabbed him by the shoulder and turned the god onto his side so Thor could better clear his airway. It gave Eir room to work on the wound in Thor's back.

"The veil can still be closed," she said.

"How?"

"*How else but by sacrifice?*" Fenrir said through Jono's wolf form.

Eir glanced at Fenrir, her stormy eyes shining with magic. "Not with Thor and not with Odin. Not with any of us, wolf. This will not be our Ragnarök."

"*I have not tasted Odin's blood in an age, valkyrie. Perhaps it is time.*"

Eir moved so fast Patrick had no time to react. She spun her spear until the point came to rest right between Jono's wolf-bright blue eyes. The spear never wavered even as she poured all her magic into Thor to heal him with her other hand.

"You will not taste it here."

Fenrir moved his head and licked the spear point. "*There is a price for everything. That has never changed.*"

"No one is paying anyone anything until we know what the *fuck* is going on," Patrick snapped.

"Uh," Wade said, staring through Patrick's shield in the direction of the broken windows. "Is that supposed to be there?"

Patrick followed where he pointed, squinting at the pillar of light that burned bright even through the snow. It hadn't been there earlier, and its presence didn't promise anything good. Within the light was a twisted shape growing and reaching for the sky with impossible branches, hints of eternity blooming between its sprouting leaves.

"It is Yggdrasil," Thor said in a voice that sounded as if he'd swallowed nails. He got one arm underneath him and shoved himself up, blinking rapidly. "It is the world tree."

The living connection that tied the Nine Realms together ruled over by the Norse gods, a myth that wasn't so forgotten if it was digging its roots deep into the earth of Millennium Park.

"Fucking great," Patrick said.

"Careful," Eir warned, her hand hovering over the barely closed wound in Thor's back. "I am not done healing you."

Thor grunted as he sat up. "I am well enough to fight. Thank you, Eir."

Patrick eyed Thor's blood-soaked button-down that had been white before Loki stabbed him in the back. "Sure you are."

A wound from a magical spear wasn't enough to keep a god down. Thor got to his feet, stripped out of his suit jacket, and ripped the remains of his dress shirt off. Blood-streaked skin came into sight, the wound from the spear a slash of pink on his chest and back.

Thor punched the air in front of him, and ball lightning erupted around his hand. Thunder ripped through Au Hall, the crackling burn of electricity so close it would've singed Patrick's hair if he hadn't scrambled to put some distance between them. Thor pulled Mjölnir from the ball lightning, gripping the hammer with bloodied fingers.

Thor's blue eyes were washed out to white, electricity crackling around him as he stared at the beacon that was the world tree. "They have taken the tithes."

"You gods need to get your shit together." Patrick stood and shoved his dagger into its sheath before lowering his shield. He flinched away from the icy, howling wind that slammed into them now that he'd drawn down his defensive magic. "Chicago wouldn't be under attack if Odin hadn't been so fucking greedy."

"We have a right to live."

"Not at the expense of *our* world."

"This is how any story is made. By the destruction of another."

"Yeah? You and the rest of the goddamn Æsir can go fuck yourselves."

Thor didn't respond to that. He merely turned his back on Patrick and ran for the edge of the building, throwing himself off it. Mjölnir was an arc of brightness that followed him down to the street. Fenrir snapped his teeth before racing after the god of thunder, the fall to earth easy to overcome for the wolf god. Patrick had to bite his tongue to keep from calling Jono back—because that wasn't Jono in control.

"What are we going to do?" Wade asked.

Patrick grabbed him by the arm and hauled him toward the stairs. "I'm going to fight. You in or not?"

"What kind of dumbass question is that?"

"It's a question, because I'm not going to force you to fight."

Wade gave him a stubborn look before beating Patrick down the stairs. "I'm not letting you fight alone. Pack doesn't do that."

Wade used his strength to shove people aside without apology, making them a path to the exit. Patrick saw jewelry, money clips, and a couple of wallets find their way into Wade's jacket pockets. He didn't have the time to argue with Wade about stealing when they were heading into a fight. It wasn't like he could pickpocket everyone at the fundraiser.

The door they'd come in was a bottleneck. Patrick grabbed Wade by the collar of his jacket and hauled him toward the broken windows. The shades had been shredded, and people were lying on the floor or slumped over tables with shards of glass protruding from their bodies.

They couldn't stop to help and kept running. Patrick and Wade vaulted the bottom of the window frame, and Patrick nearly lost his footing when he landed on the other side. His boots skidded over icy, snow-covered cement, but he managed to stay upright.

The deep revving of a motorcycle cut through the howling wind as a lone headlight shone through the dark. The motorcycle drove down the sidewalk on its own, back wheel skidding to the side so it faced Millennium Park rather than Au Hall.

"That's Töfrandi," Wade said.

Before Patrick could open his mouth and forbid Wade from going on a joyride, Eir landed beside them on the sidewalk, having thrown herself out the second-story window. Snow blew away from her landing, and she straightened up, spear still in hand. Patrick half ducked when Muninn and Huginn flew out of Au Hall over their heads and disappeared into the swirling snow.

Patrick hadn't seen any of the police who'd been monitoring the street barrier. He knew other SOA agents would be arriving soon because the Westberg mess wasn't one he could hide. Dabrowski had been there in the morgue, and the last call Patrick had taken before he'd opted to ignore his phone was from the SAIC announcing he was sending out a Rapid Response Team to deal with whatever had taken Westberg's place. Patrick hadn't been able to pull rank, and Setsuna couldn't tell a SAIC to stand down, not when this shit had happened.

"We must get to the others," Eir said.

Patrick eyed the motorcycle, decided it wasn't big enough for three people, and said, "Wade? Head for the park and shift."

"I'm gonna freeze my nuts off," Wade protested.

"You're a fire dragon. You'll be fine. Now get out there and shift, then find us."

Eir had already slung herself over the Harley Davidson, helmet nowhere to be seen. She gestured to the seat behind her. "Get on, Patrick."

"How come you get to ride Töfrandi and I don't?" Wade demanded.

"Because I'm not a dragon who can fly," Patrick retorted.

Wade muttered something under his breath Patrick couldn't hear through the wind before he ran across the street, red scales pushing up through the skin on the back of his neck.

Patrick hoped he'd catch up soon. He had a feeling they'd need some dragon flame for the fight ahead. He straddled the motorcycle, and the second he was settled behind Eir, Patrick found himself seeing the world through a complex glamour.

For all that the valkyries rode motorcycles, the machines were winged horses beneath the projection of metal frames. Töfrandi was dove gray, mane and tail braided for war, and the stallion had large feathered wings that protruded outward from his body. His leather-and-metal body armor was etched with runes that helped keep the glamour in place and others Patrick thought might be for protection.

The pegasus tossed his head, and Eir gathered up the reins with one hand. Töfrandi had no bit in his mouth, so Patrick assumed the reins were for the rider more than the pegasus.

"Let's ride," Eir said.

Patrick held on tight to Eir as Töfrandi took off, racing across the street and heading for Millennium Park. The pegasus didn't bother with park paths and barreled forward over the snow. He didn't try to fly, the wind too strong at the moment to make an aerial assault a safe form of attack.

Wade had no problem with the wind.

His fledgling fire dragon form was a little bigger every month he put behind him these days. He still had years of growing ahead of him from what General Reed had hinted at, but Wade was doing fine so far now that he had consistent care. Wade's burnished red scales reflected the light coming from Yggdrasil deeper in the park when he joined up with them. The fire he breathed at the ground ahead of them revealed a pack of hellhounds racing their way.

"Keep going," Patrick yelled as he freed one hand to conjure up a mageglobe.

He filled it and the three others he formed with attack spells, leaning hard into the soulbond that tied him to Jono. Patrick reached for the ley lines running beneath Chicago, his magic anchored by Jono's soul. Metaphysical power poured into him through the soulbond, powering his spells with a strength he couldn't achieve on his own.

Patrick sent the mageglobes spinning away from them in a defensive spiral. The magical grenades crashed into the hellhounds seeking to surround them. The ones Wade didn't incinerate were blown apart or blown backward by Patrick's attack, depending on how close they were to the impact site.

The winter landscape of the park was barren, almost impossible to see anything through the snow and wind. Patrick's heat charms in his leather jacket and clothes weren't enough against a cold driven by a hell.

Wade let out a furious roar followed by a burst of fire that highlighted his wedge head and long neck. More hellhounds were burned by dragon flame, clearing them a path farther into Millennium Park.

Lightning crashed from the storm clouds to earth somewhere up ahead, and more followed.

"I think that's Thor!" Patrick yelled.

Eir said nothing, and Töfrandi's hooves ate up snowy ground. They passed a line of snow-covered, leafless trees and entered a courtyard with no cover. Wade watched their six, focusing on the hellhounds. Beyond the courtyard was a large pavilion whose metal latticework covering crackled with electricity drawn from lightning hits.

They cleared the courtyard and were about to enter the pavilion area when Töfrandi abruptly reared up on his hind legs. Patrick was holding on to Eir by one hand but still lost his balance. He let her go rather than drag her with him. Patrick went flying, landing on his back in snow that cushioned his fall, but not by much. Snow slid beneath his shirt, freezing his skin before it melted.

Patrick scrambled to his feet, calling up a handful of mage-globes. Outside the glamour, Patrick could no longer see Töfrandi's true form. The front wheel of the motorcycle slammed back to the ground as Eir spun her spear to ward off the latest threat.

The motorcycle drove backward to dodge the snakelike tail that whipped over three heads. Cerberus' thick legs ended in monstrous claws that supported a barrel-chested body larger than the motorcycle. Blackened teeth in three mouths snapped at them, all three pairs of eyes on the valkyrie and her steed.

Patrick yanked his dagger free, white heavenly fire burning around the matte-black blade. "Eir!"

She was too close for him to cast a strike spell, so Patrick went with a blast of raw magic, pulling power from the ley lines. He didn't know where Jono was, but the other man was close enough that Patrick had no problem drawing on external magic.

That didn't mean he had enough strength to challenge a god.

Hellfire streaked toward him, melting snow during its passage. Patrick ripped his shields free, expanding them outward. They took the hit and his feet skidded over snow from the impact, bones aching from the force of it.

Hellfire dripped away from Hades' hand as the god came forward through the blowing snow. "Let's not interfere, shall we?"

"You know me," Patrick ground out. "I live to piss people off."

In the distance, Yggdrasil's branches were stretching beyond the pillar of light, shining with power. The ground jerked, rolling as if an earthquake had hit.

I hope all those brick houses don't come tumbling down.

Hades smiled, his sharp-featured face cast in shadow from hellfire light. He opened his mouth to speak, but a bone-chilling howl cut through the wind, wiping the smile off Hades' face.

A dark shape streaked through the snow, bright blue eyes burning with white fire. Jono's wolf form charged at Cerberus, Fenrir's immortal control in every inch of his body. Cerberus howled a challenge with all three heads, but Fenrir never wavered.

Jono's werewolf form might be larger than the average werecreature, but he was dwarfed by Cerberus. It reminded Patrick of their fight at Inwood Hill Park last June, only this time Fenrir wasn't hiding.

Cerberus might be immortal, but he was no god, and Fenrir went for all three throats with fangs and claws.

Hades thrust his hand at Fenrir, hellfire streaking through the air. Patrick split his shields, trying to protect Jono, but defensive magic was never where his strength had ever lay. Hades' attack crashed through his shield, the hit reverberating through Patrick's soul hard enough he fell to one knee.

He reformed his shields around himself, heart pounding in his chest as he sought to get eyes on Jono. All he could see was flashes of dark fur in what dim light the park lamps gave off around them through the snowstorm.

Red eyes came into view around them—hellhounds closing in. Eir was forced to split her attention between Hades and the hellhounds that went after Töfrandi. Patrick lashed out with a mageglobe, running toward Eir.

He never made it.

The world lit up like the after image of a nuclear blast, lightning crashing down to earth between them and Hades. Patrick's shields burned with a heavenly power not of this earth as he was thrown to the ground once more. Eyes watering, Patrick squinted at the sky, sheet lightning making the clouds pulse with brightness.

Great feathered wings the color of a storm shadowed the sky directly above them, lightning crackling along the shape of them as Hinon left heaven for earth. The Haudenosaunee thunder god crashed to the ground between them, his eyes burning like the sun, lightning trailing his pinion feathers and clenched tight in his hands.

"Hello, cousin," Hinon said, voice echoing like thunder.

Hades turned his attention from Fenrir to Hinon and let hellfire fly.

Patrick scrambled out of the way, running away from the clash of gods as he tried to make it back to Eir. The valkyrie's spear was coated in blood, and bodies of hellhounds surrounded Töfrandi. Snow spun up from the wheels as she drove toward him, one arm outstretched for his. Patrick grasped her wrist, and he was flung over the seat with bruising strength. He passed through the glamour, finding himself astride the pegasus once again.

"Hold fast!" Eir shouted.

Patrick wrapped his arms around her waist and squeezed his knees into Töfrandi's body. The pegasus launched into the sky with a powerful flap of his wings and a gravity-defying push of his hind legs.

They were airborne, in a reactionary storm that did its best to knock them back down to earth.

Töfrandi flew, buffeted by strong winds, but whatever magic lived in the immortal's body gave the pegasus enough strength to fight the headwinds. They passed low over a stretch of road that bisected the park. Patrick could make out one or two cars stalled there and hoped no one had been killed considering they had hellhounds running amok.

He looked over Eir's shoulder at where Yggdrasil had torn through the veil. The sky above the world tree's reaching branches was clear, like the eye in a hurricane. On the ground below, Patrick could make out flashes of lightning as Thor tore his way through the enemy, intent on reaching Yggdrasil. He could see, too, the spell the Dominion Sect had drawn over the earth to call forth Niflheim.

Bolts of raw magic cut through the air like anti-aircraft missiles. Töfrandi banked hard, wings pumping fast to try to gain altitude. Eir let out a furious war cry as Töfrandi rose into the storm, getting out of range. Patrick blinked snow out of his eyes, fingers numb where they held on to Eir.

"We need to get down there!" Patrick yelled.

Eir didn't respond, guiding Töfrandi with her hands and knees through the sky as wind, snow, and lightning ripped through the air around them. Patrick hated flying through clouds. He couldn't see anything, and not knowing when or where a threat was coming from made his heart pound in his chest.

It felt like forever before Töfrandi broke free of the clouds again, diving down over the shores of Lake Michigan. The Chicago skyline was to the left of them, and the vast blackness of Lake Michigan was to their right. Directly below Töfrandi's hooves was a shore of corpses as far as the eye could see in the snowstorm.

Patrick pointed at the writhing mass of the dead and the scattered bits of the veil tearing between them. "You want to explain that?"

Eir peered at the ground, spear held tight in one hand. "Hel has brought forth Náströnd out of Niflheim."

Just what they needed—the leading edge of Hel crashing into Chicago, full of the damned and ready to fight. "We need to stop her!"

"We must save the Allfather first."

Honestly, Patrick would let the greedy bastard rot if it meant Chicago would survive. Since that wasn't a guarantee, he was back at square one.

Saving the gods because they couldn't save themselves.

Still don't get paid enough for this bullshit.

The dark waters of Lake Michigan were broken by something darker and larger breaching the surface before diving back under. The dead at the shoreline didn't seem to notice or care that some of them were turning out to be dinner for a lake monster.

Something clawed at the back of Patrick's mind, but he lost the thought when another pegasus dropped out of the clouds to their left, a valkyrie astride it with spear in hand. More and more valkyries slipped free of the clouds to flank Eir on their dive toward Yggdrasil and the shadow Patrick could see hanging from its glowing branches.

All the stories Patrick knew of Odin's making flashed through his mind—of the knowledge gained from sacrifice, an eye lost forever, and the right to rule engrained forever in his myth.

But the Æsir had lost their presence on Earth, and Midgard had turned into something different and more modern, shaking free of the world tree into its own tale.

Yet here Yggdrasil grew, with Niflheim clawing at its roots, the veil torn between two worlds in a way it never should have.

Odin might hang from its branches once more, but it was the person who had tied the noose they needed to stop.

As the valkyries dove toward earth, something buried deep in Patrick's soul tugged hard, and he knew—he *knew*—what waited for them on the ground.

Hannah.

20

"Oh shit, oh shit, oh shit!" Patrick chanted as Töfrandi dodged ground-to-air blasts of magic that seared the swirling snow around them.

"Hold on!" Eir shouted.

"Like I'm going to let go?"

Patrick's yell was whipped away by the wind, the snow-covered ground rising up to meet them—and with it, Hel.

The goddess of death welcomed their approach with open arms and the ranks of Dominion Sect magic users taking aim at the valkyries. Her braided white hair whipped away from her face in the wind, and the power surrounding her was a malevolent force pulling at the corpses on the shore. Patrick knew his shields wouldn't be enough to counter the combined magic rising up to meet them.

Wade, however, had no problem with that.

He came up from the other side of Yggdrasil, mouth open wide and dragon fire pouring out of his throat. The high heat seared past a huge, gnarled root of the world tree before burning through the rear ranks of the magic users. Wade wiped them all out, but the root remained whole.

And Hel, well, she was an entirely different and difficult problem Wade had no hope of dealing with alone despite his resistance to magic. Luckily, he had air support coming in.

"I'm getting off," Patrick shouted. "Keep Hel away from me."

There were more gods than just Hel on the battlefield, but Patrick knew how to fight a multifront war. The ground rushed up to meet them, and Patrick pitched himself off Töfrandi, dagger in hand, mageglobes filled with magic, and the soulbond humming between him and Jono, wherever Jono might be on the battlefield.

Patrick let loose a shock wave spell that sent half a dozen Dominion Sect magic users flying off their feet. Patrick kept his soul open to the soulbond, channeling external magic as if his life depended on it—because it did.

And so did Odin's.

Patrick hit the ground and rolled with the impact. He crashed against a root, which was fine because it provided enough cover for the second it took to get his bearings. Then Patrick came up swinging, throwing combat magic at the enemy, holding on to his dagger with fingers that still had Thor's dried blood on them.

It was warm between Yggdrasil's roots, and the branches seemed impossibly high overhead. As Patrick looked up at where Odin hung from the branches, all he could see was the vastness of space between each leaf, and all the stars of the universe cradled there in a rainbow of colors. He could've drowned in it, and would have if Heimdallr didn't cover his eyes.

"That bridge is not yours to see," the god growled into his ear.

Patrick jerked away, lowering his gaze to the ground so he didn't lose himself. "Where the fuck have you been?"

Heimdallr swung his sword around in time to behead a hellhound trying to sneak up on them. "Searching for the Allfather, like you."

"With your eyes, I figured you would've found him before they strung him up."

"The Fates on every side all play a wicked game of blindness." Heimdallr's gold teeth were a flash in his mouth when he smiled. "Your wolf sleeps and Fenrir rides his skin. Keep that one away from the Allfather."

The pull in the soulbond told Patrick that Jono was close—and the deeper, thinner connection tangled up in everything else was a warning he couldn't ignore.

"My sister is closing in. We need to get Odin cut down *now*."

Heimdallr's gaze flickered over Patrick's shoulder, mouth tightening into a grim line. "Hel is coming. Go. I will cover you."

Patrick spared a glance behind him in time to see the goddess rounding the massive trunk of the world tree. She'd foregone the suit in favor of an evening gown, probably for the fundraiser dinner, but had kicked off her heels at some point. Hel had shed whatever glamour kept people from looking too closely at her human face. Her face was young-looking, but her body was old, skin wrinkled and bruised rotten in places.

The wind blowing over them brought the smell of death, and Patrick knew they were running out of time.

Heimdallr moved past him, the god's aura blazing, and Patrick turned away to save his eyes. He looked up at the distance between himself and the body hanging from the tree branch, careful not to stare at the eternity stretched out beyond them. Patrick shoved his dagger into its sheath and started climbing. He didn't have any gear on him to help scale a tree of this size, but he'd scaled a sheer rock face once with nothing but his fingers because he had to.

Patrick did a lot of things he hated because he had to.

Patrick poured as much magic as he could into his personal shields as he climbed warm wood with bare, half-frozen fingers. Climbing made him a target the second he left the minimal safety of the space between Yggdrasil's roots, and it didn't take long for the enemy to spot him.

Magic exploded around him like fireworks, the screams of the damned and valkyrie war cries echoing on the wind. Patrick tuned out what he could, but he couldn't completely ignore the battle.

A strike spell crashed into his shields and erupted in the air around him. Bark exploded away from Yggdrasil, and Patrick's ears popped from the pressure. He slid down the trunk, hands scraped raw over the tree bark before getting his feet back under him to stop his descent.

"Fuck," Patrick swore, forcing himself to ignore the throbbing in his hands from embedded wood and bleeding palms as he clung to Yggdrasil.

He took in a shaky breath and kept climbing.

When Patrick finally reached the branch overhead, he scrambled onto it, crouching low to make himself as small of a target as he could. They'd hung Odin from one of the lowest branches, but it was still many stories up from the ground. A fall from this height could be deadly.

More magic seared through the canopy, crashing into Yggdrasil. Patrick ducked his head and kept his shields anchored as leaves fell around him. Something crashed through the canopy, and he barely missed getting hit by a larger branch that had been shorn off.

The wood beneath his bleeding hands grew hot, and Patrick had to let go to keep his skin from burning. He pulled his dagger free and carefully moved down the length of the branch to where the rope was tied. He was halfway there when the faint connection he was doing his best to ignore tightened from close proximity.

Patrick's heat charms had been burning through their magic since he'd left the SUV. He kept meaning to recharge them. It wasn't the weather that made him freeze, but the knowledge of who was behind him, balancing on a knife edge that doubled as a tree branch hanging over the world.

For a moment, a memory flashed through Patrick's mind—of them laughing as he chased Hannah through a kitchen that smelled like cookies into a warm backyard in the middle of summer. How he followed her to the tree house someone in his mother's family had built for them.

It was a blurred mess in his mind, time having faded the edges of that home and the features of his sister's face when she'd been young and alive and not the starved thing watching him with a goddess' tormented eyes.

Patrick kept his balance on the branch, dagger clenched tight in one bleeding hand, as he stared at his twin while the battle raged beyond them.

Hannah was dressed in casual clothes not fit for winter, and her red hair, once tangled and long, had been shorn up to her shoulders. Patrick didn't have to think very hard about what spell Ethan would've used her hair for.

There'd been idols and a sacrifice and prayers to a god for a *reason*.

Hannah said nothing, but her intent was communicated through the burning magic that poured from her fingertips, the power of a nexus cradled in her body and soul from a godhead aching to be freed.

Patrick had no hope of containing Hannah and the godhead trapped in her soul—not here, not now. Persephone could want Macaria back all she liked, but Odin was Patrick's priority right now, and he clung to that mission with every last bit of him.

Bleeding fingers included.

Patrick threw himself off Yggdrasil's branch, reaching for the rope Odin hung from with his one free hand. The spell meant to kill him burned through the space Patrick had been standing in, charring leaves to ash as gravity pulled him down.

Patrick got his fingers around the rope, and momentum had him crashing into Odin's body. They swung there in the open air like a pendulum, and Patrick found himself staring into Odin's eyes.

They blinked back at him.

Patrick bit back a yell of surprise and tried to ignore the way the rope was shredding his palms. Planting one foot against Odin's chest, he levered himself upward and pressed the edge of the dagger blade against the rope. White heavenly fire flickered in its depths, along with countless silvery words giving voice to the prayers that shaped the weapon.

He didn't bother with sawing through the rope, just put his strength and the dagger's magic behind the blade to cut through the fibers with a single slice.

The rope separated and Patrick was weightless for not even half a second before they plummeted to earth.

I didn't think this through.

Patrick and Odin fell through snow and wind and bursts of magic—landing not on the ground, but caught by Brynhildr.

Patrick slammed against the back of Dynfari behind Brynhildr, the valkyrie's free hand snapping out to grab him by his leather jacket to steady him. Patrick reflexively tightened his grip on his dagger as Odin's weight where it swung in the air nearly pulled his left arm out of its socket.

"Shit! Shit!" he cried out as he scrambled to not fall off the pegasus or let Odin's body go.

"Hold on!" Brynhildr yelled.

"I'm fucking trying!"

The ground rushed up to meet them. When they were close enough he didn't think any bones would get broken, Patrick let go of Odin. The god's body thumped to the earth. Patrick's entire body jostled hard when Dynfari's hooves hit the ground, nearly biting through his tongue.

Patrick slid off the pegasus to the ground on shaky legs. He stumbled over to where Odin lay sprawled in the snow, unmoving save for his eyes that still slowly blinked, the noose still tight around his throat. Patrick's hands throbbed, wood from Yggdrasil buried deep in his skin and the meaty flesh of his palms. It wasn't enough to stop him from undoing the noose and tossing it aside.

He hooked his arms beneath Odin's shoulders and hauled the god off the ground with a grunt.

"Brynhildr!" Patrick yelled. "We need to get him out of here!"

The howling of hellhounds made Patrick swear loudly as Brynhildr urged Dynfari closer.

"The Allfather is not dead," Brynhildr said.

She didn't sound relieved, and Patrick didn't know what to make of that. "That's the whole point of this rescue mission, right? Save the god, save the world?"

Brynhildr didn't blink when she said, "Is it?"

"*Fuck* you gods and your riddles."

Snow swirled faster around them as Hinon and Eir descended, landing nearby. Hinon's wings were like an electric storm that Patrick didn't want to get close to.

Eir dismounted Töfrandi and hurried over to them. Her spear was coated in blood, but none of it seemed to be hers. "Let me aid you."

Patrick looked over at Hinon. "Hades?"

"He retreated to Zachary's side. I felt it prudent not to engage them further when you had need of me," Hinon said.

"Ethan?"

Hinon shook his head. "I have not seen him."

Patrick's gaze cut away to the vast darkness of Lake Michigan and the corpses clawing at the shore. They weren't zombies risen from their graves, but the damned who were granted no surcease from torment. The veil was still tangled between where they were in Niflheim and the mortal world where the fight was happening in.

The spell they all stood on wasn't complete because Odin wasn't dead yet.

They still had time to save Odin, but they needed more help than what they had because Patrick could see hellhounds in the distance, running toward them.

"Wade said he saw something in the Chicago River earlier,"

Patrick shouted at Hinon to be heard over the wind. "There's a monster in the lake. Can you lead it to us?"

Hinon spread his wings wide and nodded grimly. "If it is Oniare, I will bring him to you."

He flapped his wings and threw himself back into the sky with a thunderous boom.

Between Eir's strength and Patrick's stubbornness, they got Odin slung over Töfrandi's back. Then he and Eir climbed up as well, and the pegasus snorted at the extra weight. Eir patted his neck with a comforting hand.

"It will be over soon," she said.

That sounded a little too final for Patrick's taste. He looked over at Brynhildr, the valkyrie still astride Dynfari, but with her back to them as she faced the oncoming horde of hellhounds, spear resting across her shoulders. Wind tugged at her blonde braids, her biker clothes streaked with blood and snow.

"Ride," Brynhildr said, her aura shining like a star around her. "I will hold them back."

"You can't do it alone," Patrick protested.

Brynhildr turned her head just enough to smile at him, sharp and vicious against the light of Yggdrasil. "A valkyrie is never alone."

Patrick blinked, glancing at the sky. "Right."

"Make sure your aim is true, Patrick. There is only ever one way this story ends."

Brynhildr faced forward again and let out a bloodcurdling war cry that echoed in the storm—a call to arms that would not be ignored. The oncoming horde of hellhounds led by Garmr met that challenge with vicious howls of their own even as more valkyries flew to answer Brynhildr's call, their presence in the sky backlit by lightning.

Eir obeyed her commander and urged Töfrandi to turn around. The pegasus galloped away from the fight to pick up speed, wings beating hard to gain altitude. Brynhildr's words echoed in Patrick's ears as he wrapped his aching arms around Eir's waist.

"What did she mean?" Patrick shouted.

Eir ignored him and grabbed his hands one at a time to heal them. Wood pushed its way out of his skin, the pressure making him bite the inside of his cheek to keep from swearing. The pulsing rawness of his hands faded, even if the cold didn't. Patrick blinked snow out of his eyes, squinting through the stormy darkness lit by the light of a modern city to their left. To the right, lightning struck Lake Michigan in continuous bursts, a dance few knew the steps to.

From the air, Patrick could see the concentric circles of the spell that stretched away from Yggdrasil on the ground. They reached farther than they had in New York last June, the glow of the soul-driven magic broken up by nearby skyscrapers and swaths of icy water that covered them.

The spell was still active, but if they could get Odin out of the line of fire, maybe they had a chance to break it. Except when Patrick reached for the god's throat, trying to find a pulse, he felt nothing but a cold stillness that made him choke back a panicked laugh.

"Fuck, we are so fucked," Patrick gasped out. "Odin is still tied to the spell, and we need to break it."

"Have faith," Eir shouted.

Patrick's faith in anything had died a brutal death in Salem years ago until Jono walked into his life. There wasn't any left to toss to the gods and their machinations that had the power to wreck the world.

Faith, Patrick had learned over the years, was always misplaced in the end.

They were flying over the mouth of the Chicago River where it poured into Lake Michigan when multiple strike spells were blasted their way from a ground position. Töfrandi veered around the shining blasts of magic as best he could, but it was like flying through fireworks going off on the Fourth of July. The Dominion Sect was throwing so many spells at them that one had to hit.

And it did.

The strike spell slammed through Töfrandi's left wing, and the pegasus threw back his head, screaming in agony as his wing exploded. Feathers and blood turned to a bloody mist as Eir screamed in rage. Patrick held on to her with one arm, the other trying to keep Odin's body in place as Töfrandi careened toward the water in a death spiral.

Even as they fell, another strike spell shot toward them—only to be incinerated by dragon fire.

Wade's sinuous shape dove through the wind and snow, his forefeet reaching for them. They were engulfed in sharp talons that cradled them close to a warm red body, carrying them to what safety Navy Pier could provide.

It was outside the spellwork, which could work in their favor. Removing Odin from the physical location of the spellwork wouldn't break it, but his absence would weaken it.

Wade spat flame the entire flight to the ground, landing with hind legs first before he gently placed Töfrandi and the rest of them onto the ground. The pegasus collapsed to his knees, heaving for air. Patrick got to his feet, struggling to drag Odin away from the wounded pegasus while Eir did what she could for her steed. There was no saving Töfrandi though, not with a critical wound like that. Patrick wasn't surprised when Eir drove her spear through the pegasus' ribs, piercing his heart to put him out of his misery.

Odin was deadweight in his arms as Patrick dragged the Allfather beneath the safety of Wade's body. Patrick stabbed Wade in the foot with the pommel of his dagger to get his attention. "Hey! I need you to keep Odin safe."

Wade snaked his head down to blink at Patrick, golden eye bright in his wedge-shaped head. He snorted smoke through his nostrils before hissing a warning, fire flickering behind his teeth.

Patrick snapped his head around, staring through the snow at whatever had caught Wade's attention.

The neon lights of Navy Pier hadn't been turned off despite the snowstorm. The Children's Museum, Ferris wheel, and other rides provided enough light for Patrick to see the group of Dominion Sect magic users coming their way.

They'd crashed onto the side of the pier, with the buildings to their right and Lake Michigan to their left. The only way out was through the enemy. Ethan was at the forefront of the Dominion Sect mercenaries and the hellhounds flanking them, a mageglobe held in one hand and Loki carrying Gungnir by his side.

Patrick wondered where Thor had gone, if the god of thunder was alive considering the wound Eir had only half healed for him.

"That weapon does not belong to you, Loki," Eir snarled with enough malevolence in her voice that Patrick flinched.

Or maybe he flinched because of Ethan.

Patrick figured it didn't matter since no one saw, and if they did, he'd blame it on the cold.

"If Odin wants it back, he can take it from me," Loki taunted, wind whipping his laughter away.

Eir left Töfrandi's body behind to come stand by Patrick, her spear pointed at the new threat. Some of her dark brown hair had been tugged free of her braids by the wind, and the furious grief on her face was matched only by the rage in her veil-colored eyes.

"You stole something of mine," Ethan said loudly to be heard over the wind.

Patrick tightened his grip on his dagger with fingers numbed from the cold or fear, he couldn't tell which. He conjured up a half-dozen mageglobes, filling them with raw magic.

Patrick squinted through the storm at where Ethan stood, the wind tearing at his father's blond hair and the cold-weather gear he wore. Patrick didn't see Hannah anywhere, nor Zachary. The tugging in his soul had stopped—mostly because he'd done his damnedest to wall it off.

"Odin isn't yours, asshole," Patrick forced out.

Wind-driven waves crashed over the side of Navy Pier, the spray caught between the driving snow. Patrick spared a glance toward the water as the lightning storm drew closer. He flexed his fingers around the hilt of his dagger as he caught sight of pale, pale hands clawing at the edge of the pier.

The dead of Náströnd who called Niflheim home were pushing through the veil.

"We're running out of time," Patrick said, shaping the words with numb lips.

He didn't know if anyone heard him.

Thunder echoed through the sky, a never-ending sound. In the valley of silence between each lightning strike before the thunder boomed, an eerie, haunting howl echoed in the air. Loki gripped Gungnir and looked over his shoulder into the dark. Patrick followed his gaze, trying desperately to make out whatever was coming their way. Whatever was out there, it made the Dominion Sect mercenaries scatter, half their numbers holding their ground against Patrick, Eir, and Wade, while the rest turned to face the new threat.

Which meant it wasn't anyone on Ethan's side of the fight.

The soulbond twisted—sharp and demanding—and Patrick swallowed tightly against the relief that warmed him from the inside out.

Jono.

Not Fenrir, but *Jono*—and the Chicago god pack, judging by the number of werewolves that raced through the snow toward Navy Pier. Patrick didn't know how the hell they'd made it downtown in this storm, but he wasn't going to turn them away even if Naomi and Alejandro didn't know what danger they were leading their pack into.

Magic cut through the air, and Patrick strengthened his shields. Wade roared and spat fire, breaking through some of the attack, but portions still got through. Ethan's magic grated against

Patrick's shields, cutting through in a way only those tied by blood could manage.

Which was fine—because his attack knocked Ethan off his feet even as Patrick took a hit that drove all the air from his lungs and sent him flying past Eir. He crashed to the pier, rolling dangerously close to the edge with all those grasping hands of the dead. Wade whipped his tail around to stop Patrick's momentum, curling protectively around him. Instead of getting within reach of the dead, Patrick folded himself around the forked tail, trying to breathe.

The snarling howls of a fight rushed in and out of his ears as Patrick got an elbow underneath him. He coughed, getting his lungs working again. A dark shape barreled toward him, and he nearly tossed Jono off Navy Pier with magic before Patrick got his bearings.

Jono's eyes had lost the shine to them that burned there when Fenrir was in control. All Patrick could see was the wolf-bright blue he woke up to every morning in their bed and the concern in them that was all human.

"I'm all right," Patrick rasped.

Jono growled, placing himself between Patrick and Ethan. Which wasn't helpful, except for how Patrick used Jono's wolf form to haul himself to his feet. Getting eyes on the battlefield told Patrick they were fucked six ways to Sunday.

And then Hinon arrived with Thor—and Oniare.

The massive horned water serpent erupted out of Lake Michigan, teeth bigger than Patrick was tall snapping at the lightning both thunder gods threw at the beast they'd herded north.

Thor let Hinon continue to play bait and crashed onto the pier, landing near Eir, Mjölnir in hand and spewing lightning bolts. Hinon stayed in the sky, taunting Oniare with a thunderous war cry as the water serpent fell back into the lake. As its head went under, its tail rose up, and Patrick's eyes went wide.

"Run!" Patrick shouted.

He threw himself at Jono, wrapping his arms around the werewolf's neck and digging his fingers into dense fur slick with blood. Jono ran from the edge of the pier, and the pair of them missed getting crushed to death in the span of a single heartbeat. Cold water washed over them in a deluge that nearly knocked them off their feet. Patrick clamped his mouth shut against the water, shivering from the instant chill it left behind, freezing and half-numb. His teeth chattered as he struggled to bring up his tattered shields.

Wade roared a challenge and launched himself into the sky, spitting fire at the serpent in the lake. Oniare screamed at Wade when he broke the surface again, and Wade dove at him, claws raking deceptively smooth skin. Hinon threw lightning bolts at Oniare and didn't stop.

Shaking from the cold and waterlogged clothes, soaked to the bone, Patrick let go of Jono. He searched frantically for Odin, finally spying where the Allfather lay motionless farther down the pier. The wave had pushed his body toward the stairs that led up to the amusement park rides. Before he could think about moving, lightning jumped from cloud to cloud above before careening down to slam into Thor's hammer.

"You have ruined enough lives, Loki!" Thor bellowed.

"There was only one I ever wanted to take," Loki snarled, raising Gungnir over his shoulder like a javelin.

When Thor let loose the lightning bolt, it exploded from Mjölnir like a storm. Lightning arced away from it in all directions, slamming into the museum, the pier itself, Loki, and the numerous rides on the second level. Patrick leaned hard into the soulbond, and through it, the ley line. He poured magic into his shields so they would hold against the lightning storm.

All the lights around them exploded in countless sparks as lightning cut through everything. The Ferris wheel rocked on its base in a dangerous way that had Patrick yelling a warning to anyone who would listen.

"Watch out!" he shouted.

The Ferris wheel tipped forward with deceptive slowness, falling with the screech of breaking metal to the museum below.

Loki threw Gungnir with only one target in mind.

Eir dove past Thor, sliding on one knee over slick wood as she spun her spear up and around. She used her weapon to knock Gungnir out of the air, Odin's spear clattering to the pier rather than finding its target in Odin's heart.

The Ferris wheel crashed into the Children's Museum and through the underlying base of the pier, breaking the pylons that supported the entire structure. The sound echoed like a bomb in Patrick's ears, and he felt the hit vibrate through his body.

Navy Pier *shuddered*. Then it started to tip, everything sliding toward the cold waters of Lake Michigan that churned with the dead.

Eir lunged for Gungnir at the same time Loki appeared beside it, the trickster god having escaped Thor's wrath once more. Before she could get her hands on the weapon, Loki snatched it up, thrusting it at Eir. Put on the defensive, Eir scrambled back out of range, because dying on Odin's spear was a painful way to go.

"What say you, Fenrir?" Loki asked, staring at Jono but talking to the god in his soul. "Put your teeth in the Allfather, and we shall have our Ragnarök."

Lightning exploded overhead, careening through the sky to slam into Thor's hammer. It half blinded Patrick, making it impossible to see where the enemy stood.

"You shall not start our end, Loki," Thor snarled, swinging his hammer around, lightning crackling through every inch of it.

"Oh, but our end is just beginning," Loki said with a Cheshire cat smile as he turned to face Thor, still clutching Odin's spear.

When they clashed, they left a hole in the pier, the smell of burning ozone thick in the air.

Patrick twisted around as the pier shuddered and heaved beneath his feet. Heart pounding in his chest, Brynhildr's words heavy in his mind, Patrick scrambled back to Odin's side. He didn't think beyond what had to be done to break the spellwork.

He vaulted over a broken piece of the pier, scrabbling for purchase on the other side. In the flashes of lightning overhead, Patrick could just make out where Odin's body lay, protected from sliding into the water by a jutting piece of debris.

Patrick used his feet and one free hand to stop his momentum, coming to rest beside the god. Odin's eyes were open, staring up at the sky and the snowstorm churning there.

Odin's stash of souls, gathered over many decades, had proven enough of a seed for Yggdrasil to put down roots, tear through the veil, and draw one of the Nine Worlds to Earth. No soultakers had been needed this time around when Odin had done all the taking to begin with.

Last time, Patrick had sacrificed Jono's soul without meaning to in order to put an end to the madness. This time, they were outside the spellwork completely, but Odin was still tied to it, and he only knew of one way to break that connection.

Do it.

The voices of Muninn and Huginn ripped through his mind, making colored spots flash across his vision from the pain. All but one disappeared, turning into a brightly burning splotch that took Patrick a moment to realize it wasn't his eyes producing it, but Odin's.

The god's right eye burned like a Vesuvius flame, and all Patrick had to do was put it out.

Patrick gripped his dagger with cold fingers and pressed it against the palm of his other hand. One quick cut was all it took to draw blood to the blade, a back door to whatever was left of Ethan's spell buried in Odin's existence. Patrick raised the weapon high before bringing it down with an accuracy that had nothing to do with training or luck and everything to do with fate.

Because this was no Ragnarök, and Hel had no right to drag her truth into a world that had long since forgotten it.

The dagger buried itself in Odin's heart while the storm ripped Patrick's command away from his lips.

"*Close the veil!*"

For a moment, the world went silent, as if time had frozen every breath, every wave, every snowflake on its journey down to the ground and stilled the wind itself.

Then lightning flashed over the entirety of Chicago, turning night to day, and the thunder that followed nearly deafened Patrick. An explosion of glittering light erupted from the wound in Odin's chest, curling around the dagger. Power pulled at Patrick's soul, and he sank his awareness deep into the magic unraveling from Odin.

The toxic ties of Ethan's magic was curled deep around Odin's godhead, and Patrick couldn't let his father get a foothold in yet another godhead. Blood would always call to blood, no matter the years and lies separating them. Patrick used that familial connection to sever what Ethan hoped to hold on to—a chance at godhood.

"*Break,*" Patrick snarled, voice shredding on the word.

The dagger—still buried in Odin's chest—shone like a lone lighthouse beacon in a dark and raging storm. Patrick's magic, guided by countless prayers gifted by the gods, cut through Ethan's magic, giving Odin a way out. The burning essence of Odin's godhood fled his immortal body, streaking toward the sky and disappearing into the storm.

The ground shuddered once more, the backlash from the spell breaking sending everything into an upheaval. Breathing heavily, Patrick scrambled to hold on to Odin's body, not wanting it to be lost to Niflheim when Valhalla was the only hall Odin would ever sit in with the dead. His shaking fingers caught Odin by the shoulder, the dagger still protruding from the god's chest. When Patrick yanked it free, heavenly fire poured out of the blade and into the wound like a waterfall.

A couple more pylons broke, and Navy Pier collapsed in on

itself a little more. Patrick and his charge slipped farther down the broken pier, the entire structure seconds from going under.

Then teeth sank into Patrick's shoulder, scraping against skin and drawing blood. Jono held on to him and dragged Patrick away from Hel's domain and the twisting fog of the veil slowly stitching itself up again.

Lightning crashed overhead, illuminating Wade's large form against the clouds and Hinon's smaller one, the valkyries astride their pegasi, and the two huge ravens descending in a tight spiral.

Huginn and Muninn sank their talons into Odin's body when they landed, and Patrick let the immortal go. The ravens flapped their great wings, gaining altitude, carrying the god with them into the storm. Patrick didn't watch them leave, too busy trying to make it to solid land before Navy Pier collapsed completely, Jono standing steadfast by his side.

Jono hauled him the rest of the way there with preternatural speed and strength. Patrick didn't let Jono go until they had dirt beneath their feet. Bodies were strewn around them—human and animal alike—but Ethan was gone. Werecreatures kept watch, ready to attack at a moment's notice. Patrick pulled his leather jacket tight around his body, wet clothes like ice against his freezing skin even with active heat charms, and tried to remember how to breathe.

South of them, in Millennium Park, the light of Yggdrasil went out, the world tree withering in the face of a broken spell. Hel's push to regain a foothold on Earth with Ethan's help was stopped in the only way it could have been.

By the sacrifice of a god.

MONDAY ARRIVED WITH OVERCAST SKIES, CHILLY WEATHER, AND enough snow on the streets the snowplows would be running nonstop for the next twenty-four-hours.

Millennium Park was an uprooted mess that looked like a bomb had gone off. The roads running close to the shore all needed to be repaved due to the dead having destroyed the asphalt. Climbing out of a hell was rough going, and the construction cost for the street repairs was going to be high, but not as high as the rebuild for Navy Pier.

Navy Pier had been utterly destroyed, the remnants of it a crumbled pile in Lake Michigan. Retrieval of the debris would have to wait for warmer weather because construction workers would be at risk for hypothermia if they tried working on it now. Not to mention the sheer logistics of cleansing numerous parks and miles of shoreline to eradicate the lingering traces of black magic and taint from hell before anyone could set foot in it.

Dabrowski hadn't been exactly pleased with the results of Patrick managing the case, but considering the alternative, he'd let it slide. Dabrowski had just looked at where Patrick had been sitting in the back of an ambulance—stripped of his soaked clothes and wrapped in a foil blanket burning with heat charms—and shook his head.

"I said scratch the Bean and leave everything else alone, not the other way around," Dabrowski had said.

"Pretty sure the Bean got scratched," Patrick had replied.

"The Bean got struck by what looks like lightning and had a hole blown through it."

"Oops?"

Probably not the best answer to give a SAIC after wrecking Chicago's waterfront, but Patrick hadn't cared. He'd survived, and figuring out the lies to spin started in that ambulance.

That had been hours ago though, and the thirty-minute break Patrick had taken under the watchful eyes of an EMS crew felt like days. Dealing with the aftermath of a breach in the veil meant he'd declined a ride to the nearest hospital but had taken one to his borrowed SUV parked on the street. It had miraculously escaped damage.

The clothes Jono and Wade had stashed in the trunk were gone—the pair having fled the scene with Naomi and Alejandro's god pack—but Patrick's had been there. He'd gotten dressed and gone back to work because that's what an SOA agent did.

The national news was reporting on the Dominion Sect attack with a fervor Patrick usually attributed to sharks smelling blood in the water. The local Chicago news stations were focused on what had happened in Millennium Park, but they were also reporting on the news of the spellwork performed in Westberg's Gold Coast property. Patrick gave it another day or so before some intrepid reporter linked the two incidents and every SOA agent in a one-hundred-mile radius was reduced to the tried-and-true *no comment* answer for everything.

Patrick gave it maybe an hour before reporters showed up in Wrigleyville, if they managed to get through the snowy streets.

"Ready?" Kelly asked as she and Benjamin approached where

Patrick stood in front of yet another of Westberg's personal properties.

Patrick had a raging headache, more bruises on his body than unmarked skin it felt like, and was so tired his eyes burned. But he'd been in this state too many times to count after a case or mission, and he was used to pressing on. It helped that he wasn't hurt like he had been after the fight in Central Park last year. He hadn't been the one to break the spell and close the veil—that had all been Odin's doing this time around.

"Let's go," Patrick said.

As federal raids went, ransacking Westberg's fourth property turned out to be more interesting than the last two. A federal judge had practically mass printed warrants for the SOA to raid Westberg's homes, campaign office, and real estate corporate office once she'd reviewed the certified video of Westberg's resurrection. Patrick had a feeling she'd also viewed some of the cell phone videos making the rounds on the internet.

Yggdrasil had been seen for miles, a beacon in that storm many people had taken pictures and videos of. The fight was the viral moment of the week, and Patrick was just grateful none of the video was clear enough to make out much of anyone through the snow. As evidence of the Dominion Sect's intent went, it was fairly damning.

Westberg's fourth home in Wrigleyville had been bought through several shell companies. Once they made it inside, Patrick understood why Westberg seemed to want to keep his name and affiliation buried beneath layers of paperwork.

The home, when the SOA agents and workers entered, was like a museum of artifacts. It was not something a conservative democrat with a well-known record of personal anti-magic and anti-anything supernatural politician would want to be known for owning.

Westberg had paid quite a small fortune for the home to be warded so no hint of magic would seep past the threshold. Inside, artifacts were displayed as if they were works of art being show-cased in a museum. Considering the mix of magic, and the costs of individual wards to keep some of the more malignant artifacts contained, Westberg's illicit pastime wouldn't have endeared him to some of his donors.

Benjamin let out a low whistle, making sure to keep his hands to himself as they looked around the living room they found them-selves in. "Guess he was living a double life after all."

"Most politicians do in one way or another," Kelly said.

"They're announcing his death at a news conference later today after the family has been notified," Patrick said, squinting at the glass display case inside a grandfather clock. The gris-gris there looked old, but the magic in its making felt strong.

"His name is still on the ballot. I think it's too late to remove it since the election is so soon."

Benjamin pursed his lips. "That'll make for some messy voting."

Patrick straightened up and fought back a yawn. "We'll need a CSU team in here and someone from Archives. Tell them to bring a couple of warded transport vans. This is going to take longer than a day to tag, archive, and remove everything for evidence. Some of this stuff might not even be stable. The containment wards are all overlapping in a real bad way."

"Maybe Westberg was a shitty archivist," Kelly said.

"And a shitty politician," Benjamin added.

"I'll drink to that once we're off shift." Kelly sighed. "I wonder if it's too much to hope he kept the records for all of this onsite somewhere."

In Patrick's experience, people who dealt with the black market rarely kept records. The less incriminating evidence lying around, the better. Patrick didn't know what Westberg was thinking when he decided to create a veritable museum inside a house.

Three hours later, after clearing every room of any active spells meant to keep people out and do harm, Patrick decided it was all about the money.

During the course of clearing the building, he'd discovered a veritable knot of spells and wards over a portrait of Westberg's wife in the master bedroom. Judging by the structure of the walls and the layout of the room, he was pretty certain there was a safe behind the portrait.

Getting through to it took two more hours of delicate spell-work performed by a sorceress Patrick was never going to introduce Wade to because the teen didn't need to know her job existed.

Agent Sasha Kuznetsova, out of Archives, had an affiliation for spell breaking, which, in layman's terms, meant she was a thief.

"But I'm an *approved* government thief," she'd told Patrick with a cheeky grin before getting to work.

Thief or evidence collector, it didn't matter, because Sasha's ability to unweave spells got them past the portrait to the safe underneath.

And then Patrick happily blew the lock off with a focused blast spell when it was decided by the higher-ups that waiting for a day to get someone in to crack the electronics on the safe would take too long.

Once they were in, Patrick pulled on a pair of nitrile gloves, ignored how badly he wanted to sleep, and nodded at Sasha. "Ready?"

Sasha picked up her camera. The stack of empty evidence bags for collection purposes, and her clipboard of forms, were on the nearby desk within easy reach. "Let's get started."

Inside the safe were stacks of money in various currency, three bars of gold without serial numbers, a hard drive, and a small stack of files that Patrick went for first. Between him and Sasha, they managed to sort and log every file. He flipped through each one, skimming over notes in shorthand that was probably Westberg's personal code. A few had pictures of items that were probably in the house or maybe in the process of being sold.

In the second to last file, Patrick found a slip of paper that was all too familiar.

The People's Pawn Shop logo was listed up top on the carbon copy. The name printed and signing over ownership of an *invitation* was Phoebe Westberg, the cost set in return making Patrick's eyebrows creep toward his hairline.

"Idols and not money?" Sasha asked, glancing at the carbon copy receipt. "That's weird."

"Yeah," Patrick said in a voice leached of all emotion.

He reached for a small evidence bag, tucked the flimsy paper inside before sealing it, and then slipped it into his jacket pocket. Sasha pointed her pen at him. "That's evidence."

"I know, but it might also be evidence in another case I'm running. Don't worry, it won't ever leave my hands. Chain of evidence will remain intact, but I need to take it with me."

"Where are you going?"

Patrick turned on his heel. "Shopping."

"I'M DRIVING," Jono said, taking the keys from Patrick's hand. "You're so bloody knackered you might drive off the road."

"I drove here," Patrick grumbled.

"Yeah, and I'm surprised you didn't veer into a snowdrift."

Patrick rubbed at his eyes, wincing at how dry they were. The warmth of the Chicago god pack's home was seeping into his bones. If Patrick spent too much longer inside, he'd end up like Wade, who was currently wrapped up in a large blanket, lying in front of the fireplace, with his bare feet *in* the fire burning there, while playing a game on his phone. A bowl of chips was precariously balanced on his stomach. As Patrick watched, one of Naomi's god pack members approached him to refill the bowl from a bag of Doritos.

"Wade," Patrick said.

"What?" Wade asked through a mouthful of chips.

"Don't get crumbs everywhere."

"Shows what you know. The crumbs are going in my mouth and nowhere else because chips are tasty."

Patrick looked at where Naomi and Alejandro stood a little past Jono in the living room. "Sorry, he's still a little feral."

"I am not!" Wade protested before diving into his chip bowl again.

"Put your shoes on. We're getting on the road."

Wade grumbled but started to unwrap himself from the blanket.

Naomi quirked a faint smile at Patrick. "He's welcome to stay, as are you."

Patrick shook his head. "He can eat through room service at the hotel rather than your kitchen."

"She means the pack, love," Jono said. Patrick just stared at him, hoping at any moment that sentence would make sense. Jono reached out and settled his hand on the back of Patrick's neck, reeling him in to kiss him on the forehead. "Members of a traveling god pack usually stay with the local one if they reside in the city or town."

Patrick made a face. "I think the SOA would notice if I don't have an invoice from the hotel for the entire time I'm in Chicago. We're trying to keep the pack under the government's radar, remember?"

"Probably should do with a little less city destruction, then."

Patrick smacked him on the chest. "Oh, fuck you. Everything's mostly still standing."

"You destroyed Navy Pier," Naomi said helpfully.

"That's—" Patrick broke off with a sigh. "Yeah. Can't deny that. Is your pack okay?"

The mirth in Naomi's bright amber eyes faded into something more serious. "Everyone who fought with us came back alive."

"Good. That's good."

Jono held up the keys. "Ready?"

"Is Wade?"

"My shoes are on," Wade replied.

"Then let's go."

Jono turned toward the Chicago god pack alphas and extended his hand. "Thank you for your aid and hospitality."

The formality of the goodbye had Patrick belatedly wondering if he'd somehow missed any specific pack manners when he'd arrived.

Naomi looked at Jono for a long moment before taking his hand in hers and giving it a firm shake. "Chicago will always welcome your New York City god pack, and any pack under your protection from here on out."

"Thank you," Jono said with a gravity to the words Patrick would appreciate more if he weren't so tired. He knew they'd won an acceptance here they hadn't expected to get. "We'll extend the same courtesy to anyone from Chicago who comes to New York and keep them safe."

Naomi offered her hand to Patrick, and he shook it, doing the same with Alejandro. The two Chicago god pack alphas escorted them out to the SUV, not bothering with small talk. Patrick was happy about that. He was even more happy that Jono was driving.

"Where am I going?" Jono asked once he started the engine and Naomi and Alejandro had retreated back inside the warmth of their pack's home.

Patrick pulled up his GPS app and accessed the address in it from earlier in the week. He let the tinny, electronic voice fill the SUV and Jono pulled onto the street. He could hear Wade happily munching away in the back seat, having taken the bag of chips with him.

Jono turned up the heat before reaching over and settling his hand on Patrick's thigh. "Have you eaten anything?"

"I've been fed," Patrick muttered, closing his eyes and tilting the seat back a little.

"Have you been seen to by a doctor? You're moving a bit funny."

"Got checked out. I'm okay."

And he was—mostly. His soul hadn't been damaged, and being able to tap a ley line had gone a long ways toward evening out the fight against Ethan and Hannah. The aftermath of clearing Millennium Park once he'd changed clothes had taken hours, and it was still ongoing. Patrick had reported what he could to Setsuna over an unsecured line, and then again to Dabrowski in person.

Blaming the Dominion Sect for the appearance of Yggdrasil in Chicago would only give the SOA a pass for so long. The public would want to know why the agency hadn't tracked the terrorist group down before the veil tore. Patrick knew a lot of finger-pointing was going to happen. The SOA was lucky the whole mess hadn't turned into another Thirty-Day War.

"What about where we're going? What do you need to do there?" Jono asked.

Patrick curled his hand over Jono's, tucking his fingers beneath a warm palm. "I got a warrant to search the place for an item of interest."

"You're going to execute a warrant by yourself?"

"I'm bringing you, aren't I?" Jono squeezed his hand, and Patrick leaned the seat back a little more. "You guys will stay in the car. I don't anticipate there being a problem, but if there is, you'll have my six."

"Always," Jono promised. Silence settled between them, and Patrick was fighting off sleep when Jono spoke up again. "I'm sorry."

Patrick cracked open one eye, turning his head a little to look at Jono. "What?"

"For not telling you about Fenrir taking us through the veil when I met with Lucien. I meant to, but you were going to walk out of the hotel room, and I…"

Jono's voice trailed off, and Patrick opened both his eyes. "I would've come back."

The words came easily to his lips. Patrick hoped Jono could

smell the truth on him, because he meant it. Soulbond aside, walking away from Jono wasn't an option. Jono's grip on Patrick's thigh tightened.

"Jono." Patrick waited until the other man looked at him. "I would have come back."

Patrick couldn't say the words buried in his chest, in his heart, too used to being hurt by the people who were supposed to care about him to give up pieces of himself like that despite everything they'd gone through. Jono's purposeful omission about what had gone down in New York still rankled, but Patrick understood—eventually—where Jono's position had come from in deciding to keep quiet.

Patrick didn't like it, but he understood. He just needed some time to process it all, but it wouldn't ever be enough to make Patrick leave Jono or the pack they were building. Nine months of being in a relationship with Jono still meant Patrick had things to learn, but one thing he was certain about was he would never leave Jono.

"Okay," Jono said slowly before focusing on the road again.

"Are you guys done fighting?" Wade asked from the back seat. "Because it's been awkward. And weird."

"We got you your own room," Patrick muttered, closing his eyes again.

"Yeah, but I can still hear you guys."

"What have we said about eavesdropping?" Jono said mildly.

"That I should only do so strictly for pack purposes. But I mean, this is about the pack."

"Wade."

"Would you look at that? Someone slipped a candy bar in my pocket. I'm gonna need to eat it right away before it melts."

"It's snowing."

"True, but you have the heater going."

Patrick snorted softly before letting his brain go offline for however long it took Jono to drive them to The People's Pawn

Shop. Being able to fall asleep at a moment's notice was an old skill he hadn't yet lost.

Patrick jerked awake sometime later to Jono squeezing his hand and saying, "Pat. We're here."

Blinking rapidly, Patrick winced at how his eyes felt like sandpaper. He peered blearily out the windshield at the lit-up windows of the pawnshop. Patrick had been awake for a day and a half at this point; he'd give almost anything for a bed right now.

"You sure you don't want me to go in with you?" Jono asked. "Place stinks of demon."

Patrick fought back a yawn. "Owner is an ifrit, and there's CCTV everywhere. I want you to stay off camera as much as possible."

"No promises if he goes after you."

Patrick shoved open the SUV door. "Fine."

Patrick headed for the pawnshop, pushing open the doors and stepping inside. The heat was running full blast, and he soaked it in for the few seconds it took him to case the shop. No customers were present, but the owner was.

The ifrit watched him approach, his gaze flicking down to the dagger strapped to Patrick's right thigh. "You again."

"Me again," Patrick said. He slipped his hand into his pocket and came up with the warrant a federal judge had only been too happy to sign. "With a warrant this time. Now play nice so I don't have to arrest you."

Patrick held up the piece of paper he'd waited three hours to clear that afternoon. It took some finagling, needing approval by the SOA, the PIA, and the US Department of the Preternatural. Patrick had taken an hour-long phone call that had given him a headache only a potion could fix. The red tape had been worth it, if only because they were maybe one step closer to figuring out where the Morrígan's staff was.

"Let me see," the ifrit said.

Patrick placed the warrant on the glass countertop of the

display case between them and slid it toward the ifrit. The veins on the hand that retrieved it pulsed a little, looking like flowing lava beneath the skin for a second.

"You're to release whatever the owner of this receipt signed over to you," Patrick said.

Patrick pulled out the evidence bag with the receipt inside it, laying it flat on the countertop. He never took his fingers off the evidence bag.

The ifrit stared at the receipt for a long moment before laying the warrant on the counter. "If I say I don't have it?"

Patrick left the warrant where it was. "The receipt was dated two weeks ago. The Westbergs were still within their first thirty-day cycle for repayment. You aren't allowed to sell it."

"I heard Westberg is dead."

"His wife is still breathing, and she's the signatory on the paperwork." Patrick leaned forward, staring the ifrit down. "Show me the itemized invitation they left with you. Don't make me ask again."

The ifrit grimaced before shoving himself away from the display case. "Follow me."

Patrick picked up the warrant and the evidence bag, pocketing both as he followed the ifrit into a back storeroom that doubled as an office. Patrick stood in the doorway, watching as the ifrit perused a couple of shelves before finally hauling out a slender warded box. Patrick automatically strengthened his shields.

"The item number you were looking for," the ifrit said.

Patrick checked the tag affixed to the box, double-checking it against the receipt number he'd memorized. They matched.

Patrick's shields remained active when he accepted the warded box. No magic was triggered when Patrick touched it.

"Unlock it," Patrick said.

The ifrit reached out slowly with one finger and touched the center of the box. The wards withdrew into the wood, allowing Patrick to open it.

Inside lay a large cream-colored envelope. Patrick picked it up and set the warded box aside. When he turned the envelope over, the wax seal was broken. He traced the image of a globe pressed into the wax, bits blurred from being cracked. Patrick carefully lifted the flap, sliding free a single card, the thick paper embossed with gold and filled with magic.

It was an invitation to a black market auction of artifacts.

Patrick read the invitation twice more before closing up the envelope and slipping it into the evidence bag. "This was used as collateral for a set of idols. Do you know what kind?"

The ifrit shrugged, not admitting to anything. "No."

Patrick thought about the pentagram in Westberg's house, and the idols carved to carry Freyr's prayers. He refused to think about the walled-off connection buried deep in his soul that tied him to Hannah.

"I'll want the paperwork on that sale."

The ifrit smiled, biting and hard. "Got a warrant? Because the one you have doesn't cover your request."

Patrick slipped his dagger free of the sheath, flipping it around his fingers to get a better grip, never taking his eyes off the ifrit. The matte black blade crackled with heavenly fire along the edge. "Sure. I have a warrant."

"That's not a warrant."

Patrick stared the demon in the eye. "You can pretend the current warrant encompasses what I'm asking for, or I can do one of two things. Call up a federal judge and let her know the warrant that brought me here also uncovered some illegal business activity, which will just bring in more SOA agents, or I can show you how my dagger works."

The ifrit licked his lips. "That's extortion."

"I call it doing my job. I think we both know what went down last night. If I let Aksel Sigfodr know you had a hand in that mess?" Patrick shrugged. "Not my problem if you turn up dead this week."

The ifrit dropped his gaze to the dagger and stared at it for several heartbeats before giving in. "I'll get you the paperwork."

Patrick left The People's Pawn Shop a couple minutes later, carrying the invitation and paperwork showing the Westbergs had used it as collateral to purchase a set of idols that should've been in a museum somewhere. He climbed back into the SUV, knocking snow off his boots before closing the door.

Wade wrinkled his nose. "You smell like demon."

"Maybe keep your nose to yourself and you wouldn't have a problem," Patrick said.

Jono eyed him curiously. "Everything go all right?"

"Yeah." Patrick stared at the envelope inside the plastic evidence bag. "Everything went fine."

He held in his hands what might be their first solid lead on the location of the Morrígan's staff—Patrick just wasn't sure what finding it would cost them.

22

"Won't the cops see us?" Wade asked, nervously chewing on a thumbnail.

Jono squinted through the fog as they came up from the pedestrian pathway into Oak Street Beach. It was cold by the water, but the heat charms Patrick had spelled into Jono's clothes were a soft comfort. "I think the gods have that issue well in hand."

Jono removed his arm from around Patrick's shoulders, taking the other man's gloved hand instead. Patrick gave him a weary half-smile. "That's not always a good thing."

"You said it yourself, Pat. We don't need an audience for this."

"I'd rather be in bed than traipsing around the beach."

Jono couldn't agree with him more. He hadn't seen Patrick since the mage had left their hotel room early that morning. Tuesday had turned out to be just as busy as Monday for Patrick, while Jono and Wade had remained in the hotel. Since the SOA was taking lead on the Westberg case, and they'd gotten what information they needed about the Morrígan's staff, Jono and Wade were leaving in the morning.

Tonight though, the three of them had eaten dinner at a restaurant downtown, one Naomi had suggested wouldn't discriminate against them because of Jono's eyes. The food had been good, but rather than head back to the hotel like Jono had hoped to do, they found themselves returning to the shores of Lake Michigan. His plans for a night in had been derailed by a summons from the Norse gods, one which none of them could ignore.

The drive north hadn't been terrible. The reactionary storm had settled into normal bad weather that was slowly breaking up. It had stopped snowing earlier in the day, but the pileup from the storm could be seen everywhere. Jono's feet sank into the snow that covered the sand, ice pushed by the waves building up at the edge where water met land. Lake Michigan was calmer than it had been during the fight, little eddies of water finding their way to the shore and the ice there.

It looked peaceful, but Jono knew that peace was an illusion. They all knew what lived in the lake.

The city skyline to the south of them was hard to see through the fog. It smelled like normal fog, not like what lived in the veil, but that didn't stop Jono from being on edge. It was thick enough that visibility was shit until they broke into a space on the beach where the fog didn't touch.

In that spot, the beach wasn't empty.

Softly glowing witchlights hovered in the air, providing more than enough light to see by now that the sun had set in the west. The glow was reflected against the snow and the gathering of gods and immortals. The electric charge to the air made Jono fight back a sneeze.

Hinon turned at their approach, his great, storm-colored wings folded tight against his back. "Ah, so you came after all. We are about to start."

"Couldn't really say no. Did you really need us here for this?" Patrick asked.

"It would be remiss of those who fought not to see the passing of those who fell," Thor said from where he stood beside Frigg.

The Norse god of thunder looked nothing like the modern-day bartender he'd been masquerading as. Gone were the winter clothes and designer suit. Tonight, Thor wore gleaming silver armor over leather clothing dyed black. Mjölnir hung from a wide belt, the edges crackling with electricity every now and then. Thor's pale red hair was half braided back from his face, the rest falling loose past his shoulders.

Standing beside Thor, Frigg wore a simple black dress beneath a gray fur cloak, the hood resting against her back. Her hair hung in waves and braids down to her waist. A crown made of twisted gold and studded with opals rested on her head.

Brynhildr stood on the other side of Frigg, spear in one hand and a bow and arrow held in the other. The armor she wore gleamed just as brightly as Thor's. Her pegasus stood unmoving behind her in the snow, his wings furled. The majority of surviving valkyries who had fought to help retrieve Odin's body were arrayed in a half circle facing Lake Michigan.

Heimdallr stood at the shoreline, sword strapped to his back, one hand resting on the prow of a small wooden boat draped with greenery and flowers. Eir was there as well, standing beside another boat bearing the body of Töfrandi. Several other valkyries stood next to the remaining boats bearing the bodies of the dead.

The waters of Lake Michigan were a vast darkness. The stillness found there was eerie after the rough weather the last few days.

"Is Oniare still in there?" Wade asked.

Hinon shrugged, his wings spreading a little with the motion. "I did not slay the beast. What wounds we dealt him will heal in time. He will return, as he always does. That is the way of our story."

"And Odin?" Patrick asked, staring at the boat Heimdallr stood by.

Jono tightened his grip on Patrick's hand, ignoring the way Fenrir growled through his mind.

"This was not our Ragnarök," Frigg said.

"Odin is still dead, and Loki escaped with his spear. His ravens told me to kill him, and I shoved my dagger into his heart."

Frigg turned her head to look at Patrick before her gaze settled on Jono. "Loki will pay for his betrayal, as he always does. Fenrir's teeth never touched my husband. This was no Ragnarök, despite all efforts to make it so."

Jono half expected Fenrir to claw his way to control, but the god remained silent. Jono blinked, vision wavering for a second before it settled. Frigg smiled at him, the curve of her mouth secretive in a way Jono knew not to trust.

"So, what? Is he not dead?" Patrick asked suspiciously.

Frigg didn't answer him, not right away. She turned to face the horizon again, lifting her chin. "We lost our tithes, but we did not lose the people who remembered us. You broke the connection. There is no weapon available to you that could break Odin's godhead."

"Except me," Jono said.

"Fenrir chose his side," Thor said without rancor.

"To stop Ethan. Doesn't stop the furry bloke from following the path of your story to its bitter end."

Thor's smile was hard and cutting when he looked at Jono. "The day will come when we will be on opposite sides once more, but what happened here in Chicago was not that day."

"That day may never come in this world we have all lost." Hinon spread his wings. "Shall we, cousin?"

Thor nodded gravely, and Hinon launched himself into the sky without a word, huge wings flapping to keep him aloft. Frigg raised her right hand in a commanding gesture, and Heimdallr bowed to her in response. Then he and the valkyries tending to the boats pushed them into the water. Waves rippled away from the hulls as the boats floated away, leaving the shore behind. In the rippling wake of their passage, the water took on an oil-slick sheen to it, like a rainbow. The sheen overtook the boats, stretching toward the horizon in a line of multicolored light—a rainbow bridge to a heaven.

"What is that?" Wade asked quietly, sounding awed.

"The Bifröst," Patrick told him.

In the recess of Jono's mind, Fenrir howled in a mournful way.

Heimdallr and the valkyries with him stayed knee-deep in the cold water, watching the dead on their final passage. Brynhildr jammed her spear into the snow, twisting the pole until it could stand on its own. She took five steps forward, raised her bow, and nocked the arrow to the string. Fire erupted around the arrowhead, a flickering warmth Jono could feel from where he stood.

"Valkyries," Brynhildr called out, her voice cracking through the air the way ice over water did in winter when too heavy a weight stood on it. "On my mark."

Jono watched as the half circle of valkyries all raised their bows and took aim at the boats with a steadiness that never wavered. Patrick's grip tightened in his, and Jono held on because he would never let go.

When Brynhildr's count reached one, every valkyrie with a bow let loose their arrows. The burning arrows streaked through the dark sky, bringing fire to the boats and turning them into funeral pyres.

The boats drifted over the Bifröst that glowed beneath the waters of Lake Michigan, their fires growing. In the sky, Hinon followed their route, gliding low over the waters every now again, almost as if he were guarding their passage. Several of the valkyries on the beach mounted their steeds and joined Hinon in the sky.

"There is an edge to every world," Frigg said into the quiet. "Here, on Midgard, this is one of ours, because this is one of the few places we are remembered."

"Hinon isn't of your pantheon. Lake Michigan belongs more to his pantheon than yours," Patrick said.

"Our stories overlap in ways you could not understand. Hinon will ensure Oniare does not interfere with the dead. The valkyries will guide their sisters to Valhalla."

"What of Odin?"

Frigg didn't speak, merely looked up at the night sky that was no longer cloudy. Jono didn't know when it had happened, but the sky over the beach was clear and full of stars. Jono watched as two black specks grew larger and larger, blotting out the starry sky until Huginn and Muninn landed in all their strange glory in front of their queen.

Frigg knelt and extended both hands to Odin's ravens. Huginn and Muninn hopped closer to her, gently preening her hair with their beaks as she stroked their feathers. Frigg smiled at whatever they told her that Jono couldn't hear.

"Odin lives," Frigg said before straightening up.

Patrick stared at her. "I drove my dagger into his heart."

"Yes, but you didn't kill his memory. You merely broke the spell seeking to use him."

"You just lit his boat on fire. I know what burning flesh smells like."

"Odin does not burn, even if the valiant dead do. We gods lose our bodies and our lives only when we are forgotten here."

"Your lives are myths. You've already lived your age in the past. That's why you're just stories to most people on Earth."

"Midgard is the heart of the world tree, but sometimes our hearts ache to return home to Asgard." Thor pointed at the horizon. "Look. The Allfather comes."

Jono stared at the water and burning boats still drifting across the Bifröst to the edge of the world, lit by starshine. Some of those stars grew brighter, cutting through the sky like a ribbon of the Northern Lights. Jono's eyes widened in surprise when he finally realized what he was looking at.

Odin's godhead returning to the immortal vessel that housed it.

The boats never stopped gliding toward the edge of the world. When the shining brightness of what passed for a god's soul reached the boat Odin's body had lain in for the funeral, the fire there grew brighter. It flickered red, then orange, then a pure, shining white-gold before getting snuffed out by some unseen force.

Odin climbed out of the boat, standing tall on the Bifröst rather than sinking into Lake Michigan. The Allfather had been dressed in the finest suit money could buy, overlaid with a fur cloak that matched Frigg's in style and color. The crown he wore was a simple twist of gold that burned like a halo. Heimdallr was the first to greet Odin when the Allfather stepped off the Bifröst and returned to earth. To Jono's eyes, Odin looked exactly as he had when he'd swung from Yggdrasil's branch, the pinnacle sacrifice that never truly happened.

"What," Patrick said angrily, "the fuck?"

"Yeah, what he said," Wade muttered, staring wide-eyed at Odin. "Weren't you dead?"

Jono would've tried to ward off the argument he could sense was building, but Fenrir beat him to it by clawing back control when Jono least expected it. Odin smiled at them as he drew closer through the snow, his heterochromatic eyes never blinking.

"You have honed your weapon well, Fenrir Lokisson," Odin said.

"A pity I could not hone my teeth in your skin, but I know what is at stake," Fenrir said.

"If only your sister and father felt the same way."

Patrick pulled free of Jono's grip, and Fenrir let him. Jono wanted to haul him back, but couldn't. Patrick stabbed a finger in Odin's direction. "So, what? You gods just reappear if you're killed like nothing happened?"

"It is not that simple."

"Then simplify the fucking explanation," Patrick snarled. "Because Ashanti sacrificed herself on this very same dagger and she's still *dead*."

"Her body turned to ash, and her godhead had nothing to

return to. Her myth has never been one mortals have remembered well. Ashanti is worshipped amongst vampires, and they are not nearly enough to call her back. There is nothing to call her back *to*."

Jono thought it was a pity Lucien wasn't there to hear the derision in Odin's voice. He honestly wouldn't mind seeing what the master vampire might try to do to the god.

"We are remembered and have been for thousands of years," Frigg said, not unkindly, but with a warning to her tone Jono knew Patrick wouldn't heed. "What happened Sunday was not our end."

"It could've been your end because your greed enabled Ethan to try his favorite spell again."

Go back to sleep, Jono told Fenrir. *I want my body back.*

Fenrir sank back into his soul with a growling laugh, and Jono shook his head, trying to reorient himself back in his own body. Wade squinted at him before nodding. "Oh, good. You're back."

Patrick looked over his shoulder at Jono, and Jono went to stand beside him so he wasn't facing down the gods alone.

"If a godhead can return to you, what about Macaria?" Jono asked.

Patrick stiffened beside him. Jono reached for his hand without looking, interlocking their fingers together.

Odin's gaze settled on Patrick. "He already knows the answer."

Patrick wouldn't look at anyone, staring off into the distance with a bleak look in his eyes. "There's nothing left of Macaria's vessel. That's why her godhead is in Hannah's body, but it already had Hannah's soul in it."

"Mortal bodies aren't capable of carrying a godhead," Thor said.

"Hannah is still alive."

"Her body breathes. You can be alive but not living in this world."

"Mortals can damage *your* bodies to steal a godhead. That's what Ethan did with Macaria and what he's tried every chance he gets when he finds you lot," Jono pointed out.

"Ra during the Thirty-Day War. Zeus last summer. Now you," Patrick said.

"Your father did so with the backing of the hells every time. Mortal power alone will never be enough," Odin said.

"Your duty is to save Macaria. In saving her, you will save all of us," Frigg said.

Patrick scowled. "I don't know how you expect me to do that if she has no body to return to. Hannah's wasn't enough and still isn't. That's the entire reason Ethan bound himself to her."

"You will find a way." Frigg's words carried a weight to them Jono didn't like. She reached for Odin, placing her hand on his arm. "We should go, my love."

"Leaving so soon?" Jono asked bitingly. "Not going to do anything about the mess you caused?"

"Aksel Sigfodr is someone I have ceased to be. We have worshippers in Oslo who call to us, and that is where we shall go," Odin said.

Patrick snorted. "I guess dying is one way for you to get out of a RICO charge."

The bitterness in Patrick's voice had Jono wrapping his arm around Patrick's waist. "Come on, Pat. Let's go."

The gods didn't call them back as they turned to go, leaving the beach and the vigil for the dead behind them. The fog drifted back around them, and the clouds returned overhead. They walked in silence to the pedestrian tunnel that would take them back to the start of the Magnificent Mile.

"It's not your fault," Jono said, his breath coming out in white puffs beneath the street lights.

Patrick said nothing, but Jono could smell his guilt over every other scent drifting on the wind through Chicago. He tugged Patrick closer, holding on to him as they walked back to where they'd parked the car.

Patrick never pulled away. After everything they'd fought over and fought through the past few days, Jono would never take that closeness for granted, the same way he knew he'd never let Patrick walk away from him without a fight.

"I'm never flying commercial *again*," Wade announced as he climbed into the back seat of the Escalade.

Sage looked over her shoulder at him, both hands resting on the steering wheel. "I take it you enjoyed your flight home on the private jet?"

"Jono let me put in a request for whatever food I wanted yesterday, and they had it *all* waiting for me when we got on board. I ate everything."

"I'm sure you did."

Jono got into the front passenger seat and hauled the door shut. "Thanks for picking us up."

"Considering you still have a bounty on your head, you aren't allowed to go anywhere alone. Besides, I took the morning off." Sage took her foot off the brake and pulled away from the curb in the passenger pickup area of LaGuardia. "How much longer is Patrick staying in Chicago?"

Jono sighed. "At least another week. Maybe longer. He said he might have to make a stop in DC before coming home."

Sage kept her eyes on the road and the interweaving mess of vehicles. "Did you find the Morrígan's staff?"

"No, but Patrick located an invitation to a black market auction of artifacts that might lead to it."

"*Might* isn't helpful."

"Medb did say she wouldn't give up the staff unless the payment threshold was met. It's still something."

Sage made a face. "True. Did you tell Patrick about the hunters?"

"I did," Jono said slowly.

"Are you sleeping on our couch?"

"No."

"They argued," Wade said from where he sat on one of the middle seats. "And then they made up by having sex *on my bed*."

Jono rolled his eyes. "Oh, sod off. We didn't have sex while you were in the room, and we got you your own hotel room after that."

Sage glanced at Jono, arching an eyebrow. "So Patrick was angry?"

"You can say *I told you so*," Jono said wryly. "I promise I won't hold it against you."

"I'll wait until Marek and the rest are off from work. We can do it in surround sound for you at the dinner table tonight."

"Great."

Sage laughed. "You're welcome."

"Patrick was pissed, like you said he would be. But we talked through it, I apologized, and I promised not to keep things like that from him again."

"Good."

"I got us an alliance and recognition with the Chicago god pack. You have to admit I'm doing something right."

"Maybe, but there's always room for improvement."

She said it with a teasing smile, and her scent was full of happiness and mirth. Jono shook his head, laughing a little. Sage was never mean-hearted about her teasing, but their pack's sense of humor was built on a solid foundation of loving sarcasm and a bit of gallows humor. If she hadn't needled him, he'd be worried.

"Lucien called the other night. He said he wanted to speak with you when you got back," Sage said once they were on the highway heading toward the Queensboro Bridge.

"Did he say why?" Jono asked.

Sage shrugged. "No."

"If he called rather than show up in person, it can't be much of an emergency. It can wait."

"You sure that's wise?"

"We already brokered an alliance with him and the other Night

Courts. We can't jump every time he demands something from us. That's going to put us in the weaker position and piss off Patrick."

Sage smiled, a sense of calmness filtering through her scent. "Good. I'd hoped you'd say that."

Her faith in him was something Jono would never take for granted. The moment he did, Jono knew he'd be no better than Estelle and Youssef. His job as the alpha of the New York City god pack was to fight to protect the packs under his care.

Jono was finally in a position where he could stand his ground, and he wasn't moving one bloody inch.

23

 Wade said, standing on his tiptoes to try to see over the Wednesday afternoon crowd at the Arrivals area.

"Patrick's plane landed ten minutes ago. Give it at least ten more before he even gets off," Jono said.

"Marek should've let him use the private jet."

"We don't need that paper trail with the government." Jono reached out to grab Wade by the collar of his jacket and reel him back in so he wasn't in the way of the exit. "And keep your hands to yourself."

Wade tugged free with a mock-scowl before he decided to pull a Pop-Tart packet out of his jacket pocket. Jono let him snack in peace and kept scanning the people coming through the Arrivals security gate.

It had been a week since he'd last laid eyes on Patrick, though they'd rung each other every night to check in. Jono was far more forthcoming than he had been the other week, realizing his mistake in keeping Patrick in the dark.

Closing out the Chicago case had turned into a right mess that had gone all the way up the chain in command of the federal government. From what Jono understood through his chats with Patrick, Setsuna had been called in to privately brief the president. It was like New York last summer all over again with the domestic terrorist attack on home soil, and no one was pleased with that turn of events.

The Chicago mayoral election had happened yesterday. While Westberg's name had remained on the ballot, his opponent in the other party had won by a decent showing. It wasn't a landslide, and mail-in ballots were still being counted, but at least they wouldn't have Loki in an urban seat of power. That thought was enough to give Jono a headache.

In New York, the PCB was still looking into the hunter death in vampire territory. Jono hadn't interacted with the police since his interview, though he anticipated more scrutiny, especially now that Casale was aware of the god pack rivalry. Sage had assured him there were laws on the books that would cover his defense if the PCB pressed the hunter issue.

The soulbond, which had been stretched thin since Jono had left Patrick in Chicago, had settled into its normal weight in his soul once Patrick's plane had landed. It tugged at Jono's soul from close proximity sometime later, a warmth pooling in his chest.

"There he is!" Wade said.

Jono's gaze latched onto the sight of Patrick slipping through the crowd, his dark red hair standing out. He looked tired, smelled tense, but he was the best thing Jono had laid eyes on all week once Patrick got within kissing distance.

"Hey," Patrick muttered against Jono's lips. "I thought you were picking me up at the curb?"

"Wade needed a walk," Jono murmured before kissing him again.

"Hey!" Wade protested through a mouthful of Pop-Tart.

Patrick broke the kiss and laughed tiredly. He leaned into Jono with a sigh, and Jono rubbed his back with a firm hand. "Long couple of weeks."

"I can take you home before I head to Tempest if you want," Jono said.

Patrick shook his head, stepping back a little. Wade had grabbed his carry-on and was already heading toward the exit on his own. "No, it's fine. I've been gone for almost two weeks. I should show my face again. Let people know I'm back."

"If you're sure."

"You can drop Wade off first if you want."

"Nah, he said he was going to do homework at the Starbucks down the street."

"You sure that's a good idea? He might drink five lattes with extra espresso shots in each one and then be up for two days straight."

Jono laughed, curling his arm around Patrick's shoulder and pulling him close. He turned to press a kiss to the top of Patrick's head, breathing in his scent that didn't smell anything like pack, just him. Jono fixed that once they made it to the Mustang, taking a minute to press his scent into Patrick using both hands pressed to his neck. Jono distracted him from the scent-marking by kissing him and didn't stop until Wade cleared his throat pointedly.

"There are cameras," Wade said primly. "Don't give the security guards a show."

Patrick snorted. "Like Jono would ever do that. He's not an exhibitionist."

"He ran around the park in Chicago while naked. He does the same thing here."

"Not with Patrick," Jono said firmly. "Now get in the car."

Wade scrambled into the back seat, and Patrick took the front passenger one. Jono got behind the steering wheel and started the engine. Getting out of the parking garage was slow, but they eventually got on the road.

"What happened to the invitation?" Jono asked once Patrick had set a silence ward into the Mustang's frame.

Patrick stretched out his legs and reached over to rest his hand on Jono's thigh. The touch made Jono smile, settling him in a way nothing else had since Patrick had been gone.

"It's being held in the Repository under armed guards, spells, and wards. The PIA is taking lead on investigating chatter that might be related to it. The SOA will still be looking into domestic leads, but the general consensus is the auction will probably not happen on US soil."

Jono frowned. "You really think the auction will be held out of the country?"

"I think anything is possible. Ethan got his mercenary bona fides in Europe after he fled the country when I was a kid. Westberg didn't get all those artifacts in his mini-museum house from the States. He liked to travel. The SOA has a forensic accountant digging into his personal and business records right now, but that's going to take a couple of months to sort out."

"But he's dead. Is the government still suing him?" Wade asked.

"We're suing his estate and looking at other members of his family. He wasn't the only one signing off on those pawnshop receipts. The Westbergs did a lot of business with Odin's old alias."

"What about the Dominion Sect?" Jono asked.

Patrick sighed, his fingers digging lightly into Jono's thigh before relaxing. "They skipped town. Maybe even the country."

The farther the distance between Patrick and his twin, the better, in Jono's opinion.

"I'm okay with a holiday from their bollocks."

"I think that's all of us." Patrick settled a little more in his seat, fiddling with one of the air vents. "Now we just have to deal with Estelle and Youssef's bullshit."

"They've stepped back a bit from testing our territory boundaries now that every time they do they get reminded the vampires are involved. It won't keep them away forever though."

"At least Lucien's good for something. Guard dog is a good fit for him."

Jono laughed. "Never let him hear you say that."

"I'm not *stupid*."

Conversation steered away from Patrick's work to pack updates and the goings-on in New York while Patrick had been in Chicago. They hit rush hour on the drive into Manhattan, but Jono didn't mind the traffic much, not with Patrick by his side.

By the time they reached the Alphabet City neighborhood Tempest was located in, the bar had been open for a good hour already. They dropped Wade off at the Starbucks a couple of blocks away before circling the surrounding blocks until they got lucky with a parking spot.

"Who's coming tonight?" Patrick asked as he shut the car door behind him.

Jono locked the car with the key fob before shoving it into his pocket. "Everyone, I think. You've been out of town for a bit."

Patrick made a face. "They're gonna be invading my personal space, aren't they?"

Jono laughed, reaching for his hand. "Complain all you like, but you know you've missed us."

"Yeah," Patrick said a little grudgingly.

Nine months had given them both a new normal—as normal as dealing with gods could be. But their pack and the circle of close friends outside it was something Jono would never take for granted, Patrick most of all.

Tempest was already half-full by the time they arrived, and Sage had kept two barstools open for them between her and Emma. She smiled when she caught sight of them. Setting down her wineglass, she got to her feet and came to greet them.

"Got off early?" Patrick asked as he accepted a hug from her.

Sage discreetly scent-marked him before stepping back. "Yes. I'll work from home tonight to make up for it. You look tired."

"Long case."

"So we saw on the news. Come on, we'll get you a drink. Leon ordered a couple of pizzas that should be here soon."

"Only a couple?"

"More like ten."

"That's what I'm talking about."

Jono had technically taken the night off, but he went behind the bar to pour himself a pint and Patrick a glass of whiskey. He set both down on the counter in front of their seats and turned to ask Sage if she wanted a refill on her wine when an argument outside caught his attention.

The conversation in the bar dipped as Jono dialed up his hearing. What he could hear had him leaving the bar in seconds, preternatural speed getting him outside quicker than Patrick.

"Tell me you're not that sodding thick," Jono growled.

"You aren't the only one who can go where they please in this city," Estelle said from where she stood by the double-parked SUV out front, with two more waiting behind hers. "It's a public street we're on."

"It's not free territory."

Estelle smirked. "You're right. It's mine."

"Is she being delusional again?" Patrick asked as he exited the bar with Sage right behind him.

Estelle's scent never changed, but her eyes narrowed in a way that told Jono she probably hadn't expected Patrick to show up. Sage approached the woman who was the reason Estelle had driven into their territory. The dark-haired werecreature stood frozen on the sidewalk between the bar and Estelle's SUV, clutching a worn rucksack bulging at the corners, her thick curly hair cut to her shoulders and growing out a dye job. She looked to be in her late twenties, maybe early thirties, and the only scent Jono got off her was her own.

Sage pulled the woman aside and guided her closer to the bar to talk quietly. The conversation wouldn't be private, but it would get her behind them and away from Estelle. Jono left Sage to it and kept his attention on Estelle.

"I already gave you a warning," Jono said.

"You've given her several. Her dumbass keeps ignoring them," Patrick said.

Emma, Leon, and several other werecreatures exited the bar, lining up on the sidewalk in a show of solidarity. Estelle's gaze flickered over them before focusing on Jono again. She said nothing as a man climbed out of the SUV, bringing with him the unmistakable scent of sulfur. He was tall, dressed all in black, with a ruddy face. He had salt-and-pepper brown hair trimmed short, a scar bisecting his brown eyes over his nose, and a smirk that made Jono want to rip his face off.

Jono's lips pulled back in an instinctive scowl as more Krossed Knights and god pack werecreatures got out of the other two SUVs. Beside him, Patrick's hand strayed toward his dagger.

"You're not welcome in this city. Or this world, for that matter," Patrick said.

"Making deals with the devil, Estelle?" Jono asked, never taking his eyes off the Krossed Knight hunter. "Is this who you were entertaining the other week?"

"That's not your business," Estelle said. "My business is the girl."

"She's not yours. Get moving," Jono growled.

Estelle gestured in the newcomer's direction. "Soon as that one gets in the car."

Sage looked over at Jono, gaze cold and steady. "Her name is Marissa. She's from Miami. She's an independent-ranked werecreature who is looking for permission to stay and for protection."

"She'll have it," Jono promised.

"It's not yours to give," Estelle bit out. The hunters who had come with her spread out a little, and Jono tracked their movements.

"Did you miss the part where we're the New York City god pack and not you?" Patrick shot back.

Before Estelle could respond, the loud revving of motorcycle engines filled the air, the noise familiar from their time in Chicago. Jono wasn't the only one who looked down the street at the convoy of motorcycles turning the corner onto Avenue B.

Brynhildr led the way on her Harley Davidson, Eir seated behind her and wearing her cat-eared helmet. Jono relaxed a little as some of the valkyries illegally crossed the meridian to bypass the double-parked vehicles, boxing in Estelle and the hunters. Estelle's shoulders stiffened as her head moved from side to side, taking in the threat the valkyries presented. The hunters drew back, stepping closer to each other. Jono took a deep breath, curious at how the scent of sulfur seemed to diminish.

Brynhildr revved her motorcycle's engine and drove right toward Estelle's door, forcing her to scramble out of the way. Brynhildr took her time driving between Marek's Maserati and the car in front of him to jump the curb and park on the sidewalk. She killed the engine but didn't bother with the kickstand.

Brynhildr pulled her helmet off, shaking free her long blonde hair. Behind her, Eir did the same, climbing off Dynfari with a smooth motion.

"Long way from Chicago," Jono said by way of a greeting.

"We're in New York to get Eir another ride," Brynhildr said, smirking a little. "And to bring you a gift."

"Uh," Patrick said, probably thinking of how not to accept it, because Jono was as well.

Brynhildr laughed. "Freely given. No strings attached."

Jono looked in the direction she nodded and saw Skuld approaching. The red-haired valkyrie carried a crate of mead wider than she was, but she didn't seem bothered by the weight of it.

"We heard you served good beer, but were missing something from your menu," Skuld said with a wink.

"What is it?" Emma asked curiously.

"Mead."

"Do you sell it through wholesalers?"

"No. You'd purchase it direct from the brewery if you like it."

"Please don't like it," Patrick muttered.

Emma ignored him and waved Skuld toward the entrance to the bar. "Come inside so I can take a look and have a taste."

The rest of the valkyries were parking their motorcycles on the sidewalk since no street parking was available near the bar. Jono hoped whatever glamour surrounded the pegasi was enough to keep them hidden from traffic enforcement agents and anyone else walking down the street.

Brynhildr gave Dynfari one last pat on the handlebar before dismounting. She stood beside her ride and stared at Estelle and the hunter in charge, a hint of ozone drifting through the air. Jono watched the way Estelle's fingers made dents in the edge of the doorframe before she caught herself. The valkyries turned as one to face the threat on the street.

"Who is she?" Brynhildr asked with the curiosity of a hunter having found prey.

Jono thought of all the ways he could possibly respond and went with the easiest. "No one who matters."

Maybe it was a bit of a lie, but the underlying truth was a foundation Estelle couldn't break. They had alliances with the fae and vampires, and at least one major god pack in the country had acknowledged them over Estelle's. Estelle might have sold her soul to bargain with hunters, but they were as much a threat as a partner. She'd have to watch her own back with them, and that would never make her or her pack strong in the long run.

Jono watched the way Estelle subtly signaled her pack members to get back into the SUV. The hunters only followed when their leader retreated into the lead SUV as well. Whatever fight Estelle had hoped to provoke, it wasn't happening now, not with the valkyries having interrupted them.

The three vehicles drove off. Jono didn't look away until they'd turned the corner, the tension in his shoulders easing only when the threat was gone—for now.

"Is that Dynfari?" Wade shouted in glee.

Patrick peered around Jono at where Wade was running down the block toward them. "How did he even know they were here?"

"They probably drove past the Starbucks," Jono said.

"I guess it was too much to hope he'd actually do his homework."

"Dynfari likes him," Brynhildr said.

"Of course she does." Patrick raised his voice a little. "Go back to the Starbucks when you're done saying hello, Wade."

"Yeah, yeah," Wade replied, clearly ignoring them in favor of the pegasi masquerading as motorcycles.

"You're still not getting one."

Brynhildr smirked. "We know a dwarf who owns a garage. We're going there tomorrow."

"*No*," Patrick stressed, rounding on her. "Zip it. Not one word."

Wade stared at Brynhildr from his crouched position beside the pegasus masquerading as a Harley Davidson. "Tell me more."

"That's it. I need a drink. Jono, where's my drink?"

Jono snorted. "On the counter where you left it before we were interrupted. Sage?"

"Leon and I will work out where to put Marissa," Sage told him.

She was already guiding Marissa into the bar. Since Fenrir hadn't issued a warning about her, Jono figured she had a legitimate need and wasn't a plant. Jono caught Patrick by the elbow and guided him back inside Tempest.

"You're all welcome to stay," Jono tossed over his shoulder at Brynhildr.

He wasn't surprised when the valkyries came into the bar and stayed. They hailed from a drinking culture, and it was only polite to serve them. Only his pack, Emma, Leon, and Marek knew their true identities, but it didn't matter. Tempest was an integral part of their territory, the place where they officially accepted guests—immortals included—into New York City.

More than that, it was the people who filled the bar, who always showed up when the need arose, that told Jono what they were building could never be torn down.

It was strange to think this was his life now—this mix of magic and family and pack that was all he'd ever wanted since being infected by the werevirus and never thought he'd get. Looking out over the gathered crowd, Jono realized he wouldn't change anything in his past that had brought him here.

"You're thinking," Patrick said sometime later after the pizza had arrived and been devoured. "Terrible habit, you know that, right? That's why we have Sage."

"Shut it," Jono said with a laugh.

Patrick finished off his whiskey and set the empty glass on the bar counter. He kicked out his leg to hook his ankle around Jono's. Whiskey and the warmth of the bar left a flush across his cheeks, putting his freckles on display.

"What's on your mind?"

"Nothing. Just…" Jono's voice trailed off as he looked around the bar at the werecreatures, mundane humans, witches, and immortals who were all mingling. "Long way from London."

Patrick leaned forward, resting both hands on Jono's knees. "Do you miss it?"

Jono looked down into the face of the man he loved, the man he'd move every heaven and every hell for, and shook his head. "Not when I have you."

The Fates had given Jono a twisted road to walk, but he would always think it was worth every last bruising hit, every hard-won step, if it meant he made it here—standing beside Patrick, ready to fight a war they couldn't win alone, but together they had a chance.

Jono curled his fingers under Patrick's chin and kissed him, easy and sweet. Jono could taste the whiskey on his lips and smell the happiness that cut through the bitterness of Patrick's scent.

"I love you," Jono said beneath the cacophony of the bar, not caring who could hear him.

"I know," Patrick murmured softly. "Just like you know I'll always come back."

The truth in Patrick's words and in his scent was something Jono believed with all his heart. It was a promise of a future together Jono would do everything in his power to keep safe—from the gods, from hunters, from Patrick's family, and from death itself if it came down to it.

Because Patrick was every bit of hope Jono had ever wanted—bright and shining and worth a war.

~~~

Patrick and Jono's adventure continues in *On the Wings of War*.

Don't miss out on sneak peeks, exciting news, and more! Sign up for Hailey Turner's newsletter to stay up-to-date on her upcoming books.
~~~

GLOSSARY

Short descriptions of words, acronyms, and phrases used in the story that weren't readily explained in text. Included as well are character names.

Abuku, Setsuna: Witch. Director who oversees and leads the Supernatural Operations Agency.

Academy: K-12 school that teaches magic to practitioners of all affinities and designations. All provide boarding options to students.

Æsir: Immortals. Principal Norse pantheon of gods.

Allfather, the: *See* Odin.

Asgard: Location. Norse realm of the gods. A heaven.

Ashanti: Immortal. Goddess and mother of all vampires. Takes the shape of an Asanbosam vampire out of West African myths.

Beacot, Sage: Weretiger. A Diné lawyer who works for the fae law firm Gentry & Thyme. Dire to Jono and Patrick's god pack.

Bifröst: A burning rainbow bridge between Midgard and Asgard.

Breckenridge, Gerard (Captain): Immortal. Current identity of Cú Chulainn. *See,* Cú Chulainn.

Brigid: Immortal. Celtic goddess associated with fertility, spring, healing, smithing, and poetry. Spring Queen of the Seelie Court. Daughter of the Dagda and member of the Tuatha Dé Danann.

Brynhildr: Immortal. Leader of the valkyries and a shieldmaiden.

Cailleach Bheur, the: (Pronunciation: KAI-lach burr) Immortal. Goddess and divine hag. Considered a creator deity and Queen of Winter. Has various Irish and Scottish origin stories.

Carmen: Succubus. First known recorded appearance was in Venice, Italy.

Casale, Giovanni: Human. Chief of the NYPD's Preternatural Crimes Bureau.

Caster Corps: Military branch under the purview of the US Department of the Preternatural. Accepts all magic users except mages.

Cerberus: Immortal. Hound of Hades and guards the gates of the Underworld.

Citadel: United States military academy for magic users. Located in Maryland. All Academies across the nation feed into the Citadel. Mages get automatic inclusion. All other kinds of magic users need recommendations.

Collins, Patrick: Mage. Former combat mage with the Mage Corps, currently an SOA special agent. Has a tainted soul and crippled magic. Is technically a mage in name only due to a soul wound. Co-leader of the god pack he shares with Jono.

Cú Chulainn: (Pronunciation: ku CULL-ann) Immortal. Celtic god and son of the god Lugh. Member of the Tuatha Dé Danann. Irish warrior. Carries the *Gáe Bulg* in fights. Currently hiding under a mortal identity by the name of Gerard Breckenridge.

Dagda, the: Immortal. Celtic god affiliated with life, death, crops, and seasons. Member and king of the Tuatha Dé Danann. Husband to the Morrígan.

de Vere, Jonothon: God pack werewolf. Originally from London, England, currently resides in New York City. Alpha of a god pack he co-leads with Patrick.

Demeter: Immortal. Greek goddess of harvest and agriculture, fertility, and sacred law. Mother to Persephone.

Dire: A rank held only within a god pack. The moniker is taken from the dire wolf but has been shortened to account for different werecreature species. Essentially a rank held by a loyal pack member who helps enforce the alphas' orders.

Dominion Sect: A shadowy terrorist group consisting of mundane humans, rogue magic users, immortals aligned with the hells, and other preternatural creatures intent on destroying the veil between worlds so that hell and its denizens can reign on earth. Some members are attempting to steal godheads in order to ensure their hold on power in the new world they hope to create.

Eir: Immortal. A valkyrie and goddess associated with medicine and healing.

Espinoza, Wade: Teenaged fledgling fire dragon. Part of Jono and Patrick's god pack.

Fae: Supernatural beings who reside in Tír na nÓg. There are lesser or higher fae depending on their status and species. *See also,* Tuatha Dé Danann.

Fenrir: Immortal. Wolf in the Norse pantheon. Patron to a god pack.

Freyr: Immortal. Norse god of fertility, virility, prosperity, sunshine and fair weather.

Frigg: Immortal. Norse goddess of foresight and wisdom, queen of the Æsir, and wife of Odin.

Garmr: Immortal. Hel's hound.

Ginnungagap: Primordial void. Belongs to the Norse myths.

Godhead: Primordial power belonging to immortals that gives them life. The strength of their power can be altered by worship, or lack thereof.

God pack: A pack of werecreatures infected with the god strain of the werevirus. They act as spokespeople for hidden werecreature packs in their territory. They are supported by monetary tithes from the packs under their protection. Very few retain a connection to their animal-god patrons.

Greene, Ethan: Mage. Was a double agent formally employed by the SOA. Is currently a mercenary and allied with the Dominion Sect.

Greene, Hannah: Mage. Currently a vessel. Spiritually deceased.

Gungnir: Artifact. Odin's spear.

Hades: Immortal. Greek god of the dead and the Underworld.

Haudenosaunee: A northeast Native American tribe. Also known as the Iroquois.

Heimdallr: Immortal. Norse god of foreknowledge, keen eyesight, and hearing. Called the Shining One.

Hel: Immortal. Norse goddess of death.

Hel: Location. Norse underworld located in Niflheim.

Hellraisers: A US Department of the Preternatural Special Forces team Patrick once belonged to.

Hermes: Immortal. Greek messenger god and god of trade, thieves, travelers, sports, athletes, border crossings, and guide to the Underworld.

Hernandez, Leon: Werewolf. Partner to Emma Zhang and co-leader of the Tempest pack.

Hinon: Immortal. Haudenosaunee thunder god.

Huginn: Immortal. One of Odin's ravens in the Norse pantheon, whose name means "thought."

Iðunn: Immortal. Goddess of eternal youth and spring. She is associated with apples and tends an orchard that provides fruit which keeps the Norse gods immortal.

Kavanaugh, Nicholas: God pack werewolf. Dire of the New York City god pack.

Khan, Youssef: God pack werewolf. Alpha of the New York City god pack.

Krossed Knights: An organization of hunters that formed in the United States centuries ago. An offshoot of European hunter groups that came out of the Crusades.

Ley lines: Metaphysical rivers of powers that drain into nexuses.

Loki: Immortal. Norse trickster god.

Lucien: Master vampire. Was a soldier in William the Conqueror's army before being turned by Ashanti. Currently a weapons and magic trafficker. Is wanted by many governments.

Macaria: Immortal. Greek goddess of the blessed death and Hades' daughter.

Mage: Highest rank of magic users and the only practitioners who can tap external power from ley lines and nexuses.

Mage Corps: Military branch under the purview of the US Department of the Preternatural. Accepts only mages.

Magic: Emanating from and powered by a person's soul. Roughly one-quarter of the world's population has magic. Strength varies, with different titles being bestowed depending on a person's magical reach. Casting is divided into defensive wards and offensive spells.

Medb: (Pronunciation: may-ve) Immortal. Celtic goddess. Queen of Air and Darkness. Ruler of the Unseelie Court. Member of the Tuatha Dé Danann.

Midgard: Location. One of the Nine Realms in the Norse myths, generally acknowledged as Earth and the mortal plane.

Mjölnir: Artifact. Thor's hammer, capable of immense destruction.

Moirai: Immortals. Greek Fates.

Morrígan: Immortal. Sometimes depicted as an individual Celtic goddess, or more commonly as a triple goddess, of war and fate. She is particularly affiliated with foretelling of death or victory in battle. Often described as a trio of sisters sometimes given the names of Badb, Macha, and Nemain.

Mulroney, Nadine: Mage. Works counterintelligence for the PIA. Is fluent in French and based out of Paris, France.

Muninn: Immortal. One of Odin's ravens in the Norse pantheon, whose name means "memory" or "mind."

Náströnd: Location. A shore of corpses in Hel.

Necromancer: A magic user who can be of any rank. Their magic has an affinity for the dead, allowing them to raise the dead, control zombies, and manipulate the lingering souls of the deceased. Their kind of magic is heavily restricted in use in the United States and in most countries.

Necromancy: A family of magic that deals with the dead, usually involving blood magic and sacrifices. Predominately illegal or restricted in most countries.

Nexus: Metaphysical lake of power beneath the earth. Usually located in sacred areas or beneath major cities.

Niflheim: Location. A Norse realm.

Night Court: Vampire group that oversees claimed territory. Headed by a single master vampire. Several Night Courts can exist in the same major city.

Norns: Immortals. Norse Fates.

Odin: Immortal. Norse god of wisdom, healing, death, knowledge, battle, and the gallows, and is the titular king of the Æsir.

Oniare: Immortal. A horned serpent residing in the Great Lakes. The sworn enemy of Hinon.

Órlaith: (Pronunciation: OR-lah) Immortal. Daughter of Ruadán. The Summer Lady of the Seelie Court and heir to Brigid. Cú Chulainn's fiancée within the story.

Pegasus: Winged horses favored by valkyries.

Persephone: Immortal. Greek goddess of the Underworld and springtime.

PCB: Preternatural Crimes Bureau. A PCB is usually found only in the police departments of major metropolitan areas in the United States. The PCB in New York City is headed up by a bureau chief. The five detective boroughs within the NYPD all field detectives specializing in preternatural crimes through the PCB. The PCB has jurisdiction throughout the five boroughs and its own detachment of cops that work in homicide, narcotics, major crimes, and CSU. The PCB is one of the least manned departments in the NYPD due to the type of cases it handles.

PIA: Preternatural Intelligence Agency. PIA is a national-level foreign intelligence organization overseen by the Secretary of Defense directly through the USDI. The PIA's intelligence operations extend beyond the zones of combat, and approximately half of its employees serve overseas at hundreds of locations and US Embassies in many countries. The agency specializes in collection and analysis of preternatural-source intelligence, both overt and clandestine, while also handling American military-diplomatic relations abroad. The agency has no law enforcement authority. (Equivalent to CIA)

Psychopomp: Creatures, spirits, angels, or deities that appear in many religions and take many forms. Responsible for guiding newly deceased souls from Earth to the afterlife, whether a heaven or hell. Are used most commonly with necromancy and other magic that has an affinity for souls or the dead.

Ragnarök: A series of events and great battles that will bring about the destruction and annihilation of the Norse gods. An end-time myth.

Reed, Noah (General): Fire dragon. Currently hiding in human form as a three-star Army general who oversees the US Department of the Preternatural.

Santa Muerte: Immortal. *Nuestra Señora de la Santa Muerte* (English translation: Our Lady of Holy Death), commonly shortened and referred to as Santa Muerte. A personification of death associated with healing, protection, and safe passage to the afterlife.

Shields: Ward. Defensive magic used for protection on a large or small scale.

Skellig Islands, the: Location. Irish translation: *Na Scealaga*. Rocky islands in the Atlantic Ocean off the west coast of Ireland.

Sluagh: (Pronunciation: SLOO-ah) Spirits of the restless dead. Aligned with the Unseelie Court.

SOA: Supernatural Operations Agency. SOA is the domestic intelligence and security service of the United States that focuses on magical and preternatural crimes and terrorism. Employs human, preternatural, and magically affiliated people to field positions for domestic defense. (Equivalent to FBI)

Sorcerer/Sorceress: Second-highest rank of magic users and moderately more common than mages but are outnumbered by witches and wizards.

Soulbond: A binding of two or more souls to tie people together for magical needs. Illegal under the laws of all governments.

Spells: Offensive magic.

Taylor, Marek: Seer. CEO of PreterWorld, a social media platform geared toward the preternatural and supernatural community. His patrons are the Norns.

Tezcatlipoca: Immortal. Aztec god of obsidian, jaguars, war, strife, night sky, and the night winds.

Thor: Immortal. Norse god of thunder, lightning, storms, oak trees, strength, the protection of mankind, hallowing, and fertility.

Threshold: Ward. Applied to a hearth and home for protection to keep out negative magic, spirits, and demons.

Tiarnán: Member of the Tuatha Dé Danann. Carries the title Lord of Ivy and Gold.

Tír na nÓg: (Pronunciation: TEER-na-nog) English translation: Land of the Young. A place in the Otherworld past the veil where the Tuatha Dé Danann and lesser fae reside.

Tremaine: Master vampire. Headed up the Manhattan Night Court. His maker was Lucien.

Tuatha Dé Danann: (Pronunciation: TOO-ah de-danan) Celtic pantheon of gods. They are considered high-status fae.

US Department of the Preternatural: Employs all manner of magically affiliated and preternatural people for military service. Active duty combat mages are seconded to the Army, Navy, Air Force, and Marines and are required to go through BTC and joint training.

Valhalla: Location. A majestic hall beyond the veil in Asgard ruled over by Odin. Warriors who die in battle spend eternity there waiting for Ragnarök.

Valkyries: Immortals. A host of female riders who choose who live and die in battle. They guide the dead to either Valhalla or Fólkvangr.

Veil: The metaphysical barrier between Earth/mundane plane and other worlds/dimensions/planes, and versions of hell and heaven derived from myths.

Walker, Estelle: God pack werewolf. Alpha of the New York City god pack.

Wards: Defensive magic.

Warlock: Most common rank of magic users. On par with witches.

Werecreatures: Humans who are infected with the werevirus. Can change form into various animalistic shapes. Werecreatures are either infected later on in life or are born with the disease.

Werevirus: An incurable disease that makes those who are infected change into monstrous beasts. Created by an ancient Roman mage, the werevirus was one of the first recorded instances of magically created biological warfare introduced into society. People are born with the werevirus or become infected through intercourse or blood. Two strains exist: a normal strain and a god strain. The god strain has stronger magical properties which can cause the infected to be susceptible to an immortal patron.

Wild Hunt: Supernatural and ghostly hunters who steal souls. Aligned with Gwyn ap Nudd.

Witch: Most common rank of magic users. On par with warlocks.

Yggdrasil: Norse world tree that connects the Nine Realms.

Zeus: Immortal. Greek god of thunder and titular king of the Greek pantheon.

Zhang, Emma: Werewolf. Alpha of the Tempest pack.

AUTHOR'S NOTES

I know I always say it, but it really does take a village to bring a book into the world. My thank you and appreciation shout-outs might look a little familiar, but that's because these are the people who help shepherd my books once I spit out all the words. Thank you from the bottom of my heart to my friends:

Nora Sakavic, for all her support and friendship and middle-of-the-night texting sprees.

Leslie Copeland, for never steering me wrong, for being a wonderful person and an even better friend.

Lily Morton, who I finally got to meet in person (!!!) and who I'm going to hang out with in person again. You're one of my best friends, and I'm so glad we found each other.

May Archer, my bae who listened to me whine about work and writing and general real-life stress, and then told me I got this. Thank you for your support and your friendship throughout everything.

Lynn Van Dorn, for making sure I got my Chicago locations right. Please forgive me for the city destruction?

Bear, who continues to be an amazing friend and doesn't mind when I bombard her with text messages and cat pictures.

Last but not least: to my readers. Thank you so much for enjoying the worlds I get to write about so that I can write more. You guys are amazing, and I wouldn't get to do this without you.

I took liberties with police work and federal agencies in this story. I don't work in either field, and I tried to blend both into the world I created as best as possible.

I would be thrilled and grateful if you would consider reviewing *A Vigil in the Mourning* on Amazon or Goodreads. I appreciate all honest reviews, positive or negative. Reviews definitely help my books get seen, so thank you!

Cover design by AngstyG LLC.
Professional Beta Reading by Leslie Copeland: lcopelandwrites@ gmail.com
Edited by One Love Editing
Proofing by Lori Parks: lp.nerdproblems@gmail.com
Proofing by Jenni Lea at LesCourt Author Services

CONNECT WITH HAILEY

Keep up with my book news by signing up for my newsletter and get the free Soulbound prequel short story *Down A Twisted Path* and several free Metahuman Files short stories while you're at it.

Join the reader group on Facebook: Hailey's Hellions

Visit Hailey's website: www.HaileyTurner.com

Like Hailey's author page

OTHER WORKS BY HAILEY TURNER

M/M Science Fiction Military Romance:

Captain Jamie Callahan, son of a wealthy senator and socialite mother, is a survivor.

Staff Sergeant Kyle Brannigan, a Special Forces operative, is a man with secrets.

Alpha Team, the Metahuman Defense Force's top-ranked field team, is where the two collide and their lives will never be the same.

<u>Metahuman Files</u>

In the Wreckage

In the Ruins

In the Shadows

In The Blood

In The Requiem

In The Solace

<u>A Metahuman Files: Classified Novella</u>

Out of the Ashes

New Horizons

Fire In The Heart

M/M Urban Fantasy

<u>Soulbound</u>

A Ferry of Bones & Gold

All Souls Near & Nigh

A Crown of Iron & Silver

A Vigil in the Mourning

On the Wings of War

An Echo in the Sorrow

A Veiled & Hallowed Eve

<u>Soulbound Universe Standalones</u>

Resurrection Reprise

LGBTQ+ Epic steampunk-inspired fantasy:

Welcome to Maricol, where the land will kill you, kinship turns the gears of war, and burning the dead lest they come back to life is the only way to survive.

<u>Infernal War Saga</u>

The Prince's Poisoned Vow

The Emperor's Bone Palace

<u>Infernal War Saga Novella</u>

An Emporium of Hearts

Contemporary gay romance

Short stories previously published in the Heart2Heart Charity Anthologies.

<u>From the Heart: A Short Story Collection</u>

Audible

All of Hailey Turner's books are available in audiobooks. Visit Audible to discover your next favorite listen.

Hailey Turner Audiobooks

Thanks for reading!